THE LAVENDER HOUSE

In 2004 young social worker Sophia Morgan leaves the North to train as a journalist in London, where she falls in love with a tiny house painted lavender, moves in and makes friends with the occupants of her city street. There's the independent Bobbi, aged ten, whose father Sparrow seems to have vanished; the rather Home Counties Doreen, who knits for a living; dreamy architect Steve, and elderly Julia who wears hotpants and thinks it's 1969. The Lavender House proves to have a sinister history, and as its secrets emerge, events in gangland London of the 60s begins to cast their shadows forward...

THE LAVENDER HOUSE

THE LAVENDER HOUSE

by

Wendy Robertson

Magna Large Print Books
Long Preston, North Yorkshire,
BD23 4ND, England.

British Library Cataloguing in Publication Data.

Robertson, Wendy
    The lavender house.

    A catalogue record of this book is
    available from the British Library

    ISBN   978-0-7505-2889-4

First published in Great Britain 2007 by Headline Publishing Group

Copyright © 2007 Wendy Robertson

Cover illustration © Rod Ashford

Published in Large Print 2008 by arrangement with Headline Publishing Group Ltd.

Magna Large Print is an imprint of Library Magna Books Ltd.

Printed and bound in Great Britain by
T.J. (International) Ltd., Cornwall, PL28 8RW

All characters in this publication are
fictitious and any resemblance to real persons,
living or dead, is purely coincidental.

For Debora and Sean, with love.

1971

The heavy fist hammers on my front door; rat-tatting like a machine gun. Through a crack in the bedroom curtain I can see my caller; a bulky man in a long coat. The streetlight illuminates his white shirt, but his face is a shadow under his brimmed hat. He bangs the door again, then kicks the bottom panel. 'Open the door, darlin'. Chrissake.' His hoarse voice detonates through my letterbox and reverberates through the house. My frozen ears muffle his words, making them meaningless, like the barking of a dog.

On the other side of the street a low-slung Cadillac purrs to a stop and another man climbs out. His face is not unfamiliar. He bawls something at my caller, who treats my door to a final kick, rattles the letterbox, and gives up the ghost. Then he strolls as far as the Cadillac and gets into an argument with the driver. Their arms wave in the air, making long shadows on the wall of the house opposite. A light goes on in an upstairs room. The driver grabs the lapels of my caller's coat and shakes him hard, as you would a naughty child. In a second the row subsides and they jump into the car. The driver guns the engine and, after slowing by that funny house on the corner, he revs it up again and makes off at high speed.

A double-decker stops at the bus stop just outside my house. For a moment my bedroom is flooded with light from the upper deck and passengers peer in, as they often do. I stand still, counting my lucky stars. If the

11

bus had come seconds earlier my caller would have
seen me standing here, watching.
And that, I suppose, would have been that.

The Prize

2003

It all started the day Mimi Trevor threw me out of
her house. More precisely out of the flat I rented
in her house. Well, you couldn't really call it a flat,
more a linen cupboard on the fourth floor of her
elegant Georgian. My bed was a mattress on top
of packing cases, my wardrobe was the case and
sports bag I'd brought down to London with me.
Mrs Trevor, despite being a fitness freak, had
never climbed the fourth staircase, so this rabbit
hutch had swelled in her mind to an elegant *pied-
à-terre* that any girl would be proud of.

My presence in her house had started out as a
grace-and-favour thing. Mimi Trevor was an old
university friend of Malcolm, my ex-boss in Newcastle. He fixed up for me to stay with her when I
first came down to London for my course. 'She
lives in Islington, Sophia. Handy for City University. You can walk it. Save those pennies of yours.'
Malcolm, head of section in the Social Services,
could do brisk, warm, efficient very well. It was
skin-deep, though, in my experience.

On the first day I met her, when she blushed at
the mention of Malcolm's name and pressed me

12

with questions about him, I knew that Mimi Trevor must have had a thing about Malcolm way back when. But after that first darling-Malcolm-fest, Mimi Trevor began to make it clear she was bored with my presence. Being a vegetarian, she was bored with the smell of my bacon in her house, being a vegan she was bored with the sight of my eggs in her grand basement kitchen. And being an exercise obsessive, she was bored with the mere sight of my lounging, relaxed figure. So I ended up beached up in my rabbit hutch most evenings, coffee in hand, laptop on knee.

But even hiding away there did not preserve me. On that crucial morning, smelling of sweat from her early morning run, she accosted me in the hall.

'A word, Sophia,' she said, dabbing her overslender neck with a towel. 'This really is too much.'

'What is, Mrs Trevor?' I said meekly.

'You had someone in your flat.'

'It's a room, Mrs Trevor. And yes, I had someone in there. But I am twenty-five. I do have a right to have friends in my room.'

'That music of yours made my ears hurt even on the ground floor. And even down there I could smell the beer.'

'My friend Laura brought it in. Prefers it to wine.'

'A girl! Beer!' she said, folding her lips.

I tried a joke. 'You can take the girl out of Newcastle but you can't take Newcastle out of the girl.'

She didn't smile. All right, it was a corny joke, but there wasn't a glimmer from her. She walked round me and made for the cloakroom under the stairs. Then she turned round. 'It's not working,

13

Sophia, is it? We just don't gel, do we?'

'What are you saying, Mrs Trevor? You want me to leave?'

She smiled her thin smile. 'Well, not perhaps today. But I'm afraid you'll have to look round for something else, dear. I do so hate to let Malcolm down. I hope he will understand.'

I shrugged and watched her narrow back as she went into the cloakroom and shut the door very firmly behind her.

I stared at the door. Was I worried about what Malcolm felt? I felt absolutely nothing for Malcolm. Well, not any more, anyway.

I was contemplating just how much I disliked Malcolm when Mimi Trevor's head popped round the cloakroom door again. 'Perhaps by the end of the month, Sophia?'

Later that morning my friend Laura flicked her perfect curtain of black hair and scrunched her pretty smiley-baby face. 'The cow! The old cow!' she muttered as we kicked our heels, waiting for our first lecture of the day. 'Who'd'she think she is?'

I looked fondly at my new friend, warmed by her taking up the cudgels on my behalf. 'She thinks she's the owner of the house, that's who.'

'Why, what difference does that make? You still have rights, you know, love,' she growled. 'Tenant's rights.'

It was Laura's voice that initially drew me to her on the first day of the course. I was feeling a bit on my own, older than most of the graduates here, not sure I had done the right thing in coming

14

down here. The young eager voices around me were as foreign to me as the chatter of parakeets. Then Laura's voice penetrated the chatter, low and musical, rippling too fast, like the Tyne at high tide. A beautiful black-haired port in a storm.

I went across to her. 'You've gotta be from Newcastle,' I said.

'Snap!' she said, and leaped at me, giving me an unasked-for hug. I hugged her back. People think us lot from the North are dour and distant but strip one layer off and we're as tactile and emotional as any Greek or Italian. Look at our football fans.

'Snap out of it, Sophia!' she was saying now. 'What're you gunna do about it? Take her to a tribunal? Cause a ruckus?'

'Nah. No written agreement. No tenant's rights. Like she says, I'll look for somewhere. I should be able to do better than a bed on boxes.' I nodded at the door where our tutor was strolling in, black notebook in one hand and a folder with our writing briefs for the day in the other. 'Here we go,' I said, taking out my pen.

I have to say, after that uncertain start I began to love my course. An early lesson was that to succeed in journalism you had to learn to cross the line sometimes between forthrightness and rudeness. As this didn't come naturally to me the course was like a forcing ground for rudeness. When I mentioned this theory over beer last night to Laura, she laughed out loud and said how everyone here thought us Northerners had thin skins as well as log-size chips on our shoulders. She reminded me that journalism, in legend and often in reality, sees itself as a hardboiled profession. She sat cross-legged on my bed, bottle of beer in her hand and chanted, '"If it bleeds, it leads". "Don't let the truth get in the way of a good story". "Door-stepping is legitimate newsgathering". Look at it this way, Sophia. If it helps to get a good story it's gotta be worth it.'

I could see she really believed it. No wonder they thought she would go far, students and staff alike.

After the lecture we sat in the pub and considered our instructions. Laura's was a map reference in Tottenham. Mine said, 'Take a ride on the 73 bus to Seven Sisters and find a story: a colour feature about life on the edges of the city.' Not so bad. I was familiar now with the number 73. Catch it in one direction from Mrs Mimi Trevor's and you're heading for the British Museum, Bloomsbury and the West End. I'd travelled that way many times at weekends to escape my capsule of a room in Islington. But I had never travelled on it in the other direction. That would be a new experience.

Laura charged off to get started and I bought another half of beer, opened my laptop, and got on to the Net for a quick search. The 73 route was certainly not short of stories: opening of yet another gourmet restaurant; the Prime Minister lived near here; Joe Orton lived there; beggar cut up in street; East European sex slaves imprisoned in brothel; children arrested in firework scam; drug gang shoot-out in Stoke Newington – they were all news around there, once.

Our brief was to get back to college with our stories by four o'clock. They had to be good enough to please our hard-to-please tutors, a funny bunch of folks: the hard-edged ones had soft centres; the gentle ones had steely cores; they were a mixture of the professional, the streetwise and the deluded.

Writing for these exotic people was all very different from writing my own copy and being my own judge and jury, which had been my magazine experience in Newcastle. Once on the course it took me a while to live down my tutors' initial, discreet amusement at my hubris in setting up a community magazine from scratch on the New Dawn Estate in Newcastle. In fact it was my New Dawn experience that had won me a place on the course but somehow the price of this was to be forced to recognise how naff it all was: what basic mistakes I had made; how pretentious it was to think I could run a magazine from a standing start, even if it had won prizes.

I clicked my laptop shut and tucked it in my backpack. I would run to the bus stop, work up a bit of a sweat. It was not just Mimi Trevor who could keep fit. Then I would get on the bus and get my story.

Colour Feature

I squeezed on to the number 73 at Angel but didn't get a seat until we got to Newington Green. By then the heavily laden and closed-faced worker bees had peeled off and gone about their business.

I spotted this single seat at the front just behind the driver. A woman, sitting there knitting, pulled in her elbows to make space for me. I glanced at her shadowy reflection in the glass partition behind the driver. She looked like a praying mantis.

The window reflected other passengers: a stately woman in a tightly wrapped African headdress, an old man with an Arsenal baseball cap pushed to the back of his grizzled head, and a neat boy student of some kind, clutching his computer bag, his black-rimmed glasses signalling blankly into the glass.

I acquired this habit of looking obliquely at people when I first came to London. Here, direct looks cause embarrassment; seem like an invasion, a challenge. It's seen as disrespectful and can generate violence, even death. It's on the news every night: a shooting here, a stabbing there, a mugging in another place. Dark and violent but everyday stuff here.

Up in Newcastle we tell ourselves we live in a safe place. Warm. Authentic. Still, even there you can feel threatened. But there the feeling of threat is more diluted, less everyday. The press of people is less. It's still dangerous, though, if you are in the wrong place, or with the wrong family, as I know to my cost.

Here in London, this low-level feeling of threat can diminish you. But at its best it's a buzz, a challenge. It keeps you on your toes. Every look is an exchange to be dealt with. The default reaction is avoidance. And so many of these subtle avoidances generate a unique weariness, a dark exhaustion. When I first came here I used to fall into bed with exhaustion at ridiculously early hours. Of course, in those early days I was still recovering from my own dark insanity in Newcastle, so nothing was what you would call normal. So you couldn't blame London.

But I had escaped that insanity and in my newly sane frame of mind I'd embarked on a world where I would write for a living. And now to find my stories I'd had to learn to break that avoidance barrier time and time again. As Laura was always saying, if it gets a story it has to be worth it.

The bus swayed and I flinched as something – a knitting needle – poked me in the side.

The bus jolted again and my gaze dropped from the bus window to the hands of the woman beside me as she clicked away at her knitting. The fingers were long and slim, well manicured. The rings were discreet. The wool passing through her hands was pink twisted with blue. Every now and then she slipped a hand into her cloth bag, pushed a silver sequin along her wool to incorporate into the next stitch, and knitted on.

The bus turned a corner and the woman thrust her knitting into the cotton bag and stood up. She squeezed past me and made her way down the bus as it ground to a stop. When I moved into her place I noticed this other bag on the floor: one of those big checked ones that people use for all sorts of things these days.

I grabbed it and followed her. The bag was bulky but lighter than it looked. By the time I got to the platform the bus was setting off again. The conductor grabbed my arm. 'Hey, lady!' I wrenched myself free and jumped, ending up measuring my

19

length on the pavement with the checked bag beside me.

A young girl with corn rows and high boots kneeled down to help me up. She grinned. 'Yo' OK, girl? Come flyin' like that?'

I winced at the pain in my ankle. 'Fine, thank you.'

'You been to that launderette, girl?' she said, handing me the checked bag. Her fingernails were long, each one etched with a different glittering flower. 'This just like my launderette bag, I tell you.'

I shook my head. 'No.' I looked beyond her. The knitting woman was halfway across the street. 'Thanks. I've gotta go.' I managed a smile half as big as hers and limped away as fast as I could after the knitting woman.

But I had to wait. The woman had crossed just before the ever-streaming traffic was released again from the constraints of the traffic lights. It was a wide street, lined by tall houses with small front gardens that mostly harboured garbage bins and stranded domestic appliances. Some gardens had been concreted to make car pull-offs. But this was no ordinary street. It had a buzz about it, a sense of defiance. One or two of the gardens were bravely planted with dusty greenery, studded now with daffodils and crocuses. Pollarded lime trees stood guard before the low walls, filtering the air and blunting the impact of the streaming traffic. There were red, yellow and sky-blue doors as well as the peeling, faded, neglected ones. The curtained windows were mysterious, making you wonder who lived there, what their particular story might be.

I waited for a space in the streaming traffic and then followed the knitting woman, who turned into one of the houses, pulled out a key on a string round her neck, opened the door and vanished inside. I got to her gate and leaned on it to get my breath and give my throbbing ankle a rest. I looked up, conscious of being watched from a first-floor window. I blinked and looked again, and there was no one. Just a reflection of the pollarded lime tree standing by the gate.

By the door there were three doorbells with a speaker grille.

1 Selkirk
2 Marsh
3 Copeland

I pressed number 1. The intercom burbled. 'I've found this bag on the bus,' I said into thin air. 'Someone left it on the floor. I have it here.'

The ground-floor curtain twitched. I held up the checked bag. 'Come in.' A voice emerged from the crackling intercom and the door clicked open. Someone was very trusting. Mimi Trevor wouldn't have let a stranger in like that.

I found myself in a square hall floored with black and white Minton tiles relieved by a red diamond border. The stairs to my left had been boarded in and sealed by a Yale-locked door. Two mountain bikes hung on custom-made hooks on the staircase wall. There was a scattering of letters on the glass hall table. The door on my right opened, letting out a gust of heat and the smell of lilies. The

21

knitting woman filled the doorway. She had one of those faces – middle-aged, slightly horsy and innocent – that you see in Sunday supplements in front of the houses they are trying to flog in pieces that pretend they are not advertisements.

She seemed out of place here.

I held up the checked bag like an entrance ticket.

The woman smiled and opened the door wider. 'You picked it up on the bus?' The voice matched the face – crisp, well modulated. She took the bag from me. 'Come in, won't you?'

She led straight into a large room that must have once been a gracious drawing room. It had two leather couches, several low tables and a flickering faux gas fire book-ended by two big glass jars of while lilies. By the door stood an umbrella stand (full), and a shoe rack (overflowing). On the far wall there were two great bookshelves (also over-flowing); an oversize Pre-Raphaelite print hung above the fireplace. Every horizontal surface in the room was littered with books and papers – stacks of paper-cuttings and off-prints. The effect could have been charming but it felt unkempt, over-loaded, like a wizard's lair.

The woman followed my gaze. 'It's not me. My husband, Roger's, an academic,' she said drily. 'I don't doubt his study at the university's exactly like this. He lives a seamless life. Come through.' She led me through an archway into a back room. It was an enormous dog-leg space. At the far end the kitchen walls were lined with battered unfitted cupboards and there was a Swedish stove fronted by a semi-circular flowered sofa. It was calmer in that part of the dog-leg. Not a book in sight. Not even a cookery book.

'Here we are,' the woman beamed. 'My territory. Sit down and I'll get you something.' Without waiting for a reply she put the checked bag on the large table under the window and busied herself with a very large coffee pot.

'I'm Doreen,' she said over her shoulder. 'Doreen Selkirk.'

'My name is Sophia Morgan,' I said. I sat down on a wooden chair beside the large table. 'We pronounce that *So-f-eye-ah* where I come from. Down here in London they say *So-f-ee-ah*, so I always have to tell them.'

'And Morgan? Is that a Welsh name?'

'Probably. But I come from Newcastle, in the North.'

'I can tell. Our name is Scottish,' she said mildly. 'Three generations down, I'm afraid. More Home Counties than anything else now, I suppose.' She poured the coffee into two heavy, hand-thrown mugs and brought them over. 'You drink coffee?' she said, sitting down at the table. 'I didn't ask. Roger says I rush at things. Like a bull at a gate.' She nodded at a frizzy photo on the wall, of a man in combat fatigues. 'He thinks I'm unsafe. He sees robbers everywhere, old Roger. Robbers are his thing. Robbers are his *bêtes noires*.'

'Coffee's fine.' I sipped it. 'And I'm not a robber.'

'I could see that. I remember you from the bus. You sat beside me. Thank you so much for saving my bag.'

I nodded. 'A pity for you to lose it.'

'Right! My living's in there.' She leaned over and

23

upturned the bag, tipping three glittering woollen waistcoats onto the table. 'Gilets. Worth more than a hundred pounds to me. I sold the other three but these didn't make it. Poor darlings.'

She didn't seem like someone who had to do sweated labour for a living. More your Ladies' Circle kind of things – bridge and all that. My gran used to call them Kept Women. I stroked the purple mohair, flicked a silver sequin. 'You sell them?'

'Indeed I do. To this West End company called Big and Bold.' She paused. 'I sell them to them for forty pounds, they sell them on at a hundred and fifty.'

This didn't sound like the Ladies' Circle. They would never talk about money like this.

She went on, 'Of course, Roger says they're exploiting me and I should sell them on eBay for a hundred. But Websites! Selling!' she shuddered. The shudder was very Ladies' Circle.

'How did you get to sell them in the first place?'

She smiled and her face lit up. 'Well, I was in the café at the British Library, killing time because I really suffered with cabin fever when we first came here from the country. Have you been to the British Library?'

I shook my head. 'I've only been here a couple of months. Very tied up with things.'

'Yes. Well, there I was in the café, wearing one of my gilets, and this girl (slender as a wand, I may say), asked me where I'd bought it. I said I made them myself. Anyway, turns out she's the Bold bit of Big and Bold. She gave me a card. We made a deal. Now she buys half of what I make and the rest I knit on commission for people who've already bought.'

'So it's a living?' I said, my journalistic talons emerging.

'Living?' She laughed. 'I don't think of it as that, my dear. I like doing it and it brings in something. That's helpful, the way things are for me just now.'

I wondered what these things were for her.

She was in her stride. 'I have always knitted. My mother insisted when I was little. Idle hands and all that. She embroidered beautifully herself. My grandmother knitted. That and golf. They were both great golfers. Little else to do in Berkshire if one didn't ride.' She pushed a silver-grey gilet towards me. 'You may have that one, Sophia Morgan. Have it for your kindness.'

I must have blushed.

She blushed too. 'Perhaps I'm being tactless. Not the very height of young fashion?'

'No ... no ... honestly, Doreen.' I was digging a hole for myself.

'I know!' She leaned over, opened a long drawer in the dresser. I could smell her perfume, flowery and lemony at the same time. She hooked out a pair of grey gloves tied with pink bobbles. 'How about these? Have these. They'll keep you warm on those long bus journeys.'

The gloves were neat. I tried them on and made the right noises. Then I put them in my bag and, having drunk my coffee, I became what the course required of me: direct to the point of rudeness. I asked her how she came to live here, how she liked this part of London.

She shot me a startled glance, then sat back in her chair. 'Well,' she said, 'Roger is my second husband. We moved in here a year ago. All we could afford, if I were to be honest. Second marriages are poverty machines. Divorces are money pits. And then Roger lost his tenure at the university. So we are playing poor town mice these days. He does have a room at the university and this commission to write some scholarly tome about the eighteenth-century growth of the city. His interest is crime, particularly the highwaymen who roamed the Hackney Marshes and robbed rich people as they made their way out of London travelling north on the Kingsland Road. There's still a Kingsland Road. The old Roman road, you know.' Doreen sighed. 'But now the old boy's got this bee in his bonnet about those gangsters who ran in London in the 1960s. Making some kind of academic comparison with the highwaymen.' She yawned. 'Nonsense, of course. Robin Hood my eye! These people are the spawn of the devil, if you ask me. Psychopaths. But you cannot tell Roger. Oh, no!'

'And you like it here, Doreen? Better than Berkshire?'

She stared at me for a moment. 'Absolutely. I'm here with Roger and that's my choice. And the thing I thought would be awful, I find myself liking. I like the kind of subdued anarchy that is under the surface here, you know what I mean? The rich and "the rest" living cheek by jowl, their worlds barely touching, yet each sharply conscious of the other? In this very street you can go right across the social scene, from lords to ladies

26

of the night. In Berkshire one lives very separately. The nearest one gets to "the rest" is when they deliver milk or serve in Tesco's. Stifling. So much more lively here, don't you think?'

She stood up and a sequin floated out of the folds of her clothing. My cue to leave. She gave me her card, in case I knew anyone who wanted a custom-knit gilet. For someone who didn't care for selling she was not doing a bad job.

I pulled on the grey gloves and adjusted the pink pompoms. 'Thank you for these, Doreen,' I said, standing up.

'Thank you for saving my bag.' Her smile was kind. 'Come and see me again. Listen to me! Mae West. Come up and see me sometime!'

I was through the door before I realised that although I knew a good deal about her, she had not asked me a single thing about myself. She had not broken my line of avoidance. But I liked Doreen Selkirk. She had this comforting, engaging, self-absorption that's easy to be around and makes no demands except a listening ear.

And, anyway. I didn't want my line broken. I certainly didn't want to answer questions about myself to strangers.

Did you see that young woman with red hair falling off the bus and that black girl helping her up? There are lots of them round here now, black people. You never used to see a black face in the old days. But they're always immaculate. You never see a scruffy one. Not like the people who sit by the banks, begging. Always white, they are, man or woman. And scruffy.

27

Not like the people in the shops in the street, those Indians and Turks. Immaculate, they are. Polite. And glamorous, often. Film star looks, especially the men. The man in the newspaper shop always wore jeans and T-shirt, very modern, until the planes went into those towers in New York. Then he grew his beard and started to wear white linen. Even more glamorous, if you ask me. But still so polite.

And did you see the girl following that woman into the Copelands' house? That house is flats now. Teeming with people. Old Mrs Copeland would be mortified. They keep bicycles inside. I've seen them wheel them in.

I wonder why the girl followed her. They were on the bus but not together. The girl followed her. I saw it clearly. She fell down, the black girl picked her up, and she followed the woman into the house. Dangerous, if you ask me.

A Mint Girl

The door to number 83 clicked behind me and I stood looking out at the passing traffic, processing the idea of the Selkirks and their life in London. There was a colour piece there, surely. 'Temporary Londoners', or 'Doreen Selkirk Knitting a Life for Herself in North London'…

'They're not from round here, you know. Mr Selkirk's from Scotland and Mrs Selkirk is from some posh place out in the country. You can tell.' The voice was deep but the speaker was female.

28

A golden-faced child sat on the wall.

Children sitting on a wall like a line of crows. That's when I first noticed. I first suspected. The children knew about it. The neighbour had said that at the inquiry in Newcastle. *The children knew about it. They had been watching.* Her daughter told her. She knew something was wrong before it all came out.

This girl had tousled black hair, gleaming eyes, a flat chest, short skirt and big trainers. She sniffed and nodded at the door behind me. 'I got some gloves like that. She gave me them. The posh woman.'

I smiled widely. It usually works, especially with children. This friend of mine who still worked on the New Dawn Estate always said a big smile was a better weapon than a pepper-spray any day.

'Yes,' I said to the girl. 'I was just talking to her. Mrs Selkirk. She's very kind.'

'They're called Doreen and Roger. I call them Mr and Mrs Selkirk. She makes fairy cakes, you know. Dee-licious.'

I nodded. 'A kind woman.'

'That Roger saved my life once. That Mr Selkirk.'

I glanced across at the traffic.

'D'you wanna know how?'

I recognised that this was a titbit to keep me there. I hitched my bottom onto the wall and instantly regretted it. The wall was damp and cold from the morning rain. The girl must have felt it too. Her narrow thighs were mottled with the cold.

'Well then,' I said. 'How did this Mr Selkirk save your life?'

She stood up and went across to lean against

the pollarded lime, so she was facing me. She glanced at the closed front door. 'Well, it was like this, see? There's these three girls in my class think they're hard. Do martial arts. Got belts and things. Slap you all about. Kick you as soon as look at you.' She said this in a chanting rhythm.

'For defence?' I'm all for martial arts for girls. Didn't I set up two classes for girls on the New Dawn? How could a girl walk those mean streets up there in Newcastle, or these mean streets down here, without so much as a red belt, and all that implied? Mine had stood me in good stead from time to time. It gives you an unassailable walk.

This girl snorted. 'Defence? For attack, more like.'

'They attacked you?'

'Well, this girl did, see? Called May-Bell Ott, she took a flying leap, kicked me on the back and I was in the gutter. Then she kicked my arm and my leg. There, see? There's still a mark.'

I winced.

'Anyway, there I am, in the gutter and they're all crowding round, May-Bell and her friends, nudging me with their feet, tipping my bag all over me. Laughin'. May-Bell picks up my mobile and my new protractor and compasses. She has the compasses through her fingers like knuckle dusters. Then her eyes go back like this...' The girl rolled back her eyes so only the whites were visible, then returned to normal. 'Then I am for it. No sweat.'

In my time I'd heard stories at case meetings of child-on-child violence – some of which hit the headlines. But this was a London story. Could

30

make copy for my colour piece. 'So what happened then?'

'Well, that Mr Roger Selkirk came along and scattered these girls about, like it was some American film.' She giggled, showing very white teeth, as yet too large for her child's features. 'That Roger don't look like no Brad Pitt, though.'

I thought of the photograph on Doreen Selkirk's wall. 'No. I can see that.'

'Well, he flung these gikes off. They swore at him and called him a pervert but they backed off and slinked away like so many wild cats. But, like I say, that gike May-Bell took my mobile and my best protractor. Curse her!'

I raised my eyebrows.

'My nana Mary used to say that before she died, against people who disrespected her. Before she died, that was. My mum died too, but she never said "Curse them!" Never cursed nobody, my mum.'

I started to feel uneasy. I glanced up at the house.

'Me? I live here,' she said. 'Halfway up. See that big window in the middle? That's ours.'

I looked up at the tall house. She must have been the one watching from the window when I rang the bell. And she had come down here to wait for me. 'That one?'

'I live here with my dad. He's called George Marsh. They call him Sparrow because he's so big. I'm called Bobbi. My mum named me after that girl in *The Railway Children*. She liked reading, my mum.'

'Shouldn't you be at school?' I said. Christ! I

31

sounded like some maiden aunt. Or a social worker, which I had been but was no longer.

'No, I shouldn't, I've got bronchitis.'

I looked at her mottled thighs. 'Well, you're taking a chance, sitting on this wall. That tree must be damp too.'

She stood away from the tree and groaned. 'Oh, ain't that a shame? I came out here to see my dad off to work at one o'clock and stayed.'

It was not about me, then. How self-centred am I?

She went on, 'Sometimes it's too bloody quiet up in there on your own.' She nodded towards her window. 'D'you know what they call me now at school?'

'No. What do they call you?'

'Yank! Yank! They say Brad Pitt – no, sorry – Roger Selkirk was my dad. And because he has a funny accent they said he was an American. Now they're blaming me for the invasion of Iraq, stupid gikes.'

'Gikes? I've never heard that before.'

'I made it up. But that's just what they are, though.' She stood away from the tree and turned towards the door. 'So what're you called?'

'Sophia. Sophia Morgan.'

'That's a nice name. "Sophia-Sophia, your pants're on fire." Do you live round here?'

'No. I'm just visiting.'

'You should live round here. You'd like it. It's mint, living here. You should meet my dad. You'd really, really like him.' Bobbi Marsh fished a key out of her pocket. 'Will you be around here again?'

'I don't know. Maybe.'

'You should. Like I say. It's mint.' She stood back, tipped her head and looked right to the top of the house. 'There's this man lives in the top flat. Now *he* really is nearly like Brad Pitt. Only thinner. You'd like him too.' Then she slipped into the house and the door closed behind her.

I walked on, buzzing. The stories were coming out of the walls in this place: 'One parent families'. 'Bullying'. 'Anti-Americanism in Schools'. I should make some notes. Time was ticking away. I reckoned if I walked to the end of this road, turned right and right again I'd be on to the High Street. I could go into a café and get some of this stuff down while it was in my head. One part of my head said that if I were a real writer I'd have had my notebook out already, checking facts, getting verification. Not to worry. I'd have to blag it. Be creative. That was another thing I was learning on my course. There was a lot of blagging creativity about. Everyone was at it. In the rush to the deadline the truth is the first casualty.

That child is off school again, Pusscat. Talking to the falling-down girl. Too much of that, wagging off. There are shoals of children lurking around the streets during the day. There should be someone to sweep them up with a net, like in the film. It's nothing new, of course. All that started in 1963. Sex. Truancy. When everyone suddenly started to feel their oats. Chris used to say all that new freedom came too late for him. Called his posh boarding school 'Borstal With Carpets'. Funny, that. Of course, those men he ran with around here had known the real thing. Borstal, that is.

33

I should get on, Pusscat. There are the new bulbs to water. Then there's Chris's suits to brush and his shoes to clean. Did I tell you he used to call me Matron when we were playing our games? How we laughed. But still his high standards were no joke. Standards. That's what he had. He was class among rags, was my Chris. Class among rags...

Oasis

I waited for the sanity pause signalled by the lights changing on the corner, crossed the road diagonally to the bus stand and took my place in the queue. Up behind the bus stop a woman was standing in her garden. She was wielding a brush, harassing detritus from the bus stand into a heap, before shovelling it into a black bin. The crazy paving path was laid with white marble tiles, irregularly shaped like chocolate mis-shapes. It wound into a spiral around a central patch of garden filled with meticulously kept dark green-ery, relieved by clusters of daffodils that seemed to emit light rather than reflect it.

A lithe grey cat lording over this oasis was pos-ing on a deep windowsill, eyeing the queue with sleepy disdain.

The woman caught my admiring gaze, as gar-deners do. I'd seen this in Newcastle: people who make beauty where there was none. I'd written an article, 'Oases in the Urban Dust', for the New Dawn community magazine. Fascinated by gardens ever since. I even started to cultivate my own garden at my ground-floor flat in the West End of that city. Those plants have probably withered away now from neglect.

(At my course interview, Jack Molloy, ex hard-news journo on the old *Express*, had read this piece, rolled his eyes and said, 'Gardening! Jesus!')

'Those tiles are amazing,' I offered now to this woman. 'Unusual. You know?'

She stared down at the tiles beneath her feet. 'I suppose they are.' Her voice was very London – high-pitched, slightly nasal. 'Chap before us – that would be in the 1930s – he worked in Abney Park Cemetery. My guess is these are off-cuts from gravestones.' She contemplated them. 'My mother told me that. She should know, she was married into this house. She always thought they were creepy.'

Suddenly the path was not so attractive. I nodded towards the slightly dusty forsythia hedge undercut by hellebores. 'Lovely garden. Are you a keen gardener?'

She leaned on her brush. At close quarters she seemed older: she was thin to the point of scrawny. Her boots were knee-high and her skirt was far too short for what must have been her fifty-odd years. Or more. She had a deep fringe over her eyes, which were lined with kohl. Her hair flowed down her back: a cross between an ageing Brigitte Bardot and Joni Mitchell. Only thinner. My friend Paula, who mostly writes about style and fashion, had been banging on about the sixties look being back in. Seemed it had never been out for this woman.

35

The woman's chalky pink lips widened into a smile at my continued attention. She was not fazed by my staring. 'This is nothing compared to my real garden, out the back. Out here I just plonk things in that'll tolerate the fumes from the cars and the buses, and the rubbish coming from that lot.' She nodded at the queue, all standing with their backs to her. 'Daffs are good for that. Iron-clad. There are tulips in there too; they'll show in a week or two. Now my back garden's better. Out there my philadelphus, she'll give a show by June. And *Lavendula* – you can rely on her.' Her voice had this thread of gentility, politeness counterpointing the sharp London tones. 'Out the back it's a different world.'

'So, you must be a keen gardener,' I offered, feeling my way in.

'Keen? My mother says I'm an obsessive. A madwoman over my garden.'

I waited. The bus came. The queue filed on and settled in their seats but I didn't join them. The brakes creaked again and it lumbered off.

The woman leaned her brush against the wall and stood still for a second as the grey cat launched itself from the bay windowsill and settled on her shoulder. She made her way down to the gate and opened it.

'Would you like to see my back garden?' she said. Two sets of eyes – hers, black-lined, panda-like; the cat's, clear, round and haughty – bored into me.

'Yes. Wonderful. Yes, I would.' I subdued a quick mental flash of the witch in *Hansel and Gretel*.

The woman led the way down the substantial

hall, through an old-fashioned scullery down a bit of yard and into a long garden surrounded by tangled hedges of budding honeysuckle. The low box hedge that defined an elliptical lawn held back deep borders. Halfway down the garden were two raised beds joined by a pergola that marked the entry to a section at the back of her garden, which centred on a small sundial set in an ellipse of gravel, also contained by a box hedge. In the back corners of the garden were two buildings: a garden shed, painted yellow, and the smallest of greenhouses.

The borders were filled with daffodils and the last of the crocuses, interspersed by clumps of cutback perennials and evergreen shrubs. It was neat and orderly and pregnant with spring delight.

In this small, immaculate space the roar of the traffic on one side of the house and the rattle of trains beyond the gardens faded into insignificance.

The cat leaped from the woman's shoulder and raced down the garden after some invisible prey. The woman took my arm and walked me down the garden, intoning the names and history of every plant as we passed them.

In front of the yellow shed were two old-fashioned wire chairs painted dark blue. She sat on one of them and nodded at the other. I sat down. The cat leaped on to her lap and she started to stroke it.

'It's a lovely garden,' I said. 'A kind of surprise. A secret. Have you always been a gardener?'

She was already shaking her head. 'Absolutely not. Up till five years ago this space was a slum.

A stub of lawn with honeysuckle and magnolia sprawled halfway across it. Smelled heavenly. Then I kept meeting this old man on the seventy-three bus. He lived on the top of some flats in Essex Road and had no garden. He just loved gardens. Jamaican chap. Warm, like they are. He came in here and we transformed it between us. I'm grateful to that man. Gregory, he's called.'

'Does he still help you?'

'No. Got the chance for an allotment across town and took it.'

'That's a pity.'

'Not really. I'd got the bug by then. Gregory had me growing vegetables down this end.' She nodded towards the sundial. 'Vegetables? I never eat them. Had to give them away. So when he went I dug out the bed for gravel and got the sundial in.'

'It is nice. Kind of frames the plants. I bet it looks fantastic in summer.'

'You are right there. I opened it to the public, you know. *"Small Town Gardens, June the twelfth."* For charity. Gregory came that day, brought his friends. It was like Mardi Gras. We made one hundred and twenty pounds last year. Breast Cancer.' She stood up abruptly, scattering the cat from her knee. 'Sorry, dear, but I have to get on. I'm meeting a man at the council about the waste bins.'

I followed her back down the stepping-stone path. 'Are they a problem, the waste bins?'

She sniffed. '*No* waste bins, that's the problem. Been fighting nearly a year for a bin at that bus stop. The stuff that comes off that bus stop! Ends up in my garden like so much flotsam and jetsam.' She opened the front door to let me out. 'But we're getting somewhere. They've promised me one. Now they just have to get it here from the warehouse. Hooray to that.' She shook my hand with a hand that was surprisingly hard and horny. 'Julia Soper. Miss whoever-you-are, come tomorrow, at two,' she said. 'We'll have cocktails.'

'I'm Sophia M...' As I stared at the closed door it dawned on me that Miss Julia Soper was quite a hustler. She'd got the Jamaican man Gregory to transform her garden. It would certainly get me back here tomorrow for cocktails.

For cocktails. Jesus!

Back home – if you can call it that – my landlady met me at the door. 'The room, Sophia, I must...'

I charged past her. 'I'm looking, Mrs Trevor. I'm looking.'

Well, Pusscat, what do you think of the girl who knocks on doors? She knows more than you'd think about gardens. She looks anxious, needy. Too thin. Mother would say she needs feeding up. My mother was always on about people needing feeding up. Chris used to say she wouldn't be happy until I was bouncing around like a Michelin man. He used to help me hide the food away. 'Slender as a wand, darling.' That's what he used to say. 'I like my women slender as a wand.' He used to bring me clothes, Pusscat. Always the right size. Once he even brought me a Chanel suit. It's in the wardrobe. Black and cream check with black braiding. It had the label removed, of course, but you could tell. You can always tell good design. My Chris taught me that.

Cocktails with Miss Soper

The next morning, after sitting through a sparkling lecture by a famous magazine editor who was obsessed with F. Scott Fitzgerald, I was itching to be off again. I turned down an invitation from Laura to join them all in a pub for the usual session, and by one thirty I was on the 73 bus with the intention of visiting Miss Julia Soper for cocktails.

My assignment yesterday turned into a story about a child being saved in the street by a stranger. I buffed up my conversation with Bobbi into a real interview. I invented an interview with Roger Selkirk, calling him Robert Simpson. I padded it out with statistics and other stuff from the Internet archives of child-on-child violence and urban alienation. Jack Molloy said it needed a few tweaks but was quite sound and 'might even see the light of day'.

I was relieved to find, when I knocked on her door, that Miss Soper recognised me and remembered our appointment. Her eye-skimming hair was unchanged from yesterday, but today her knee-length boots were white and she wore green tights and a green miniskirt with a white polo-necked sweater. The kohl round her eyes was leaking into her crepey skin and the varnish on two of her nails was chipped.

She led the way into her immaculate sitting

room, which sported two leggy sofas, a teak coffee table and that kitschy Tretchikoff *Portrait of a Green Lady* hung over the low tiled fireplace. She slipped behind a shelf arrangement in the corner, lined with bottles like a bar.

'I've already mixed it. It's called French Riviera. Whisky, apricot brandy, fresh lemon juice. My favourite. Gregory liked rum, so I used to make him Black Devil – dark rum, dry vermouth, black olive. But I still gave him this from time to time.' She held the shaker shoulder height and shook it. Then she poured it in two cornet-shaped glasses on to ice, which cracked and crazed. Then she added a maraschino cherry. The whole thing smelled of danger.

'There.' She handed me a glass. 'Taste that. It was invented by Chris, a friend of mine. I call it Nectar of the Gods.'

It was delicious. Not like alcohol at all. Therefore, as we all know, dangerous.

She sat down, knees close together, and sipped her drink. 'Now, my dear, I didn't catch your name?'

I told her.

'So, Miss Sophia Morgan, what brings you to this neck of the woods? You're a stranger. I thought so yesterday when I heard your voice and saw you wandering across the road out here after the large woman.'

Not Hansel or Gretel but Babe in the Wood, I thought. Babe in the Wood, watching.

So, my tongue well oiled by the Nectar of the Gods, I began to talk about being a stranger in a strange land, then went on to tell about being a

41

social worker on a hard Newcastle estate. About setting up the New Dawn magazine and, at first anyway, having to write everything myself. Then, with a little prodding and a second cocktail, about winning the prizes for the magazine and being tempted to sell up and come to London to try this course, with the wild thought that I could make my living in journalism. By my third cocktail I was telling her how everyone else on my course, apart from my mate Laura, seemed so sharp and metropolitan, so hard-edged. How my take on life felt provincial and passé. And then how the 73 bus had planted me here on Barrington Street, which felt good. How much I liked this street...

But even half drunk I didn't tell her about the wild events up in Newcastle that led to my breakdown.

'Are you married, Sophia?' she cut in sharply. 'You're old enough to be married.' She was good at the direct question, as good as any aspiring journalist.

'Well, I nearly got married once when I was twenty. But felt like – well – avoiding *not* being married.'

The door creaked and the grey cat flowed into the room. It leaped on to the windowsill, coiled down, turned away from us and concentrated on glaring at the people in the bus queue.

'Well, Sophia, marriage isn't everything,' she said.

I nodded. 'That's what I thought.'

'I was nearly married once, you know,' she said, wandering back towards the cocktail shaker and reaching for the bottle of grenadine.

'Did you call it off?'

'No, *he* did. He was our lodger. Nice man. A gentleman. Name of Chris. Public school. Something in the City. We were engaged but he got cold feet. I'm sorry to say he couldn't face me. One day he just didn't come home. Left me alone.' She sighed and turned the shaker upside down, then upside down again. 'D'you want to see his room? I bet you'd like that.'

The Nectar was making my eyes burn, my cheeks flush. 'I really don't think...'

'Come on. I'll show you.' She led the way up to the first, then the second floor, now treading on a threadbare stair carpet. Then into a large back bedroom. The bed, a high single, was fully made up and laid out with green silk pyjamas. The dressing table was set with two brushes, a tub of Brylcreem, a packet of Players Full Strength, a silver cigarette lighter and a half-bottle of whisky holding down a racing paper. It was dated 13 June 1969.

Miss Soper went across to the wardrobe, opened it and passed her hands along the row of dark suits, making the wooden hangers rattle. It was like a benediction. 'He wore a different suit every day, you know. Clean shirt. Handkerchief in the pocket. He was very particular.'

My mind felt fuzzy.

She shut the door with a clatter. 'Well, that's it.' She sniffed. 'More Nectar awaits us.' She charged past me and went back downstairs. By the time I was back in the sitting room, she had two Martinis set up.

'I don't think...' My protest was weak.

43

She waved a beringed hand. 'Nonsense, Sophia. Just one for the road.'

I pulled myself together and took out my notebook. 'I thought I might do a piece for my course about opening the garden to the public.'

She sipped her Martini, crossing one leg elegantly over the other. 'Bit early for that, dear.' The cat decamped from the windowsill, leaped on to her lap and eyed me with moderate malevolence. 'It won't happen again till June.'

My brain was too fuzzy to handle that. 'But ... but ... still, just tell me about it.' I waved my gel pen in her direction. 'Your garden. And ... er ... opening it to the public.'

She sipped her Martini again. 'Well, this woman knocked on the door, very jolly hockey sticks. She'd seen my garden from the train and tracked me down.' She giggled. 'Tracked me ... train ... tracks. That's good. Anyway, I've done it for three years now. I do it every year.' She spread out her long fingers. 'You wouldn't think they were gardener's hands, would you?'

'Well, no...'

'My mother, she says my hands are ridiculous. She hates nail varnish. Calls me a tart, you know.' Her tone became confidential.

I looked towards the door. 'Your mother...?'

She shook her head. 'No longer with me, I'm afraid. Now finish your cocktail, dear.'

My mind was fuzzy by now but the story of Hansel and Gretel flashed back into my mind with Miss Julia Soper in the role of the witch enticing the children with sweets. I remember wondering if this was how she enticed the Jamai-

44

can Gregory to come and transform her garden. She read my thoughts. 'Like I say, Gregory said he preferred rum,' she said. 'But he got to like my Nectar in the end.'

What happened next was a bit of a haze, but I do remember being on a bus and catching sight of this very small house, round the corner from Barrington Street. Painted a very pale dusty lavender, it had a small door and a single arched window. It seemed to glow in the late afternoon light. It would not have been out of place in Hansel and Gretel. A big 'To Let' sign was nailed across one of the dusty windows. I must have had enough wits about me to write the number of the agent on the back of my hand because it was still there the next morning when I woke up with a very gritty mouth.

The rest of that night is a blank. I only remember waking up in the early hours with a blinding headache, drinking a litre of water and vowing never to accept cocktails off strange women ever again.

Do you know, Pusscat, it took Mother only a short time to admit that she liked Chris. She said he was smart without being flash. Talkative without being loud. She liked his tales about his family house in Yorkshire and the stuff about shooting and horses. But when he started taking me about, buying me clothes at Biba, taking me to Vidal Sassoon to get my hair done and teaching me how to make cocktails, she became disenchanted. She was suspicious about his job in the City and said he kept bad company. She

45

used to say he had stolen me from her, even though we were all still in the same house and clearly he hadn't.

Still, she put on a cheerful face when we got engaged, even gave us a party. You know she wasn't a bad woman, my mother. And she didn't crow when Chris left me so very suddenly. The two of us just went back to how we'd been before, although now I was different. Her Julia was a very different kettle of fish now. I might still be her daughter but now I was still Chris's girl too. She and I had this tiff about me keeping his room for him. But I won that, and Chris and his room were never mentioned between us. I think the girl Sophia liked Chris's room. Bound to, really.

I am not demented. Don't think that, Pusscat. You're going to say that by now Chris must have married some county girl up in Yorkshire. He could have had children, even grandchildren now. I'm still not sure. What if he's still waiting to come back to me? I will be ready for him, Pusscat. His room is there. I'm here. Waiting.

Property

Of course Jack Molloy told me to ditch the idea for a piece on gardens opening to the public. He drew hard on his thin cigar, then waved it about, trailing smoke in the air.

'I know gardens are something of interest to you, Sophia, but surely there's something more … er … immediate? It might *just* be a story in June when the gardens are open. But now, it's a dead duck. In journalism timing is everything, dear.' He was middle-aged, distinctly heterosexual but, in Laura's observation, has clearly adopted the current fashion for homosexual style.

The 'dear' still rankled, but I swallowed the offence. Still rather fragile from the Nectar, I was in no fit state to take on Jack Molloy. He mended fences, suggesting a piece on gentrification of the London urban villages. 'It should suit you, dear. Not exactly hard news but one has to admit everyone's interested in property these days. Take Stokey as your model, dear. Booming, that old place.'

It was certainly an idea. The next day I went back to Stoke Newington and interviewed three of the numerous estate agents. I listed the restaurants (from Turkish through Thai and Russian to Afro-Caribbean); the organic shops and the chichi decorating emporia. I went on to the Internet and learned of Stoke Newington's evolution from a village on the road north from London, preyed on by highwaymen and opportunistic robbers. I learned that the bricks – used to build houses here and further afield as the suburbs grew – were made from clay from the old brickfields on land not far from Barrington Street, an area now itself covered with houses. Pooter-fication of the village then, gentrification of the suburb now. Even alongside this process, the highwaymen and robbers had given way to sixties gangsters and present-day drug gangs.

So far, so complicated.

Consequently I was pumped up with information as I walked Barrington Street again, past

47

houses that had been featured in lifestyle magazines, cheek by jowl with darker moth-eaten places, squats, drugs dens and worse. And there was this special brand of ethnic gentrification: brilliant houses curtained in stunning sari silk and larded with bright paints in fantastic shades gleaming out at me like beacons through the dull spring afternoon. The gentrified houses now outnumbered the dark dens and squats, so I suppose we were at a point of change. Not hard news, of course, but worth a comment.

Weird, on two days' acquaintance, that I seemed to have acquired a feeling of ownership of these streets. So it was with proprietorial anger that I observed front gardens that could have been small gems (as was Miss Julia Soper's), crudely covered with concrete to make car pull-offs. Even worse, some of the pull-offs had no room for cars because of the plethora of bags of rubbish, discarded sofas, battered filing cabinets and the doorless fridges.

Even so, I liked Barrington Street. The trees in most of the gardens were in their spring green, and even with the roar of traffic you had the sense that it was a real street, not the way through to somewhere. I turned off Barrington Street and came to a halt in front of the little lavender-coloured house I'd noticed from the bus the day before. Though it didn't glow, it looked no less engaging in full daylight. I was drawn to it with the feeling I had seen it a hundred times before. That feeling you get in cathedrals or in the middle of standing stones.

I shivered and pulled up my sleeve to see the letting agent's number still on my unwashed wrist. I had seen it. Just once. Last night from the bus. I can't have been that drunk as the number was accurate.

It was far from perfect. The railings round the narrow front garden had snared every bit of flying paper for weeks. The pale lavender paint on the walls looked like an apology beside the bright reds and dense ochres of its neighbours. But the arched window was very pretty. You could see straight through to a back window so the house must be very shallow – just one room deep – and narrow, no more than one and a half rooms wide. It was a tiny house, much older than its neighbours.

I was suddenly very hungry. I turned quickly and took a short cut on to the High Street and found a narrow restaurant called Bodrum not far from the police station. The four burly men in anoraks devouring full English breakfasts at the next table could only be policemen.

I tucked into soft Turkish bread, honey and yoghurt, my mind teeming with thoughts of the Lavender House. The aches in body reminded me of last night when I tossed and turned, dealing with a surfeit of alcohol as well as my lumpy mattress in Mimi Trevor's boxroom.

No contest. The Lavender House was a palace in comparison. I wanted it. I wanted it more than I'd wanted anything for a long time.

'Back again, Sophia?' Young Bobbi Marsh slipped into the seat opposite. She was in school uniform. 'Can't keep away, seems like. I saw you through the window of the caff.'

The sight of her made me smile. 'Seems like that...'

49

'So, what're you doing here?'

The pretty Turkish waitress, uncued, brought Bobbi a glass of milk and some toast.

'Now, Bobbi, how're you? Your dad OK?'

'He's fine, Rina,' Bobbi said. Then she caught my glance. 'My dad has this deal with Rina and her uncle. I come here after school for my tea and he pays them every month for whatever I have. It's usually milk and toast.' She sighed. 'That's all I can stand after school.'

It was two o'clock. Not really *after school*. 'Is it that bad, school?'

'It's not that bad. But I have to keep waiting for people to catch up with me so often that it's boring. And there's the Yank thing. All that, like, name-calling. I don't like that.'

'Is that girl still bothering you?'

She shrugged. 'Not any more. She was taken away.'

'Excluded?'

Her dark hair bobbed as she shook her head. 'Nah. There's a few worse than her. Nah. It's like this. My dad went to see her dad. And *he* took her away to another school.' She gulped at her milk.

I suddenly wished I'd had a father like that, galloping to my aid whenever I needed it. But for me, my father was an unknown quantity If he'd galloped up to save me I wouldn't have recognised him from Adam.

She put down her glass. 'Anyway. Why're you here again? You don't come from round here. I can tell from your voice.'

'I've been looking at property.'

'Property?' She beamed. 'You're moving in

round here?'

It was too complicated to explain about the gentrification article. 'I saw a To Let notice on a house when I was here yesterday. Round the corner from Barrington Street. So I thought I'd check it out.'

She leaned forward, fixing me with her gaze. 'It's nice round here, Sophia. Mint. Can I check this house out with you?'

'Shouldn't you be at school? Haven't you any homework to do?'

She sighed. 'I told you. I've done it. I'm always waiting for people to catch up. Not missing anything.'

'I'm a stranger to you, Bobbi. You shouldn't hook up with strangers. It can be dangerous.' Old professional habits die hard.

She shook her head, then pulled out her mobile phone and rang a number. 'Dad? Yes. I'm fine. I'm in Mehmet's... Finished early... It's only Citizenship, then Modern Dance, yugch! Listen! You know I told you about the woman who came to the house to see Mrs Doreen Selkirk...? Sophia... Yeah...Yeah... She's OK. I told you. Well, I met her here at Mehmet's again and, well, I'm gunna hang out with her a while. I'll get Rina to check.' She waited, then handed over the phone. 'You gotta give him your name, address, and telephone number.'

The voice on the phone was deep, resonant, unaccented. 'Bobbi told you?'

The knight on the white charger.

'Yes, she told me,' I said faintly. 'Name, address and telephone number.'

'Well, Miss Morgan, my daughter's an independent soul and I like that in these besieged times. But I always check.' His tone was deep, cool. It flowed through my ear into my brain and right down to my toes. It occurred to me that I must still be hung over.

I gave him the information and meekly assured him I was trustworthy. Then I handed the phone back to Bobbi. She took it across to the waitress, who came back with her and asked me for my card or some ID. I complied.

She spoke into the phone. 'The woman's OK, Sparrow. Her name's Sophia Morgan. Don't worry, I tell you.' She clicked the phone shut and grinned at me. She had one cracked tooth. 'I tell him you are all right,' she said. 'Bobbi is a wild child but we all take care of her here.'

Bobbi stood up. 'Now! Can we please see this house you were talking about?'

The estate agent, a smart plump woman called Mrs Slack, took some persuading to show us the house there and then, but I flashed my press card at her and talked about the gentrification article and she became rather more co-operative.

Inside, the house was even smaller than it looked from the outside. You walked straight into a living room, and the capsule kitchen was a step away through an open arch.

'Fully carpeted, as you see,' said Mrs Slack, rubbing the toe of her high-heeled shoe along the speckled heather carpet that stretched as far as the kitchen tiles. A downstairs bathroom led off the kitchen. There was a veil of dust on the inside of every window. The place smelled like rotting apples. Upstairs there was a small bedroom with a double bed base wedged into it and a tangle of shelves. The other, even smaller room could only take what looked like a child's bed. A coat rack blocked the window light.

'Like a doll's house,' said Bobbi. 'Great, that.'

'It's let furnished,' said Mrs Slack, flicking off a piece of dust that had settled inconsiderately on her immaculate suit. 'But we got rid of the mattresses. We always advise changing mattresses. There's an allowance for the purchase of new ones in the deposit.' She lifted the corner of a drooping curtain with her little finger cocked as though she were drinking tea. She wrinkled her nose. 'Can't think why she left these grotty curtains.' They were slippery, paper-thin yellow silk, appliqued with butterflies in all shades of blue and pink.

I thought the curtains were lovely but I kept my face straight. 'So will there be an arrangement on the deposit to replace these curtains?'

'I could contact Mr B about it. It's possible he might make a concession.'

Back downstairs, I looked around again at the long leather sofa that had seen better days, the chipped black glass coffee table and the table under the window. The kitchen had a stained stainless-steel sink unit and a 1950s kitchen cabinet and that was that. I peered through the glazed back door at the narrow yard and a high wall. In the far corner was a wire garden chair, very like those in Julia Soper's garden. On it, in a dusty pot, a leggy pelargonium was just surviving.

Bobbi had started another tour of the house. I could hear her clanking around upstairs. I stayed to talk to Mrs Slack, who was standing in retreat

53

position by the door, scratching marks on her clipboard. The rental was not much more than I was paying for my hutch-bedroom in Islington. The deposit was a shock but with a couple of hundred off for the curtains and the mattresses I could do it, even if I had to raid my precious survival fund. This was still pretty healthy, bulging with the profit from selling my flat and car in Newcastle, but I needed it to keep me through this year and even further, so I couldn't throw money away.

Bobbi came bounding downstairs. 'It's a brilliant house, Sophia. Dinky. You've gotta have it.'

'D'you think so?'

'Course I do. It's near Barrington Street and everything. Near me. Think of that! Mint.'

I looked around. 'I don't see why not. Anything's better than where I am now.'

Bobbi grabbed my arm and hugged it to her side, a kind of partial embrace. Mrs Slack, standing guard by the door, relaxed. I could read her mind. A sale! This late in the day. So she hadn't wasted her precious time.

I told her I wanted the keys as quickly as possible.

We went back to the office and Mrs Slack got on to the phone to Mr B. I heard the word 'press' mentioned, and something about 'good PR'. She returned to say if I paid the deposit by Barclaycard, paid the first month by cheque and set up a direct debit for the rental, then I could have the key directly. Now.

'I feel I can trust you, Miss Morgan.' She hesitated. Clearly they were very keen to get the place off their hands. 'We do get numerous enquiries,

54

but they're all tourists. Just nosy about the house. You know.'

I didn't know.

Bobbi clutched my arm. 'Do it!' she said.

So I did it. With Mrs Slack on one side of me and Bobbi on the other I seemed to have no choice. But really, to say 'no choice' is to cop out. I wanted this little house more than I'd wanted anything for a long time. More than I'd wanted my boss Malcolm to leave his wife and marry me.

Worse, I wanted it even more than I wanted the chilly Darren and Josie Parnaby to get a long sentence for killing their Drina, who had always meant more to me than just part of my case load. It was when I told Malcolm that the Parnabys should be garrotted, not imprisoned, that he said he thought it was time for me to take a break. He arranged for me to take paid leave and fixed up the New Dawn community magazine thing. Malcolm was very considerate towards me in those months after he dumped me. Bastard.

Outside in the street Bobbi said we should go and look at the house again without 'that woman' hanging around.

'I can't, Bobbi. I have to get back to write an article on gentrification. For this course I'm on.'

'Is that what you're doing? Gentrifying yourself?'

She was clever. In some children this can be irritating. But in her it had a kind of directness, an engaging simplicity.

'That'll be the day!' I said.

I saw the 73 coming and ran.

Jack Molloy did not dislike the piece, entitled

'Gentrification Is No New Thing'. 'Nicely anchored in the history of the place, dear, but not too pedantic. Informative.'

That night I went out with Laura, her friend Tariq and some others from the course to drink cheap beer and sit back and listen to these sparkling, self-confident souls, talking their day, telling their future. They had all had more interesting lives than me. One lad, the son of a leading African dissident, had done a piece about a corrupt British policeman, another (whose father was a Liberal peer) had written about a fight in a nightclub involving a famous Arsenal player whose name I didn't know. Laura had interviewed an eminent French chef whose wife she had met at the checkout in the Sainsbury's on her map reference. I didn't like to say I'd just written this piece about houses. I kept quiet, stuck to my beer and let it chase yesterday's alcohol out of my system.

I was on to my third beer when I realised I had totally recovered from Miss Soper's Nectar and could think purposefully about the Lavender House. After having a quick proprietorial gloat I faced a few facts and did some planning. The place was pretty squalid really, needed a good scrub right through. I'd have to buy a new mattress, and some bedding, of course. The rail would do for my clothes. I would change the pretty butterfly curtains from upstairs to downstairs. I would buy some bright wool blankets from one of the Turkish shops, throw them over the horrible sofa and use them for curtains around the place. A rug from the same shop would cover that horrible carpet. Ideally I should pull the carpet up and sand the floor. A house that age would be sure to have wooden floors. I'd go across to clean it up on Friday. By Saturday, with a bit of luck, I'd be ready to move in.

'Sophia! Where are you?' Laura shook my shoulder. 'Stop daydreaming, will you, flower?'

'What? What?' I shook my head back to the here and now and the warm beer.

'We're going to pick up a takeaway and go back to Tariq's to hang out. You up for it?'

Of course I was up for it. Anything was better than that rabbit hutch at Mimi Trevor's. They were kind to me, this clutch of kids, but they didn't quite get me. Their experience of life had been different from mine. They were metropolitan types, high flyers, selected on merit and natural glamour. I was, if you like, the charity case on this course: a field-trained social worker who had been involved in a couple of headline cases and set up a prizewinning magazine. Selected by social conscience. Like I said, a charity case. I knew that they, as well as my tutors, were puzzled that – with my experience – I didn't tackle pieces of gritty social realism that abounded down here, instead of soft-centred pieces on gentrification. I could see that, for them, it proved I wasn't a journalist after all.

I fished a fiver from the back pocket of my jeans and put it in the kitty for Tariq, who was going to Oddbins for the wine. Yes, hanging out and not saying very much would just be my bag tonight. I would simply sit in a corner, drink my wine and think about my Lavender House. My lovely, lovely Lavender House.

I saw the young woman twice today, Pusscat. Once on her own, and another time in a car with that child from across the road. They got out and went into the house on the corner, the one that's To Let. I remember that house so well, Pusscat. But it was empty for ages, wasn't it? Then those squatters moved in, the ones with the painted van. Took the police to get them out. Then that pair of Russian prostitutes. Then that young girl. Looked no more than fifteen, didn't she? The one with the baby in the pushchair. Nice little thing with white curls. I do wish I'd had that baby of my own, Pusscat. Chris said we would have one, sometime. But not then. He fancied a boy but all I ever wanted was a little girl, do you remember? Like my mum said, it just wasn't to be. Not that time. Of course, the clinic was very superior. Only the best was good enough for me. Chris always said that. But after he'd gone back north like he did, I wished I had had my little girl beside me. She would have been grown up now. A comfort, like I was to my mum. But it wasn't to be. All I have is you, Pusscat. And I fear that's very little consolation. You're not even a girl.

Clearing the Decks

Having skipped Friday's obligatory attendance at Highbury Corner Magistrates' Court on the excuse of a stomach upset, I caught the 73 to Stoke Newington and bought buckets, sponges, black plastic bags, Flash and toilet cleaner at the Pound Shop on the High Street. Miss Julia Soper was there at the checkout, paying for cat food and string. Beside her was a cane shopping trolley which, as well as a quart of milk and a loaf of bread, contained her grey cat. He was not tethered, so must have been there for the ride: a willing passenger.

Miss Soper's glance dropped to my basket, but she didn't comment on the tell-tale contents.

'And did you write the article about the open gardens, dear?' she said. 'I would quite like to see it.'

'It didn't come off, Miss Soper. My tutor said it was before its time. He said better to do it nearer the time of the opening.'

She nodded. 'Now that does make sense.' She paid for her shopping and waited for me to check out. 'It was nice the other day, talking,' she said in her tinny nasal voice.

'Those cocktails of yours, Miss Soper, they're lethal.'

'They are, aren't they?' She smiled. 'The Boys always liked my cocktails. Swore by them.'

'Boys, what boys were they?'

She waved her hand. 'Oh. Just some boys who used to call. A long time ago.' She turned on to the crowded pavement.

I fell into step beside her. 'I'll walk with you, if that's all right, Miss Soper? I'm walking down Barrington Street.'

'Are you?'

'I'm renting a house just past there. That little one just round the corner, painted lavender blue.

59

You might be able to see it from your house.'

'I know it. I can see it from my front bedroom window. I saw you go there with the woman with the car. I know that house.' She nodded at my carriers. 'I see you're doing some cleaning,' she said.

'It needs it,' I said. 'The house is cute but it's pretty filthy.'

'Cute? I wouldn't have said that, dear. It will be dirty, though. They've had all types in there recently. All types. Prostitutes, even. Russian, Latvian, something like that. Poor unfortunate girls,' she sighed.

When we got to her gate, the cat leaped out of the basket and stood guard at the door, waiting for her to follow.

'So I suppose I'll be seeing you,' I said. But she didn't turn round and I walked on.

The house was even dirtier than I'd expected so I hurried to open the windows, pour toilet cleaner down the loo, fill the bath with soapy water and bleach before I set to with my plastic bags to clear everything from the rooms that was dirty, kitsch or just undesirable. I turned on the tiny water-heater. In an hour I had three full black sacks outside the front door. I filled another sack with the blown-paper detritus in the garden. I had washed the kitchen cabinet and had just set about washing the kitchen floor when there was a bang on the door.

I opened it and blinked. 'Miss Soper!'

She stood on the step in her black patent boots, a matching handbag under one arm. She was wearing blue Marigold gloves trimmed with marabou, and was carrying what looked like a shiny silver bomb.

'It's my old Hoover, dear. Sucks up dust like nothing else. It was a present from Chris, my friend. I should think it fell off the back of some lorry. I never used it after he left. But I thought it might be useful to you here.' She fished in her handbag. 'I've got a washleather and vinegar. I've come to do your windows. And if I'm cleaning your windows you'd better call me Julia. Miss Soper sounds likes my Aunt Kit. And she was an *old* woman.' Her voice was full of contempt.

I had no choice. I opened the door and welcomed her in. She walked round the house with me, saying it was very neat, very neat. Then we spent a harmonious afternoon cleaning and scouring, hoovering and polishing. In the process I got dirtier and dirtier, and she remained immaculate. As we worked the spirit of the house seemed to lift and the sun began to stream through the shining windows. And the house no longer smelled of rotten apples.

Julia agreed with me about the beauty of the butterfly curtains and helped me to thread them on to the cane pole over the window of the downstairs room. But first she insisted on shaking them in the back yard.

'Couldn't wash them,' she said. 'Too fragile. They look Chinese to me. Perhaps those girls were from further east than I thought.'

At four o'clock precisely Julia peeled off her Marigolds, repaired her lipstick and picked up her handbag. 'Must go, Sophia.' It was the first time she had used my name. 'I have Pusscat to feed and some antirrhinums to pot up. And

61

there's Mum to see to.'

I still didn't know whether she was talking of her mother in spirit or in flesh, but I let that go. 'Thank you, Julia. You've played a blinder.'

'Blinder?' She frowned. 'Oh, well, if it helped...'

After she'd gone I walked through my empty house, shutting the windows. I started to gloat again. It was a gem, this house of mine. And I was here to stay. I locked the door behind me, ran out on to the High Street and bought tea-towels, a job lot of white crockery and steel cutlery, four woven rugs, four cushions and four pillows from a Mr Ayhan. He said he would deliver the mattress the next day He looked at me standing there surrounded by all these parcels, laughed and sent his son, just in from school, to help me carry them back to the house.

At the house I pushed a fiver into the protesting boy's top pocket and shut the door behind him. I threw one of the rugs over the nasty leather sofa, heaped it with the cushions and laid another rug out on the flecked carpet in front of the electric fire. I folded the other rugs and put them on the bottom step, ready to take upstairs. I arranged the crockery and cutlery in the kitchen cabinet and put the tea-towels in the drawer of the sink unit.

After that I lay back on the sofa and thought about how we always need to mark our space to say we are here. We exist. This is where we are, who we are. There are dozens of magazines now that exploit that deep desire. Everyone has this desire, even those cool lads like Tariq, who buy black leather chairs and huge plasma televisions and hang knives and guns on walls. I knew this man once, in Newcastle, who slept rough, but wherever he slept he laid out the goods from his sacks and bags in the same precise manner. The way we lay out our stuff is an expression of ourselves, as unique as our fingerprint. It is our décor DNA. Where does that, I wondered, leave people who buy show houses, lock, stock and loo-paper? Does that mean they have no selves?

It dawned on me then that here was an idea for a good colour piece. I should interview five people who had bought furnished show houses and see if they really do exist as people separate from the house. I'd try the idea on Laura. Interiors were her thing, after all. I might even make her a present of the idea. She could write it.

I leaped up and went to my *own* bathroom to wash my face, and fixed my hair and make-up in my *own* mirror. It felt good. I picked up my rucksack and locked my *own* door behind me.

I jogged along to the High Street, feeling light as air, not tired at all, despite the hard work. I'd have an early supper in Bodrum before I jumped on to the 73 to go 'home' to Islington for the last time. Of course I'd have a battle with Mrs Mimi Trevor to avoid my next week's rent. But then, first thing tomorrow, I would bring my bags and boxes across here in a taxi and be rid of her for good.

As I passed number 83 I saw Doreen Selkirk standing knitting in her bay window and I waved madly at her. She waved back. I looked upwards and there was Bobbi, standing grinning and waving in her bay window. It crossed my mind that I should go and see Doreen and talk some more. She had the confident sheen of a middle-class woman, but there was something more to her, I was sure.

I was so busy looking upwards that I bumped into a tall man getting out of a battered Volvo. He clutched my arm to stop himself falling. I had the impression of grey-gold hair, rimless glasses and muddy wellingtons. I pulled myself away. 'Sorry!' I gasped and ran on.

This girl called Sophia has set herself up in the house on the corner that I know so well. And she has met that Copeland boy. Stephen. In fact they just knocked into each other. He's different now from the little boy that Chris liked so much in the old days. Do you know, Pusscat, he used to stand Stephen up on the wall and do this trick with a silver coin, producing it from his ear. Then he'd stick the coin in the boy's pocket and send him on his way. He used to say that if ever he had a boy he wanted one like Stephen. That day we first met, at Esmeralda's Barn he bought me a cocktail and showed me this picture of himself when he was eight. A funny thing to do to a stranger, wasn't it? This picture of himself, all blond curls like Stephen Copeland. Just before he went away to school, he said. Then he laughed. 'Before the Fall.' That's what he said. 'Before the Fall.'

I knew at that moment that he was for me, that poor boy. Surely I could save him, make him forget that awful time, after the Fall.

Rubbing along without Fireworks

The next day Bobbi raced the taxi all the way along Barrington Street and, the lights being in her favour, was sitting on the wall of the Lavender House when the car rolled to a halt. Fortunately the mini-cab firm didn't take their name literally, as they sent a people carrier with lots of room for my boxes and cases, my computer and my sound system, my books and my posters. My room in Islington had been something of a Tardis.

As it was Saturday Mrs Trevor had helped me to load my things into the cab. Having grown more and more chilly in recent days, she suddenly became all affectionate again, just like she'd been when I first arrived. She said we must keep in touch. We could have coffee one morning at The Dome perhaps? I said what a great idea, but we both knew that was that. Mimi Trevor was relieved to have her room back and I was relieved to get away from her. My tenancy had been a bit of a shotgun wedding, with Malcolm as the anxious father.

'You don't have much stuff,' said Bobbi.

'There's enough,' I said. I looked down at the two huge cornflake packet boxes, full of clothes and linen, my old computer and printer in their boxes, and two suitcases full of books.

Taking charge, Bobbi emptied the cases and arranged the books in size order on the battered

65

bookshelves at the back of the room. We put the computer and printer on the table under the window. Bobbi was sorry for me because I didn't have a proper desk like hers. 'Mine's custom-made for my computer. You should see it. A space for everything. It's so good. My dad got it for me in the Tottenham Court Road.'

I flicked her hair with my finger. 'No need to be so smug.'

We put the clothes into the suitcases, which we then placed at the bottom of the stairs.

'My dad was arrested last night,' she announced.

'What?' The man on the white charger comes crashing down.

'Don't worry, it's all a mistake. This guy had a gun and a shot was fired. My dad jumped off his motor bike to help. Then the cops were there, grabbed everyone in sight, then let them go one by one. My dad was at the cop shop. He didn't get in till half-nine this morning. Too bad if it had been a school day,' she said philosophically. 'Then I wouldn't have seen him.'

For a second I lost the power of speech. Then, 'What do you feel about that, Bobbi? Your dad being in a police cell?'

She groaned. 'Don't you start that counselling stuff. I've had enough of that.'

'You've had counselling?' I'd have thought she was as steady as a rock.

'Not what you think. I had to talk to them after my mum died. My Great-nanny Elsie wanted to take me away to live with her in the country. Suffolk. It's very pretty there. All sea and big pebbles. She told me she thought life was poison round

66

here. Dangerous. You know. Pollution. All that stuff.'

'You convinced the counsellors?'

She shrugged. 'I was a proper show-off really, but it was worth it. I played my guitar for them. I showed them my schoolbooks and this project I'm doing about Jamaican folk stories. I talked to them all about my dad. Lots to say. It was easy. My great-nanny cried. She was really nice, but I think she missed my mum even more than I do. You could tell that, 'cos my mum was her granddaughter, see? She was dead by then, like I say. I go to see my great-nanny a bit in the summer holidays. Throw a few stones at the sea. It's all right round there, even if they do stare at you a bit. Well, they stare at me. But mostly I live here with my dad.'

'I can see that.' Bobbi could be quite unnerving, but the more I knew her, the more I wanted to meet this father of hers.

As we worked on, Bobbi started to tell me about the other people in her house. As well as the Selkirks there was the man who lived at the top of the house. 'Mr Copeland. He told me to call him Steve but he's really old so it didn't seem right. He's even older than my dad and *he's* thirty-three. So I still call him Mr Copeland. He's the tall one, skinny with grey hair. You bumped into him yesterday.'

The Volvo man. I could only remember the hair and the glasses. And the hair wasn't all grey. And he hadn't been skinny. He'd felt quite solid as we collided. And he smelled of lemons. The smell of lemons came to me now. 'So what ... does he do? Does he work at something?'

67

'Well, Mr Copeland's our landlord but he doesn't do anything about that. He has the whole house but you wouldn't think that. He thinks nobody knows, but my dad knows all about it, 'cos he's his good friend. Everybody knows it's his house, but pretend they don't.'

'Is that all he does, sit there and be a landlord?'

'Nah. He's an architect. My dad says he designed a new bank in the city. And a church. He designed another church but that's a long way away. In Wolverhampton or somewhere. And another in Canada. Nobody's ever seen them but I've seen a picture in a magazine. I think he would like you very much.'

I blushed. This impossible child made me blush.

'My dad told me Mr Copeland plays badminton. My dad says, *"Badminton!* You could understand it if it were *squash."*' She wrinkled her clear brow. 'What do you think he means by that?'

'Men say some funny things.'

'They sure do.'

We heaved the cases upstairs, opened them and hung my clothes on the single rail.

'So, what does your dad do, Bobbi?' I needed to know much more about this man.

She looked at me, her eyes opaque. 'My dad? Well, he rides his motor bike. He keeps it inside the back hall. Mrs Selkirk's not too pleased about that but she doesn't say anything because Mr Copeland's in charge and he's cool about it. Him and my dad talk motor bikes sometimes. But anyway, Mrs Selkirk still doesn't say anything. My dad says that's because he's black and she's one of those Bleedin'-Heart White Liberals.'

'Does he now?' Another part of the Bobbi-jigsaw clicks into place. 'So where does he work, your dad?'

Again, that opaque glance. 'Well, it varies. This year he works for this gangster up West. On security. And he delivers things all about the place on his motor bike. Kind of.'

'Gangster?' I tried not to sound too surprised. Not your business, Sophia.

She eyed me slyly. 'Don't like that, do you? Dad says Oliver –that's his boss – is *legit* now, but he was in prison once. They're old mates, him and my dad. Went to school together up Bethnal Green before my dad's family went to Bristol.'

'*Legit?*' I said faintly.

'Proper business. Books and everything, my dad says. You don't need to break the law to make money these days, he says. Look at those boys in the City. My dad says Oliver's not a gangster in any way you'd know. People with real names go to his club. People whose names are in the papers. The princes go there. Their girlfriends. The paparazzi love that place. They're always there. My dad calls them maggots.'

'He must work funny hours, your dad.' I concentrated on keeping my social worker self on a tight leash.

'That's right. He just gets in when I wake up. He brings my breakfast and we talk for ages. Then I go to school and he goes to bed. Then he gets up twelve-ish, cleans the flat, does the washing and ironing, makes my tea and leaves it in the fridge, then brums off on his bike. Some days I come home dinnertime, to see him.'

'You must be up there a lot on your own.'

'Yeah. But I don't really mind that. But there's Mehmet and Rina at Bodrum. I always go there after school and Mehmet checks with my dad. Then Mr Copeland always knocks on my door when he comes back from work to make sure I'm all right. And even Mrs Selkirk stops by sometimes. And Mr Selkirk saved me from the witch-girl. And my dad's never off the phone to all of them, just checking.'

'But you're on your own a lot?'

'Yeah. Like I say, I like it.'

'No friends from school?'

'Some of them are great. But some of them are weird. And mostly they can't keep up with me so they think I'm weird. Call me nerd and that. I pretend not to notice so they keep off me. Mostly. That and my dad. He keeps them off me as well.'

'So what do you do up there in the flat?'

'I play on my computer, do homework. I draw. I read stuff. Lots of stuff. I have to do that because I'm going to Bristol University when I'm eighteen. My dad's saving up for it. He says I have to go because my mum went there.'

'Did she?'

She grinned. 'There. That surprised you.'

I thought of the children I'd met in my job in Newcastle: fearful, aggressive, abandoned, mistreated, some of them wild, even feral. Some were as frightening as their parents. Many had absent fathers, even absent mothers. But Sparrow Marsh was a very present father; even in his absence you could tell that.

I was saved from further comment by a great

hammering on the door. It was the man and boy from Mr Ayhan's, delivering the mattresses and the bedding. They lifted them upstairs and then the man went out to the van and brought back a big bunch of lilies and a bag of peaches. He brushed away my thanks. 'From Mr Ayhan for the house, Miss Morgan,' he said. 'For the house!'

After they had gone, Bobbi and I jumped up and down on the new mattresses, testing their bouncability, then we laid on the bigger bed staring at the navy-blue ceiling on to which someone had pasted silver stars.

'Now you!' said Bobbi.

'Now me, what?'

'You know about me now, so what about you? What are you doing here? Why is an old person like you still at college?'

'Old? I'm twenty-five!'

'That's too old to still be going to school, even college.'

'Well. I missed my chance of going to college from school.'

'So what did you do then?'

'I had to stay at home and take care of my gran. And then I was a social worker.'

'Oh, sugar!' Bobbi groaned and sat up. 'One of those?'

'We're not all bad, you know.'

'Then what?'

'It didn't work out.'

'Why didn't it work out?'

Why? I couldn't tell Bobbi about Drina Parnaby. I couldn't explain about the crossed wires, and the missing case notes. I couldn't plead with Bobbi –

71

as I had with Malcolm and the police – about the number of times I'd knocked on the Parnabys' door and been refused entry by the belligerent surface-civilised Mr Parnaby. Bobbi wouldn't grasp the adult euphemism of 'slipping through the net'. The fact was that Drina Parnaby had slipped slowly through the net over several months and had ended up dead. That the Parnabys had finally been put behind bars was no solace for me. The year's enforced sick leave produced the magazine but yielded no respite for these dark feelings. I knew then I was finished as a social worker.

'Why?' repeated Bobbi. 'Why'd you stop?'

'I just discovered it wasn't for me. I liked writing things, so I thought I'd go back to college and get better at writing.'

Once there, I found that hard news was not for me. I had lived the hard news and found it not to my liking and knew it was never really about the truth. It was about scapegoats and hot stories. It was about people lying in wait for you at your door, saying that people wanted to hear your side of the story. It was about feelings of vengeance and not forgetting.

So on my course I stuck to colour pieces.

Bobbi sat up straighter on the bed and peered out of the window. She groaned. 'Uh-oh! Here's Mrs Doreen Selkirk bearing gifts. She even has a basket with a cloth over it! She really thinks it's Red Riding Hood country not London town.' She jumped off the bed. 'I'm off! My dad'll be out of bed now and he's taking me up West with him. We do that on Saturdays.'

'To his job?' He was there, at the house. Perhaps today I would see him.

'Nah. But he doesn't start till eight tonight. We're going to have lunch at the Savoy and then we're going to the Odeon, Leicester Square and then shopping. I need some new trainers.' She looked up at me, her face bright as a bird, a sparrow. Perhaps her father was the same. Perhaps that's where he'd got his nickname.

Bobbi was only two years older than Drina Parnaby but had so much more power. She had her own safety net comprising Mehmet and his niece at the café; Stephen Copeland; a middle-aged couple of which the wife thought she was in Red Riding Hood country. And she had her dad. And now me. Bobbi Marsh had constructed her own very powerful safety net.

I gave her a hug. She felt hard, wiry. 'Thank you, Bobbi. Thank you for all this help.'

'My dad'll put me in a taxi home tonight at half-six. Can I come and see you then?' We made our way downstairs. Bobbi opened the door for Doreen Selkirk, said a bright 'Hello!' and fled.

Doreen bustled in, bringing the smell of apples and spices with her. 'Bobbi told me you'd got hold of this house. You're truly a fast worker. I'm full of admiration.' She smiled slightly, then un-packed her basket on the table under the window. Two stainless-steel flasks. 'One coffee, one leek and potato soup.' An apple pie. 'My grandmother's recipe.' Two crystal glasses and a bottle of wine, the cork half out. 'To bless the house and for the stomach, to misquote St Paul.'

And ten squat candles.

'Thank you, Doreen. You're really kind.' I was

puzzled by the candles.

She glanced around. 'The candles are for cleansing. Two in each room opposite corners. They will bring balance to the house. Karma. They will clear all the shadows away.'

I laughed. 'There are no shadows here, Doreen.'

She glanced around the room then back at me. 'There are always shadows, dear,' she said soberly.

We started upstairs and lit candles in the bedrooms and on the landing; two candles on the stairs, two in the kitchen area, two in the bathroom. The scent of almonds, honey and nutmeg seeped through the house. She placed two of the candles on the mantelpiece of the sitting room and tried to light them. They wouldn't light. She frowned and glanced round, then tried again. Finally, after four goes, the candles stayed alight. But they didn't flare up like the others. They sat there, tiny static peas of light on a wax cushion. Doreen shook her head. 'Something wrong in the making, perhaps,' she murmured, and left it at that.

Then she poured the wine into the glasses, handed me one and we toasted each other and the house. As we clinked glasses the candles flickered and flared into life. She told me she got into the karma and candles thing shortly before her divorce. 'It was a great help to me then. There seemed no pattern to things. The good old C of E was no help, but I had this cleaner who was a great support. She knew about these things and they were a help.' She looked round. 'It's nice here.'

I told her about my speedy decision-making and the kindness of Mr Ayhan. 'I like it here.'

She nodded over her glass, her chins wobbling slightly. 'This is a wonderful place. Not like Berkshire. This is an amazing square mile. So many people living in harmony, getting on with their lives. All kinds of British, Caribbeans, Asians of all kinds, Turks, Greeks, Kurds, Burmese, Irish, English...' She counted them off on her fingers like a child.

'But–'

'Oh, I know you'll tell me about the gangs and guns, the drugs. And all those things about it being a risky place where it really doesn't work in one way or another. Pockets of anarchy. Even the dark religious stuff. But all cities have their criminals, dear, their people outside the law. But when I'd been here a few months I realised how special this place is. Here we're all living cheek by jowl, getting on with our lives. Living parallel lives. Rubbing along without fireworks.' She smiled, suddenly looking very pretty. 'When I take my walk down the High Street among all these people I feel like whooping. This is the way forward. The only way. No matter what.' She nodded. 'I thought Roger was bringing me down in the world when we had to live here. But I bless the day he brought me here. Truly. What's the alternative? Ghettos for the rich and the poor. Gated communities insulated against anything, anyone different. Psychological barriers. We betray our own fundamental decencies in the face of this threat of unseen terrorist–' She caught my gaze and shrugged. 'Sorry, dear, I'm on my soapbox. That really used to get my first husband's goat. Said I was an embarrassment.'

'Never.' I was thinking of Sparrow Marsh calling

Doreen a 'bleeding-heart white liberal'. But that was not fair. She was passionate. Her heart was in the right place and she was no hypocrite. I raised my glass. 'Here's to living cheek by jowl, Doreen.'

She raised her glass, drank off her wine and stood up. 'Welcome to Barrington, dear. It's unique, as you will discover. I have to go.'

At the door she turned round. 'Are you doing anything tonight?' she said.

I shook my head. 'Just settling in. I might ring my friend Laura and see if she'll help me finish your lovely wine.'

'Come to dinner,' Doreen instructed. 'It's smoked haddock chowder. You like fish? That man Johnny at the Fisheries got hold of some divine haddock just for me. Bring your friend Laura. Stephen upstairs is coming and the child Bobbi will join us for a little while. I passed her escaping from here. Her father – lovely man though he is – is never there. He comes and goes like a will-o'-the-wisp.' She vanished, then put her face back round the door. 'Come at eight, sharp. No excuses.'

See that to-do across the road, Pusscat? Flowers. Baskets. Candles. Always the same routine. There'll be music later. Quite nice that, the music drifting across. A change from the drumming that cuts through across from the railway. And they'll leave the curtains open, a picture-gift to passers-by. You can see the people on the bus turn to get a better look.

It's not like I don't like parties, Pusscat. Chris used to like our parties here. He liked to play master of the house, although he wasn't. Cocktails and crisps and sausages on sticks stuck into a pineapple. Beer and vodka on the sideboard. The Boys were always, always late. My mother had an early nap so she was fresh for the fun. They would come in, maybe half a dozen of them, with strange women on their arms, smelling of the night after an evening in special pubs or their gambling place in the West End. We'd have Al Martino on the radiogram and the air was drenched with this dusty excitement, this expectancy.

Chris's friend, that Roy Pinder, would sit nursing a beer on the best chair by the window with the prettiest girl lounging on the chair arm beside him. The big Scotsmen they always had with them would sit on the settee watching the other girls dance together. You'd want to laugh – but you didn't – at this small square-built man who always got up to dance, his chin level with his partner's cleavage.

Roy's brother, Richie, usually poured himself a tumbler of vodka and enticed my mother into the kitchen, where she made him bacon sandwiches and they talked about the old East End. Before she married my father and moved up in the world she was a Bethnal Green girl and the two of them would lounge there in the kitchen, reciting lists of streets, pubs, names and families like some Bible litany.

I have to say my mother adored Richie and would never believe any wrong of him, even when he'd been sentenced. He was, she said, a natural gentleman. People were out to get him. That was the only explanation.

In the ordinary way of things my Chris always preferred Roy. Said he was a businessman; you could talk to him like any chap. But when Richie was *around it was like walking a tightrope over hot coals. 'Richie's a rum cove,' Chris would drawl. 'Distinctly warm, darling.' But like the rest of the men Chris was still bewitched by Richie. Like all of them, he kept his eye on Richie even when he was not talking to him.*

You might wonder Pusscat, where a man like Chris met boys like that. Where did he meet those boys, Pusscat? In a gambling club in the West End. He'd been a bit of a naughty boy over gambling, had my darling Chris. He'd gone through a pile of money from home and was losing as usual, and Roy Pinder subbed him and his luck turned. The three of them ended up drinking together and Richie asked where he got his shirts and then the next day went out to Jermyn Street and bought six of them. Six at once. He told Chris he never paid a penny for them.

When the Boys opened their own gambling club the brothers liked to have Chris there to give the place a bit of class, to talk to the rich patrons they'd enticed down from the West End: men who'd been to the same kind of school as Chris and the same weekend shooting parties in Yorkshire.

Before long Chris had used up all the money from his family and was stony-broke. Then he was entirely beholden to the brothers, obliged to do their bidding at the drop of a hat. They were clever, you know, by turns very cruel and very kind to the poor boy. That kept him close. Money was the pole around which they all danced. Chris was often broke, only rarely paid rent for his room here, but – occasionally flush with funds – he'd buy me jewellery or a new dress from Biba, pick up a big bunch of flowers and a bottle of sherry for my mother, and everything was all right.

My mother liked Chris nearly as much as she liked

Richie Pinder but still said now and then that he had us for suckers. But I didn't care. He was a sweet man, my sweet man, and exquisite in bed. Wonderful. Breathtaking. I know you will keep that secret, Pusscat. Best of all was when he got the key to this place where we could be out of Mother's earshot. Quite a love nest that was, Puss. That's what I missed most after he went away: those times in bed with him in the early hours, breathing in his scent of cigars and gin all mixed up with the scent of my Estée Lauder perfume necklace. He bought me that on our first proper date. Silver chased with brilliants. It's still half full of perfume. I still have it, tucked away somewhere.

Hospitality

I rang Laura but she was not interested in coming to dinner. She said she'd love to see my house and clock my new neighbours but she was meeting a radio producer for tea on a river-boat café and the encounter might just, with luck, spread out to the evening, with a film and who-knew-what?

I wasn't too sorry. I'd always preferred to keep the different bits of my life separate. It was the only way I could keep sane in Newcastle. I was very cautious. When I met new people up there I would usually say I was an administrator at County Hall: a much more neutral subject than bruised children. Either people were horrified or too interested in that experience. Or both. One thing for sure, it didn't make for good relationships.

I thought it was worth trying to make a good impression for Barrington Street. I decided to wear my cowboy boots (a treasured legacy from an otherwise ludicrous relationship with a bloke from Byker obsessed with country music), my newest stone-washed jeans and a white linen shirt from Next. I softened this look with an Aztec pendant, a gift from my first real boyfriend, who, after experiencing my obsession with the bruised children in my care, ran away to the soup kitchens of Mexico City.

My guess was that on this kind of visit to virtual strangers you should come bearing gifts. (I suppose this works if you are not a Greek with a horse in tow.) So I took a bottle of wine from Sainsbury's and a little tray of baklava, sweet Turkish cakes from δzenplia in the High Street.

I left my own curtains closed with a light burning in the window so that when I returned I would know I was coming home to my own home. Then I walked along and rang the door of number 83. Doreen's curtain twitched and I was buzzed straight in. Her flat door was open and I let myself into the long room, which was now lit by armies of candles marching on every surface. They stood guard on the mantelpieces, presented arms on the low tables and bookshelves. They kept watch over the long table from an elaborate candelabra. Smoke and the scent of vanilla filled the air. The glowing, diffused light was eerie rather than romantic. It was rather more India than Berkshire. Doreen had certainly seen the light.

She had thrown a woven rug over the table and topped it with a delicate lace runner. The knives and forks had horn handles and beside each place setting were two hand-thrown ceramic goblets. The theme was obviously medieval feastery.

I curbed an instinct to applaud.

Roger Selkirk introduced himself to me. In well-pressed designer fatigues he had the cultivated look of a TV archaeologist, complete with beard, and hair that floated out in the air around his overlarge head.

'Hi! You can only be Sophia.' He smiled, took my gifts and nudged me further into the room. 'Come on in. Doreen's making the usual mayhem down there in the kitchen but Stephen's here.' His voice was deep, much more attractive than his person.

At the other end of the room I could see Doreen's back, a tea-towel thrown over her shoulder. She was stirring something in a pan. She raised a hand. 'Two minutes, dear.'

The man standing by the marble fireplace, thick glass goblet in hand, was gazing at me as though I were the first course. He put out a hand. 'Stephen Copeland,' he said. 'We bumped into each other the other day.' His thick short hair wasn't grey, more gold with threads of silver. 'Good to put a face to a back,' he smiled. He grasped my hand.

'Sophia Morgan.' I pulled my hand away. 'Sorry I fled.'

He grinned. 'I have that effect on strangers. I've learned to deal with it. Doreen says you've just moved in? That funny little house round the corner?'

'It's not funny,' I said with some belligerence. 'It's lovely. I like it.'

'Sorry. Perhaps I should say intriguing.'

Without asking my preference, Roger poured me a glass of red wine from a stoneware jug and thrust it into my hand. The wine was thick and spicy. The second sip was much better than the first. Then, jug in hand, Roger wandered down to the kitchen end of the long room to peer at Doreen, who was garnishing plates with bits of lettuce.

'Be careful with that drink, Sophia,' said Stephen Copeland. 'Old Roger here is a bit keen on his medieval recipes. I reckon he says incantations over it.'

Bobbi was wrong. Stephen wasn't old at all, despite the strands of silver in the golden hair. He was attractive without being showy. The eyes behind the rimless glasses were bright hazel. In his polished brown shoes, his black T-shirt and jeans under a battered linen jacket, he looked like the arty understated types you often came across here in London. Two of the tutors on my course paraded the same uniform. One was thirty and one was sixty. One was gay, the other wasn't. It was a style that owed nothing to age or sex.

'Young Bobbi says you're a journalist,' he said.

I was already shaking my head. 'Not quite. Not yet. I'm on a course. One day maybe I'll write for a living. But I'm still not sure. Not sure at all. Some of it ... well, I'm not sure about it.'

'So you're escaping from somewhere?'

Escaping! I glared at him. 'I never mentioned escape.'

'Well, you're obviously not a Londoner.'

I groaned and clutched my throat. 'Oh dear, I thought I'd covered my tracks so well.'

'It's in the lilt,' he said. 'That music in the voice. You can never lose it. I'm always saying that to Roger here, who was claiming that Shakespeare spoke with a Northamptonshire accent. I say it's all down to music. No accent, no music, I say. We metropolitan types have had the music beaten out of us. We're very thin metal. The only music in London is that brought in by the incomers.'

It was a nice thought that just missed being patronising. I was spared the embarrassment of responding to this by a row erupting at the other end of the room. Doreen was laying something out on plates and shouldering Roger out of the way. He was murmuring angrily in her ear.

'Trouble in paradise muttered Stephen.

'Ready!' Doreen's voice trilled down the room, filtered by gritted teeth. 'Roger, dear, if you'd just lay out the pâté?'

His shoulders down, Roger clashed round discs of pâté garnished with tomato and dill down on the table. Doreen washed her hands and came along the room to kiss me on the cheek as though we were old friends.

'Sophia, dear. Excuse my manners. I am such a fool. I made this pickle dish from one of Roger's old recipes and, would you believe it, it tasted foul. It tasted like the soil of the earth.' She laughed a little too shrilly. 'Poor boy was just a bit peed off that I threw it away.' She put her arm through mine. 'Now then, dear, where will you sit?'

We were all seated when Bobbi let herself in, nodded at everyone and said she couldn't stay because she had something bubbling on her computer. Doreen insisted on giving her a bowl of smoked fish chowder and a hunk of home-made bread. Bobbi took the tray and looked across at me.

'D'you wanna see my computer table?' she said.

I glanced at Doreen.

'Sophia can't come now, Bobbi,' she said. 'We're just about to eat.' Her easy tones were laced with pure steel.

Bobbi was still gazing at me. 'All right then. You have to come up to mine after. I'll still be up.'

'All right, dear. She will,' said Doreen, irritated. 'Now go!'

I winked at Bobbi and turned to see that Stephen had caught my wink. I felt like a naughty schoolgirl.

'That child's too precocious by half,' commented Roger.

'No she isn't,' I leaped to her defence. 'She's unusual, that's all. Very self-sufficient. I'd say that was a good thing nowadays, not a bad thing.'

'Sparrow's done a good job there,' said Stephen. 'You can't deny that, Doreen.'

'I suppose so. But sometimes she makes me uncomfortable. One would think a child like that should be more ... well ... needy.'

'Like I say,' Stephen reached for a knife, 'Sparrow's done a very good job.'

It seemed that this Sparrow was all around us. I have never known anyone who was so present in his absence as Bobbi Marsh's father.

The starter, some kind of herby crab pâté, was delicious, despite Roger moaning about offering fish for two courses. The fish chowder that followed was wonderful. It tasted of the sea. You could almost hear the tide.

I managed to get through the evening without having to say very much. There was some discussion about my name and its northern versus southern pronunciation. Roger announced that it was very old-fashioned, smacking as it did of the Restoration comedies. Then he took centre stage, talking about some new documents he'd found in the London Museum that were provision bills for two of the inns on the Kingsland Road out of London – now our High Street. He went on about the cost of provisions then and the difference between beer houses and inns. And, even more exciting (he said), there were assize records of highwaymen apprehended on this road for holding up the carriages of the rich.

'It lists the things stolen – rings, a gold casket, fine luggage, a sword in a Spanish leather case...'

Doreen finally interrupted. 'Oh, my love, take a breath, will you! Everyone is not engrossed in these things as you are.' She smiled across at me. 'My dear Roger never did quite get the hang of living in the here and now. He goes around London with people from these other worlds, other times, at his elbow, in his ear. That's why London is *his* place. He lives with a regiment of its ghosts.'

Roger glared at her with a look of such pure dislike that I shivered.

Stephen Copeland laughed. 'It's not exactly a dead tradition, is it, Roger? There are plenty of criminals and bad boys round here even today. Of course, we're a bit insulated with our locks and bolts and wooden shutters, but think of all those drugs and guns lurking in houses just streets away from here. Almost got to open war on the Green Mile last year, if you remember. Like that film *Gunfight at the OK Corral*.'

Roger shrugged and smiled slightly. 'The more it changes the more it remains the same.'

'It has changed in a very particular way, I think,' Stephen went on. He glanced at me. 'When I was a kid, this was virtually an all-white place – dingy middle class and working-class respectable. But even then the wide boys and gangsters lurked around. The Pinder brothers – remember them? – even had this club down the road here. The Verandah. Talk about flyblown glamour! Villains came from right across London to rub shoulders in there with upper-crust thrill-seekers. And vice versa. All Crombie coats and homburg hats. Into every kind of racket, according to my mother. And worse. There was a killing just round the corner in Evering Road. That was all down to them. I suppose it was a dark place even then, below the surface. In that way it was the same as it is now.'

'Here?' I frowned. 'It's too far out, surely? I thought all that sixties gang stuff was in Soho, the West End...'

'Don't believe it. These flash cars picked up from some garage they were "protecting" would take them anywhere. Up West. Down East. The Pinders were based in Bethnal Green but they had flats up Stamford Hill at one time. And that's no distance from here.'

Roger, mopping up the last of his chowder with a lump of bread, pulled the attention back to himself. 'That cottage you're in, Sophia, is of interest,' he intoned. 'Much older than the rest of Barrington Street, nearer seventeenth century, even sixteenth. I reckon it's something to do with the clay pits. Brickmakers. Gatekeeper's place, perhaps. Or horsekeeper's. On one map there are stables alongside. I checked it just today.'

Stephen caught my gaze. 'Talking of the sixties and seventies,' he nodded towards the window, 'Miss Soper, who lives opposite, was associated with those bad boys for a while. My mother and hers were acquainted. Our Miss Soper was apparently quite a wild girl. My mother was horrified, but old Mrs Soper thought it all quite a lark. She was a strange old bird.'

'Well, her daughter's an eccentric soul too,' said Doreen. 'She takes her cat for a walk in her shopping trolley. Talks to it!'

Roger nodded. 'And have you seen the clothes? The dear woman's the sixties in aspic. Thinks she's Joni Mitchell.'

'I like her,' I said. 'She showed me her back garden. It's exquisite.'

Now they were all looking at me. Stephen's brows were raised. 'You got inside the house? I was born here and haven't been inside that house since I was a child. Not even after her mother's funeral.'

'Her mother's dead?'

'Ten years ago, at least. Why?'

'It's just that once or twice she mentioned her mother as though she were still around somewhere.'

'Insane!' said Roger gloomily. 'The woman's breaking up.'

Then Doreen got up to clear. Roger filled up our goblets again and started on about the history of the drains in Stoke Newington and the dedication of Clissold Park. Stephen glanced at me and I realised he'd heard it all before.

Doreen came back with steaming apple pie and custard, and I made a mental note to fast tomorrow. No wonder Doreen was as round as a butterball. I cut into Roger's endless lecture to ask about himself and Doreen, how they came to be here in London.

He grinned. 'She picked me up.'

'Roger! For goodness' sake!' said Doreen.

'I broke down on the way to a WEA lecture in Reading. *The Impact of Clean Water on Town Planning*. I delivered that lecture all over the Home Counties.'

Doreen looked at him over her laden spoon. 'And he broke down on the road so I picked him up and delivered him to his lecture, which I was attending anyway.'

He touched her arm. 'She rescued me on the road. And I rescued her from...'

'...a peculiar marriage, said Doreen. 'My husband then was a GP who was wedded to his clinic. He hated my candles and my incense.'

'And Doreen, having just discovered karma and its related delights, decided there might be more life balance living with me.'

'So you didn't have any family?' I said to Doreen.

'We don't talk about Doreen's child,' said Roger firmly. 'You get too upset, don't you, darling? Now then, is there more of your delicious apple pie?'

88

'I have a daughter, Sophia,' said Doreen defiantly. 'Helena. She's fifteen. Stayed with her father.'

'Doreen, darling!' said Roger. 'More apple pie!'

I put my napkin on the table and stood up. Stephen and Roger politely got to their feet. 'That was absolutely marvellous, Doreen,' I said. 'I wish I could cook like that. D'you mind if I pop upstairs to see Bobbi? I did promise her. I won't be long.'

And I fled, before I threw my hand-thrown pot, half full of home-made mead, right into Roger Selkirk's smug, hairy face.

That man who delivers the post in his shorts and that hat with corks hanging down, we know he's not Australian, don't we, Puss? When he delivered that pile of plant catalogues you could hear his accent. North of England. A lot of that about nowadays. That and Poles.

Shorts! When I was young the postmen wore proper uniform. Before your time, Puss. Flower power had not yet reached the Post Office. Of course, they still called it the Post Office then. It was a man in proper uniform who delivered that last card from Chris. It had a picture of a very threatening spotted orchid on the front, and on the back, in block capitals:

'DARLING! OFF TO THE COUNTRY. BACK IN 24 HOURS. WAIT TILL YOU SEE YOUR PRESENT!!'

Chris always talked about presents, Pusscat. He used to bring them all the time. Jewellery. Good stones. Gold. Of course he sometimes borrowed them back to sell, when his money dribbled away, as it often did. To be honest I didn't mind that. For me it was not about the presents. It was all about the life he brought to me, brought into this house. It was about the difference between him and the office boys and swaggering retailers I'd been out with before him. Compared with him they were munchkins.

Between us, it was never about trust. Trust never arose, even when we had to stop the baby. I didn't really worry. It was just as though we had all the time in the world to have another one. Then another. Our future together was a given fact, a taken-for-granted.

But it's still always nice to see that man in his shorts and his bobbing hat at my door. I watch for a letter from Chris every day. Of course, I get very little post nowadays. Utility bills. Seed catalogues. Bank statements. Letters addressing me by my Christian name telling me I've won £10,000 if I agree to do certain things. Odd, that. To be known only by strangers, that's my fate.

But now, Pusscat, the fact is, I may be known by that girl called Sophia. Hasn't she been in my house? Hasn't she drunk my French Riviera? I think I'll try the Honey Bee on her next. Gregory loved that. Roy Pinder liked it too, on a good day. I still have the recipe in the drawer. That Sophia knocked them back, Pusscat. Chris would have been pleased. He liked women who could take their drink.

I have turned up my recipes. Isn't that good? I might give them to Sophia to copy out.

Darling Julia! I have written them down for you!

French Riviera
1 oz rye whisky

90

½ oz apricot brandy
1 tsp fresh lemon juice
Shake with ice, pour into a cocktail glass. Add that very important maraschino cherry. You know how much you like that cherry!

Gordon Cocktail
2 oz gin
½ oz dry sherry
In a chilled cocktail glass pour in sherry and swirl around glass. In a mixing glass filled with cracked ice chill the gin. Then strain into prepared glass. Hang a lemon or lime curl on the rim. Sharp but good.

Honey Bee
1½ oz Jamaica rum
1 oz lime juice
½ oz honey
In a shaker with ice combine all ingredients. Shake well and strain into sour glass filled with cracked ice. Caribbean sunshine in a glass.

Black Devil
2 oz dark rum
½ oz dry vermouth
black olive
Combine spirits in a mixing glass filled with ice, stir Strain into our gorgeous cocktail glass. Add at least one olive. Secrets, secrets!

C.

The Man at the Door

Life followed its usual rhythm. Home, lectures, research forays, court attendances, writing, writing.
I wrote a piece on strangers settling in London for
Jack Molloy. Doreen Selkirk was interested in the
idea and introduced me to an American friend of
hers from the Alternative Therapies Centre, who
lived in a barn of a house in Islington and sent her
children to the Lycée as she didn't think the
English school system sufficiently rigorous. After
we'd had mugs of gritty decaffeinated coffee she
showed me a small, ornate, loaded gun in her
eighteenth-century chiffonnier. Her husband
insisted they kept it. They went nowhere without
it, she said. Nowhere in the world.

Jack Molloy damned the piece with faint praise.
It was a fair enough piece, well enough written,
he said, though without the gun it would have
been lame and old hat. No hard edge to it. That
was the problem.

Hard edge. Why did there always have to be a
hard edge? Sitting there in his office I was
suddenly weary at all this hunger for the hard
edge. Life was hard enough without creating new
edges. It made me uncomfortable. Perhaps I was
on the wrong course. But if not this course, then
what? I enjoyed the actual writing, and I really
thought I'd been getting sharper, tighter. Even
Jack Molloy said I'd lost my provincial fuzz,

whatever that meant. But I was still phobic about the telephone, and my single placement on a magazine had been a minor disaster. At the other end of the scale I couldn't really get worked up about retro furnishing or the positioning of a cushion for a photo-shoot. That was very soft edge and I couldn't care about it at all.

But I had been reconciled to all of that until I took the bus to Barrington Street and found the Lavender House. Of course, after I moved there I still hung out with Laura, Tariq and the others. But the highlight of my day now was when I went home to my Lavender House on the 73 bus. I always looked out for Bobbi and Doreen in the windows of number 83, and for Julia Soper across the road. When I saw them I felt I was home.

So coming home to Lavender House became peculiarly precious. Living on Barrington Street now seemed like living in a village. But before when I lived in a village, all I wanted to do was escape. Up in Northumberland I could pop out of my grandparents' village house and bump into three familiar people within twenty yards. In those days, though, I couldn't get away fast enough from such sticky familiarity. It was better in my little flat in the West End of Newcastle. I was more anonymous there, and had some good times before getting pregnant and breaking up with Malcolm.

But my liking for that flat was entirely spoiled during those black days when I couldn't get out of the door without tripping over a journalist or a man buried in a parka, flourishing a camera. 'Tell us your side of the story, love,' they would chant. 'This is your chance, Sophia. We want your side of this story.'

But the Lavender House was different. It was special.

One day after lectures Laura stayed on the bus with me and came out to Barrington Street. In the High Street we picked up some wine, olives and cheese from the Italian deli, took it home and had a picnic in front of my gas fire. She lounged on the couch and I sat on the floor, my legs straight out in front of me.

Laura looked around the room. 'It works, doll. Improvisation. The signature style. You certainly have it, Soph Morgan.'

I raised my glass. 'Why, thank you, madam editor. But it's Sophia. I keep telling you.'

'Sophia, then. But no kidding. I know you hated your magazine attachment, but you do have a touch. I'd have thought...' she hesitated.

'I'd be living in some squat, some replica of Mimi Trevor's rabbit hutch?'

She giggled. 'Watch that chip, Sophia. Your right shoulder's already two inches lower than your left.'

I glowered at her, then laughed. 'I've gotta say, Laura, that every other place I've had has been a bit of a tip. But here I suppose I'm a bit new-fangled. Or maybe it's that this house is different. Begging for a bit of TLC.'

She nodded and peered round the room again. 'The domestic ghost in the machine. Some houses have one.' She took a sip of her wine and looked at me with narrowed eyes. 'Why in heaven did you do all this, Sophia? Why'd you come down to London and do this course? Somehow

94

you don't...'

'...fit? Seem the type? I know that. But I had to do it. Do something.'

'Why?'

'Well, they did give me the chance, almost out of the blue. I told you. The magazine I ran up there won me the prize that paid for the place on the course. It meant I could get away with a purpose, I suppose. And I wanted to get away.'

'It just seems sort of strange. You're not like the rest of us.' She left a silence then, like a seductive velvet net, an inviting trap for the unwary. No wonder the tutors loved her. She was born to squeeze secrets out of people. Now, even though I knew about her, I fell into her trap. I stumbled into telling her about my doomed affair with Malcolm and the inconvenient pregnancy. She squeezed out of me the facts of the depression, the sleeping all day and the revulsion for the telephone.

'Malcolm was really good about helping me out of all that,' I said brightly. 'He got me this kind of attachment on the New Dawn Estate and the magazine project. And that got me out of the black hole.'

'That Malcolm's a bastard,' she said soberly.

'That too,' I said.

She looked at me again. Such a careful forensic gaze. I made an effort to shut myself off from her, to resist the temptation to tell her the real cause of my despair. This was not the run-of-the-mill pregnancy. Not even the nasty run-of-the-mill abortion. The real cause of my despair was the image carved on the inside of my skull of Drina Parnaby in her cage in the corner of the Parnabys' garage. It was the sound of Darren Parnaby's calm posh-Geordie voice telling me with sure confidence that he'd moved Drina's cage from the kitchen as a punishment, to cure the kid of her evil whining, her defiant ways. I couldn't tell the beautiful Laura how on that last day I got into the cage with her and cradled her chill, fragile, stinking body in my arms as I scrabbled with one hand for my mobile to telephone the police.

I was saved from blurting all this out by a heavy knock on the door of my house here in London, my Lavender House. In the Here and Now. Today.

Laura leaped up. 'Stay there, pet!' she commanded. 'I'll get it.'

She went to answer and I heard the skitter of voices. She looked back round the door at me, managing to scowl and wrinkle her pert nose at the same time. 'You'll have to come, Sophia. It's this man. He wants to buy your house.'

'This man' was fortyish, either bald or shaven-headed. He was wearing a dark anorak in soft napped fabric and a scarf tied high round his neck.

'You the owner?' he asked.

I hesitated. 'Yes,' I said. 'I am.'

'Is the house for sale?'

I shook my head. 'No, it's not. I've only been here a short time.'

The man craned his neck to peer past me. 'Can I just take a look?'

'No. There would be no point, would there? It's my house. I'm not moving.'

He sniffed, his mouth turning down at the corners. 'I was only asking for a look, darlin'.'

I was already closing the door. 'Sorry, no. This is

96

my house.' I shut the door and leaned against it.

Laura peered through the butterfly curtain. 'He's still there, staring. Creep.'

I sat on the sofa and picked up my glass. 'What did he want?' I said.

Laura took my spot on the floor. 'A slice of you, pet, if you're not careful.'

I shuddered.

'Nah,' she said reassuringly. 'Just some flutter. This city's full of them. I tell you what.' She reached in her bag for her phone. 'I'll tell Tariq and the others to come over with a bottle of champagne and we'll launch the house. What do you think? Get the taste of that pervert out of our mouths.' She put a hand to her mouth. 'Oops! Less than delicate.'

Of course that's what happened. No way of resisting when Laura is in full flight. We all drank, talked and played music till late. I can't remember what was said. And just how late it lasted I'm not sure, as the last hour was a bit fuzzy. I do know I ended up in the bed the wrong way round. And I do know Laura stayed, as in the early hours, before the traffic started up again, I could hear her snoring in the other room.

It took a month or so, Puss, but Chris did become a fixture in our house, even though he might go missing for days at a time. Mother got her weekly flowers and her kisses on the cheek. I got my nights out, our wonderful times in our little love nest, my presents and my cocktail lessons. I lost two office jobs because when Chris was here he liked me around. He brushed away

97

my protests and packed pound notes into envelopes with my name and a made-up number on, saying anybody could have a pay packet. Then when he was skint he would borrow the money back, kiss me and say we would have to live on love and we had that in abundance, didn't we?

Then things eased a bit when Richie was put away for a while on a trumped-up charge about a car. Chris said poor Richie had been in the wrong place at the wrong time and the police had fitted him up. Then his face lit up with that lovely smile of his. 'Ironic, isn't it, darling, that old Richie should go away for something he didn't do when we all know how much he gets away with.'

So for a time things quietened down. Chris was home more. Roy enjoyed getting on with the less dramatic side of their business. He ran things along the lines of a legitimate business, even though everything depended on this underlying smell of violence and any money was under the counter, no tax paid.

Chris used to tell me they looked after people and made them feel safe, which meant they were very grateful. Chris himself was still gambling and running errands for Roy, legal and illegal. But this meant that he had regular money and was out less at night. And there were fewer late-night parties with Richie queening it over the men and the women in a huddle in the corner, clutching their gins and tonics. There were fewer riotous assemblies designed to show everyone just who was the cock of the walk.

Chris told me Roy had even started courting this girl properly, talking about marriage, a thing that would never have happened with Richie around. He would brook no rivals, not at home, not away.

98

There was this night when Richie was still 'inside', Chris came home by taxi and dragged a sailor's heavy kitbag into the house. There was a banging and clashing as he lumbered it upstairs. My mother doing needlepoint in the front bay window, looked across at me. 'What's that boy doing now?' Like I said, she liked him, but she never was a fool.

When I get to the bedroom he has this big sack on the bed. 'What's in that?' I say.

He laughs, his white teeth gleaming. 'Ask no questions, my darling, and you'll get no lies.'

I pout then. It usually works.

He shakes his head. 'No resisting you, my darling.' He lifts the bag up, loosens the cord and tips the contents on to the floor Out of its narrow neck come perhaps thirty knives, large, small, long, short, all glittering in the light of the bedside lamp. An Eastern scimitar with a curved blade, two cutlasses. One of the cutlasses and one long knife have what looked like rust along the blade. Blood. 'Christ!' I don't often blaspheme, Puss, but I did that night.

I can see Chris is quite pleased with the effect that has on me. He can be perverse sometimes. He runs his hand over the hilt of the scimitar. 'They're Richie's,' he says. 'His mother asked me to store them for him. The filth are down there at the house all the time, all over them like a rash. Mrs P doesn't want these in her house. She says Richie sent a message out for me to take them. Just for the time being. Makes sense.'

I touch the rusty blade and shudder He takes me in his arms. 'Oh, baby,' he whispers, 'you're safe with me, you know that.' And would you believe it, Puss? We make love there and then on the bed, with the knives on the floor and my mother downstairs banging pans,

99

making bubble and squeak because it's Monday.

I was still very young then, Puss, but even as we melted into each other's arms and lost ourselves in our usual joyous wrestling, I found myself wondering how you could feel so safe with a man who wasn't even safe himself. I suppose you'll tell me it's all about love.

Missing

The hammering in my head transformed itself to a hammering in the outside world. I'd been dreaming of a long garden with tall trees bowing at its edges and the ground in between turned over and raked into neat rows, like Japanese gravel. Here and there were dark islands of black tulips. Not black, of course, but the deepest maroon, sucking out the light and reflecting nothing.

Not black. As I jumped from my bed I was mumbling 'Not black, not black...' As I passed the open door of the other room I glimpsed a neatly made bed. Laura had gone. I raced down the stairs. Perhaps it was that anorak man at the door.

'Not black,' I muttered again, opening the door. It was Bobbi.

'My dad's not home,' she said, walking straight into my living room. 'He hasn't come home. I waited and he didn't come.'

I glanced at my watch. 'You should be at school.' My mouth was dry and my head was raging. 'It's eleven o'clock.'

'I never go to school until he's back home,' she

said. 'Or until he rings and tells me to go to school. He did leave me this message telling me not to worry. But when people say you shouldn't worry you know you should be worrying. Mr and Mrs Selkirk are out and Mr Copeland has gone to work so I came here.' She collapsed on to the couch. 'It was here or Mehmet's, and he'll be busy with lunches.'

'Ring your dad now! Try again!' My shrill voice hurt my own ears. 'Wait!' I rushed to the sink and poured myself a very long glass of water, drank it and poured another.

Bobbi moved through to the kitchen end and stood looking at me. 'You have a hangover,' she said soberly.

This child knew too much. At this moment I could quite dislike her.

'Ring him now!' I repeated. She took her dinky phone from her pocket, hit a single number and held it out to me. I listened to the dulcet tones of some woman inviting the caller to leave a message for Mr Marsh.

'I'm gunna go up West and find him,' said Bobbi, pocketing the phone. 'An' I want you to come with me.'

'I have places to be, Bobbi.' A lecture on libel law, no less.

'D'you think I care?' She peered up at me through her curly fringe. 'Jesus, you look rough. Your hair looks like a barbed wire sunrise.' She smiled. 'I saw them come to your party last night. Your friends. I saw them through the window.'

'It wasn't a party. It was ... well, a gathering of friends.'

101

'A party, like I said.' She paused then sniffed, suddenly the worried little girl she really was. 'You've gotta come with me, Sophia.'

Which is how Bobbi and I, face washed, hair brushed (and polished with that very pricey serum Laura got me from Molton Brown), ended up in front of a narrow door in an alley behind Brompton Street that smelled of dead fish. I don't know what I expected. Some pink neon strips, perhaps. But there was only a plain, dark green door with a discreet brass plaque engraved with the word 'Kazoo' at eye level. Underneath the plaque was an Entryphone. Bobbi leaned forward and pressed it, and as she did I glanced up and saw the small camera above the door.

'Yeah?' a voice, rough, sexless, crackled through the speaker.

'We're looking for–' I began.

Bobbi piped up, 'We're looking for George Marsh. You know. Sparrow. He's my dad.'

'Yeah. Right. Wait!'

We waited for ages before we heard the sound of chains and the turning of locks. Then the door swung open and we were staring at this woman. She was anywhere between forty and seventy, and although she was smaller than I, her face, made up and well powdered, was large, out of proportion. She wore some kind of turban that pulled up the corners of her eyes. Only a bouffant fringe of bleached hair was visible. The red-nailed hand that held the door was weighed down with rings. 'Yes?' she said.

'My dad,' said Bobbi, 'he works here and did not come home. I've come to get him. You know

102

Sparrow Marsh.'

'Sparrow?' The woman pursed her lips. 'Sparrow's long gone. You say you're his kid? You're not like him. Not so dark.'

'I'm like my mother,' said Bobbi patiently. 'Where is he?'

'Went off early. Five, six o'clock. Hared off on that bike of his.'

'But he didn't come home. And he's not answering his phone.'

The woman nodded, compressing and stretching her crepey neck like a cockerel. 'Wait here,' she said, then vanished.

'That's Oliver's mum,' said Bobbi. 'She don't know me but I know her. I seen her once when I was out with my dad. In Harrods.'

Out on the road the searing scream of an ambulance cut through the roar of the traffic. A woman in a long dress and battered trainers meandered down the narrow alleyway, pushing a shopping trolley. You could smell her from twenty yards.

Oliver's mum came back with a small silver mobile phone in her hand. 'Sparrow left this,' she said. 'It was on Little Oliver's desk. Can't think why.' She pushed it into Bobbi's hand and shut the door in our faces. Then she opened it again. 'Where d'you say you live again?'

Bobbi clutched my arm. 'Not sayin',' she said.

The door clanged up and we could hear the chains and locks going on.

Bobbi fiddled with the phone and looked at me. 'My calls are on here. All missed. Now what should we do?' For the first time that morning her voice wobbled. 'He wouldn't leave his phone.

He wouldn't.'

I took her hand. 'People leave their phones around all the time, Bobbi. Really they do. What we should do now is go back to your place. Sparrow might be there already. Looking for you. If he's not there we wait. And if he doesn't get back we ring the police.' I was talking as though I knew this man. This Sparrow Marsh.

She shuddered. 'He'd kill me if we called the police. I am never supposed to contact them. He says that would muddy the waters. I'm not to contact them. Even though...'

'Even though what?'

'Nothing.' Her face closed down.

'Let's just wait and see. I bet he's there already.'

But he wasn't. We waited in the flat for him all afternoon. We played backgammon and chess. We sorted out Bobbi's many books. We ate cornflakes in milk and apple sandwiches. We looked at the photos of Sparrow with Bobbi's mother on some pebbly beach, windswept and gleeful in each other. Bobbi played her guitar and her bass recorder for me. She asked me to sew on a button that had come off her jeans in the wash. She surveyed the result and told me I was better than Sparrow. 'At sewing, anyway.'

Sparrow Marsh was all around us in that space but still he wasn't there.

Suddenly from below there came the sound of raised voices and bumps and thuds. I looked at the door. Bobbi shook her head. 'Not him,' she said. 'That's Mr and Mrs Selkirk. He's beating the crap out of her.'

That was the first time I had ever heard Bobbi

104

say an ugly word. If you worked around children as I had you were used to hearing them use the Anglo-Saxon oaths like God bless you. But Bobbi had an unusually clean mouth.

Then the noises faded and all was quiet.

I thought of Doreen, a big woman, round as butter. And Roger, stringy and slight. It occurred to me that Doreen must have been having a bad time with her first husband to choose this one.

We watched the news on television. Something about a study showing how many people could be killed by anthrax in a letter in a new scare in the USA.

'Webb and Blaser estimated that over 5,000 unwitting recipients received cross-contaminated letters, and that despite the low levels of contamination – the vast majority of letters contained between ten and a hundred spores – the sheer number of letters meant that two or three recipients could be expected to fall victim...'

'Just think of that, Sophia,' said Bobbi. 'Anthrax! I think I'll Google it.'

By six thirty Sparrow still wasn't back and I had my hand on the house phone.

'We do need to tell the police, Bobbi. It's the only thing.'

Bobbi took it from me, shaking her head. 'No, Sophia. He wouldn't want that. We'll wait. I'll wait on my own if you can't be bothered.'

'Of course I can be bothered. I can't leave you here alone.'

'I'm mostly alone. It doesn't bother me.'

'But Sparrow's not mostly *missing*.'

'OK then. You gotta stay here with me. But don't ring.'

'I can't do that, do nothing.'

'*We* can do anything.' She grabbed my arm, tears in her eyes. 'What if I stay at yours and we come back here in the morning and wait for him again?'

I found myself doing as I was told. Bobbi typed a large notice on her computer telling Sparrow where she was and stuck it on the door. She stuffed clothes at random in a backpack.

In the hallway we came across Doreen, pink and a bit dishevelled, taking out the bin. She held it up. 'Man's work!' she said, smiling slightly. 'I try to tell Roger but he says we feminists are simply not allowed to have our cake and eat it.' She looked at us, one to the other. 'What is it? You two look like thieves in the night.'

We explained what had happened. 'Good heavens!' she said. 'The poor man might be...' her glance dropped to Bobbi, 'well, *kidnapped*. Surely you have contacted the police?'

Bobbi shook her head. 'He won't want the cops. Things must have got hot for him.'

'Hot?'

'My dad says the Kazoo's no kindergarten. Even if his friend Oliver's legit now.'

Doreen frowned at me. 'No place for a child,' she said. 'I tell Roger that's no place for a child. When I see Bobbi here on the back of her father's bike I could faint. The size of it! Like a tank. Roger says the child's at risk.'

At risk. That familiar phrase. Alarm bells ringing in my head.

'Is that a bruise on your cheek, Mrs Selkirk?'

said Bobbi, suddenly very solicitous. 'Did some-body hit you?'

Doreen touched her cheek. 'This? Silly me. I had the cutlery drawer open, bent down to pick something up and wham! Came up with this stunner.' She laughed sheepishly. 'Roger says I should look where I'm going, that I'm a dizzy trout. Listen to the man!'

'Anyway, Doreen,' I said firmly, 'Bobbi thinks Sparrow will be back tomorrow and he won't want the police. I'm respecting her wishes on this, Doreen. Just for now.'

'We're going to Sophia's,' said Bobbi. 'I left a notice on the door for my dad. He'll be back soon.'

'Well, I hope so, dear,' said Doreen. She smoothed a curl off Bobbi's broad brow. 'You take care, now.'

'Doreen! What is it?' Roger's voice came from inside the flat. 'Where's my coffee?'

Doreen's face hardened. 'I must go.' She put a hand on Bobbi's shoulder. 'He'll turn up, child. You'll see.'

I gave Doreen my mobile number in case Spar-row did turn up, and she vanished into the flat.

As we made our way out of the house Bobbi told me how much Mrs Selkirk missed her own daughter. 'You can hear it all if you sit on the stairs. She rings her every day when Mr Selkirk's out. Then he sees it on the phone bill. He doesn't like it. So he gets mad. You can hear it. D'you think that's fair?'

'No I don't. Definitely not. Still, I don't think you should listen to all that. It's not polite.'

'I asked her about it, you know. But she said it's

fair because she deserves it.'

'No one deserves to be hurt like that.'

'Mrs Selkirk says it's her punishment for leaving her daughter behind. But I said Mr Selkirk wouldn't let her bring her here so he should be punished. And she said things didn't work that way.'

'Doreen shouldn't be talking to you like that.'

'Mrs Selkirk has nobody to tell. So she tells me. I'm the only one.'

Across the road Julia Soper was wheeling her shopping basket through her gate, her cat on board. She beckoned us across. 'Sophia! I have this new azalea called Girard's Hot Shot. You must see her. She's just out.' She hustled us up into her house and through to the back. She led me into her garden. Bobbi didn't follow.

We examined the azalea and spent a further five minutes admiring a rather luscious Manchurian lilac before coming back in to find Bobbi just emerging from the cellar.

Julia looked at her sharply. 'You've been prowling, you minx. I hope you didn't disturb Mother. She'll tell me, you know.' I caught the merest hint of a twinkle in her eye.

Bobbi held in her laughter until we got back on to the pavement. 'She's bonkers,' she spluttered. 'Just bonkers. There was nobody ... nothing down there.'

'Just a bit eccentric,' I said. 'She's teasing you. Don't mock.'

'There's no mother there. Why did she talk like she was?' Her eyes were sparkling.

'Well,' I struggled. 'I think she feels her mother's

there, in a kind of spiritual way.'

The humour drained from Bobbi's face. 'That's impossible, isn't it? Even *I* know my mum's not there. My mum died from this tumour in her head, you know. Me and my dad have talked about it lots. We believe in reincarnation, see? And she's reincarnated now into a humming bird that lives on Jamaica. My dad's grandpa came from there so my dad knows all about it. But they don't *talk* to you. Old Miss Soper's crackers, I'm tellin' you.' There were tears in her eyes.

I put my arm round Bobbi and held her tight. It was too hard on a child, all this. I wondered how long we'd have to wait before Sparrow Marsh came home. Or how long we would have to wait before the police got involved, whether Bobbi liked it or not.

Later that night Stephen Copeland telephoned to ask if he could do anything for Bobbi. He'd seen the notice on the door and Doreen had told him what had happened.

'Is there anything I can do? Does she need to be here? Perhaps I could sit in with her.'

'No. Bobbi's fast asleep on my sofa. I'll keep her here and we'll decide what to do in the morning.'

He gave me his mobile number. 'If you or Bobbi need anything, any hour, just ring. I mean it.'

I clicked off the phone and looked at Bobbi's tousled head beside me on the sofa. And even in the middle of this crisis I thought what a very nice voice Stephen Copeland had. Deep and kind of plain. I wasn't falling for him. I knew that. But he had a very nice voice.

That's the first child that's been in here, Puss, since Chris brought young Stephen into the front room to show him some magic tricks. Years ago. And I did not feel bad about letting her in even though we left her to her own devices while we walked down the garden. When we came back I mentioned Mother to her and she looked startled. Now they'll both think I'm a crazy woman. Don't know why I did that, really. Mischief, I suppose. Or force of habit. I was always talking to Mother before you came, even though I knew she was six feet under and missing from my life. I never talked to Chris, though, after he went. Silly to talk to someone who was swanning about up in Yorkshire or even on one of the Costas with his shady friends. Of course, he could be dead now, anyway. It is forty-odd years, after all. But I don't feel that. It's as though it was all yesterday. I feel he's waiting. Don't look at me like that. Now you think I'm a crazy woman, Puss, never mind that little girl.

Those people in the bottom flat have been at it again, did you see? He gave her such a bang across the face, first one way, then the other. Right there in the bay window. A funny chap. One day rescuing the little girl from the monster-kids, then hitting out at his wife. Heroes, villains, it's in us all, Pusscat. There's just no telling with people, is there?

110

A Crying Shame

Bobbi spent the next twenty-four hours just waiting. We stayed in my house. Laura rang and I said I had a bad stomach and she said, 'Oh yes, I've had those meself from time to time, pet.' Her voice was like balm. I put down the phone and wished I'd asked her to come over.

Doreen called at the house with a bag of *baklava* and sat and ate them with us. The sweetness made my teeth ache.

Stephen Copeland called to try to convince us to go to the police but we all stood around helplessly in the face of Bobbi's stubborn resistance. 'I have to get into work. Ring me if there is anything,' he said at last.

Bobbi and I mooched around, read and ate boiled eggs at lunchtime. Then, at two o'clock in the afternoon, Stephen called me again.

'Where are you?'

'Still at mine.'

'Wait there. I have news.'

'News? How can you have news?'

'Wait!'

He arrived half an hour later, breathing heavily. 'Had to park right up on Brooke Road.'

'What?' demanded Bobbi. 'What news?'

He took out his mobile. 'I was in a meeting at one of our sites. I always turn this off when I'm on a site.' He set it down and clicked on to messages. Sparrow Marsh's voice, very deep but strangely contained, belled into the room.

'Hey, Steve. Can you get this message to Bobbi? Don't want to talk to her directly. Tell her I'm quite all right but am lying low. I saw something I shouldn't have at the Kazoo and need to go to ground. Tell Bobbi to keep her head down just for a while, will you? No one's got any idea where she is, so that's OK. Tell her to keep things normal. An' can you keep your eye on her, Stevie? Keep her by you. Tell her I love her. I posted something to you at your office. Give it to her, Steve. Tell her ... tell her she gotta go to school just like normal. Just like normal. I tried the house but she wasn't there...'

The voice faded. Stephen Copeland placed an envelope on the table, opened it and flicked through a pile of notes. 'Two hundred, I'd say.'

When I looked at Bobbi her face was beaming. 'I told you,' she said. 'He's all right. He's safe in Bristol, I bet. That's where he comes from, you know.'

I was angry. 'How could he? How could he have done this to you? Leave you like this?'

She looked at me with barely concealed contempt. 'He's not done nothing to me 'cept take care of me. He trusts me. We're a team. Always were. No police, no Social, Sophia.' Her voice was firm.

They were both looking at me. My social worker self drained away. I gave in. 'So, things being normal, will you go to school?'

'Yep,' she nodded. 'And everything. Just normal, like he says. I'll put on my uniform. Be a bit

112

late but they won't notice. We had better get back to the flat. I should change into my school uniform.' As we walked along Barrington Street she whistled a tune.

'Listen to her! Not a care in the world.' I looked helplessly at Stephen.

His deep-set eyes gleamed. 'She's in charge. Hadn't you noticed? Look. What do you want to do? I brought a stack of drawings so I can work at home for the next few days until this thing sorts itself out. You have to go to your course...'

'Yes.' I felt myself colour. He was dismissing me. I didn't like that. 'I just missed a lecture on libel law.'

He grinned. 'Essential info for a journalist, I'd have thought.'

I was still hesitating.

He put a hand on my arm. 'Look, Sophia, go to your course and come straight back here to check things are OK. We'll sort this between us. As long as Bobbi's safe Sparrow's more than capable of taking care of himself.'

I relaxed. 'If you think so. I've never met him, though at this moment I feel like I could murder him.'

'He's quite a guy. True blue. You'd like him.'

At the flat I waited until Bobbi came out of her bedroom, bandbox fresh, in her uniform.

'Right!' she said. 'Now, school.'

At the gate, before we parted, she clutched my hand. 'See you s'afternoon, Sophia. In Mehmet's. At half-past three.' And she skipped away.

When I got back to the Lavender House, Julia Soper was already there in my front garden. She

113

had tipped out the dead earth from the derelict pots on to a black sack and was filling them from a sack of fresh potting compost. She waved her trowel at me, her hands, in skin-tight medical gloves, catching the light.

'This front garden's a mess, dear. I've split some of my plants and potted them up for you. And I have a new azalea for you. We'll soon bring this desert back to life.' She bent down again. 'Don't hang around, dear. I'm sure you've more to do than hang around watching me. Nearly finished here. We'll do your back yard another day. That place really does need cheering up. You could start with painting those walls.' She turned her back on me and bent down over the last pot.

Rendered numb from my morning, I went inside and rang Laura to check on our commitments. She swallowed my repeated tale of a tummy bug with a sceptical, 'Oh, yes!' and said we had a lecture on placements at eleven. She would watch for me.

I scrubbed my face hard and sat brushing my hair, rubbing in even more serum to tame it, trying to reassure myself that I was not becoming obsessed with Bobbi Marsh. And her father. Bobbi didn't need my protection. She wouldn't fall through the cracks like Drina. She was in a strange set-up but she was not neglected. Even if she was, I was not really responsible for her. Not like I had been for Drina. That was when the tears started to fall down my cheeks. To be honest I was used to it, bursting into silent tears every so often. I was resigned to it.

In my job in Newcastle I'd had to learn to be

rational and stoical, even if I wasn't as hard and pragmatic as some of my colleagues. I was no more a born social worker than I was a born journalist. But this crying had been a built-in part of my life since those events around Drina. I'd cried Lake Windermere for her, for me, for all the lost children. At first I cried all the time. Then the doctor gave me the pills. While I was taking them I didn't cry all the time. I merely cried at certain triggers: a mother chastising her child in a supermarket; a mother skipping with her child in a playground. A Benetton advert for children's clothes. The television was the worst: a child crying in a street in Iraq; an NSPCC appeal with a child crouching in a corner; a sentimental presentation of some tragic child in a soap opera. In the end I just stopped watching television and stopped taking the pills. Couldn't afford all those paper hankies.

But I hadn't cried at all since I'd been in London. Not until today. Now at last I sniffed hard and blinked and the tears stopped. Julia was nowhere to be seen when I set out to catch the bus and came across a man standing in the road looking up at the house. He was wearing mousy clothes. He had a mousy face and thin mousy hair.

I tucked away my key and went down my path.

'You live here, darlin'?' he said.

'Yes.'

'Is it for sale?'

Another one. 'No. I live here. It's not for sale.'

He put his hand on the fence and I shuddered, as though his hand were on me. 'D'you rent it?' His face was whiter, harder.

115

'No business of yours.'

'You do, then. So it could be for sale?'

'No. Like I say. I live here. I have a contract.'

'Can I just have a look round it?'

The man must have thought I was a fool. 'You most certainly can't.'

He grinned suddenly, showing bleached, over-white teeth. 'Don't get your shirt off, darlin'? His face had taken on that mild mouse look again. 'I'll be on my way then.' But he still stared at me.

'Yes. You'd better be on your way.' I pulled out my mobile phone. 'Of course I could get the police.' I turned back and let myself in the house, locked the door behind me and raced upstairs to watch him through the curtains. The man was walking away slowly. Then he turned round and stood in the road, his hands on his hips. He stared at the house and his glance drifted up at me in the window. He looked so much like a pantomime villain that I laughed and shook my fist at him. He turned and walked away round the corner, quickly now.

I breathed out, relief flooding through me. My gaze was pulled to the far end of Barrington Street where Julia was decanting her garden spade and fork from her basket. I thought per-haps I'd call at Mr Ayhan's on my way back from the lecture and buy some outdoor paint. I'd get Bobbi to help me paint the yard. That would keep both our minds off this bizarre situation. And off Sparrow Marsh. I didn't know the man but somehow these days he was filling my mind.

Then I decided not to bother with the seminar on new placements. As I walked down Barrington Street I enjoyed a mild feeling of pleasure at playing truant. Then I felt guilty about not feeling guilty about it.

Look, Puss, quite a lot of coming and going between the house opposite and Sophia's little house on the corner. Stephen too, he's definitely taking an interest in Sophia. She could do worse than get on with Stephen, as my mother would say.

I don't know whether Mother was pleased or sorry, Pusscat, that I didn't get on with some other chap after Chris went off. Apart from an occasional mutter about people wasting their lives she left it at that. I think she was pleased to have me back to herself. She and I got on with things. Me in my little job working for a taxi firm off Church Street, her keeping the house nice and jumping on the bus to go down Dalston to meet my Aunt Madge for their weekly bingo.

For years that went on, then her dementia set in and there was no more bingo. Just me talking into thin air. Gets to be habit, that, Puss. Good thing you turned up, Puss. I've got you here to talk to these days.

Mum came from Dalston, you know. So, even doolally as she was, I knew she must have missed those trips. She liked Dalston but she liked it here on Barrington Street best. Thought it was a step up. Mr Copeland's family had been on Barrington Street from way back, even before the First War. He was a bit of a stick, was Mr Copeland. I remember him going up to the City every morning with his bowler and umbrella, marching to the station as though there were still a war on.

Mrs C was a different kettle of fish, Pusscat. Tall as

117

a heron, just like the boy. Her hair turned from blonde to silver overnight. Or so it seemed to me. And she had staff there. A housekeeper who lived in, and a skivvy who scurried in at half-past seven every morning.

That party across there made me think of the Copelands, who had these parties in their drawing room, in that room where the Selkirks live now. The women who came wore cocktail dresses and the men wore those lumpy post-war lounge suits, not too well cut.

Then every Wednesday Mrs C would have friends round to play bridge and afterwards had a meeting that was something to do with refugees. Apparently she wanted Mum to join this meeting. She even offered to teach my mother bridge. Mother, though, was too shy to join in all this. Wasn't having any of it, see? As I see things now, Pusscat, Mrs C was grand but not at all condescending. But my mother had come out of the East End and was proud of it. She told me my father used to call her his little Cockney Sparrow. But that's only hearsay, so I never knew that. Dad was old North London and his people were Jewish, well off enough to buy this house for him before the war, even though my mother was goy, not Jewish at all. Then I was born and he went off to war and never came back. Killed in Burma, like so many of them. His family settled a bit of money on Mother and me, but we never knew them. I could pass them in the street and not recognise them. How odd is that, Puss?

Mum and I got by. She had this little job cleaning insurance offices and when I was old enough I got jobs in town. I ended up in this record shop off Piccadilly. Of course, that's where I met my Chris. He was looking for a record of Al Martino and I laughed at him and said how square was that? Told him he

118

should try the Kinks or the Beach Boys. He told me I was gorgeous and should be a model but he still bought the Al Martino.

Then he was waiting outside when the shop closed and asked me if I'd like to go to the pictures to see Cool Hand Luke. I turned him down, saying my mother was expecting me home. He said he would come home with me and ask her.

And he did. We didn't go to the pictures. We went to Esmeralda's Barn and he introduced me to the Pinder boys. That was how it all began.

Dropping Out

Taking refuge in a 'sickie' was a new experience for me. I have always been known as a very good girl. Dropping out of anything was always anathema. Growing up with old people in Northumberland meant being socialised with phrases like 'If you can walk you can work', 'Work's a devil but you must give the devil his due', 'Missing work for no reason is a living lie'. My grandmother loathed the friendly term 'sickie'. She thought it made light of a serious thing. Claim a sickie and the gods would have their revenge and you would really get sick.

So, until I got pregnant I never missed a day at school or a shift at work. In my professional life I always worked to excess, meticulously attending meetings, writing up case notes, pinning down my clients, watching those weaker people floundering around me with pity and sometimes

119

condemnation. I was commitment personified. To be honest, I verged on the sanctimonious.

It couldn't go on, of course. I had to move out of my grandmother's generation into my own. The evolution started when Malcolm, my boss for three years, stepped out of his mentoring role and slowly ensnared me. Late meetings would end with drinks at the pub; drinks at the pub led to deep, meaningful, very personal conversations; such talk ended up in my bed in my flat. Or in a seaside hotel at some convenient conference. When I got pregnant Malcolm was thrilled with me for a whole minute and we had a wonderful 'what if...' session. Then he treated me to one of his very powerful 'let's be reasonable' talks. He was a wonderful talker. After that he was very helpful over the termination. Naturally I thought it was all my own fault and I had to claim a justified 'sickie' for that day off.

It was while all this was happening, when I was evolving personally at cataclysmic speed that, despite all my efficiency, Drina began to slip through the net. Dealing with the early queries regarding reports of non-accidental injuries I'd had reasonable contact with Drina and her parents. Her parents seemed rational, bewildered, at a loss to explain the vindictiveness of their neighbours. Soon after my second visit, in the flurry of the business of my termination I lost notes, missed calls, missed meetings. (*Absolutely out of character*, as my evaluation report said to the inquiry.) The Parnabys dissolved away from me into some kind of a black hole. Then there was this urgent call from the school welfare officer about Drina's continued absence from school, on the same day that I finally listened to a second message from the Parnabys' neighbour about a strange noise in their garage.

Later on, the newspapers were full of how plausible the Parnabys were, both well-paid IT consultants, good car, living on a chichi suburban estate. Behind the scenes there was much satisfied huffing and puffing about how naive it was to think that cruelty was the domain of the poor and the dispossessed.

Of course, Malcolm was very supportive in the ensuing row. He was forced to suspend me until the inquiry, and when it was all over he really did understand that I couldn't go on in the job, even if they welcomed me back with open arms. I sat at home watching daytime television and drinking too much.

Malcolm rang me one night and I had to put down the phone because I couldn't quite frame any coherent words to say to him. That was when he put me forward for the community magazine project funded by the Lottery, which seemed right out there among the poor and dispossessed these days. The New Dawn Estate had qualified for a lot of assistance.

I took the offer like a blind woman accepting her stick, and it saved me.

Even then, though, I knew that it wasn't Malcolm who was my saviour. What saved me was the energy and bustle of a group of ferocious people on the estate led by a Blyth woman they called Big Emma. These people, mostly women, who did not see themselves as the poor and dispossessed, had banded together to make the New Dawn a better place to live in the face of an apathetic council and a disbelieving and accusing world.

In the company of these women my deep sadness and remorse about Drina – as well, I think, as my own lost child – began at last to retreat. I buried myself in the astonishing stories of these women, which told the history and degradation of the estate. I recorded how they had secured funding, built a garden and a playground partly with their own physical efforts. I noted how they literally lit up sections of the estate that had been in the dark for a generation, insisting on a particular design of secure lighting that did not succumb to any passing stone. Doll Wharton, handy with her grandson's digital camera, took photographs only accessible to an insider.

The fact is that it was Emma and Doll and the others who deserved the magazine prize. But on that last day, Emma, always the biggest and boldest of the women, tucked her arm in mine. I still remember every word she said.

'Go on, pet, it's yours. We got our magazine, haven't we? And we got the council worried about their image. It's not finished here. Doll can mind the magazine now. Not much to it, is there? Dinnet forget us, Sophia-pet, but you've had your own troubles and now's the time to get on with things for yersel'. You do that. Right?'

Who needs counsellors?

So I came to London with their blessing. Now here I was, playing truant. Letting down Emma as well as the memory of my grandmother.

Disrespecting my prize. Claiming a 'sickie'.

But it seemed to me that events in Barrington Street were pulling me further and further away from the sterility of the course. I had begun to care less and less whether I finished yet another piece of writing about some alienated misfits who turned up in court, and I resented the need to curry favour with strangers in order to sub-edit copy or make coffee for sharp, talented people on a magazine, who were no older than I.

What surfaced strongly now was my resentment towards the profession that had been thrust on me. And my annoyance at myself that I had taken it on so blindly. By what wilful slip of the imagination had I forgotten those journalists hammering on my door when Drina died? They were unrelenting. I couldn't have spoken even if I'd wanted to. I had been gagged by the department, even though, apart from speaking at the Parnabys' trial, I was for ever now labelled as the 'social worker concerned'. Excited journalists, both local and national, made much of the deviousness and plausibility of the Parnabys. There were pages and pages on the underfunding of the social services.

In the end I was grateful that the Court and the inquiry were so even-handed. The fault was never seen as all mine. Except by me.

Now here in London I had begun to feel irritated by the artless certainties of the younger students around me. Their ambition and witty, conscienceless insight floored me; their background, nurtured in university halls, away from the realities of people like Big Emma and her crew of women, seemed irrelevant. I felt this even while I liked them. I truly appreciated their forthrightness, their miraculous skill with words, their pragmatic abandonment of the literary and the metaphorical for the zippy, everyday phrases demanded by metropolitan editors. I was so very fond of these kids. But living here on Barrington Street had intensified the yawning distance between me and them, even lovely, talented Laura and funny, clever, cynical Tariq, who had taken me under their wing from day one.

These truanting thoughts buzzed and buzzed around in my brain for days before I made my decision. I resisted the desire to talk it over with Laura. It was up to me. So, on the third day of my watch over the deserted Bobbi, I picked her up at Mehmet's at three thirty and took her on the bus with me to the university. I left her on the seat outside Jack Molloy's office and went in to tell him I was giving up the course. He sat there and listened patiently as I tried to explain the random way in which I had ended up on the course, my growing doubts and my present certainty that the course was not for me. As my defensive explanation went on, my gaze fixed downwards and I noticed that under his desk his big feet were bare. And he had beautifully formed, very hairy toes.

When I'd finished he was scowling. 'If you're giving up now, Sophia, even though you're doing OK, why in Christ did you sign up for the course at all?'

I thought I had explained that. 'I suppose I was flattered. I'd enjoyed writing for and with the women on the estate. And I thought this might be something I'd be able to do. A new career.

124

Away from all that.'

'Journalism is anything but away from it all. If it's anything, it's slap-bang in the middle of things. Do you hate it all?'

I shrugged. 'The actual writing I like. It's the scrabbling around for a subject, any subject, the cynical, partial view of people's lives that bothers me. The transitory nature of it all.' I clapped myself on the head. 'Oh God, I sound so bloody po-faced.'

He grunted. 'Well, you said it, kiddo. But don't you see that's just what it's all about? That's why it's so bloody fantastic. Living in the moment. Today's news, tomorrow's fish paper. If you don't get that...' He rubbed his brow hard, then ran his hand through his already spiky hair. Then his tone changed. 'Of course, I'd forgotten. You've been on the other side of the fence, haven't you?'

'Haven't I!' I said gloomily.

'We did talk about that here before you came. Me, I thought that might give you a kind of edge on the course. Others were not so sure.'

'I thought so too. I felt certain then. But now I've changed my mind. Things have changed my mind. Sorry.'

'You're not a *dreadful* writer, Sophia.'

'Why, thank you, sir! Like I said, the writing is OK. The rest, well...'

Then he seemed to relax. His tone changed. 'It's your life, kiddo. So what'll you do? Go back North? Safe home? Back to your roots?'

'Not at all.' I was red, angry that he saw my actions as a retreat, a childish attack of homesickness. 'It was the best thing I could do, coming away. I was right about that. Away from those legendary roots. I'm happy here. I like it. I've got this new place and I'm settling in. I feel at home here. Isn't that what London does? Allows you to reinvent yourself.'

'Right!' Jack sat up straight, his feet feeling for his sandals. 'So what'll you do now, then?' He stood up.

I stared at him. Then an idea came out of my mouth that had not even been in my head a minute before. 'Well, I'm all right for a while. Sold everything I had, car, flat... So I'll not starve for maybe a year.' I drew a breath. 'I think I might write about the estate. Stories. Those women. You know.' I stood up, ready to go. Now I knew what I would do. 'Stories.'

He frowned. 'Some kind of documentary fiction?'

I was already shaking my head. '*Not* journalism. Stories. Kind of fiction but the truth, you know. A kind of patchwork.' I was uncertain of the details but my mind was racing on like a rattling, creaking train. I could write about Emma and her crew. Maybe I could even write something about Drina, something that would bring her to life, not leave her lifeless in her cage.

'Won't you need a job? To keep yourself?'

I shook my head. 'Like I said, I have this bit of money. Survival money.' I stood up, my head spinning with this new idea that I'd made up on the spur of the moment. I was buzzing. I wanted to start. Here. Now.

Jack scowled, then shrugged, then grinned widely and shook my hand. 'Good-oh! This

126

game's not for everyone. Bit between the teeth, Sophia? If that book shapes up, let me know. I might have a name or two for you. No promises, though. It's a cut-throat world.' He followed me to the door and put a heavy hand on my shoulder. 'Keep in touch, won't you?'

That touch was the first really personal contact between him and me. I nodded, but felt I probably wouldn't. Get in touch, I mean. The stories might be some mad dream brought on by Bobbi and Sparrow Marsh, and the Lavender House.

Outside Jack's door Bobbi leaped up and almost careered into him.

'Is this your daughter?' He looked puzzled.

How many months had I been here?

'No, she's my ward,' I said.

'What's a "ward"?' said Bobbi as we went through the double door.

'Someone whom one is bound by law to protect,' I said.

'*Whom one is bound by law to protect.* I like that,' she said, tucking her hand in mine. 'Brilliant.'

We made our way across to the Lion, where I knew Laura was waiting.

She scowled her disbelief. 'Bloody hell, lass. You're f... kidding!' She glanced at Bobbi. 'Are you crazy?'

It was even worse facing her with my decision than Jack Molloy. I found myself going through my reasons one by one.

'You mean you're too good for this game? Well, I admit writing about cooks and curtains is not world shattering...'

'You're a great writer, Laura. You'll affect the

way people see their world. That's not trivial. You'll be famous. Me, I'm not that good. I don't believe any of it. If it feels false to me how can I really do it?' I could feel Bobbi's beady eye on me.

'But you're gunna write this thing about the New Dawn?'

'That's not false to me, it's unfinished business.'

'And if nothing comes of that?'

I had never known Laura so intimidating, so tight-in angry.

'It'll be there, outside me,' I said. 'Then I can get on with my life.'

'Another book?'

I shook my head. 'Not necessarily. I could stack shelves, sell books, be a pole-dancer.'

She stared at me. Then her face melted into a broad grin. 'Your life, pet. But you're not getting rid of me that easy. Should we have a beer to celebrate your escape?'

'Yes, please,' said Bobbi.

Laura looked at her blandly. 'You pipe down, small fry. You're the one who started this farrago.'

It might not sound like it, Pusscat, but in the end I was under few illusions about Chris. I'm not a fool. Once I'd actually met Richie and Roy Pinder I got to understand what an edgy world my Chris inhabited. The Pinders treated him like some kind of poodle, showing him off, patting him on the head, bringing him to heel. No. When I think about it they treated him more like a retriever. They were always sending him on errands. Amsterdam. New York. You know, Chris said the Americans liked to talk to him, and mimicked his plummy accent. He also said Richie liked to order him about when the aristos and Americans were sitting there. Especially when I was there. Of course, I blustered on about this but Chris just shrugged. 'Beggars and choosers, darling. Beggars and choosers. He who pays the piper calls the tune.' He softened that savage truth with a gift of a Fabergé egg that had fallen off the back of a Rolls-Royce the previous weekend.

I fingered those bright enamels, Pusscat, that sharp gold, and went quiet. I was not just angry with the Pinders, I was angry with Chris. But I couldn't say this to him. He would only leap to their defence and look very hurt. Like a beaten dog.

Only once did I really push him. Just once. I asked him why he couldn't give up gambling altogether. Go away. Out of their reach. He looked me in the eye and shrugged. He said it didn't work like that. Once they had you, they had you. You could never get out of their reach. The ones who tried to get away ended up being chopped up by one of the Scotsmen and being fed to pigs on some farm in Suffolk.

I said, 'They can't do that.'

What he said then, Pusscat, was, 'As long as you believe they can, they've got you.' So much despair in his voice, Pusscat.

I got even braver that night, Pusscat. I asked him if the Pinders had ever asked him to do something really bad. 'Bad like what?' He smiled this very thin smile. 'Bad like chopping up some poor pilgrim? Or bad like tipping another poor pilgrim into the concrete footings to these new flyovers?'

I clutched him then and told him I knew, just knew, he would never do anything like that. He kissed me hard on the cheek. 'You know me so well, darling. To be

129

honest the most they ask for me to do is entice some reprobate lord or nubile starlet to their soirées, or deliver shady goodies here or there. They are shrewd, those two. Clever. They know their men and I have my uses.'

I longed for him to get away from them. And that's what I thought when he didn't come home, Puss – that he'd escaped. That he'd gone on some errand and not made it back. When he first went off, Mother asked if he'd run away from her or run away from me. I said I didn't know.

She missed him. She said that more than once. Sometimes she would say she missed the parties. And that Richie was quite a lark, wasn't he?

The Yellow Book

On our way back from town to the Lavender House, Bobbi and I stopped at Art-A-Print in the High Street and I bought a yellow notebook (feint lined, perfect bound), and three gel pens. I left Bobbi at number 83, went to the Lavender House, sat down straight away at the kitchen table, took out the book and laid the gel pens beside it.

It was like my first day at school, exciting and terrifying in the same measure. On those first pristine pages I wrote chaotically, inspirationally, everything I could remember about Big Emma: who and how she was; what she did, most importantly what she said. Emma had this tight, pithy way of saying things that stuck in your head. And then Doll, with her sharp eye and unerring instinct for the picturesque in dark places.

When I had exhausted that first flight of inspiration I turned to the back of the book and made a straight list of all the things Emma, Doll and their crew did to change the New Dawn Estate: their battles and dramatic confrontations, their wily manipulations and inspired pleadings, their sheer articulation of who they were and what really mattered in life.

Three hours later, when I looked at my scrawled pages, I knew I had enough here to work on right past the end of this year, right past what would have been the end of my course. And more. Here was *my work*. This, the Lavender House and Barrington Street would make me a life. It seemed a long time since I'd had a life.

The money lying in the bank, profit from selling my Newcastle flat and my little car, would give me the time to see if I could do it.

I should have been exhausted but I was buzzing again with energy. So I put on my oldest jeans and briefest, oldest T-shirt, covered my hair tightly with a green silk scarf and went out to paint the back yard.

I had just painted half of the back wall when Julia Soper put her head over the fence and held up a basket. 'More plants for you, Sophia.'

I opened the gate and she came in. Her grey cat was coiled round her shoulders like a fox fur.

'I have a climbing hydrangea here for you. *Hydrangea anomala*. It'll show up very nicely against that cream wall when it's painted. I've brought my gloves. I thought I'd give you a hand with the painting.'

131

No permission asked. No by-your-leave.

The cat leaped on to the wall and Julia pulled on her pink gloves. She raked around in my box for a spare brush. As we worked we talked. She told me it was a nice little house. It had character. She was pleased I was making something of it. As we talked I savoured my decision to stay closer to this house, closer to her, instead of going haring off each day on fools' errands. Fools' errands! I had fallen out with the idea of journalism.

We were finishing the second wall when someone rattled at the front door. I peered through the kitchen window right through to the front window, and there was another of those men standing back and looking at the house. This one was wearing a trilby and a short white mackintosh.

'Shall I go?' said Julia.

'No.' I picked up my paintbrush. 'Leave it.' I told her about the house stalkers.

Julia's brows climbed into her Joni Mitchell fringe. 'They're stalking you, dear?'

'No. It's not me. There's something about the house. They want to buy it, or look round, or something.'

'Shouldn't you tell the agent?'

I shook my head. 'No way. She might sell it to one of them over my head.'

'So we'll lie low?'

'Exactly.'

We worked on. When we were finally finished she lit a cigarette, drawing on it gratefully. Keeping it in her hand, she used the other to sort out the biggest pot from the pile in the corner. Then she filled it with some compost from the yellow plastic sack she'd left me last time she was here planting, and crouched down to plant the hydrangea up against the back wall.

'There she goes.' She teased out the tendrils tenderly against the wall, then kneeled back. 'You're in and out of number eighty-three a lot,' she stated, squeezing her eyes against the smoke of her cigarette.

'Of course, you must see me,' I stated, matching her neutral tone.

'I'll say one thing for that black fellow.'

'What's that?'

'He sends that child out to school immaculate. Immaculate.'

I wanted to tell her what was happening, but it was not my secret to tell. One part of me was pleased, though, that Sparrow was alive in her mind too.

Tenderly she patted down the compost around the roots of the plant. 'Haven't seen much of him lately. He's either a will-o'-the-wisp or has a cloak of invisibility. Or–'

God, she could qualify for the FBI. 'This house,' I interrupted her. 'My Lavender House. Did you know anyone who lived here before?'

She stood up, stretched her back, and looked up at the house. 'Well, it's hard to say. It has always been a coming-and-going sort of house. Even when I was little. Then I was in here myself a very long time ago.'

'Yourself?' My interest sharpened.

'And,' she swept on, 'I think there were working girls in here last year.' She drew hard on her cigarette. 'Foreigners. Sharp faces. Too pretty to

133

be home-grown. A good deal of coming and going when they were there, as you'd expect.' She frowned. 'My mother used to call it a den of thieves. She had what you might call an accusing way of seeing the world.' The cat suddenly leaped on to her shoulder and I jumped. She stroked it. 'There, Pusscat, you frightened Miss Sophia. Shame on you.'

'Would you like a cup of coffee, Julia? A glass of wine?' I had my hand on the door latch.

She shook her head. 'Thank you, but no. Pusscat and I require some sustenance and I have cooked chicken all ready at home.' She gathered up her basket. 'This courtyard is shaping up very nicely. I'll find you some more climbers. Campsis or clematis, perhaps.'

As the gate clicked behind her I relaxed. Sometimes conversations with Julia Soper were just a bit too spooky. I went in and changed out of my paint-spattered rags. As I came downstairs I decided to go along and check on Bobbi before I settled down for the night. The yellow book sat invitingly on the table under the window, but I resisted it. When I came back I'd read through what I'd written and have a good think about Emma and her crew

I locked the door behind me and was walking along the road when the man in the short white mackintosh appeared beside me. 'That your house, is it?'

'Yes.' I walked steadily.

'Is it for sale? Could I take a look?'

I stopped and faced him. 'For Christ's sake, what is it about this house? What is it?'

'Don't you know?'

'It's the house I live in. That's what I know.'

'Well, love, you live in a notorious house. Notorious.' His face was too pale, just running to fat. 'You should know that.'

I thought of the prostitutes. 'Well,' I said, 'it's not notorious now. It's mine. So just keep away.' I turned and strode on.

'There's a cellar,' his voice pursued me. 'Have you seen the cellar?'

'There's no cellar,' I shouted behind me. 'No cellar.' I ran up the path of number 83 and rang the bell.

He had followed me and was standing at the gate. 'You check, love,' he said. 'You just check.'

Doreen opened the door and stepped outside. She folded her arms and stared at him. 'Will you get off my path?' she drawled. 'You're spoiling my view.'

He glared at me, turned on his heel and stalked away, his coat flapping slightly.

Doreen turned and looked at me. 'House stalker?' she said.

I nodded. 'House stalker.'

'Well, Sophia, is it me you want or young Bobbi?'

'I'm just checking on her,' I said.

'How're things up there? No sign of her pa?'

I shook my head. 'It doesn't seem like it.'

'Perhaps one shouldn't say it, Sophia, but surely it's illegal for her to be there like that? On her own?'

'Strictly, yes. But I watch her. And she sleeps at my house. And you and Stephen are here. We've talked it over. She's anxious just to wait for her father. There is no going against her.'

Doreen nodded. 'She's a forceful child, in spite of those dreamy ways of hers.'

'She's confident he'll be back. Stephen's in some kind of roundabout touch with Sparrow and he thinks it's all right.'

She led the way into the house. 'Well, if Stephen thinks that perhaps we should go along. You two are getting to be quite a little team, I think.'

I did wonder if Stephen was in from work yet. 'Nothing like that Doreen. It's all just about Bobbi.'

'Of course it is, my dear,' she said soothingly. 'Of course it is.'

Sophia calls that little house the Lavender House. Don't you think that's romantic, Pusscat? It's changing back again now, back to what it was in those days. But not quite. Today the bedroom is not quite the Aladdin's cave, the sheik's tent it was. Chris had such an exotic eye. Of course, Mum was always very nice about Chris being here but it was really good to have the Bolt Hole. She calls it the Lavender House, we called it the Bolt Hole. It's all in the name, Pusscat, isn't it?

It was our secret place. Even the Boys didn't know we went there.

Anyway, the best times, those dizzy fun times, finally ended when Richie came out of prison, having caused havoc and been put on drugs in there to keep him quiet. Chris said Richie had always hated the quiet life and did anything he could to stir it up. Same when he came out. He didn't care how good the money was now from the Pinders' shady enterprises.

136

Such discreet villainy held no buzz for him. He liked to operate in the spotlight. Well, more a black light for him. A cone of darkness. I saw that once in a comic. The Dandy, I think. Korky the Cat in a cone of darkness that struck the core of darkness in other people. A bit like Hitler.

When I mentioned this thought to Chris he said I could be very deep but my trouble was that I didn't get Richie. It wasn't all bad stuff. He created this buzz around him that other people fed off. Kept them buzzing.

I looked at him then, right into those big blue eyes. 'Even you?' I said.

He shrugged. 'Even me, my darling. I'm a fool for that man. Roy is too. Now even he's saying it's been too quiet. Now he's buzzing up again himself. He's listening to Richie again. More alive himself.'

'Weird,' I said.

'Like I said, darling, you don't get Richie.'

I knew there was real trouble ahead, Pusscat, when I caught Chris coming down the stairs with the sailor's clanking kitbag full of knives. 'Richie wants them by him,' he said blandly. 'I've got a taxi waiting. See you later, darling.' He kissed me on the top of my head and whirled away, knives and all.

As a kind of way of showing me how special Richie was, Chris started telling me about things that were happening. It seemed Richie thought they needed to extend their operation further south to show just who ran things in London. And he got his wish. Before long there were set-piece knife fights in pubs and grudge-led battles in empty warehouses. Bloodied heads and injured limbs. Vanishings. Meetings in glamorous West End clubs set up with no hope or

137

intention of compromise.

The Pinders began to win their battles for bodies, hearts and minds. Richie was the driving force. Roy was riding shotgun, Richie was buzzed up with it all, and I saw much less of Chris, whose bed some nights was rarely slept in now. There were no transports of delight in the Bolt Hole. Then one night Chris brought Roy home with his suit covered in blood. I hustled my mother back into her bedroom while he stripped off and took a bath. I remember he whistled in the bath. Can you believe it, Puss. Whistled!

Then he padded along to Chris's room, draped in a towel, and emerged dressed from the skin outwards in Chris's best suit and shirt, and the Guards tie that was Chris's prize possession. After that the two of them went down my garden and burned Roy's clothes in an old iron water-butt.

I went into Mother's bedroom to find her standing at the window, staring at flames leaping up by the dense honeysuckle hedge that was there then. Even from here you could hear the mumble of their voices and their laughter.

'What are those boys doing, Julia? They'll set fire to my hedge. I do love that honeysuckle.' I remember her exact words. She loved the honeysuckle and when I went to look in daylight, it was badly singed.

I led her back to her bed and tucked her in. 'Don't worry, dear,' I said, lying in my teeth. 'Don't worry. There was this car accident but nobody's hurt.'

When I came downstairs Roy was walking along the hallway with his usual cocky squaddie's walk. He looked up at me, handsome in my Chris's best three-piece suit. He grinned. 'Your boyfriend's a long bugger darlin',' he said. 'The belt on these strides is right up on my fuckin' chest.' I remember the words exactly.

Chris was standing behind him, wearing his long Crombie, the one with the military buttons. When he got that coat he thought the leather buttons boring so he got me to replace them with ones with the insignia of his old army regiment.

I looked him in the eye. 'You're not going out again, Chris. Not really?' I couldn't believe it.

Roy moved his head into my line of vision. 'The night's young, darlin'. Me and Chris here are goin' up West. My Richie's waitin'. Ain't that so, Christopher?'

Chris nodded, his eyes not quite meeting mine.

Roy grinned. 'You go and get your beauty sleep, darlin'. Every little helps, know what I mean? Not that I'm sayin' you need it. I'm always tellin' your Christopher here he's a lucky one. Nice girl like you. Bit of class. Ain't I sayin' that, Chris?'

But Chris was fumbling with the front door lock, still not looking at me. I remember thinking he was Roy's man, lock stock and barrel. Not mine at all.

When I shut the door behind them, Puss, even though I felt chilly and very worried, I didn't think that's the last time I would ever see him. That would have been too ridiculous, wouldn't it?

The Hare

In the next few days, Bobbi spent much of the time in the flat on her own, Doreen and Stephen within calling distance. Most nights she stayed over with me. During the day she went to school,

139

then, as usual, called at Mehmet's for tea. If I'd written enough that day I would join her. Then I would walk round to the flat with her and stay with her for a while as she did her homework with her usual meticulous care. She could get bored with the television, but she was very slick about using the Internet to look for certain kinds of music or to search for information about whatever bee she had in her bonnet that day.

One day it was hares.

'Did you know, Sophia, that they are hermaphrodites, sometimes male and sometimes female? The same hare! Did you know that they are born with their fur on and their eyes open? Did you know that the mother keeps each baby in its own separate nest for safety? Hares are always alone and they like it.'

As Bobbi herself did. If she'd been any other child I should have been concerned at her sitting alone all those hours in the flat with just her computer and books for company. I felt I should worry about the dangers inside that computer, which could be as harmful as the street to vulnerable kids.

But you just had to know Bobbi to know that this wouldn't be the case with her. The children I knew in Newcastle who had ventured down the murky path of risky chat rooms had all been needy in some ways, made lonely by the admonition not to 'play out', or left with the light-box in the corner while their parents and minders 'played out' themselves in the pubs and clubs of Newcastle. Bobbi was not like this. I'd rarely even met an adult so self-sufficient. Like the hare, she was comfortable, not deprived, in being alone. She was quite formidable in her innocence.

I tried talking openly with Bobbi about my concerns. She laughed. 'Don't worry about me, Sophia. I don't *do* email at all. And I don't *do* texting.'

'You must be unique then.'

'Not really. Me and my dad talked about it like we talk about everything. There was this girl, see? She was in my class. She was a bit, well, fat. She got these gross emails and texts and topped herself, hung herself from her own staircase. Well, she tried to. She was in hospital more than a week. Me and my dad went to see her. Took her some magazines, *Hello!*, *Heat* and that. You should have seen the machines she was hooked up to. Gross.' She paused. 'She wasn't my friend or anything. Just my dad said we should go and see her.'

Clever Sparrow, I thought. You had to like him for that, even while you were condemning him for staying away.

'Anyway, after that happened, me and my dad talked a lot about her. We decided I needed neither of those things. The emailing nor the texting. I've got my Google. That's all I need. You can find out anything with Google. And we phone all the time. That's enough.'

'So you found out about hares on the Net?'

'Nah. There's books as well, you know. I found this hare book in the bookshop in Church Street. It has pictures. Chinese hares. Egyptian hares. D'you know where we have a man in the moon, the Chinese have the hare in the moon? Hares are magic. How great is that?'

Looking at her fondly, I thought Bobbi herself had a touch of that magic. Then, in a rush of panic that started somewhere in my gut I contemplated the savage waste of my abortion. That little one, girl or boy, would have been three now. Walking. Then, like the tick of a clock, my thoughts turned yet again to Drina. She would have been ten, now. Like Bobbi.

'Don't cry, Sophia.' Bobbi handed me a tissue. 'You've gotta smile, not cry at all this magic. You're not quite right, are you?' she said kindly.

'No, Bobbi,' I sniffed. 'I'm not quite right.'

I was saved by a knock on the door. It was Stephen Copeland. He glanced at me. 'Sorry, I was checking on Bobbi,' he said stiffly. 'Are you busy?'

'We are talking about hares,' I said, dropping the tissue into the waste basket.

'What? Oh.' He looked across at Bobbi. 'I have another message from Sparrow, Bobbi. He asked if you were OK and I said you were, and that we were looking after you. And he said to send his love and he would be back soon.'

'How soon?' said Bobbi.

'He didn't say.'

'Was he all right?'

'He sounded fine. He said not to worry about him.'

'Good.'

There was an awkward silence. 'Sophia's painted her yard cream,' said Bobbi, her tone helpful. 'It looks nice. And Miss Soper has given her some blue flowers. You should go and see it. It's mint.'

'Bobbi, for heaven's sake!' I warned.

He glanced at me. 'These houses are organic. They repay in spades, any care you give them,' he said briefly. 'Can I have a word with you, Sophia?'

'I have to go now anyway. You'll be all right, Bobbi?'

She nodded, her eye wandering back to her computer screen.

'Come along to the Lavender House when you've finished.'

She ignored me.

Stephen walked with me down through the house and lingered in the hall. 'I have to go to Zurich for a few days. I've told Sparrow you're keeping a close eye on Bobbi. Was that OK?'

'Of course it is.'

He frowned. 'There's the matter of your course. You'll be out part of the time.'

'I've given my course up.'

'What?' He frowned. 'For Bobbi? I'm sure Sparrow wouldn't–'

'It's not about Bobbi. It's about something else. Just a coincidence. I would have done it without Bobbi. The course wasn't right for me. I'm not the only one. The registrar told me three or four people drop out every year. Self-selection, they call it.'

'Seems a pity.'

'I chose to do it. The decision wasn't thrust on me, you know. I wasn't sacked.' I kept my voice cool, telling him it was *not* his business.

'So ... what're you doing with yourself?'

I wasn't going to tell him about the writing. 'I'm watching Bobbi and doing up the Lavender House. Just for now.'

143

'Mmm. If there's anything I can do for you in the house, just say. Not much I can't do in a building. I've got the hands to prove it.' He held out his hand, large-palmed, long-fingered.

'I thought it was all drawing on big sheets of paper, being an architect.'

'I started out hands-on. That was my choice, really the best way. I like to get my hands dirty. And when my mother died and I came back here I did all the conversions on this house. Pulled down and rebuilt walls, stripped floors. Did it myself. The lot.'

His almost childlike pride made me smile and relax. I couldn't think why I was so tense around him. He'd done me no harm.

'I'll remember that when I come to stripping the floors in my house. Wouldn't know where to start, in stripping a floor.' I looked up at him. 'And I did want to ask you something.' I liked the way he listened. He was one of those people who gave you his full attention when he listened to you.

'Ask away.'

'Not about the house. It's about Sparrow Marsh. Why on earth doesn't he talk to Bobbi directly? Can't she ring him? Couldn't you get a number from him?'

He stared at me, frowning. 'It's not possible, Sophia. Really.'

I stared back at him. 'He could just give her a number to call. Then she could call him.'

'It's complicated, Sophia. He's keeping her safe, out of danger. He thinks this is the best way. If she has his number, if he's traceable through her, she's in danger. Even I don't have his

144

number. He rings me at my office.'

'Danger?' I laughed to cover my anger. 'All this cloak and dagger. Gangsters! It's ridiculous.'

'It's no joke, Sophia,' he said evenly. 'I do suspect, though, that the police are involved.'

Now I came to the defence of a man I had never even met. 'The Sparrow Marsh I've heard about can't be mixed up in something like that. I can't imagine him like that. Not the way Bobbi talks about him. Not the way he comes to me through her. If he were that kind of man she would be unbalanced, all over the place. But she's steady as a rock.'

'Right. So you're an expert on children?'

'I was, once. And an expert on children who were all over the place, if you want to know.' Oh, no. I'm not going to tell him. 'It is really him at the end of the phone?' I asked. 'You're not making this up?'

He stared at me. 'I don't tell lies, Sophia. He's there, all right. Although even I don't know where there is.'

I shook my head.

'He moves in the shadows, does Sparrow. And, as you say, he's no criminal. In fact you could say he's the opposite of a criminal. And I'm not saying anything further, no matter how you flash those brown eyes at me.'

Even angrier, I turned away and stomped to the gate.

'Stop!' His voice came from behind me. 'Can I give your mobile number to Sparrow, Sophia? He asked for it.'

'Of course,' I said.

'Thanks. But when he does ring, the thing is just to take the message for Bobbi and talk to him about her. Don't harass him with questions. Please.' He saw the look on my face, backed off and shut the door carefully behind him.

I turned away and looked up, and there was Julia Soper, waving away at me with a trowel from the other side of the street. I dodged the cars and buses and walked across.

She was wearing a bright green outfit today and her Joni Mitchell hair was gleaming. 'Tiff with young Master Copeland?' she said with a small knowing smile.

'Not at all,' I said. 'We had matters to discuss.'

She opened her gate. 'Well, dear, don't worry about that. Come and see the buds on my philadelphus. She's coming along very nicely.' She led the way through the house. 'And when we've seen her we'll have a nice–'

'No cocktails, Miss Soper. Not those cocktails. They were gorgeous, but I really, really suffered the next day.'

'I was going to say a nice glass of single malt. I've just opened it. It's old, very fine. You'll like it. I promise you.'

So, Puss, for four long days I worried about Chris. I cleaned his already clean room. I raked the ashes of Roy Pinder's suit out of the garden boiler and dug them in under the honeysuckle. The garden was a bit of a muddle in those days, Pusscat, but the honeysuckle was outstanding. I kept the burned belt buckle I found in the ashes. It's there now in Chris's top drawer

146

It was on the fifth day that Richie Pinder came calling, at two o'clock in the morning. He banged on the door and shouted at me through the letterbox. Even from my bedroom window I could see he was ugly-drunk. He kept rattling the letterbox and screaming and shouting. I remember being pleased that Mother had had her Mogadon.

Then Roy Pinder's Cadillac purred to a stop at my gate. He jumped out and quietened Richie down, his voice whining, conciliating, his arm round his brother like he was a toddler. Then, with this kind of brother's gentleness, he led him to the car, ushered him in and swept him away. The car roared to the end of the road, slowed down slightly, then roared away.

Then, 'What's all that about?' My mother was standing in my bedroom doorway, her eyes blinking. 'What's that uproar? Is this a dream?' Her voice was groggy.

'Nothing, nothing.' I took her arm. 'A car back-firing, that's all, Mum.' I hustled her back to bed, then went downstairs. On the doormat was a brown envelope, its edges ripped when he pushed it through the letterbox. I could see the Queen's head through the tear. I went into the dining room and laid out £400 in five-pound notes. A lot of money now, Pusscat, but really a lot of money then.

I turned the wrapping over and looked in the folds, turned over every single note. There was nothing from Chris. Not a letter not a word.

Two days later Roy Pinder telephoned to ask how I was and to explain that Chris had had to go away.

'Did somefink naughty, and they're on to him, see? Needs to lay low.'

'Where is he?' I shouted on the phone. 'Where is he?'

'Scotland? Spain? Who knows, darlin'? Old Chris always had places to go.' He went quiet then but I could hear his heavy breathing. Then, 'So don't go and talk to the filth, will you? Don't make waves, darlin'. Worse for old Chrissie-boy if you do. They'll have him banged up, no time.'

I could hardly breathe, much less say anything. Then he asked if I'd got the package. 'Richie insisted on the money. Very fond of old Chris, was my Richie. And your mother. Had a soft spot for your mother too...'

Christ. He wanted gratitude, Puss. Gratitude! Perhaps I should have told him I had burned the money in the old boiler like his suit. But I just thanked him, tame as milk. All I wanted was him off my phone.

I can hear his voice like it was a record. 'What you need now, darlin', is a nice little job. We could fix one up for you. The club–'

'No, Roy! I've got a job waiting at the record shop. They say I can go back any time.' I was lying, of course.

'Right, good. But don't forget, Jules. Me and my Richie'll always take care of you, no matter how long Chris is away. We'll keep our eye on you. Remember that, doll. Mum's the word.' Then he giggled. Such an ugly sound, Puss. 'Yeah. Think of your poor old mum.'

After that, every month or so, brown envelopes were shoved through the door with fifty pounds in them. That came to an end when both Pinders went away for a long time for murder The papers were full of them, Pusscat. Made them seem glamorous, like some kind of Robin Hoods. But I knew them, as far as any woman could. They weren't glamorous, Pusscat. What they were, was strange. Even from prison you could feel their power, like the tide rising. So I didn't ask the

148

police about Chris or he might have been in prison alongside them. Better in Spain, or Scotland, or South America than rotting in some gaol with those two.

Once they were in prison, though, the money envelopes stopped, which was just as well. It was tainted, that money, and it didn't make up for losing Chris. Not at all.

But I stayed hopeful. I just thought if I kept myself nice and kept his things in order Chris would come back and we'd start again. But it's been such a long time, Pusscat. Such a very long time.

But here I am. And I'm good on my own. But then I'm not on my own, Pusscat, am I? At least I've got you to talk to. That's something.

Columbia Road

The following Sunday morning Stephen Copeland drew up at my gate in his dusty old Volvo and knocked on my door.

'Stephen. What is it?' My mind raced straight to Sparrow but still I was conscious of standing there at the door in the long Snoopy T-shirt that served me as a nightie.

'Sorry, Sophia. Did I wake you?' He looked uneasy for a moment. 'I had this idea that you and Bobbi might like a jaunt. Columbia Road. It's an old flower market. Flowers and other things. Perhaps we could get some plants for your yard. Isn't Bobbi with you? We could all have breakfast there.'

My mind was doing somersaults. 'Yes, yes.

149

Wait.' I shut the door in his face, then shouted up the stairs. 'Bobbi? Rouse yourself, love. Get dressed. We're going out for breakfast.'

My hair was a mess. I had to tie it up in scrunchies to control it at all. Still, within seven minutes we were in Stephen's car, Bobbi in the front, me lounging in the back seat.

As we drove along Barrington Street we passed Julia Soper meandering along, bag in hand, cat on neck. Stephen backed the car up and leaned out of the window.

'Morning, Miss Soper. We're going to Columbia Road for breakfast. Care to join us?'

She sniffed. 'Not what it was, Columbia Road. Used to be a proper market. Flowers, plants, everything. Real people. Proper market. Now everyone goes. Hordes of them. It's even been in the papers, Sunday supplements. Glossy magazines.' Her tinny voice was drenched in disgust.

'If you don't want to go...' He started to wind up the window.

She put out a beringed hand to stop him. 'I didn't say I wouldn't go, Stevie. Just let me dispose of Pusscat.'

In a minute she was beside me on the back seat and the car was filled with her slightly sticky perfume. Bobbi sneezed. As we drove through the streets Julia and Stephen carried on this decorous conversation about their mothers and old times in Barrington Street.

Sitting there beside her, I suddenly had a vision of the boy Stephen and Julia as a young woman, a fleshed-out Joni Mitchell with black-rimmed eyes.

'My mother was so very fond of your dear mother,' she was saying. 'I was just saying to Pusscat, I wonder what she would have made of you ... er ... splitting up the house like that, Stevie. She so loved it. Such an elegant house.'

He glanced into the rear-view mirror and met my gaze. 'The house was far too big for me, Miss Soper. It makes sense to double up on homes in this day and age.'

She sniffed. 'Spoils it somehow, breaking it up like that.'

'I have to say I don't think so, Miss Soper.' He was not having any of it. 'Each flat is very nice. The Selkirks have made a lovely job of theirs.'

'And so have we,' Bobbi chimed in, staring up at him, beady-eyed. 'Our flat is lovely. It's very modern. Huge. And you should see Mr Copeland's. Like something out of a magazine.'

Stephen glanced at me again through the rear mirror and smiled. 'A ringing endorsement,' he said.

Julia lifted the hair away from her mandarin collar. 'Do you think you could open a window, Stevie? This car is stifling.'

The first sign of the Columbia Road market was the waving of tall trees and plants above the heads of the crowd. Some people had custom-made plastic carriers packed with plants – grasses, secretive perennials, blazing boastful annuals. One woman was embracing what looked like a thousand tulips. A tall black man was hidden behind a giant flowering honeysuckle.

It was the city celebrating the country. Bright

151

and very sad at the same time.

Julia started naming the species as we passed the stalls in between repeating the refrain about the market not being the same, not the same.

Bobbi stopped at a narrow yard doorway where a girl in a bandanna was selling necklaces of shells joined by cleverly coiled silver wire. Stephen offered to buy Bobbi one but she turned him down, saying she had money herself if she really wanted one.

'I was just interested in how she made them. I think I could do them myself, actually.'

We stopped at another doorway where a young French girl was selling oysters from Chichester. Stephen insisted on buying us two each. Julia ate hers with a relish that must only have come from practice. Bobbi swallowed hers, declaring them mint. 'Like swallowing the sea. I've had them in Aldeburgh where my great-nanny lives.'

I was not even sure how to eat them but I took a breath and gave them a try. Bobbi was right. It was like swallowing the sea. Neither pleasant nor unpleasant. Just the sea.

Then Stephen led the way down an alley, past a bric-a-brac stall and a stall manned by an expansive Australian plantsman. Now we were in a corner where people were queuing for fresh bacon sandwiches and gourmet coffee. While Stephen joined the queue, Julia and I waited on a mildewed garden bench with Bobbi perched on the arm beside me.

A boy in the queue in front of us was wearing an immaculate denim jacket wired together with safety pins threaded through steel eyelets. *'Very* designer!' whispered Bobbi in my ear. Then she clutched my shoulder. 'Uh-oh!' she said. 'Danger to starboard. It's Oliver and his ma.'

Surging towards us like tankers through the tide were an enormous man and, clutching a bunch of funereal lilies, the woman whom we met at Kazoo. The old woman spotted us and reached up to whisper in her son's ear. He scowled for a second, then rolled towards us, smiling widely.

'Well, if it ain't young Bobbi. You buying flowers, darlin'?' He was wearing a well-cut linen jacket that nearly succeeded in hiding his stomach.

'Hello, Mr Cowell.' She threw out a hand encompassing the whole of the crowd waiting for coffee. 'Me and my friends came here for breakfast...'

I stood up and put an arm around her. To my right Julia Soper stood up and set herself shoulder to shoulder with me.

'...Just hanging out,' finished Bobbi. 'Me and my friends.'

Oliver surveyed us, his eyes glinting sharply above his full cheeks, then glanced at the queue. 'Your old man with you, kid? Old Sparrow ain't been to work for days now, you know. No word. Is he crook or something?'

'Crook? What's that mean?'

'He means is he sick,' I said in her ear.

'Nah...' she hesitated. 'He's all right.'

'Right. So I suppose he'll be at home? Blighter never left his address nowhere with us. I checked. Fuckin' inconvenient, that is.'

His mother tugged his arm. 'Oliver! The kid!'

'Excuse my mouth,' he said, without a note of

remorse. 'But Sparrow's at home, is he?'

She shook her head vigorously, her fine black hair rising and settling in the air. 'No. I think he's in ... Scotland. Something about business. He didn't say where.'

Oliver's mother nudged his elbow. 'Kid's lying. Look at her, Olly,' she said. 'Ain't nothing so sure. Know nothing of the truth, kids nowadays.'

He shook off her hand and dipped into an inner pocket in his immaculate jacket. He pulled out a card, gleaming black with gold lettering. 'These are my numbers, darlin'. Day or night. You tell your old dad to give me a bell when he gets back from Glasgow. Or wherever he is. Or if he rings you. And be sure to tell him how me and Ma met you out and about.' He glanced up at me and Julia, and Stephen who had joined us, balancing steaming cups of coffee and bacon sandwiches. 'You and your friends.'

We stood and watched the two of them depart, past the Australian plantsman and the bric-a-brac man. Then we drank our coffee and ate our sandwiches while Bobbi explained the phenomenon of Oliver and his mother briefly to Stephen.

'He's called Little Oliver because his dad was called Big Oliver. It's not about size. Anyway, my dad told me Big Oliver was shot in the olden days so he says Little Oliver was more to be pitied than laughed at.'

We had our coffee and sandwiches while I told Stephen about meeting the old woman at the club when we went looking for Sparrow.

After that Julia insisted on buying some plants and Bobbi returned to the stall in the alleyway to buy a shell and silver necklace. But somehow the savour had gone out of the morning and we were all glad to get back to the car.

We'd gone only a mile when Stephen drew up beside a small supermarket. 'Nip into there, all of you.' He rapped it out, like an order. 'Wait five minutes, then come out and get a bus back home. I could be wrong but I think Oliver and the crone are following us. Watch for the blue BMW. I'll drive back into the city.'

We crowded into the little shop and lurked by the window. Seconds later the blue car passed. Oddly enough, the old woman was driving, crouched over the wheel like a vulture. Oliver was lording it in the back, his ear to a mobile phone.

Bobbi burst into laughter. 'It's like *Road Runner*, Sophia!' she gasped. 'Remember that old cartoon?'

I smiled at this, then went down the shop aisle and picked a packet of rice and some sweet potatoes off the shelf as a gesture of payment for our refuge to a turbaned man who was looking at our antics with some amusement.

As we walked on to find a bus stand, Julia put an arm through mine. 'That old witch,' she said. 'The woman with that Oliver? I'm sure I've seen her somewhere. I'm certain of it.'

Stephen was waiting for Bobbi and me at number 83. He leaned over the banister and told us to come up to his floor.

'Wait till you see his place,' said Bobbi, her eyes gleaming. 'It's absolutely mint.'

So it was. Mint clean. Mint fresh. Mint sparkling. There is a cliché that homes are imprints of their owners but here Stephen had worked hard to keep you guessing.

He had opened up the whole of the top floor, right to the rafters. The space was lit front and back by the Victorian windows, by curious horizontal slit windows that lined the walls like tacking stitches, and a big skylight over a vast plank-wood table that obviously doubled as a drawing board, a bureau and dining table. The kitchen – plain white and a kind of grey-lavender – was enclosed in a steel half-circle against the middle of one wall. At the other end the circle was repeated in two semicircular black leather sofas set around a low circular table in the same heavy plank-wood as the giant table at the other end of the room. It was all clearly designed rather than accidental.

The far wall was lined with cupboards that must serve to hide all the detritus the rest of us spread around our living space – things like televisions, videos, sound systems, books, CDs. Above us, reached by a plank-wood ladder, was a wide shelf where his bed must be. But even that space was obscured by a steel mesh, like expensive steel knitting.

All the things that might tell you something about the person who lived here were hidden. The one bright obvious object that sprang out at you was a large painting on the triangular end wall – a kind of bird's-eye view of an Aztec palace. At least I thought that it was.

All you had to decode Stephen Copeland was this sparse, elegant space with a very large obscure painting.

'What d'ya think?' said Bobbi, perched on the

156

back of one of the black sofas.

'Well...' I truly did not know what I thought.

Stephen put his head to one side. 'You don't like it?' His tone was neutral.

I glanced around. 'I love the space and the light. I like all that wood. But ... but...'

'But...?'

'It's beautiful but it's like a puzzle. The only thing here about you is that work spread out on your desk.'

'So you're curious about me?' he said without smiling.

'Course she is.' Bobbi jumped off the sofa and came and put her arm through mine, making me think of Big Emma. 'Show her, Mr Copeland!' she commanded. 'Show her the magic doors.'

He went across the wall with the vast cupboards and touched a switch. Very smoothly, one after the other the doors swivelled and changed their faces, revealing the shelves of books, equipment, computers, screens stored behind them. Then the cupboard doors turned completely and showed us their back side. Now the cupboard fronts were collages with different themes. One was lined with images of buildings, some very farfetched. Another had an elaborate collage of photographs from school and university, team pictures and family seaside snaps as well as sepia images that must have gone back to the turn of the last century. Another door was pasted up with drawings of people. Large and small, head and full-length studies, of men and women of all ages. Bobbi moved across to this. 'Look, here I am! And Sparrow. And Mrs Element, who lived downstairs before the Selkirks. And Miss Soper with her cat-in-a-basket.' She peered closer. 'Crikey! And here you are, Sophia. With your big hat and boots.'

There I was. I flushed and glanced at him. He was grinning. 'So, Sophia. I'm not quite the blank sheet you thought I was.' He glanced around his space. 'I needed to make big changes here when I did the conversion. I grew up in this house. These rooms were my bedroom and play-room. Don't you think it would be too sad just to live like I did when I was small? I had to do something.' He moved to the kitchen. 'Now, something to drink. Juice, Bobbi? Tea, Sophia? Or something stronger?'

I relaxed. He'd done something for me. He had shown me the two sides of himself and was mak-ing me tea. There was no harm in him. Still, I found myself discreetly peering at the wall of doors to find clues about other women in his life, past and present. There were women there, young and interesting enough. But no real clues. I would have to stifle my curiosity – well, just for the present.

My gaze returned to the drawing of Sparrow Marsh. It was not like the clear colour snaps in Bobbi's flat. It was like a portrait in smoke. He was as alive and mysterious there as he was in my imagination.

Later, when he walked Bobbi and me down to the street door, Stephen suddenly asked if I'd be interested in going with him to some event to do with architecture. At the Savoy. 'A presentation kind of thing,' he said.

'Are you getting a prize?' Bobbi said.

'Well, me and a few others. Medals, not prizes.'

'Go, Sophia!' ordered Bobbi. 'You have to go and tell me all about it.'

Why not? I had seen his 'mint' side. I had seen his cupboard doors. I could trust him. 'All right then,' I said. 'I think I'd like that.'

He smiled broadly, a young, bright smile that made me lurch somewhere inside. 'How could I fail with Bobbi on my side? How could any of us fail?' It was then that I realised that he'd had to stir up the courage to ask me. And I was touched.

As Bobbi and I walked along to Lavender House my mind started to race. I hadn't been on a date for years. Not since breaking up with Malcolm. And going out with him had been like being in the Secret Service. No matter how far we drove we had to do the usual tour of the car park to check there was nobody inside that we might know, and Malcolm always cased the joint first. During those months I consumed buckets of scampi or chicken goujons that all ended up tasting the same. Amid all these undercover operations I turned down some engaging and quite exciting men. One of Malcolm's juniors once suggested I was worse than a nun. Did I have no interest in the opposite sex? Or was I 'like that'? If so I was foolish not to come out. These days we all had to be true to ourselves or breakdown beckoned. Had I not read the magazines?

Malcolm and I had been almost too good at keeping our secret. Our whole affair went unnoticed. That was its tragedy.

I thought it would be nice to go out with Stephen on a proper date, out in the open. It felt like a brand-new thing. But I held back, even to myself. Don't make too much of it I said to myself. It's only dinner at the Savoy.

Sorry to dump you, Pusscat, but I have to tell you it was a very nice outing. These plants are from the Columbia Road market. Of course you know nothing about that. Your territory's here, on the High Street and the railway line. Anyway, I went to the market today with the child, Sophia and with Stevie Copeland. Those two seem quite cosy now. See there now, Pusscat, how he touches her arm as he shows her out of the house! Just like Chris.

That market's not at all the same these days. All too busy, commercial now. Anyway, we were just in there and we saw this woman, a proper old crone. She spoke to the child. And Sophia. Now then, Pusscat, I was sure I knew her. Then, just as I was coming in through my door here, it came to me. Around that time Richie Pinder came out of prison that first time, me and Chris went to this party down near Sloane Square, at the town house of some viscount It was unusual because there were women there with the Pinder boys. Proper women, not just club girls. Even the common-looking ones were proper women.

Anyway this viscount, he'd been creative with his invitation list, got together this mongrel mixture that teemed and tottered through those gracious rooms. He lorded over us all on one side of the room, all velvet waistcoat and overlong hair. On the other side of the room his wife, half his age, queened it like some exotic bird under one of those Victorian glass domes. She didn't talk much, but then her English wasn't good and

160

people got weary of trying to talk to her. You know, Puss, she was kind of there to be looked at, not to talk to. Decorative rather than useful, you know what I mean.

Most of the men there had a woman with them, all scrubbed up, with just enough leg and cleavage showing. My Chris whispered in my ear that I outclassed them all and they were just a load of tarts brought in for the night. 'Class among rags,' he said. It was a favourite saying of his.

I'd pushed out the boat for tonight and bought a knock-off copy of a Courrèges shift dress that was like an abstract painting. Plenty of leg but no cleavage. And long purple patent boots. You've seen the dress, Pusscat. In Chris's wardrobe. Safe in one of his suit bags.

The Pinders were at the party, of course, in identical DJs, flashing white shirts and matching bow ties and silk hankies. They hovered on each side of the viscount like a pair of exotic cuff links. It was hard to decide whether he was wearing them or they were enclosing him in a tuxedo vice.

The mongrel sort and the great and the good, with their worthy wives, rubbed shoulders with actors and comedians and women floating in that misty world between prostitution and the legitimate stage, hanging on the arms of worn-out old men who still had the glow of money about them.

Now then, Pusscat! I'm coming to it. That crone I saw today, in the market, that Melanie Cowell, was one of these tarts. I remember her now. She had this perfect body encased in a sheath dress slit up to her knickers, and that big head of hers was like a cartoon, piled high and back-combed and already out of fashion. So high, she towered above this bloke she was with, a ferrety type

161

spilling out of his suit, who would have looked tall beside any other woman in the room, including me.

Chris catches me looking at them. 'Big Oliver Cowell,' he says. 'Queer old coot. Slot machines and other unmentionables. Nice little earner for us.'

'Us?' I pick him up.

'Well, the Boys,' he says.

I remember thinking then how much Chris felt he was part of the Boys, somehow inside their skin. Or they in his.

I shivered. Chris was all concern. 'You cold, darling?' He had this lovely ringing voice, like James Mason, an actor you saw a lot of in those days.

'Not really,' I say. 'I was just wondering if we could go. Go on somewhere else.'

Chris glances at Roy, who's moved and is standing with his arm round his girlfriend, a pretty doe-eyed girl who looks tense and is not like any other of the women in the room. 'We'll hang on just a bit, darling,' says Chris. 'Just bear with me, won't you, darling?'

It was while I was 'hanging on' that I saw Big Oliver and Melanie Cowell move to stand close to the viscount. I saw Richie's eyes bulge just a little and observed him cut in front of Big Oliver and with a lift of his black brow indicate that he should 'get lost'. It was clear to anyone there. Big Oliver spat out some words, took a step back and then stalked out of the room, Melanie tit-tupping behind him in her high heels.

It wasn't long after that that Big Oliver was shot in a so-called gangland killing and Melanie was left on her own to bring up her young son the best she could. Money by the boatload, but he didn't have much chance, that boy, when you think of it. Little Oliver.

162

He was there with his mother today, a hulking man like his father. Not pleasant. Things do tend to go round and come round, don't they?

The Jean Muir Dress

Although I've never met him I'm becoming quite well acquainted to George Sparrow Marsh. There's that smoky drawing in Stephen Copeland's flat. And Sparrow's there in the studio photograph on the mantelpiece in Bobbi's flat: tall and thin, slightly heavy-jawed, in a gleaming white shirt with the sleeves rolled up. His muscular arms shelter Pamela, Bobbi's mother, whose round bespectacled face stares up at him in adoration. He's there in Bobbi's smile, in the cocky set of her head. He's there in the tones of calm respect in Stephen's voice when he speaks of him. He's there in Doreen Selkirk's liberal relish at living side by side with a black man. He's there in the faint, tangy smell of petrol that still impregnates the back entry of that house, in the scent of pimento, Caribbean allspice in his kitchen. And he's there in this indistinct aura of dark, pantomimic threat around Oliver Cowell and his mother.

He's there in the fact that Bobbi remains calm, even in this situation. She clearly trusts him. She only falters one day when I let myself into the flat with a key she has given me. She looks blankly at me for a second before her brow clears.

'For a minute I thought you were my dad.'

Now I'm really angry at Sparrow but I smile at Bobbi. 'No, it's me, pet. Come to sweep you off to Mehmet's for your tea.'

The next day I was sitting with Julia in her garden, drinking a Honey Bee cocktail ('Jamaica rum, lime juice and honey – Gregory loved them'). I had just finished telling her about Stephen's invitation to the architects' dinner when Sparrow rang me on my mobile.

'George Marsh here, Miss Morgan. I understand you're watching over Bobbi.'

My breath caught in my throat. My heart was thumping.

'Miss Morgan? Are you there?'

'I'm here. And it's Sophia, not *Miss* Morgan.' Beside me Julia put down her glass on the rickety garden table and watched me closely, making no secret of the fact that she was listening to every word.

Joy, anger, relief, were doing a tom-tom dance inside my head.

'Stevie says you're a great person, Sophia. He gives you a good report.' Sparrow's voice was soft, as though filtered through gauze. 'Thank you for watching over Bobbi for me. How is she?'

'She's very good. Fine. But she's worried about you.'

A pause. 'Now that surprises me, Sophia. Bobbi never worries.'

I know, I thought. I am the one who is worried. 'She *is* calm. She's going to school, keeping to the routines. We're watching her, but of course she's keen to know where you are.'

Another silence. Then he said, 'Perhaps it would make her feel better to know that. But I'm moving around. Tell her that. I'm moving around.' He paused. 'Just tell her I've been to all the places we know. Tell her she can imagine me there. But to say exactly where, well, Sophia, that's dangerous.'

'Dangerous?' I glanced at Julia, still watching with bright birdlike interest. 'What is it, Mr Marsh? Are you a policeman? Are you a criminal?' God, that sounded pompous. 'I'm sorry... I...' My voice crumbled away.

This time the silence at the other end went on too long.

'I'm sorry, Mr Marsh. That was ridiculous. Are you still there?'

'Hey, call me George. Or Sparrow, like the others.'

'Why Sparrow?' I took refuge in trivialities. 'Why do they call you Sparrow?'

'We-ell. I was born in London before we decamped to Bristol. My ma called me her Cockney sparrow. My brothers started calling me Sparrow. It stuck. Ironic, isn't it?'

I didn't know what to say.

'Anyway, Sophia, I've been talking to old Stevie. He tells me you're watching over my Bobbi like a guardian angel. That you've given up this course you're doing...'

'That's not because of Bobbi. That was because of me. I would have done it anyway.'

'So what're you doin' now?'

This was bizarre. We might have been having a conversation in a bar on singles night. 'I'm kind of ... well, writing something.'

165

'Oh-oh. Great stuff. I hope you ain't writing about this po' little girl who's left all alone in the Smoke by her evil pa–' His pastiche of a Jamaican accent was ridiculously bad.

I interrupted him. 'No, I'm ... I'm... I don't know what I'm writing. It's about...'

Perhaps it was that we were on the phone or that he was a stranger but somehow the dam was breached. I told him about Newcastle and the break-down that led me to know the women on the New Dawn. At the other end of the phone, Bobbi's father just murmured and made soft assenting noises as the words flowed, flowed from my mouth. Then my words faded to a trickle. I felt ridiculous.

'Why am I doing this? Why am I doing all this? Who are you, for God's sake?' I put down the phone and Julia reached out and laid a thin hand on my arm.

The phone rang again.

'Don't put down the phone on me, Sophia,' he said quickly. 'There is nothing wrong with talking to me. Nothing at all.'

'Don't you see?' I said desperately. 'You don't want someone like me watching over your daughter. Much as I adore your Bobbi – she really blows me away – I'm not fit to watch over her. You should be here, Mr Marsh – George – Sparrow. Really, you have to take care of her yourself.'

A warm chuckle flowed down the telephone like honey. 'Clever girl. So you've poured out all this stuff, Sophia, just to bring me to heel? To get me home for Bobbi.'

I was suddenly calm. Icy. 'How can you say

that? How dare you?'

He sighed, this big deep sigh. 'I'm so-orry, Sophia. Not fair. It's just my Bobbi's on my mind.'

'Well. Your Bobbi's fine, Sparrow. She's showing us all the way to go.' I paused. 'She's showing me the way to go.'

'Well. Sophia, she's kept me going since – well, for the last six years.'

'She told me about her mum.'

Silence. 'She's so like Pamela, Sophia. So like her mum.'

I came back to the present, to my coping self. 'So. You still won't tell us where you are?'

'Not just now. I'll be back soon, when all this is cleared up.'

'Is it about the police? Are the police involved?'

'Not in the way you think, I promise you. Trust me.'

'It's about Bobbi. I'm doing this for Bobbi.'

'No better reason. Look at this: I know something about you now, Sophia, and I trust you. Now will you trust me?'

I sighed. 'How can I not trust you? What other option have I?'

He chuckled, somewhere deep in his throat. 'Well, Sophia Morgan, if we trust each other the only way is forward.' I wanted to ask him about Oliver and his mother, to say they seemed threatening, but the phone clicked at the other end and I was talking into thin air. I thrust the phone back into my pocket.

'Damn! Damn the man,' I said.

Then I remembered Julia was there. Her bright eyes were on me. 'Well, dear. You've had an interesting life, haven't you?'

'I am not the only one.' Mind racing, I tried to deflect her. 'Stephen was telling me how ... social you were. In the sixties, seventies. You had an exotic life.'

'Ah, did he?' She took a sip of her cocktail. Pusscat jumped on to her lap. 'Well, I suppose it was quite exciting. All down to my friend Chris, of course. Before him I just worked in a shop. Then he went missing, like Mr Sparrow Marsh. Never to be seen again. My mother said he'd gone back to his family in Yorkshire. She said they had made him turn his back on all this. On me and those boys he ran with. It made sense, really.'

'Boys?'

Then she went on to tell me an extraordinary story of meeting this Chris in the shop where she worked: how he romanced her with presents that sometimes he took back to pay for his gambling debts; how for a while she had drunk the best champagne and danced to famous bands dressed in clothes by great designers; how he told her she was class among rags; how he hung out with the Pinder gang, running errands for the notorious brothers. I'd read about them, the Pinder brothers.

She called them 'the Boys'. 'They were not nice people, the Boys. I'm afraid they had Chris on a leash. That was their way. He was in debt to them, poor dear.' She sighed. 'But he was so beautiful. *He* was the class among rags.'

She stood up and the cat leaped with acrobatic agility on to the windowsill. 'I've got something for you, Sophia. I think you'll like this. Come!' She led the way through the house upstairs to

Chris's room. I watched her open the wardrobe wide and push to one side the line of shirts and men's suits. Half the hanging space was occupied by dresses. From the far corner she pulled out a dress in a plastic cover and spread it on the bed. It was a brown, full length, long-sleeved dress in a soft crepe, with a low round neck and covered buttons on the cuffs and shoulders. It was very finely made. She stroked it.

'Jean Muir,' she said reverently. 'The best. Chris loved me in it.' She picked it up. 'Try it on, dear. It'll just suit that hair of yours.'

'Julia...'

'Try it on.'

So I stood there, in that mausoleum of a room and stripped to my bra and knickers, conscious of my bare white skin and scrawny frame. Then I slipped the dress over my head. It fell over my breasts and thighs in one smooth sliver. Julia zipped it up at the back. It touched my body and flowed away in just the right places.

'Look!' said Julia, turning me round to see my-self in the mirrored door of the great wardrobe. 'I knew it would fit. We are exactly the same size.'

This grown-up stranger stared back at me. The deceptively simple brown dress somehow in-tegrated with my rusty hair to create an elegant person who could go anywhere, do anything.

'It's gorgeous, Julia.'

'You are to have it,' she said.

'No. I couldn't...'

'It's time it came out of the wardrobe,' she said. 'Things have been in there too long. I was just saying so to Pusscat.' Her usually pale face was flushed, her eyes sparkling.

'Julia, this is a precious vintage gown, I can't–'

'You can wear it for that architects' dinner with young Stephen. Or would you rather have something briefer? There's a Mary Quant shift dress in here somewhere.' She moved to open the wardrobe again.

'No. This is fantastic.' I hesitated. 'Perhaps I could borrow it.'

'No,' she said firmly. 'Take it. It's yours. Here, I'll unzip you, dear.'

Later, walking down Barrington Street clutching the Jean Muir dress in its plastic bag, I thought how intrigued Laura would be at the treasure trove in Julia's wardrobe. Vintage fashion. Just her thing. I would ring her and ask her to bring a bottle and view the Jean Muir dress. And we would talk about Julia and her butterfly years.

As I walked along it occurred to me that I should go on to the Internet to find out a bit more about those 'Boys'. Julia's Chris might even get a mention there. He could not be a nice man, holed up now in his Yorkshire lair. Probably a grandfather now. It was so cruel to leave Julia alone, set in aspic all these years. His leaving had left her unchanged and entirely eccentric.

Today, though, Julia had given up the Jean Muir dress. That was something.

As I turned the corner I caught my breath at the sight of another of those dratted stalkers sitting on the wall of my house. When I got nearer I realised it wasn't a house stalker at all. It was Roger Selkirk in his archaeologist's fatigues topped by a khaki baseball cap. He looked for all the world like one of those American backwoods-men you see on television papers who are fight-ing to keep America White and Right.

He stood up. 'Doreen's in trouble, Sophia. Will you come and see her?' he said. His pale eyes were bloodshot and you could see he had been crying. 'She won't talk to me.'

Dear Chris,

I am suddenly inspired to write to you because so much is happening in my life and I feel you would like to know directly. I don't know whether I am Rumpel-stiltskin or Rose Red, but something has woken me up. You'll be sad to know Mother died, although she wasn't really herself at the end. Then I was in a kind of dark prison for years. Then I was saved by this cat who walked in and has been a good companion. But today the naughty thing scratched me and drew blood, and I thought perhaps he had got bored with my ramblings. So now you are my last resort, my companion of choice, as you always were.

All my eternal love,
Julia xxxx

Stand-Off

'Slow down, will you?' Roger jogs along behind me, out of breath. 'Doreen isn't going anywhere.'

I glance down at him. He smells of aftershave and superglue. Must have been mending something. 'Maybe she wishes she was.' I couldn't resist it.

'There's no need...' he puffs.

'I've heard that you hurt her,' I say grimly.

He grabs my arm and makes me stop. 'So young. So wise. You don't know, Sophia.' His voice squeezes into a whine. 'She's a very difficult woman. She hits me too. I have stitches to prove it.' He drags up his sleeve to show me a scar on his forearm. 'Skillet,' he says briefly.

I pull my arm away. 'She must have been defending herself.'

He snorts: a strange piggy sound. 'What do you think *I* was doing? She gives as good as she gets, does Doreen.'

I set off again. 'It's no way to solve a problem.'

He laughs now and lengthens his stride to catch up with me. 'You're very young, Sophia. Ain't you so clever for one so young?'

I ignore him and charge on. The house and the flat doors are wide open. An invitation to crime in this part of London. Crime-savvy as Roger is, he must just have wanted desperately to get out of the house.

This being an upside-down flat he leads the way downstairs and stops just by the bedroom door. 'She's in the bathroom.' He nods towards a door leading off from the room which, with its drapes and embroidered panels, has a look of a Moroccan souk. He looks me in the eyes, his normally guarded eyes quite bleak. 'She has pills in there, Sophia. Pills.' He turns out his hands upwards to the ceiling. 'I'll go up there and make some tea,' he mumbles. 'That should help.' And he flees.

My mind goes back to the first time I heard about Roger from Bobbi: how he saved her from the girl about to gouge her with her own compasses. I don't like Roger but there is more to him than I can see. Doreen left her husband for him, after all.

I try the bathroom door and it rasps against the lock. 'Doreen! What is it? Why are you doing this?' There is no response but I can imagine her in there, listening. 'Open the door, love. Roger's gone now. It's just me. What are you doing in there?'

'Phhchashth!'

'What's that? Are you talking Cherokee?'

The door opens and Doreen is standing there, her black hair damp, wearing a voluminous purple kaftan. 'Navaho, my dear, if you want to be correct.' She glides past me on her large bare feet and sits on the bed in a buddha-like pose. The calmness does not deceive. Her eyes, like Roger's, are red-rimmed with crying.

I sit by her feet and lean on the wall. 'Roger came for me. The lad's at his wits' end. He said there were pills in there.'

'Huh! O ye of little faith.'

'What does that mean?'

'Easy way out. He thinks I would take the easy way out. He doesn't know me at all. What am I doing with a man who doesn't know me?'

'Hardly an easy way out.'

'D'you want some advice, my dear?'

'Somehow I thought I was here to give advice.'

'Don't ever, ever give up yourself for another person. Not even the love of your life.'

'Why not? Sounds ideal.'

173

'Because it's the death of romance. I know because I've done it twice. It's the end of voluntary intimacy. There's no one to mediate that sticky space between you. No children, no true friends, no complicated sisters and aunts to filter that void. You're there in the full glare of their attention, dealing with the detail of their obsessions. You notice their bare ugly feet. You become too aware of the scrape of their razor on their morning chin. You notice how pernickety they are about small things, how they use those small things to pull you into line. It ain't surprising you hit out. Or have a child to bridge that chasm.'

'Roger told me you hit him.'

'He did? Well, that's the truth.'

'And he hits you?'

'This marriage is a two-way game. He frustrates me with his fussiness, his pedantry; I frustrate him because I don't seem to care. Well, I don't care so he's right. So – wham! Game, set and match. One on the other. The other on one. Fireworks. Of course we're both so sorry for what we do. And that usually ends in bed so we can remind each other of just why this happened in the first place.' She sighs. 'I'd give up a week in bed with him, complete with the most spectacular sex, for one clutch of my daughter's hand. D'you know this Saturday's her school dance? She texted me that her father's girlfriend helped her choose her dress.' The words shoot out in icy gusts, her mouth frozen with the attempt not to cry. 'Girlfriend!'

'And Roger doesn't get this?'

'Oh, Roger knows. I wanted to send her a corsage to go with the dress. But he goes on about keeping things in proportion. Stupid man. I am so bored...' she hiccoughs, 'with him and his proportions. Bored. Bored. Bored. And I think he is too. With me and the click of my needles. That's why we come to blows. To break the boredom.'

I don't know what to say. What can I say?

'I'll be truthful with you, my dear. I did look at those pills in their little blue jar. But what for? I don't want to leave *life*. I want to leave *him*. And I'm worried that this is getting to be a habit.'

'That's a relief. I didn't fancy giving you mouth -to-mouth resuscitation.'

She laughs reluctantly, her chins wobbling. 'A glorious thought.'

'Perhaps you need some time apart from each other.' God! I sound like an agony aunt in some red-top.

She ignores me. 'D'you know what alarms me the most, Sophia?'

I shake my head.

'That this is exactly – but exactly – how I felt about Helena's father when I left him. And he couldn't have been more different from Roger. I was so-o bored that I fought with him too. Hit him too. So-o bored I fell for Roger, who at that time was so into his studies he was bereft of any useful carnal knowledge and so had a lot to learn in that department. So-o bored that I left my Helena to the tender mercies of some geography teacher regarding the choice of dress for the school dance.' She slaps her plump hand on her brow. 'Now I'm doing it again. I'll end up like the Flying Dutchman moving from man to man rather than place to place, never staying for long.'

175

'Roger's very concerned, Doreen. I hadn't thought he–'

'Was so mad about me?' She laughs now and the tension in the air slides away. 'Of course he is, my dear. I rescued him from the dry valleys of nerdish bachelorhood, from the inexorable turn of the academic treadmill. We created such a scandal that the only way was out, away from the alma mater that had been his home, man and boy. Away from my Helena.'

'He sacrificed a lot then?' I make the question sound innocent.

'Me too, honey. I sacrificed my Helena. And isn't she the innocent in all this?' Doreen's not laughing any more.

'So what will you do?' I take the bull by the horns. 'You can't keep hitting each other, Doreen. There could be an accident. One of you could be ... well ... seriously injured.'

Her large round shoulders move in a shrug.

'Couldn't you get some counselling?'

'Always the social worker!'

I am stung. 'Well, what will you do?'

'I was just reading this thing in a magazine that's beached up in my bathroom. Where you sit down with each other and each of you writes down three things that you promise to do and three things that you promise not to do. Then you look at what you've written and make it a mutual list to go forward. And you do that every month.'

'Sounds like common sense.'

'Roger will say it sounds like gobbledygook. Or Gobble Dee Gook. One of his favourite insults.'

'What if I ask him to do that with you?'

'He won't.'

'Let me ask him.' I go and pick up a notebook from the bedside table. 'Here. You do it. Now. Three things.' She takes the notebook and pulls down a pillow to lean on.

Back in the living room, Roger gulps back a sneer when I insist how serious the proposal is, how his wife is really at the end of her tether.

I pick up Doreen's kitchen list book and push it towards him. 'Now, Roger!' I say. 'Do it now.'

He pushes the scrappy notebook back at me, goes to a drawer and pulls out a bound notebook and a fountain pen. 'OK. OK,' he mumbles. 'I'll try anything. If it gets her out of that fucking bathroom.' He pauses and looks at me. 'Why are bathrooms such menacing places? Something to do with *Psycho* gettin' into the collective un-conscious, d'you think?'

I didn't tell him she was already out of the bathroom.

'Write! Do it while I wait,' I say quickly, before he gets into some psycho-social dissertation. 'I'll take it to her.'

He glances down at his combat boots, sniffs, and starts to write in his careful hand. 'I want to see hers.'

'You will.'

In five minutes Roger's promises are well laid out, the writing neatly lined up on the unlined paper:

For Doreen Selkirk
1. I promise never to lay a hand on you except in love.

2. I promise to talk less about the historic past.
3. I promise not to question your talking to or about Helena.

I went downstairs. Doreen's sheet was covered with overlarge elaborate scrawl but in essence was equally brief and self-knowing.

Dear Rodge,
I promise not to drink more than three glasses of wine.
I promise not to hit you with my hand or anything else.
I promise not to go on too much about things I can't do anything about.
D.

When I show Doreen's sheet to Roger he takes it to the window to read it, his back to me.

'Seems reasonable,' he says over his shoulder. His voice is muffled by the epaulettes on his shirt. 'Mere common sense. When you think about it.'

Downstairs Doreen's reaction to Roger's note is sober. 'See? See, Sophia? He knows. It's not as though he didn't know.'

'Can you keep it up for a month?' I say. 'D'you think he can?'

She hauls herself up off the bed. 'Who knows, dear?' Her voice is weary. 'Who knows?'

'I really do think you need a bit of time away from this flat, Doreen. A break.'

She shakes her head. 'Where would I go? I know no one here in London. And we run things on a shoestring, you know.' She got right into bed

178

and pulled up the covers. 'Tell Roger I respect what he's written here. But tell him to leave me awhile. I could sleep for the whole of England.'

Roger nods when I tell him, extracts his laptop from his briefcase and sets it up on the kitchen table, pushing a pile of Doreen's knitting wool on to the floor. The sight of those tender colours melting together on the floor makes me want to hit him. It's obvious that these two do need some time apart but I'm at a loss to see how this can be contrived.

In the end it's Bobbi who presents us with the answer, who gives Doreen a temporary route of escape. She tells me she wants to go to see her great-nanny in Suffolk.

'I need, need to see her, Sophia. I woke in the night and knew that's what I want. I would like to see my great-nanny.'

Of course I agree. For myself, I wonder if the person she really wants is her mother, and Great-Nanny is the nearest she can get to that.

Dear Chris,

I have made the acquaintance of this young person and I think you might quite like her. She is bold and enquiring and has no fear of me. I have realised for some time that people tend to be afraid of me. I don't bite, but there must be something. Anyway, I have shown this young person my garden and we have been sampling your cocktails. The French Riviera is her favourite. There is this very strange thing. Since she has been around I have felt you around here as well. More than for many years. Strange. Hence these letters. It's not just that Puss has become a scratcher.

The girl has hair like red-gold wire, full of life. Her face, though, is smooth and closed off. Mysterious. But I think she likes me, so her face lights up now and then. There is something about her that makes me feel alive, part of this world. I have been dead to it for so long.

When you come back you must meet her. Her name is Sophia, like one of those girls in the Georgette Heyer books. Did you read them? No, I suppose you'd be more likely to read Dashiell Hammett. All that exotic crime.

I feel closer to you every day. When you come back you can make cocktails for my friend Sophia. She would like that.

My love to you always,
Julia

A Ticket for Mrs Selkirk

So, the next day I found myself in Aldeburgh, looking out on that North Sea so familiar from my childhood. But here, instead of that long glorious Bamburgh beach there is a shifting pebble landscape that echoes sea music: unsettling, compelling.

The great-nanny's house is by the beach at one end of the town. The taxi driver points to a path leading to a drowned village and a Martello tower. Bobbi leaps out of the taxi and leads us to a tall house tacked like an afterthought on to an even taller hotel.

180

Doreen stays with the taxi, having insisted on paying the fare. 'It's the very least I can do, Sophia. I can't think why you want me tagging along but I have to say I'm enjoying myself.'

Perhaps it's Bobbi, reminding Doreen of her Helena, or perhaps it's just the idea of a jaunt, but this Doreen is a different person from the defiant, crumpled heap on the bed yesterday. Or perhaps it's just being away from Roger. That would cheer anyone up.

The day before, Bobbi had burst in on me and the tearful Doreen, looking for me.

'Aldeburgh, Sophia! We have to go to Aldeburgh. My great-nanny lives there and my dad loves her; loves the place. He liked to walk the edge of the water. I dreamed of it, Sophia. It's all pebbles, silver and blue shelves of pebbles. I dreamed my Sparrow was there. Walking the edge of the tide.' She held up papers clutched tight in her hand. 'I've booked the train tickets online. Printed these off. We've gotta go, Sophia.'

'Great-nanny?' asked Doreen, tears forgotten.

'My mum's nana,' said Bobbi patiently. 'She loved my mum. My dad's always saying that.'

'We can't go,' I said flatly. 'I can't leave Doreen, Bobbi. There's been this problem.'

'I know,' said Bobbi. 'I heard. Through the floor.'

'I can't leave Doreen,' I repeated.

'No problem,' said Bobbi, and vanished. Five minutes later she was back, waving another piece of paper. 'A ticket for Mrs Selkirk. We'll all go.'

Doreen loved the train journey, exclaiming at the broad landscape and the wide skies. 'I've heard of Suffolk, of course, but never been. Brit-

181

ish. Romans. Witches and witch hunters. Ghosts. A coastline that moves,' she muttered, all the time knitting something in deep blue with wine-coloured sequins.

As we waited for the bus to take us to the railway station we saw Julia with her wheeled basket. I explained that we were going to Aldeburgh to visit Bobbi's great-grandmother. Her face fell.

'How long for?' she said.

'Just overnight.'

'Well, that's all right then,' she said placidly.

Doreen was bubbling, clearly pleased to be out of the house. 'Come with us, Miss Soper. This is an excursion. A ladies' jaunt.'

I looked at Bobbi, who shrugged and grinned. 'More the merrier,' she said.

Julia glanced back across to her house, where her cat was sitting on the wide windowsill, his beady eye on her.

'It's something about Bobbi's father,' I said hurriedly. 'Just business, you know?'

Julia shook her head. 'Couldn't desert Pusscat, anyway. He'd go berserk.'

We settled on the bus and Doreen murmured, 'No bad thing, I suppose. We can hardly have two mad women on the same jaunt.'

So here are just three of us, standing on Bobbi's great-nanny's doorstep, cringing at the sharp breath of the easterly wind licking its way along the coast path.

Bobbi lifts the heavy dragon knocker and clashes it down.

The person who opens the door is tall and

slender, her hair in weblike silver fronds either side of her narrow face, her pink skull shining through. Her eyes are large, round and blue, netted in fine lines. She looks blankly at Doreen, then her glance drops to Bobbi and her face is transformed, wreathed in smiles.

'Roberta! Glory be. Is it you, sweetheart?' She puts her hand into the pocket of her faded print dress and pulls out glasses, places them on her nose and peers again at Bobbi. 'So it is!' She opens the door very wide, giving us a glimpse of a wide hallway lined in faded panelling, treating us to a gust of polish and dust and genteel neglect. 'Come in, come in.'

She leads the way through the house to a kitchen at the back that is twice the size of the ground floor of my house. A big table dominates the centre of the room and the fire in the high grate is blazing, despite the warmth of the day.

She sits in the carver chair, then waves a veined hand for us to sit at the table with her. Her print dress is missing a button at the waist and we can see the taut line where her waist is held in, just above her navel.

Bobbi sits on the arm of the carver, her own arm casually draped over the old woman's narrow shoulders, and tells her who we are and why we're there. The old woman tells us to call her Elsie.

'Housemaid's name, I know. But there you are. That's what I was in my first world.'

'We're on Sparrow's tail, Nana,' says Bobbi. 'He's done a bunk, you know. What is he like?'

'Sparrow's tail? That's a good one, dearie.' Elsie clasps Bobbi's smooth brown hand in her blue-

183

veined white one. 'Well, dear Roberta, I have to admit that reprobate was here. Just one night. If I didn't know him better I'd have to say he was running from something. But we all know Sparrow. He is not afraid. He runs from nothing. He said you might come and he said to tell you he is safe, gel, and you too are to keep safe.' Her soft voice drawls, soft-edged like sand.

'I dreamed of him here on the beach, Nana, the tide running over his lovely long toes and back down the pebbles and out to sea again.'

'You dreamed well, dearie. He was here. But I fear the Sparrow's flown. Didn't settle this time.' She smiles at her own wit, her false teeth gleaming. 'But you are not to worry, Roberta.'

'Did he say where he was going?' I try to keep the urgency out of my voice.

Elsie shakes her head. 'No, m'dear. He said our Roberta here was in safe hands and I was not to worry, even if she turned up to see me.'

'She is in safe hands...' I say.

'...There is nobody more responsible than Sophia here, I can assure you,' puts in Doreen.

Elsie peers at me. 'Are you his girlfriend?'

'No, no.' I find myself wishing I were. It would all be so much simpler. 'But I'm taking care of Bobbi and she thought her dad would be here with you. She was very keen to come,' I add.

Elsie shakes her head, still smiling that death's-head smile. '"Too late too late, it was the cry!"' she declaims. 'You go home, dearie. And sit tight with Roberta. And he'll come. When the dust settles.'

'We've just arrived, Nana,' said Bobbi indignantly.

'It looks so very interesting, Aldeburgh,' murmurs Doreen.

Elsie turns the beam of her blue eyes on her. 'Has Sparrow deputed you as well, dearie?'

Doreen goes pink. 'Not exactly Mrs ... Elsie. There was a ticket, so I came.'

Elsie beams. 'Good idea! Now that's a good idea. Travelling around.' She looks up at her granddaughter. 'Do you know, Roberta here, her great-granda came from Ohio. He's still there in my heart, a golden youth who never came to dust.'

She catches me glancing round the room, and out of the window at the long courtyard behind the house. 'You're wondering how I came to be here, in this house?' she says. 'I was housemaid for this lovely old fellow, then I married him. Better an old man's darling than a young man's slave. He loved our Roberta's nana, my daughter, Mary, like his own. She was only little then, of course.'

'Great-Nanny's always saying that, about being an old man's darling,' says Bobbi. 'Drums it into you.'

Elsie nodded slowly towards Doreen. 'I met that golden boy in the war, of course. Lots of Americans hereabouts in the war. They were welcome here, m'dear. My golden boy wrote a book on Suffolk churches. Even while the war went on. Can you believe it? Rode around on his bike and looked at churches. I've got it somewhere.' She glances casually around the room.

'I'd love to see it,' says Doreen.

'I'll root it out for you.'

Then they both stay silent. They are comfortable together, like old friends.

'So,' says Bobbi. 'Can we stay, Nana? Just for one night?'

So this is how the three of us stay in Elsie's spare bedroom, head-to-tail in an enormous bed by a window, which looks out only on the sea, as it comes in and goes out, the pebbles murmuring as they rearrange themselves again and yet again.

It is also how I discover that Doreen snores: the delicate, restless snuffle of a small animal. And how during the night Bobbi takes up more and more of the bed, her young limbs twitching, spreading and colonising the space. Eventually she ejects me and I go downstairs and sleep on the long bergère couch in the front room. It's not warm down here but I get my stretch. Still I can't sleep, so after a while I get the yellow book out of my pack and write about my own grandmother, a tough old woman who is very different from Elsie in her large house by the sea. But they are alike in some ways.

Then the day lightens and I go out to sit on the sea wall. The shingled beach is deserted, but out on the early tide I can see heads bobbing, at first with, and then against, the tide. After a few minutes a figure in a dressing gown appears from the narrow streets behind the strand, a towel over one shoulder, and makes its way down the shingle shelves, and dives into the curling tide. Only when he discards the dressing gown and towel do I realise he is male. Surveying the bobbing heads, I now count three female swimmers in tight caps, and two bareheaded males. Not one of these people is under sixty-five.

There is a rustle behind me and out comes

Elsie, a yellow rubber cap enclosing her fine skull. Her high-necked costume is in some kind of black jersey. Her arms and legs are nut-brown whipcord. Her smile is toothless. Obviously she thinks her dentures will not survive an encounter with the North Sea.

She joins the bobbing throng and proceeds to make seven passes, executing a stately breast-stroke, head held high like some ancient sea horse. Then she rises from the sea, traverses the tide lines of shingle and treks back past me without a word, her towel round her shoulders, her face glistening with salt water. Five minutes later she joins me on the sea wall in canvas trousers and an ancient T-shirt, which must have campaigned to save the whale in 1960. Her gleaming dentures are in place and she is carrying two steaming cups.

'Here,' she says. 'Coffee. Black to start the day. I always say, it's the only way.' She hitches on to the wall beside me, swings her legs around and draws up her knees in front of her. How her young spirit belies the lizard skin and alien teeth. 'Roberta is keeping well with you, I see,' she says, her eyes boring into me. 'Wonderful of you to volunteer, m'dear.'

'You might say I was volunteered. Or chosen. I am something of a pressed man. Or woman. Bobbi has kind of adopted me, if you like.'

Her blue eyes narrow. 'You don't come from London, do you? The North, p'raps?'

And here's me thinking I have no accent. People like Big Emma and her mates have accents. Laura has an accent. Not me. 'Yes I say,' conceding my roots, 'I do.'

She nods, the loose skin on her neck contracting and stretching again. 'Reliable. Sturdy. People from the North.'

I groan. 'Really we're a lot of light-minded scallywags in the North, but it's a secret.'

She shakes her head and a strand of drying silver hair releases itself from her skull. 'I know better than that, dearie. I was evacuated there in the war with my baby Mary, Roberta's nana.'

'Right. I see.' I look up at the house with its many windows and its peeling wooden balustrade.

'You won't find her up there, m'dear. I lost her and my Roberta's mother, Pamela, within two years. This dratted plague that's about now.'

She means cancer. I know that.

'So, Bobbi...?'

'...has visited here many times, with Pamela and George – Sparrow. My Mary lived here with me. Always.' She flashes a grin. 'Children out of wedlock have been a tradition in this family. No strange thing. Till Pamela stopped the rot and actually married Sparrow before she had Roberta. He's a treat, that Sparrow. A real treat.'

I think of the photo in the flat, of Pamela and Sparrow wound round each other, she gazing adoringly up at him. Suddenly I want to know Sparrow so much it's like a physical pain.

Elsie catches my thought. 'Sparrow was this great surprise at first. Stupid old me thought he was a gangster or drug-dealer or something. My decrepit mind, of course. But Sparrow forgave me that almost at once. He was quiet and charming, and those two were so much – so much – in love. And now their child, our Roberta, is so special.

188

Like her mother in everything except looks. She's much prettier than Pamela. She was plain. A bit of a bluestocking. But he adored her like we all did.' She sniffs and lifts her T-shirt to dab away a tear, giving me a glimpse of her flat brown belly.

The fresh morning makes me daring. 'Tell me about Pamela,' I say.

She sniffs away the last of her tears. 'Pamela? Well, she was the sun and the moon for Mary and me. Clever. Dogged. Flew through school at the top of her class. Turned down Cambridge because it was too near here and went to Bristol University. She loved to study and she loved to dance. Those two things. They met, dancing, her and Sparrow. He once said to me, "The minute I saw her move, Nanny, I knew she was the one for me." He loved how clever she was but most of all he loved how she danced.'

She turns her head and we watch as, further down the beach, a man and a woman are trying and failing to get a kite away. The man is holding the toggle and the woman is running, slipping and sliding over the pebbles, throwing the red kite into the air again and again. Their laughter rings out in the clear air.

'So how did Sparrow come to be over there, in Bristol?' I need to know more about him, not just for Bobbi, but for me.

She frowns. 'I think his family were there. His father worked for some kind of importer, and Sparrow worked for a wine importer as a boy. He was very smart to look at, and inside his head too. Sparrow was a lesson for me, so late in life.' She sighs. 'I am too much a child of my time.'

189

I jump in with both feet. 'So when he called here this week, what was that about?'

She frowns. 'He just wanted to say hello, m'dear. To sleep over. He has always kept an eye out for me. I asked about Roberta and he said she was in safe hands. We talked about Pamela and Mary. He swam in the tide. Came out all sparkling. A change from the usual early morning wrinkled crew.' She nods towards a silver-haired military-looking guy who is marching towards the sea.

'Didn't you ask him what he was doing, wandering the country like that?'

She finishes off her coffee. 'Course I did. Do you think I'm decrepit, dearie?'

'What did he say?'

'He said ask no questions and I'll tell no lies. Policeman, like I say. Very secretive.'

So he was a policeman. A jigsaw piece clangs into place. 'I thought you said he worked for a wine importer.'

'That was before. Once he met Pamela he made sure he got himself a career.'

'I thought he worked in security where we were in London.'

'Cover, m'dear. Deep cover. Don't you watch television?' Her tone is kind. 'War stories, police stories, they're all the same.' She jumps off the wall, wincing a little as her feet hit the ground. 'I do love that man even though sometimes I worry about Roberta. But now I've seen you I know she's all right. Thank you for bringing her.'

'She's an amazing girl. Self-sufficient and innocent at the same time.'

'Like her mother and her grandmother. But my

190

Mary couldn't dance like Pamela. Nor was she as good as Pamela at picking her men.' She points up into the sky. 'Look!'

Along the beach the man and woman have the kite up now and it is straining on its leash, dashing about, quartering the wide Suffolk sky. 'It's a good beach for kites,' says Elsie. 'Kites lift the spirit, don't you think? Even an old spirit like mine.'

When we get back into the house I tuck the yellow book back in my backpack. The sound of a flute ripples through the open kitchen door. The music seeds the words in your head. *Cockles and mussels, alive, alive-oh.*

Bobbi is in there, elbows up, playing the flute, and Doreen is sitting at the table, looking slightly the worse for wear. 'Oh, my dear,' she says, 'the sound of the sea. Kept me awake all night.'

Bobbi catches my gaze, winks, and lowers the flute, cutting the music out of the air.

'I don't think so, Doreen,' I say. 'You were sleeping very soundly when Bobbi finally kicked me out of bed.'

Her face falls. 'Did I snore?'

'Just a little sniffle-snaffle.'

'That's right,' says Bobbi, 'just a little sniffle-snaffle.'

'Roger says I snore like a warthog,' she says.

Bobbi looks interested. 'Do warthogs snore?' she says.

This makes us all giggle, and when we get our breath back Bobbi turns to Elsie. 'So you really, really don't know where he is, Nana? My dad?'

Elsie touches her cheek. 'I really, really don't know, dearie.'

191

'Then why'd he come here? To you?'

Elsie moves her thin shoulders in a shrug. 'I'm not sure, Roberta. Really. P'raps just to see me. He always liked to come and see me.'

Bobbi's body suddenly tenses. 'He came to say goodbye, didn't he?'

Elsie shakes her head, her hair, now dry, lifting in a sparse halo. 'Not that. Not at all. P'raps to reassure me about you? To talk about your mum? Sparrow has always liked that. To talk about her.' She glances at the photo on the wall by the window. 'To go through the photo albums.'

'Where else would he go?' Bobbi is being unusually demanding. 'After this?'

That shrug again. 'He might go to Bristol. He still has uncles there.' Elsie puts her hand on Bobbi's arm. 'But don't dream of haring off there, dearie. You would just miss him there, like you've missed him here. What if he's back this minute at your place in London? Go back with your friend here. Sit tight. That's what Sparrow would want, dearie.'

Slowly Bobbi puts the flute back into a battered leather box embossed in gold with the name Pamela Armitage. Her mouth trembles. 'What's he doing, Nana? Why's he doing all this? Dodging around.'

The old woman folds her in her arms and strokes her hair. 'There, dearie. Your daddy's all right. Have faith in him. He would want that.' She takes a tissue from a box on the table and dabs away Bobbi's tears. 'Now then, shall we check on the trains?'

I stand there, helpless.

Then Doreen pulls us all out of our sadness with an unexpected statement. 'Is there a bed-and-breakfast place near here, Elsie? I might stay awhile. The sea here is very restful and I'm not ready for dear old Roger yet.'

Dear Chris,

You'll be interested to know that Sophia has made friends with the little girl who lives in the middle flat in the Copeland house opposite. She is a very attractive child. Looks Italian, but her father is black. He's a very smart fellow who drives a shiny motor bike. I have not seen him at all lately. I think there is some issue about his being missing but I'm not clear on the details. Of course, our Sophia watches out for the girl. Takes her responsibility seriously. She has a way with children, I think, and I feel some tragedy in her own past. But that is confidential. She will tell you about that in her own time. But this is a risky situation with the child. I cannot say this to Sophia because I am from another world and have no right to say anything.

I was with Sophia and the child at the market when I met that Melanie Cowell. Remember her? A very common type, I'd say. Do you remember, her husband was mown down in some kind of raid, not long after you went away? I have to tell you she does not improve with age. She and her dreadful son – the image of his father – are somewhat in pursuit of this child Bobbi's father. (I fear there is darkness around now, just as there was then.) We had to take a detour to avoid them. Sophia and Bobbi laughed about the whole thing. But I did try to tell them not to underestimate that pair. They have the smell of evil

about them.
Only you know what I mean, Chris.
Where are you?
Always with love,
Julia x

A London Mile

I looked out of the smeared window as the train purred and rattled through the East Anglian countryside. Beside me Bobbi's head was buried inside a Dean Koonz book she'd bought at the station.

As the train chugged and chased through the countryside I thought about how much I'd learned about Bobbi, and about Sparrow. Now he fascinated me even more. Now I was even keener to meet this monster, this paragon, this unusual person: to rage at him, to accuse him of child-neglect. To meet him.

Perhaps I was too fascinated with him, like one of those sad souls who fall in love with complete strangers: women who become close to men on death row; lifetime pen-friends; stalkers who get involved with actors, celebrities; risky intimate relationships established in cyberspace. The not-knowing in the true flesh renders the relationship close to fiction, where both writer and reader should be in love with the imagined hero. Ridiculous.

I wasn't in love with Sparrow Marsh. No. Not at all.

I wondered if Bobbi was trying to make me fall in love with him. But then as she snapped closed her book and we drew into Liverpool Street Station I smiled.

'What are you smiling at?' she demanded.

'Nothing.'

I was smiling at my own simplicity. All Bobbi wants to do is find her dad.

'You should be careful, Sophia. Only lunatics smile at nothing,' she said.

It was funny, then, that having been fantasising all the way from East Anglia about falling for a man I'd never met that when we got off the bus in Barrington Street a flesh-and-blood candidate for my affection potential was sitting on the wall by the bus stop talking to Julia Soper.

'Hello, you two,' he said. 'I heard you'd gone adventuring and assumed our date at the Savoy was off, Sophia. But Miss Soper here assures me our date's on, as you've got a particularly elegant frock to wear.'

Sitting there on the wall, he didn't look in the least bit like an imagined hero. He looked like a man I would meet anywhere: fit, clever, early thirties but kind of unemphatic; not at all like a glamorous figure only glimpsed in photographs and in other people's tales. That might be a problem but it was also a kind of relief.

I grinned. 'Well, we're back and yes, the dress is perfectly lovely. Vintage delight.'

Julia looked up at me. 'Did you get what you wanted? Out there in Suffolk?'

I shook my head.

'My dad wasn't there,' supplied Bobbi. 'But he had been. My great-nanny gave him breakfast and he swam in the sea. He left a trace. That was nice.'

Julia leaned sideways a little to peer behind us. 'No Mrs Selkirk?'

'She decided to stay awhile in Suffolk,' I said.

'She told me she'd fallen in love with the place,' said Bobbi. 'Me too. I love it.'

'What will Roger think of that?' murmured Stephen, nodding towards the road, where Roger was dodging the traffic to get to us.

Roger did not think very much of it. 'I trusted you!' he said grimly. 'I trusted you to take care of her. To bring her back safely.'

'I am not my sister's keeper,' I said wearily. 'She liked it there. It calmed her down.'

'Mrs Selkirk is going to ring you,' announced Bobbi. 'She told me. "Tell Roger I'll ring him tonight." She said that.'

He glanced round. 'I'd better get back then. Don't want to miss her call.' Then he went back, dodging the traffic again.

'Ain't he a funny one?' said Julia. She looked at me. 'I've put another climber in your yard for you, Sophia. Honeysuckle. A cutting from my own. Just two sticks now but should get some height next year. You'll like it.' She was obviously planning on me staying. 'Oh,' she went on. 'And there was another of those men hanging round. I saw him off with my trowel.'

'Good for you,' I said.

Then we had to explain to Stephen about 'those men'. He suggested the police.

'They have better things to do,' said Julia.

'There was a drugs raid down behind the High Street last night. Shootings off Brooke Road. It's like Chicago round here sometimes. The poor police have enough to keep them busy.'

His eyes were on me. 'Well, give me a ring,' he said, 'if it happens again.'

I smiled at him. 'Only if you promise that your trowel is as effective as Julia's.'

Bobbi picked up her rucksack. 'I'm going in, Sophia. Things to do.'

'Me too,' I said. 'I just want to see my little house again. I've missed it.' I had. I was dying to go through my door again, to throw myself on my sofa and just think. About Sparrow Marsh, probably.

Stephen jumped off the wall. 'Well then, Sophia. Seven o'clock tomorrow night?'

'Seven o'clock.'

Julia put a hand on my arm. 'Sophia, I wonder if you'd do something for me?'

'Anything, Julia. What is it?'

'I wonder if you would cut my hair for me?' She must have seen the alarm in my eyes. 'Not now. Any time will do. Tomorrow afternoon?'

I swallowed. 'Yes. Right.'

I walked along the road. I knew that my job tomorrow was to persuade her to go to one of the proper hairdressers on Church Street. I couldn't even cut my own fingernails, much less anyone's hair. Especially someone who had settled into her style in the 1960s.

When I got in the phone was ringing. It was Laura. 'Seems like you've fallen off the edge of the world, babe. We're missing you loads.'

197

'No you're not.'

'All right, me and Tariq're missing you a bit.'

'I'm only a mile away. Come and see me.'

She groaned. 'It's a London mile, babe. A London mile. That's a long, long way. Not like Gosforth to Heaton.'

'Where are you now?'

'Islington.'

'Jump on a bus. Pretend it's a Newcastle mile, pet. I'll put the kettle on.'

When Laura arrived we sat out in my little back yard among the pots and greenery that seemed to have bred while I was away. It was warm enough to do that here in London. Laura once said that London was two top coats warmer than New-castle. Today she brought the gossip from the course. Tariq had a new boyfriend and Marina had a placement with the *Daily Express* and was loving it despite the fact that its politics were poles apart from hers. Laura herself had a placement with an interiors magazine where the editor wore odd shoes and talked to herself.

I told her about my date with Stephen Cope-land and wowed her with the Jean Muir dress.

She whistled. 'Look at that quality, Sophia! Look at those seams. Pristine. Worth a mint, pet, dresses of this vintage.' She whipped out her ever-present camera and took a picture. 'You said there were more? More in that wardrobe of hers? I've gotta meet this Havisham creature, love. Simply got to.'

I was already shaking my head. 'Not the right time,' I said. 'Really, it's not the time at all. She gave me this dress because she's keen for me to go out with Stephen. She knew him when he was a boy and I think she's connecting up with him again. The dress is all part of that.'

'That sounds kooky.'

'The story is that she had this boyfriend who used to show him magic tricks when he was little. It was this guy that was mixed up with the Pinders, those gangsters years ago.' I regretted the words as soon as they were out of my mouth. Here I was, handing Julia to Laura like some little titbit, some morsel to seal our friendship. I waited for the quickened interest, journalist's spark of excitement.

Laura stared at me for a moment, then let it go. 'Well then, when the old dear's more ready to part with the stuff make sure I'm the first to know, won't you?'

But still I blundered on. 'Giving me the dress and getting to know Stephen again, I have this feeling Julia's moving on in time. Out of the chrysalis. Did I tell you she has this long Joni Mitchell hair? Well, now she wants me to cut it.'

'So, you can cut hair? You're a girl of many talents.' Laura sipped her coffee.

'Can't do it for toffee, love. Have you seen my hair? The only reason I grow it is because I can't cut it. I'm bound to make a pig's ear of Julia's hair.'

'I can cut it for her,' Laura said calmly.

'You? How can you cut hair?'

'Grew up with hair,' she said calmly. 'My mum did hair. My auntie Marge did it. I was sweeping up cut hair in their salon from the age of nine.'

I was relieved. 'Would you really come and do it?'

'She won't mind me bringing my own scissors,

will she?'

Later that day I called at Julia's on my way to pick up Bobbi. I told her about Laura, whose mother had been a hairdresser and who was – I said – a brilliant haircutter herself.

'I would make a real mess of it,' I said. 'You'd hate it if I did it. Laura would be much better.'

Julia wasn't sure. 'I don't know this girl. Is she from round here?'

'She's from Newcastle. Like me.'

'Well, that's all right then.' She frowned. 'Does she drink?'

I laughed. 'Well, not to excess. But she'd probably love one of your cocktails. She likes a bit of style, does our Laura.'

'Right then. You can bring her here tomorrow teatime, before you go to the Savoy. Tell Stephen to collect you here.'

She walked me to the door. 'I've stopped it, you know.' I noticed that she was quite pale. There was something unusually quiet and still about her.

'Stopped what?'

'Stopped talking to Pusscat. One day I caught myself doing it and thought it was silly. So I don't do that now.'

'Are you all night, Julia?' I said.

'I'm fine. It's just that I miss it.'

'Miss what? Talking to Pusscat?'

'No. Talking to him about Chris, my friend. I used to do a lot of that.'

Later, walking with Bobbi back to the Lavender House, I thought that my instinct that Julia was moving on might be right; letting me into her

200

house and garden; helping me with the Lavender House; giving me the Jean Muir dress; sitting on the wall talking to Stephen; having her hair cut. Now she had stopped talking to herself – or to Pusscat, which was the same thing. She had moved on from the recluse she was when I first arrived. But as I let myself and Bobbi into my house I wondered whether this was entirely a good thing. If she dismantled that self that had been her shell for forty years, what would there be underneath?

'What's this?' Bobbi held up an envelope that was on the doormat, then without asking permission she tore it open. 'Oh,' she said sadly, handing it over. 'It's not from Sparrow.'

The note was on crisp mustard-coloured paper, with a computer-generated border of curlicues, and word-processed in capitals.

DEAR HOUSEHOLDER I WONDER WHETHER YOU KNOW OF THE VALUE OF YOUR PROPARTY. LET ME IN TO CHEK AND I WILL SHOW YOU JUST HOW MUCH IT IS WOTH. RING ME ON THE NUMBER BELOW. A WELL-WISHER.

It was a mobile number.

'What a nutter. Will you ring?' said Bobbi, her wide eyes stretched even wider.

'I will *not*,' I said, screwing up the letter and throwing it in the bin.

But when she had gone to bed I retrieved the paper and smoothed it out. Then I turned on my computer, Googled 'Pinder Brothers' and turned up dozens of sites, some more serious information, some adulatory cult-type pieces that really did talk about 'diamond geezers' and threatened retribution on people who misinterpreted the facts as they saw them. It seemed they had ways of getting back at you, even now, in the present day. They even said they could find out where anybody lived. They really did talk about the Pinders 'Keeping order on their own turf', people getting a 'good kicking' for being naughty boys, and miscreants 'just getting their due'. Some talked about the injustice of the long prison sentences and the missing Pinder millions.

One – a more articulate American article – argued that the Pinder phenomenon was a cult with rules and myths and magic of it own. The same man wrote an article about the men who, at one time or another, ran with the Pinders until their fickle favour ran out. On the list, among the Ms was 'Muncaster, Christopher'. I clicked through to a brief paragraph alongside a photograph of a handsome tall man in his thirties in an elegant, slightly draped-lapel suit:

Christopher Muncaster, petty gambler. Father Yorkshire entrepreneur, mother a Polish refugee. Attended Ampleforth College and dropped out after one year at Magdalene College, Cambridge. Acted as a bagman for the Pinders and introduced both Roy and Richie to useful school and college contacts, at that point part of the establishment. Faded from the picture in 1969. Research in London, Yorkshire, Spain and Brazil has failed to uncover any trace of this man. He just dropped out of sight, like others who in their day caught the Pinders' fancy. It was acquaintances like Muncaster who allowed the Pinders to traverse with such apparent ease that mile between the culture of violence in the East End and the culture of wealth and privilege in the West End of London in the sixties.

'Dropped out of sight', 'faded from the picture' – crikey, what a fate for Julia's Chris. I printed off the pages and put them in the folder with the nutter's letter. I would decide what to do about all that after Laura had cut Julia's and I had been to the Savoy with Stephen Copeland.

Dear Chris,

I thought you'd like to know I gave my young friend Sophia that brown dress you so liked. I have to say she looks lovely in it, like a bright brown bird with a golden crest. It didn't look the least bit old-fashioned although it's more than thirty years old. Think of that! But that's couture, isn't it? Quality sustains. You always said that.

A revolution is afoot! After all these years I have decided to change my hairstyle. Between you and me I am quite frightened about this. Was I with you when I saw that film about Venice and a masked ball? There was this one man who, when he took off the mask, had no face behind it. What if that happens to me when I change my style? What if I somehow vanish?

Anyway, I asked Sophia to do it but she suggested her college friend Laura, who has experience with hair. She will do it tomorrow before Sophia goes off to

the Savoy with Stevie Copeland. He was a nice boy,
Chris, but he really has grown into a charming man.
You would like him.
   All love,
   Julia xxxx

The Cinderella Corporation

Laura persuaded me to let her do my hair before
we went along for her to cut Julia's. She rubbed
in lots of wax and pinned it up with a kind of
peacock's tail spread out at the back. When I
objected to the peacock's tail she pinned that to
my head so that the whole effect was a kind of
corrugated copper helmet.

Bobbi viewed the proceedings, gimlet-eyed.
'Now that's brilliant. Like black hair only ginger,'
she said approvingly. 'Shows up your cheek-
bones. And your eyes are like a car's headlights.
Enormous.'

'Don't know whether that's good or bad,' I
scowled.

'It's good, good,' Laura patted my arm. 'Now,
Sofe, let's get ourselves down to Miss Havisham.'
Clearly doing my hair was for her a prelude to a
much more exciting event.

Julia was ready for us. She had a chair on a
spread of newspapers in the middle of the
kitchen floor and her hair was wet, hanging down
in rat-tails. Over her shoulders, where Pusscat
more usually resided, she had a long green towel.

There was no sign of Pusscat.

Julia surveyed me, her eyes travelling up and down the elegant brown dress. She herself was wearing hotpants today. 'What a good idea that was, Sophia, dear,' she said. 'You look lovely. The hair, a bit severe, but very sophisticated.'

Laura led her to the chair, sat her down, and took out her scissors and comb. Julia's hair was surprisingly thick and challenging to cut, and Laura worked her way through it, taking the thinner ends off, layering it just a bit around the crown, taking a razor to the long fringe. Then she whipped a brush and a small hairdryer out of her bag and blew it dry, lifting it and pulling it and letting it fall in glossy layers, glittering gold and silver in the light of the single bulb hanging from the ceiling. The transformation was dramatic. Julia looked younger and more distinguished. Her eyes, formerly hidden under the awful fringe, were luminous.

Bobbi took her hand. 'Look, look, Miss Soper! You should see yourself.' We followed them to the hall and stood like some kind of jury as Julia surveyed the effect for herself in the large mirror. She ran her fingers through her hair and it settled down again beautifully. It was a very modern cut. Her eyes met mine through the mirror and there were tears in them.

I put a hand on her arm. 'Julia...'

She pulled her arm away and turned to walk steadily, steadily upstairs. We watched her helplessly.

'That's blown it,' said Laura gloomily. 'She hates it. Won't let me see her clothes now.'

205

'It's brilliant, said Bobbi. 'You wouldn't recognise her.'

'We'd better clean up in the kitchen,' I said glumly. This was only a matter of rolling up the newspapers over the cut hair and putting the bundle in the dustbin. Then, as I did this I noticed that the dates on the newspapers were in the 1970s. 'Senators Contact Nixon Urging Him to Resign', 'President Rejects Demands for Tapes', 'Arab Guerrillas Slay Two Israelis. Olympics Halted'.

When I went back inside to tell Laura about the newspapers Julia had reappeared, dry-eyed. She had changed out of her hotpants. She was wearing neat black slacks and a man's white shirt – one from Chris's wardrobe, I was sure – with its sleeves half rolled up. She had pulled it in round her narrow waist with a black snakeskin belt.

'That's better. Rather goes with the hair, don't you think?' She looked round. 'Now then, will you please go and sit down and I'll find the wherewithal to make us a very fine Honey Bee. It'll do to celebrate my entry into the twenty-first century.'

We were just sipping the drinks, staring bug-eyed at the transformed Julia, when the doorbell rang. Julia leaped to her feet, vanished, and came back leading Stephen by the hand. He looked taller than ever in a black dinner jacket and a white silk polo-necked, shirt.

'Here you are, Sophia,' she said. 'Someone for you.'

'Cool,' said Bobbi. 'You look just like that first James Bond, Mr Copeland. Saw him on telly.'

I stood up and Stephen blinked. 'What's happening here?' he said. 'Is this the Cinderella Corporation?'

We all laughed nervously and stood around while Julia poured Stephen a Honey Bee. I was relieved when he drank it off and asked was I ready. I looked at Laura, who was going to stay with Bobbi till we got back.

'Let the girls stay here for a while,' said Julia firmly. 'Didn't you say Laura likes those old frocks? We can look at the others and have another Honey Bee. Then they can go back to your little house.'

'Girls! I like that,' Laura grinned, showing all her perfect teeth. 'Let's do that, Miss Soper. You two young things go off and enjoy yourself, why don't you?'

As we walked down the hall I saw Pusscat glowering down from the seventh stair. Perhaps he didn't like all the changes. Perhaps he didn't like to be disturbed. But then the thought occurred to me that he might be missing his conversations with Julia.

Dear Chris,

I met Sophia's friend Laura today. Charming. A sparkler. Very clever, I should think. From the same neck of the woods as Sophia. She's all set to be a fashion journalist. I showed her my clothes and she absolutely loved them. Took a photo of each one. Said I could sell them for a fortune. I would never do that, of course. You know that.

Anyway, she cut my hair. I told you that was the

207

arrangement, didn't I? Her family are all hairdressers, apparently, so I felt I could trust her. (I hope you are not upset. I have kept it just the way you liked it but I caught sight of it in the mirror the other day and thought how old I looked. I didn't like that. Nor would you.)

And this Laura did a lovely job. It is shining and soft and not that much shorter. I think you will like it.

Oh! And Sophia came all ready for the Savoy. She looked beautiful in my Jean Muir dress. Laura had done her hair too and she had a kind of glow about her. Stevie called here to collect her. They made a very handsome couple, I can tell you.

As I saw them off I had the forbidden thought that if our baby had been allowed she would be just like that. I – we – would have waved her off to university, to dances and balls, feeling just as proud as I did tonight of Sophia. Of course, I can't let Sophia know this as she would probably think it very weird. And then she'd stay away. We can't have that.

I just wish you had been here with me to wave her off. It was never to be, of course.

All my love,
Julia xx

At the Savoy

We went to the Savoy in Stephen's old Volvo, which still had building-site mud on its wheel arches. We parked in a mews somewhere near Oxford Street.

'Friend of mine lives here in the week,' said Stephen. 'Said I could use his parking spot. I thought a walk in the night air might suit you.'

We walked awkwardly, like the strangers we were: no fit between our bodies. I felt quite formal in my Jean Muir frock, not at all like myself. Like some grown-up who really had a life. This made me very quiet.

Then he took my arm, and walking was easier. Our paces began to match. 'So. Have you made a start on the house yet? Ripped any carpets out?'

I shook my head. 'I've spent the week chasing round after Bobbi. And Sparrow. And I've been trying to write something. Not a minute to think of the house. Although I do love it. I feel like I've lived there for ever.'

'So, what is this thing you're writing?'

That was a hard question. 'It's about a few things. About my grandmother. And some women I knew at home. Fantastic women on an estate called the New Dawn.'

'Fact, then?'

'Well, yes. But I'm taking some liberties.'

'Is that allowed?'

'I don't know. That's how it's getting on to the page. I have this yellow book that seems to allow me to take liberties.'

'I'd have thought it was all computers and cut-and-paste these days.'

'It probably is. That's why I'm probably not a writer.'

'D'you have a publisher?'

'No. Well. My tutor at college might know someone.'

'I'd like to read it.'

'So would I. If ever I finish it.'

We turned into the set-back entrance to the Savoy and Stephen led the way up the wide shallow staircase like he knew where he was going. We rose into a wide reception area throbbing with people talking and waving their hands about, and waiters weaving around with trays held high. I hadn't experienced such a thing before but I suppose it was like any group of professional people gathering for a formal dinner. Most of the women were older than me, showing a lot more flesh. Most of the men were in dinner jackets, but there was a sprinkling of less conventional souls. A number of them had, like Stephen, opted for the less formal silk rollneck. Quite a few men wore coloured dinner jackets. One oldish man was wearing a dinner suit made of what looked like curtain material.

As we entered the throng a few heads turned towards us. I felt stiff, like a governess from some TV costume drama, in my Jean Muir dress and tight, pinned-up hair. I asked a passing waitress for the location of the powder room and fled. A stout grey-haired woman was in there, carefully outlining her mouth with lip pencil. She watched through the mirror as I tore out Laura's carefully placed pins and pulled my hair down. I ran my fingers through it and looked in vain in my small bag for a brush.

The woman fished one out of her tapestry bag. 'Would this help?' she said.

'Thank you.'

She watched with open interest as I loaded the

brush with water, bent over from the waist and brushed my hair with punishing strokes, making it crackle like the beginning of a thunderstorm. When I finally stood up my hair was standing out a foot from my head. I looked like a circus clown. I ran more tap-water over the brush and worked the frizz back down to a sensible height. It was not bad, although it still had bizarre bends in it from all that pinning.

I handed back the brush. 'Thank you. You saved my life.'

The woman was obviously very amused. 'No problem, my dear. I have to say it's a great improvement. Greek Warrior to Cathy Earnshaw in one fell swoop. A transformation.'

Cathy Earnshaw! As always, the North reveals itself.

Stephen smiled as I approached. 'That feel better? More like you?' He handed me a glass of champagne. 'There was this and some special cocktail. I thought that this would be best. Nothing should compete with Miss Soper's firebomb specials.'

'Stephen!'

An older couple were bearing down on us. The woman, perhaps a bit older than Stephen, was elegant in a beautifully cut black gown, which did justice to her generous proportions and showed off a flawless neck and throat. It took two glances to realise she was pregnant. Stephen introduced her as Emily Sillitoe, senior partner in his firm.

'My inspiration, my mentor,' he said, kissing her hand.

She in turn introduced her husband, Jerry. He

was a good few years older than she, heavily built but quite fit, with curly grey hair and glinting blue eyes. I wondered if he too were an architect. No, he just didn't have that look. Too solid about the shoulders, too bristly about the hair.

He shook my hand warmly. 'Sophia? That's how we say it back home. Nice old-fashioned name, that.' His voice had a comforting Lancashire lilt that flowed like cool water against the edgy metropolitan tones of the professionals around him.

I had just decided that I liked him but was not sure about the woman when, on some unseen signal, the crowd started to move and we moved with the two of them. My alarm at the sight of place-names abated when I found myself beside this same Jerry Sillitoe at one of the large round tables that filled the banqueting hall. Stephen on the other side of me and at his side, round the curve of the table, facing us, was Emily.

Over the first course, talking to Jerry was easy. He talked about Emily and her brilliance, her exceptional nature, her beauty. It was clear that Jerry was not only in love with her but in awe of her and wanted the world to know it. It was a late marriage.

'Life in the army, then the police force. Not much time to make liaisons, to be honest. I liked my work too much.'

His enthusiasm made it easy to ask questions. 'So how did you meet Emily?'

'Well, I ran this police charity that took city children into the country. Lots of people involved. Film stars. Media. People you'd know by sight. Emily's firm paid for the transport. We met

212

and that was it.' He rubbed his bristly cheek. 'Like I say, she's quite a woman. Always ready to take a risk. Took a risk with me. And now she's taking a risk having this baby. I thought I was a risk-taker but she's teaching me to take risks. She is a lovely lass. The best.'

I looked across at Emily, who was talking enthusiastically with Stephen, her eyes gleaming, her lips on the edge of a smile. 'I can see that.' I leaned sideways so the waiter could serve the vegetables. 'So, are you still in the police?'

He shook his head. 'Retired two years now. I do some consultancy – foreign police services, home security – lots of that these days. I work with a couple of other lads who've retired. But mostly I look after Emily.' His fond gaze wandered again across the table. She raised her glass to him.

It's funny, I'd only known him an hour but I was certain I could trust him. 'Can I ask you something, Jerry?'

'As long as it's not how to break the law, love.'

'It's not that. But there is this man I know ... know of ... who I think might be a policeman. Or working for the police...'

So, I gave him an edited version of what I knew of Sparrow. As we talked Jerry's whole demeanour changed from loving spouse to policeman. You could almost feel him hardening, sharpening up. He asked again about Oliver Cowell and his mother. And asked Sparrow's proper name and where he lived. I didn't mention Sparrow leaving Bobbi to God and good neighbours but, even so, I started to worry that I was talking out of turn. 'I'm not sure about this, Jerry. Talking about him like this. I could be entirely wrong. I was just wondering.'

His eyes bored into me for a second, then he relaxed, making me relax too. 'Don't worry, love. I might come across something. You never know.'

To distract him again I started to talk about Julia's Chris Muncaster problem and the Pinders, and the house stalkers. He laughed at this. 'Nutters. All of 'm in love with the Pinders. There are dozens of books about those bad lads. Hundreds of sites on the Net. Hero worship. Those brothers left a long dark trail. Anywhere their feet have touched becomes holy ground. D'you know, there are Pinder tours in the East End! Quite an achievement for a pair of amoral quick-witted chancers.'

'Did you know them?'

He chortled. 'How old do you think I am, love? The force was cleaned up – well, relatively – by the time I got into the Met. No – well, I suppose *less* – police corruption, and by then simple murderous villainy and protection by assault was no longer what it was all about. It was big-time drugs, international gangs, cyberfraud, all inter-national stuff – more shocking and less romantic, p'raps, than London gangs knocking each other off and playing Bugsy's turn to run the show.'

I was just going to ask him about Bugsy's turn when Emily called across the table, 'I hope you're not talking shop to Sophia, Jerry darling.' She looked at him fondly. 'Not everyone understands the labyrinthine ways of our boys in blue.'

'Are you kidding, Em? Everyone here is talking shop.' He nodded round the room. 'Only their shop is likely to be about shops, or cathedrals or factories, or some other building. My shop's more about the meaning of life. And death.'

Both Stephen and Emily were looking at me now. 'And just what have you found out about Sophia?' she said. 'Did you get to know about her "shop"?'

To my relief at that point someone chinked a glass at the top table and the room fell quiet, ready for the speeches. These were not too long and were quite witty, as far as I could tell from the laughter. Most of the humour was in-house and went right over my head. Then came the awards with, thankfully, very short citations but no speeches. I clapped till my hands hurt when Stephen went up for his medal, having learned from the citation that it was for an exciting project in Leeds, converting industrial buildings to social housing. Emily stood up and kissed him soundly as he got back to the table so I had to do the same. He clutched me tight and pinned his medal on to my Jean Muir dress.

'The star of the evening!' he said, kissing me again, on the cheek this time. 'Thank you for coming.'

Later, we walked through the crowded streets easily together, his hand on my elbow. The pavements gleamed with recent rain but the air was warm and soft. People were wandering round with the eager, benevolent aimlessness of those who had enjoyed one part of their evening and were going on to a next, more mysterious phase.

Newcastle, at this stage of night, would be much more boisterous. The crowds of mostly young people would be chummier and louder, the loosening impact of alcohol more significant. The nihilistic Viking spirit lives on there to the fortieth generation.

Here, the crowd was all ages and all nationalities, turning night into day as a holiday present to themselves. But then, as we cut through one side street, we saw darker places with menacing door-men standing guard in suits and black polo-necks, walkie-talkies in their ears. As we walked past one door there was some kind of shift change as one man greeted another with a slapping handshake, head and shoulders ducking towards each other in a no-body-contact hug. Was this what Sparrow Marsh did? Was this how he greeted his fellow workers? It was hard to reconcile this clean-cut menace with that soft voice on the phone and the photograph on Bobbi's mantelpiece.

The very uniformity of these men made me think that although there were no Pinders around, these days someone was running it all very efficiently, perhaps still on the borderline as far as the law was concerned.

Walking along, Stephen and I talked about the Sillitoes, what easy company they were. Stephen told me Emily had been his mentor when he first started and had brought him into the partnership five years before. 'At that point she was a single, thrusting career woman. Brilliant. That was before she met Jerry, of course.'

'That can't have made her any less brilliant.'

'Oh, yes. But she's a lot easier to be around.'

I wanted to ask him about himself, whether he was simply a thrusting young career man, and whether there had ever been an Emily in his life. Or whether for a time Emily had been the woman in his life. But I didn't.

We turned a corner into the mews. 'Now,' he said, turning to me. 'I'm honestly not coming on to you, but I have a key to my mate's house just there. The one with the yellow door. We could go and have coffee and chill a bit. If you want to. Just seems a pity to go back to Barrington Street so soon.'

I hesitated.

He hurried on. 'No, perhaps not. Bobbi's back there, and your friend Laura.' He opened the car door. 'Jump in!'

I couldn't then protest that, yes, I would like to go in for coffee, to chill, whatever that involved. I could ring Laura, she could stay... But I couldn't do that. It would be like giving myself to Stephen on a plate. And no girl would do that even if the diner was someone as special as Stephen. And although I really liked him I was waiting for something else to happen. Some spark. That hadn't happened yet.

He solved the inevitable tension inside the car by driving back the very long way, along the quieter Embankment, across Blackfriars Bridge, along beside the river, back across London Bridge. I blinked and blinked on the glittering river, the gleaming Babylon of the City, the quieter glimmer of St Paul's, offset by the dark mass of buildings and shadow street canyons.

'Look at that!' I said, my eyes widening in the dark to take it all in.

'The best time to be in this city,' Stephen said

briefly, 'is at night. Then the flesh melts and the bones emerge.'

'Newcastle is magical at night,' I said. 'On the Tyne, there is this succession of bridges, brilliant new buildings reflected in the water. But this is something else.'

After that, the drive out to Stoke Newington was an anticlimax. By the time we were pulling up outside the Lavender House the magic between us had faded. I thought of the lost opportunity of coffee and whatever else in the mews house. I was still not sure whether it was he who lost his nerve or me.

We sat there quietly. Then he said, 'So, when are you starting to rip this house apart?'

Rip my house apart? I wasn't going to do that. I dragged my thoughts away from the glamorous evening and my extra special city tour. My house is safe territory. *Tell me about Emily or whether she and you were lovers. Is that why you're on your own?*

'The floors? As soon as I can get myself organised. It'll have to be on a shoestring, though. My bit of money needs to stretch like chewing gum.'

'You need to rip the carpets out and sand the boards. Cheap enough.' *I'm sorry I cocked it up tonight. I lost my nerve.*

'Huh! Hiring a sander costs. And man-handling the thing.' *Me too. I've never been with anybody for far too long. Hard to handle. Man handle. Woman handle.*

'I can borrow a sander for you. Find you a man to do it.' *I really, really like you but am not sure how to start this thing.*

'But that will cost...' *Just start. Just start.*

218

'Not if the man is me.' *We have to take time over this.*

'But, but...' *But ... but*

'But what, Sophia?'

'All right then.'

'So we'll start soon? On the floors? I'll supply the labour.'

'Yes.'

He leaned over and kissed my cheek. 'I had a great night, Sophia. You're great company.'

I turned my head and kissed him on the lips, mouth closed. 'You too.'

Then I leaped out of the car and let myself into the house. I watched from the window as he drove away, the old Volvo bouncing a bit on the uneven road. I touched my lips and tried to feel his on them again. But there was no echo of that feeling. Still no residual spark.

It took me a second to realise that Laura wasn't there. I found her upstairs sleeping beside Bobbi, an open copy of Alan Garner's *The Owl Service* dropping from her hand. I crept back downstairs, made myself a cup of coffee, got out my yellow book and spent the next hour burning off my adrenalin by writing a story about the time Big Emma's friend Mrs Drew fostered two brothers from care and stood by them even though they robbed her twice and took drugs in her back room. Of course, I didn't call her Mrs Drew but I was stuck with a happy ending because that was what happened in real life.

It was only when I was getting ready for bed at three in the morning that I realised that Stephen's medal was still pinned to the Jean Muir dress.

219

Dearest darling Chris,

I'm afraid I've done something rather daring. My haircut must have gone to my head (only an accidental joke, that). I decided I needed a change of style and I have raided your wardrobe. I found some black slacks of my mother's that had never been worn. They just about fit – she was so tiny. Then I got one of your white G&T shirts, rolled up the sleeves a bit and belted it with your black snakeskin belt. Of course I had to put in a fresh hole – managed that with a nail and hammer. It worked very well. Laura – the one who cut my hair – and my Sophia really liked the look and the child Bobbi said it was 'neat', whatever that means now. I have to say I was pleased. I must be getting vain in my old age.

I felt so pretty that I knew you would like it. I longed to feel your arms around me again, and your lips on mine.

I have been sitting here thinking about you, but I can't for the life of me think of you in old age. I can only think of you as you were – slim and smart in your G&T shirt and your snakeskin belt. Elegant is the only word.

All this is making me sad. I will have to close.

Yours always with a thousand kisses,

Julia x

PS. Pusscat has gone missing, which is very worrying. I think he is feeling offended, neglected, poor thing.

Debriefing

When I finally raised myself the next morning my house was deserted. There were notes from Laura and Bobbi: Laura's note about setting out for an early lecture, Bobbi's about going home to get ready for school.

A fine one I am, to be in charge of anyone.

When I got along to number 83 Bobbi was already at the gate in her overlong parka and with her rucksack on her back.

'I'm sorry, Bobbi. Slept in.'

She grinned. 'What for? Having a good time out with Mr Copeland?'

'Have you had your breakfast?'

'What do you think?'

Of course, I was talking to Miss Self-Sufficiency.

'Rough night?' she said helpfully. 'You look dragged.'

'No. I was writing till three o'clock.'

'Writing. Ha-ha-ha.'

'I was! And no need to be sarky.'

She grinned. 'I'm off. Don't wanna be late, do I?' She raced away, then turned back round. 'Mr Copeland was up and out an hour ago. And he's ages older than you, i'n'he?'

I shook my fist at her but let her go.

'Sophia?' It was Roger Selkirk, standing in the doorway of number 83. His army fatigues were badly creased and he had dark circles round his eyes. 'So pleased to have caught you.'

'I can't tell you where Doreen is, Roger,' I warned.

His eyes gleamed. 'No need, Sophia. She rang and gave me the number of this mobile she's acquired. A mobile! Doreen! There's a change. We had a long talk. She's got a room with this old lady, some relative of young Bobbi's? She needs money and I'm going to take her some.'

'Can't she just get some from a hole in the wall?' I said, not quite believing him.

He shrugged. 'I'm afraid she can't. Doreen knows I take care of all the important things. Particularly money.'

The pig.

'Here. Here's her number. She said you should ring her. Do it now, if you want.'

On the phone Doreen, sounding relaxed and calm, assured me everything all right now. Roger was excited about all the things she'd told him about Aldeburgh. 'All those witches and wailing sea-ghosts and things. He'll love it, Sophia. He needs a break. We need a break together.'

I gave up. I turned to Roger. 'She sounds well.'

Roger came closer. 'Thanks, Sophia.' He looked me coldly in the eye. 'I know you're watching out for Doreen, but how long have you known her? A few weeks? Give me a break. I've known her five years and, strange as it may be, I love her.' He turned on his heel. The door slammed behind him.

I turned away to someone waving at me from across the street. Blimey! The newly shorn Julia. She was wearing the shirt and trousers from last

222

night but had added a fancy waistcoat (man's) and a single string of pearls. Very little make-up: mascara, lipstick. No meandering eye lines. Overnight she'd changed her style from sixties icon to ageless Katharine Hepburn. It was quite a switch.

I waited for the lights to change and crossed over.

'Didn't recognise you, Julia,' I said.

'I didn't recognise myself, dear, when I woke up this morning. All this change might be desirable but it's very disturbing.' She opened the gate wider. 'I thought you might like to see my Compassion.'

I must have looked blank.

'Climbing hybrid tea rose. First blossom.'

I followed her through the house and down the garden like a lamb. She showed me the climber with several buds and one blossom just breaking out. Then it started to rain and we dashed back into the kitchen. She sat me down and made me a coffee, complete with a shot of brandy. 'You look as though you need it, dear.'

She sat down opposite me at the little Formica table. 'Now then. Tell me about your evening.'

I started my tale backwards with the walk through midnight London. Her face brightened. 'I used to love the city at night. Innocent revellers, but so much of the real place underneath, layers and layers right down to the bad boys, then the working girls and pimps, then even further to the waifs and the strays and people in doorways.'

Startled by her perceptive description, I told her about the doormen I'd seen, wired up with their walkie-talkies. Creatures of a criminal half-world. 'It made me think of Sparrow. I think he does that kind of thing. The shady side of things.'

'The child's father? Oh, no, dear. I don't think he's one of those.'

I was startled. 'How would ... how d'you know that, Julia?'

'You forget, dear. I see it all. I can tell. He's not a shady person.' She glanced round the kitchen, then through the door to the hall. 'Pusscat is no bad person either, although he's gone AWOL. I think his little pussy nose is out of joint.'

'Why d'you think that?'

'Well, for a year or so I only talked to him. When he turned up he was a godsend because I'd got to talking to my mother, although I knew very well she was no longer with us. But now...'

'Now?'

'I talk to you. And Stephen. And last night I talked to your friend Laura, who is quite delightful. D'you know she took photos of all the dresses in my wardrobe? We had great fun, she and I and the child.'

A creeping sense of alarm stiffened the flesh of my face. 'Did you talk to her about Chris Muncaster?'

Julia treated me to a look of great severity. 'My dear Sophia, she is your friend, not mine. There are things one only mentions to one's friends. Anyway, tell me about the Savoy.'

I told her about the set-back entrance and the sweeping staircase and the long bar.

'It hasn't changed then. Chris and I went there twice. Once on my birthday and once to a party the brothers threw for their auntie when she was sixty. That was what you might call "a knees-up". I don't know whether the staff of the Savoy were amused, but money was splashing around like rain in Manchester, so the worst excesses were smoothed over. Money is a great salve.' She poured me some more coffee. 'Now, dear, tell me about the do. Were they all fancy-dans?'

'Well, they were smart but a bit, well, bohemian, you know? Artistic. Not so conventional as a gathering of lawyers would be.' I told her about the dinner and showed her Stephen's medal, still in my pocket from my abortive attempt to return it.

'He gave it to you?' She frowned.

'No, no. It was just an extravagant gesture in the heat of the moment. You know?'

'I think he likes you,' she said, her large pale eyes sparkling. 'I thought that last night.'

'And I like him.' Then more words came out that were true, but seconds before I didn't know I felt that truth. 'But not in that way. No real spark, Julia.'

'That's a pity then,' she said gently. Then she said, 'Was that woman there?'

'What woman?'

'Dark. Dramatic. Older than him. Slightly heavy, Jewish-looking. Can one say that nowadays?'

She meant Emily Sillitoe. She did see everything.

'How d'you know about her?'

'Well, years ago, when he was pulling that house to pieces she was always there. You could tell – well – by the way they came in and came out of the house that they were close. I said so to Mother. But of course Mother wasn't there. This

225

was before Pusscat landed on me.'

Julia saw a good deal from her window. I decided that somebody who knows they're dotty in fact can't be dotty: a contradiction in terms.

'I did meet her. And I liked her. They seemed on very good terms. But she's married now to this lovely man, and she's pregnant.'

'I'd have thought she was a bit old for that. But they do that nowadays, don't they?' She closed her eyes. 'I was pregnant once. But nothing came of it.'

Me too, I said silently. *Me too*. 'He's even older than she is,' I said aloud. 'The husband. Fifty-ish.'

'Crikey!' she said.

'He was very nice. A policeman. He knew all about those Pinder brothers. It was still canteen gossip when he enlisted. He called them dark legends.'

'That's ancient history, of course.' Her tone was dismissive but a shadow crossed her face.

'Well, anyway, I asked about your friend Chris Muncaster, whether he could find him for you.'

'Muncaster. Good old Yorkshire name.' She frowned. 'Or is it Lancashire? He came from Yorkshire. Had a place in Yorkshire.'

'I'll mention that, if I see him again.'

Her lips folded into a very thin line. 'Sophia! I will not have big-footed plods scouring Yorkshire for Chris. Too embarrassing. As I say, Sophia, it's all ancient history.'

I distracted her by asking if she thought the hybrid tea rose called Compassion would flourish in my back yard, and finished my coffee while she lectured me on the horticultural impossibility of such a proposal, before dismissing me by asking me if I wanted an umbrella to get me home as it was raining cats and dogs outside.

As soon as I got into my house I rang Laura and asked her what did she think she was doing, photographing Julia's clothes and was she sneakily working on a Miss Havisham story by the back door? If she did that I would never speak to her again, or possibly even strangle her.

'Whoa, whoa, pet! Hold your horses. First, I have no sneaking tabloid designs on your dotty friend. Two, she insisted on me photographing the clothes. Three, she said did I know anyone who would buy them as one day she might just sell them. And four, she asked if I would find the time to take her somewhere where she could buy some new clothes, how she always loved clothes and thought she might like something more up to date. I told her that the gear she changed into last night was right on the button and her instinct was great. And I did tell her I'd take her shopping any time. And she said to me she could tell my instinct was great too and could she have my address so she could drop me a line about the shopping. No phone! I ask you. She said she no longer needed one. So I told her when she was ready she should tell you and you would tell me. By phone.'

For a second I couldn't say a thing. Then I said, 'That's me told.'

'Too right.'

'I'm sorry, Laura.'

'So you should be. Anyway, what happened with the elegant Stephen? He's not bad, by the way. In fact quite a doll.'

'We had a good night.'

'But...'

'I met the love of his life who, alas, is wed to another. And to my great disappointment there was no spark between us.'

'Pity, that.'

'Doesn't matter. He has the makings of a very good friend. And friends last longer. The good news is...'

'What?'

'He's gonna sand my floors.'

'Brilliant. Much more useful than even a good f–'

'Don't say it, Laura.'

'The puritan from the North rides again.'

'I blame my grandma. Brought me up out of my time.'

'Just like my auntie Maud.' We both laughed then, friends again.

When I put the phone down it rang straight away. 'Laura, what is it?'

'It's George Marsh, Sophia.'

The room flashed. Trumpets sounded. 'Oh.' I wrestled with my image of the doorman last night on his walkie-talkie. 'How are you?' What a stupid thing to say.

'I'm fine, Sophia, but I was wondering what the hell you were doing talking to Sillitoe?'

Crikey. That was fast.

'He's retired.' What a stupid thing to say. 'He told me he was retired.'

'Police tom-toms never retire. And Sillitoe was always a very big wheel. Famous in his own way.'

'I just happened to meet him last night,' I said frostily. 'I talked about you. I'm concerned about

228

Bobbi. And you. I suppose I thought he might help.'

'Well, now he thinks he is ... helping. Look, can we meet?'

I swear my heart missed a beat. I'd be swooning next. 'Of course we can.'

'Look, do you know Clissold Park? At the top of Church Street?'

'Yes. I've seen it from the bus.'

'Well, there's a little café in there. Basic. The families go there to walk and to see the animals. I'll meet you there in two hours. One thirty.' The phone went dead. I stood up and prowled around the house, a surge of excitement flowing through me. Perhaps I could go early and just sit in the café, killing time till he came. Get the feel of the place. I peered out of the window at the steady rain. No. That would be really stupid. I'd wait until the rain stopped.

My wandering eye dropped to the yellow book on the table. Yes. I would kill some time looking through my story about Mrs Drew. I turned the pages, pencil poised. It was a very basic, even sloppy, draft, but the energy and charm of the New Dawn and its people came flowing back to me. I slashed out lines and added more detail with abandon, buzzing with energy.

Then, without warning, Drina was in my mind. Her estate was a much grander, less caring estate than the New Dawn. There, curtains twitched but people didn't really watch out for their neighbours, or their neighbours' children. Until it was too late. Poor Drina. How lucky Bobbi was compared with her. She had Julia watching from across the street and Stephen upstairs and Doreen downstairs. And me and Laura.

It was only when I was shaking out the umbrella to go out again into the persistent rain that it occurred to me that was the first time I'd ever really thought of Drina with sorrow and regret, but without the deadening pain at the pit of my stomach and the searing guilt in my head and my heart.

Dearest Chris,

I thought you'd like to know that our young Sophia is getting on very well with Stephen Copeland but there is nothing in it. She says there was no spark. As I said, he took her to the Savoy. You remember you took me there for a treat on my birthday? There was a spark between us, all right. Didn't we go back to our little hideaway and make love right through the night, only sleeping at dawn? My mother was so cross when I came in with the morning post and you were nowhere to be seen.

You'll be pleased to know that Stephen has grown up very well. Remember the magic tricks? Well, now it seems he's a well-known architect. Doreen Selkirk told me that. She's the woman who lives in the lower flat opposite. She's quite nice for an outsider although now it seems she has run away from here. Her husband is quite distraught. A strange little man.

You wouldn't recognise that house now, Chris. Old Mrs Copeland will be spinning in the cemetery. Stephen has it made into three flats. Incredible. I would hate that to happen in my house. I went to see Mr McAdams. You remember his father, who looked after my mother's affairs? Anyway, he has assured me that I can make a will which can ensure that does not happen. So we did it there and then. The will was quite complicated because at first everything was left to you. But Mr McAdams explained the difficulty with you going missing for so long. I told him our story but he kind of pressed me to designate another heir and in the will instruct them to take care of you should you turn up. I have designated that other person now, a person about whom I've been telling you. And I have left my clothes to a person whom I know will love them. I have to apologise to you for this change, but I know my own darling you will understand.

Your ever loving
Julia xxx

Sparrow

I stood my dripping umbrella beside a buggy that was parked outside the café door, its translucent cover glistening. Inside the café the buggy's owner was sitting at a corner table breastfeeding a baby, a toddler beside her drawing a house in a book. The breast-feeder had the *Guardian* features page open in front of her. She didn't look up.

I bought a coffee and went to sit in the opposite corner, my back to her. I stared out of the streaming window at the deserted park outside. So much green. There was so much green in this part of London. I remember what a surprise all the greensward was when I first arrived. My glance sharpened as people drifted into my eyeline and departed – all swimming along indistinctly in the rain. A woman under an umbrella. A younger woman with a buggy so well protected it looked as though it had been wrapped in clingfilm. No one came towards the café.

Then a chair scraped and Sparrow Marsh was sitting beside me, bone dry in a navy jersey sweat suit with a hood. He leaned across and shook my hand in a tight firm clasp.

'You're dry,' I said with a vast lack of consequence. 'How can you be dry?'

I rescued my hand.

'I came earlier,' he said, nodding at the kitchen door. 'Waited to see you weren't followed.'

I frowned. 'You do know you show all the signs of paranoia?'

He laughed at that and I finally really looked at him, took him in. He was not what I expected. He was thinner, older and more grizzled than his photographs scattered around the flat. But he was also more vibrant, alive, than anyone I have ever met. He had a tight elegance, a containment that put him under a spotlight. People looked at him. 'In a word,' as I said to Laura later, 'he was gorgeous. Just gorgeous. My knees were buckling under the table.'

The girl behind the counter brought him a small black coffee, unasked.

'So you think I'm paranoid?' he challenged.

'I didn't say that. I said that the way you act shows signs of paranoia.'

'Would an explanation help?'

'Of course it would. Particularly why you had

232

to leave your daughter like that.'

'It happened so quickly, that's why.' He fell silent. 'And I always go on the principle that the less people know, the less harm comes to them. It has worked with Bobbi so far.'

In the window I watched the reflection of the woman putting her breast away and wrapping the baby tightly in a shawl before hunching back down over her newspaper.

Sparrow ducked his head into my eyeline. 'I'm not one of the bad guys, Sophia, if that's what you're thinking.' His voice had a slight drawl and I remembered he was from Bristol, not London.

'I was not thinking anything other than why the hell were you not with Bobbi. Why did you leave her like that? Seems like you can't care about her.'

He looked at me very directly. 'Now that's not true. I think you know that.'

It was my turn to be quiet.

'I have to trust you so I have to tell you the truth. The truth is simple enough, Sophia. For two years I've been buried – in deep – conning a set-up where this unsavoury fish has built up a ring of security men like some kind of praetorian guard. Protection, extortion, arms dealing right up to nuclear stuff, money laundering, govern-ment tampering – they'll do it, clean as a whistle. Kind of internal army for sale.'

'Oliver Cowell?'

He laughed. 'Olly? Oh, no. He's a very small fish. Bottom feeder. But he's in on it down there in the depths. But his club is some kind of headquarters for them. Room behind a wall. All that stuff.'

'Blimey!'

'But they sussed me and I legged it, and when he saw you and Bobbi he got very excited. Big price on my head, see? He's a bottom feeder but as greedy as the rest.'

'Megalomania *and* paranoia?'

He laughed again. 'It's like this. The big fish lives behind walls and walls of protection. Not literally. It's legitimate business this, legitimate business that. The one we're after walks round like a regular guy. He talks like an accountant. I came across him. Mild, proper salt-of-the-earth gent. Then I made the connection and he knew I did. There was one shooting where I was the target and I knew I was blown.'

'If you're one of the good guys why don't your friends arrest him?'

'They will, but me knowing this fact does not mean they can prove it. They – we – are still gathering evidence, turning people, until we get something on this deceptively mild guy. We've enough to arrest dozens of this man's praetorian guard, and a few fish like Little Olly, but it's the big fish we want. And he wants me, hence the price on my head.'

'Sounds like some TV fantasy.'

'Actually it's much more mundane than that, Sophia. You ask your friend Sillitoe. Much more routine and pedestrian. Information gathering, computer searches. Clerkish stuff. And it's much more dangerous too, because it's real life. That's why I've never even told my employers where I live, or anything about Bobbi. As far as they – or any of the fish – know I live in a flat in Hoxton. That was the first thing to be torched.'

234

'That's why Oliver Cowell and his mother followed us. To find you?'

'That's right. Or Bobbi, to force me into the open. But you were too wily for them.'

'That was Stephen.'

'Ah. Stevie's a good bloke. The best. A good friend.' Sparrow leaned nearer. He smelled of cinnamon and clean laundry. 'I'd guess you and he are close?'

I shook my head. 'I wouldn't say that. He's nice but we barely know each other. He's very protective of Bobbi.' I paused. 'I was with him last night at this architects' do at the Savoy, when I met Jerry Sillitoe.'

'Yeah. I heard whispers that Sillitoe had got together with this architect woman. A love job, they say. Stars in their eyes. Good thing he's retired. But he's still connected. And very efficient. He rang a man who rang a woman who rang me.' He looked across at the girl behind the counter and she brought us both more coffee.

'You're a writer, Stevie says?'

'I wouldn't say that. I write.'

'What do you write?'

'I write about ordinary things. People. I'll never set the world on fire.'

He leaned over, took my hand and turned it over. I was surprised my hand didn't spark like a firework. Our palms lay side by side: his the colour of almonds, deeply scored with lines, mine a mottled pink with its long, long lifeline. 'One day you'll raise the temperature all around, Sophia, and make people understand things. I feel it in my bones.'

I curled my hand tight into itself. 'What are you, a fortune-teller as well? You know nothing about me.'

'I talk to people. Stevie. He likes you. And Elsie. Now Elsie really rated you. And that's some wise woman. And now,' he put his hand over my tight fist, 'I've seen for myself.'

I breathed evenly to hide the fact that it felt like my whole body was crackling. 'I really liked Elsie. We got on.'

'And that tells me something about you.' He stood up, still holding on to my fist. Then he kissed me on the forehead, as if I were a child. 'Watch over my Bobbi for me just a little while longer, Sophia. We've nearly hooked this big fish. A week, two at the most. Stay cool, Sophia. For Bobbi.' He stared into my eyes. 'For me too.' Then he vanished again through the kitchen door.

The café was a chilly vacuum now that he had gone. The girl in the other corner must have felt the chill because she looked up from her newspaper and grimaced. 'Men, eh?' she said. The baby whimpered and she untied his woolly hat and tied it again.

I couldn't have put it better myself.

Dear Chris,

Sophia has that house just on the turn of the road. Our Bolt Hole. Do you remember it? It's had all kinds of people renting it but now Sophia has certainly made a nice little home of it. You can tell she loves it. She and I have turned her back yard into a very lovely courtyard garden. You can sit out there again.

You would like it.

The thing I liked about Sophia on that first day was the way she took me so seriously, the genuine interest she showed in my garden. She knows quite a bit about gardens but not as much as me. Never that. You never knew I was good at gardens, did you? I found gardening many years after you left when I met this man called Gregory. So much has happened since you were gone. I have this big garden day in June when lots of people will come and view my efforts. Laura and Sophia and even little Bobbi will be helping this year. I am thrilled about this, of course.

I wish you could be there, my darling, with your arms around me, kissing my brow, my ear my lips. I miss you more than ever before, even though now I am more resolved than I have been in years,

All my love, my own darling.

My bones miss you,

Julia xxx

Ghosts

The afternoon when I met Bobbi in Mehmet's I looked at her with new eyes. I noted that she was tall like Sparrow, and she had the same long narrow hands. Her full lips curved in just the same way. I didn't tell her I'd seen Sparrow, not just because he'd told me not to, but because it might hurt her that she had not shared the secret rendez-vous. She broke off telling me about this new girl at school who was Somali and was truly mint.

'What are you staring at, Sophia? Cut that! It's weird, I'm telling you.'

'I was just thinking how extraordinary you are.'

She put her hands over her face. 'Stop being weird. What are you doing?'

Rina came over. 'You all right, Bobbi?'

Bobbi took her hands from her face, grinning. 'It's this one. She's going mad.'

'More toast?' Rina picked up the empty plate.

'Nah. Plenty, thanks.'

I picked up my bag. 'Shall we go?'

'Am I safe? You haven't turned into a ghoul?'

'Come on, silly, you don't need to ask that.'

I left her in her own flat, doing homework on her computer, and as I was passing the lower flat I noticed the door was open. I thought Roger had galloped after Doreen. He couldn't be still there. I knocked at the open door.

'Roger? Roger, are you there?'

No answer.

I pushed the door open and went in. It was cluttered, and familiar, but it smelled fusty, unaired. Looking closer I could see it was much more cluttered than the last time I was here. There were cans, dead coffee cups scattered across the magnificent table. At the far end of the room the sink was overflowing with possibly every dish and container in the house. In the bathroom the bath was still half full of scummy water and the mirror was speckled with shaving cream. The bedclothes were screwed up into a kind of corpse in the centre of the bed.

So this was the man who 'took care of things': Doreen's pretty, casual house reduced to a dosshouse in a few days. I emptied the bath, then washed and cleared the dishes. Doreen couldn't come back to this. Then I locked the door, pocketed the key and went back up to Bobbi to ask her for her great-nanny's phone number, telling her I wanted to check that Doreen was all right.

'But she has her mobile,' said sharp Bobbi. 'You have the number.'

'Well, really I want to ring Elsie to ask how she thinks Doreen is. Outsider's view, you know.'

She accepted that, but the truth was I didn't want to phone Doreen with Roger at her elbow.

'Give Nanny my love,' said Bobbi, turning back to her computer.

Back home I rang Elsie's number. 'Hello? Hello?' she shouted into the mouthpiece, making me put the phone a foot away from my ear.

'Hello, Elsie.' I curbed the desire to shout myself. 'This is Sophia.'

'Oh, hello, dear,' she shouted. 'Are you well? I was just talking to Sparrow on the phone, saying good things about you.'

'Thank you for that.' There was a pause. 'I was wondering about Doreen. Did Roger get there?'

'Oh, yes, the odd man,' she shouted. 'They're out now and can't talk to you. They've gone to see some churches. Mad for the old and dead, some people are.'

'Are they all right? Is Doreen all right?'

'Well, dear, she's all right, but the man? Don't care for him, m'dear. Talks to a person as though they're deaf or daft, as far as I can see. Not just me, but Doreen too. And all the rubbish about things being quaint like he was in a museum, not a house. Now me, I like outsiders. But he lets them down. Gives me the willies. I told her so. An' I told her that if they were staying in Aldeburgh they couldn't stay here. Now he's been up on the big caravan site and says they can live in a caravan while he does his researches. Researches! In a caravan! I ask you.'

I was at a loss for words. 'Anyway, Elsie, can you tell Doreen that I found her apartment open so I have locked it and I have the key? Can you tell her that? Elsie?'

'No need to shout, m'dear. I ain't deaf. Of course I'll tell her.'

Five minutes later my phone rang.

'Doreen?' I said, reminding myself not to shout.

'It's not Doreen,' said an unknown male voice.

I took a breath. 'Then who is it?'

'It's Jerry Sillitoe, Sophia.'

Now I recognised the voice. 'Jerry. Great. Thank you for getting hold of Bobbi's dad for me. We met and talked. It was very helpful.'

'Good. Good. It was about that other matter. The Muncaster chap you asked me about.'

'Gosh, that was quick.'

'The delights of retirement and the possession of a little black book. Time to sweat the small stuff.'

'You found out about Chris Muncaster?'

'Mmm. Not good news for your friend, love.'

'Not good news?'

'Dug all around with a good friend of mine who is still in harness. Very junior to me, once. Access to files and all that. According to them, your Mr Muncaster dropped out of sight in 1969 and has not emerged in any guise, any alias. Not here, not in Spain, Brazil, Australia. Unofficial history has it that he was making a bob or two informing our lads of a few things on the side, and he went the way of quite a few of the boys who offended the Pinder brothers. Devoured by pigs, supporting some flyover, something like that. Definitely eliminated.'

'Not living in county comfort in Yorkshire then?'

'Hardly. We would know.'

Poor Julia. But then perhaps not-so-poor Julia. She had not been deserted as much as deprived, robbed by those toxic brothers. It was not because he had rejected her. Her missed life was what they now call co-lateral damage in a war not of her making. 'Thank you for going to all this trouble, Jerry. Perhaps it'll at least settle my friend's mind.'

'Remember it was all a very long time ago. But not for your friend, I suppose. Glad to be of help, love. Oh, by the way, I'm under instructions from Emily to ask you to supper on Saturday. Very informal, barbecue on the roof. A few friends. I'm in charge. Em's asking Stephen and a few of the office crew. To celebrate the gong.'

'Gong?'

His hearty laughter came down the line. 'Blimey! I'm showing both age and army, aren't I?' He paused. 'I'm talking about Stephen's medal. So you'll make it. Emily's very keen. Very fond of young Steve, she is. But it's rare to see him with a friend. A female friend, that is. Just between us he was so squeaky clean I thought for a while he might bat for the other side. A few of Em's mates are like that. Nice fellers, don't get me wrong. But she assures me that Stevie's not like that. I think,' he added drily, 'her certainty's down to personal experience, but she's not saying and I don't ask. Do come, Sophia. It'll be our last do before the arrival of the sprog. After that ... well, who knows?'

I gave in. 'That's very nice. I would love to come.'

'Great. Steve'll give you the SP, the when and the where.'

The phone went dead.

He was really nice, that Jerry. You could see why Emily was mad about him. It would be intriguing to see that interesting pair on their own ground, to find out more about Emily and Stephen. To find out more about Stephen. Last week I'd have been even more keen about that. But that was before I actually met Sparrow Marsh in the flesh. Before the fireworks.

Minute by minute I was consumed with thoughts about this man. I kept getting flashbacks to the way he sat on the café chair, the way he flipped a glance to the waitress and she brought coffee. I felt like a changed creature, as though all the molecules, every atom of my being, had been shaken sideways and up and down a bit before settling down again in their familiar shape; but not quite.

It was dawning on me that my early near-misses at marriage and my secretive, edgy affair with Malcolm were counterfeit experiences, experienced by me as 'love' without really knowing what love is. But now I knew.

In these last few days, when I spent time in the

flat with Bobbi, I found myself prowling around like a stalker, opening drawers, scanning photographs. Yesterday Bobbi went out to buy a pencil sharpener and I went into Sparrow's bedroom, opened his wardrobe and ran my hand along the row of lightweight jackets, the soft sweaters. There was one in a particularly nice shade of blue. I counted his shoes. He had small feet for such a large man. Three pairs of trainers; two pairs of loafers: one black, one brown; one pair of black leather boots, highly polished; one pair of climbing boots, badly scuffed.

Then I heard Bobbi come in downstairs and at the same instant I caught sight of myself in the long mirror in the wardrobe door. I pulled my hand back from the clothes as though I had been burned. Christ, I thought, I am a besotted person. Now I could identify with Julia and her obsession with Chris Muncaster: I knew why she has kept his clothes for thirty years, how she must go to *that* wardrobe, running her hands over *his* clothes. Mad. But then I now knew the madness. It dawned on me that being obsessed like this was a kind of haunting.

I slammed the wardrobe door and came out to find Bobbi at her work table.

'What was that bang?' she said.

'I think a draught must have filtered through and slammed the kitchen door.'

She stared at me. 'Impossible. This is the least draughty place in the whole world. Mr Copeland's good at things like that. Into "no waste, conservation" and that. No unwanted air.'

I laughed uneasily, placatingly. 'Maybe it's a

243

ghost,' I said.

'A ghost?' she grinned. 'Cool, that.'

At least she didn't say it was mint.

I sat there scribbling in my yellow book while Bobbi finished her homework. But it was hard to concentrate. I was getting used to the idea of myself changed now for ever by a single meeting in a park café with a man who so far had been a ghost in my life. A ghost from the future.

Dear Chris,

One thing I really liked about the way we were – that's yet another film you've missed, The Way We Were – was how kind we were to each other. You were kind to me. You knew. I was not like some women in that clique around Richie and Roy – some of those poor girls had to lard their faces with make-up to cover the bruises. The woman across the road, Doreen, she sometimes has bruises on her face, you know. I saw her with a shiner once. But then another time I saw her through her window with a pan in her hand, batting the man around the room like he was a fly. It was a small pan, I admit. It might be amusing if it were not so tragic.

But now, Chris, I have started to wonder if we would have kept being kind to each other through all these years. All these years? I've always loved you in your absence but now this thought has hit me like a thunderclap. These last few days I've been wondering whether I would have continued to love you in your presence. Funny, the things you think about, isn't it?

But I finally decided I would have loved you and you would have loved me. And I feel nearer to you than I have in a long time. I would have loved you

244

*into eternity. I am sure of that as I am sure that you
are and always will be, class among rags.*
   I will love you for ever and think of you kindly.
   Your Julia xxx

The Cleft Stick

On Friday afternoon I sat at my table under the
window and read right through my yellow book.
As I read it I started to remember all kinds of other
things about the New Dawn, and inserted bal-
loons on the blank right-hand side with new dia-
logue, new directions for the stories and new
questions for myself. Then for the first time it
occurred to me that I could invent other stories
around places other than the New Dawn: more
salubrious settings, in some cases with less salubrious people. Then like a crack of thunder, an explo-
sion in my head, I knew I could write something
about Drina and the toxic feeling of guilt the
thought of her induces in me. I had the terrible
thought that in this parallel fiction the social
worker loses her own child in an accident and sees
the events around Drina as atonement for her own
guilt.

   I was just sitting transfixed by this thought
when Stephen, complete with muddy wellies,
turned up at my door flourishing a note.

   'From Em. She wants you ... well, us ... to go
to a barbecue.'

   'Yes. Jerry rang. He asked me to the barbecue

and I said yes.'

'Good.' He glanced at the yellow book open on the desk. 'You're working? Sorry if I disturbed you.'

I closed the book. 'You didn't. I'd just finished.'

Stephen sat down on my couch, his long legs spread before him. He made the room looked small. 'So why were you talking to him? Jerry?'

'He rang me. Helping me to "pursue my enquiries".'

'Enquiries?'

'I'd asked him at the Savoy about Julia. About that man who set Julia in aspic. The one who ran with the Pinder brothers and vanished. Jerry phoned me about it.'

'Any joy?'

'Nothing. Not a whisper. Not here, not abroad. Jerry says he's probably underneath some bridge or some multi-storey car park. Like a few others, I think.'

'Poor Miss Soper. D'you think she knew? Knows about that?'

'She talks about him as though he's still alive but somehow delayed in Yorkshire.'

'I think Jerry would know. He's got his nose to the ground, very well connected.'

I was suddenly tempted. 'You like him? Jerry?'

He shrugged. 'Nothing to dislike about him. Good bloke. Sound.'

'I thought perhaps with Emily ... Emily and you...'

He met my eyes. 'Is there something you want to ask?'

I hesitated. Here was a cleft stick. My mind was

246

full of Sparrow and my life seemed full of Stephen. Now, showing this kind of interest in Stephen might put out entirely the wrong signals. But what the heck. 'I think that you and Emily have been more than good friends. I was puzzled before. You, at your age, not gay, not attached. To the outsider it's a bit, well...'

'Odd?' He smiled slightly and at that moment was more attractive than he had ever been; for that moment he blotted out the presence of Sparrow that had been there behind my eyes since that day in the Clissold Park café.

How fickle am I?

'Well, to be honest I fell for Emily the first time I saw her at the office. I was very green in those days. She was senior to me, ten years older and buzzing with life, power – creativity, if you like. For the next ten years I loved her and learned from her. Not just about architecture. About love. Life. Sounds like a cliché, I know. Problem with clichés is that they're usually based on some kind of truth. Then,' he paused for a second, 'for the last two years of those ten we became even closer. Funnily enough, that kind of spoiled it all. Can't quite say how. In the end I moved back in here and she met Jerry. At first we all smiled. How unsuitable was that relationship? A policeman from Lancashire! Of course, we were wrong. They couldn't be better suited and were – are – mad for each other.'

'A love job, we call it at home,' I murmured.

He shot a glance at me. 'A love job? I like that.' He looked me in the eye and I kept my gaze steady. 'Anyway, I think one of the better achievements of my life is the fact that Emily and I are still close friends and still learn from each other. Not that I carry a torch for her. That's totally over. But we are buddies. That counts for a lot.'

After that there seemed nothing to say. Then he looked round the room and broke the silence. 'What about these floors, Sophia? D'you want to make a start on them?'

'Today?' I glanced at the sunburst clock on my wall. 'I'm meeting Bobbi in Mehmet's at four.'

He shook his head. 'No. Let's say tomorrow. The carpets need lifting and there'll be some preparation before we sand them. We could do the prep over the weekend and I'll borrow the sander Monday–Tuesday. That should do it.'

I frowned. 'Someone would have to show me how to use the sander.'

He laughed. 'I'll do it. I think Emily'll spare me for a couple of days. Especially if it's for you. She took quite a shine to you.' He saw the look on my face and held up his hands in mock defence. 'Don't worry. She's not matchmaking. I can make my own matches, thank you very much. All I'm talking about now is a bit of house renovation. Meat and drink to me. I like hands-on stuff.' He stood up. He gazed down at his muddy boots. 'None of this when you have your new floors, Sophia. Boots off at the door. I'll come round tomorrow morning and we can get Bobbi to help us rip out the carpets. Then tomorrow night we'll brush off the dust and go to Emily's barbecue. We'll go early and take Bobbi with us. The kid needs an outing.'

'But–'

'Emily won't mind. She'll be interested. And Bobbi can't fail to charm her.'

When he'd gone I thought how clever he was to hold back like that, not to push things. But his friendly aside about removing his boots for the new floors showed that he saw himself as part of my life one way or another. And I was pleased. Even while I was daydreaming about Sparrow Marsh, I was glad I knew Stephen Copeland.

Like I say. How fickle am I?

I realised when he'd gone that I'd not told Stephen anything about talking to Jerry about Sparrow. Or about meeting Sparrow in the flesh. Probably a serious omission.

At that point the phone rang and my heart jumped. But it was not Sparrow. It was my tutor, Jack Molloy.

'How's things, Sophia? Freelance life suiting you?'

'I'm fine, and yes it is.'

'Work coming along?'

I thought of the scrawled-on yellow book, now quite tatty. 'Yes. I'm plugging away. Enjoying it. How good it is I–'

'Well, that's what I'm calling about, love. Met this woman last night in a pub. Some do for an artist who's up his own elbow. Anyway this woman there was talking about the market in stories from the depths of humanity. Misery memoirs they're calling them now...'

'Charming. And you thought about me.'

'Well, yes. She said you wouldn't believe half of the stuff that comes across her desk – did I tell you she was an agent? – is ill-written shit without a spark of imagination or grace.'

'And you thought about me?'

'Not in the way you're implying. I was thinking what a sound writer you were. So I told her about you and the things you've done, and she said if you could get a chunk of this material to her she might just be interested.'

'Jack, it's in draft! Scribble!'

'Then get a chunk of it into good heart and let her have it. Be the pro, Sophia. Don't degenerate into one of those genteel fucking hobby writers. It'd break my heart.' Everyone knows Jack's leathery, shrivelled old heart is unbreakable so I knew I was safe there. But I found myself taking the woman's address and promising to ring Jack next week and tell him I'd sent something off.

'Right, Sophia. If you don't ring me, I'll ring you. So be very afraid.'

He rang off and I looked at the phone. Just how I was going to manage carpet lifting, floor prepping, sanding and sealing as well as hammering my pages into shape I didn't know. But I would do it. For Jack. But most of all for me.

Dear Chris,

The funniest thing happened today. My young friend Sophia came with the most wonderful bunch of flowers from the Turkish flower shop. Lilies and roses. Gorgeous. They were the first flowers I'd had from anyone since that fancy bouquet you got me on the first anniversary of our meeting. That and the new Al Martino record. Do you remember?

I'd been down on my knees snipping the box hedge

around the gravel. We put the flowers on the dining table and she came out to watch me finish the box. Then we had a cup of tea together She was chattering on about changes to her little Lavender House. Did I tell you about that? It seems Stephen's going to sand the floors for her. Apparently it's the latest thing. Seems rather rough to me. Give me a nice carpet every time. To be honest, I thought Sophia was a bit odd today. Not like her. A bit strained. One minute she seemed on the point of saying something, then didn't say a thing. Then I thought the strain might be in me. I was wondering whether I should tell her I've made her our heir – well, heiress – but decided not to. Can't have her feeling she's being bribed into something, can we?

It was very nice to see her but I can't think why she came, or brought flowers.

(Apparently Mr Sparrow Marsh is still AWOL. As she told me about him, I suddenly thought that the two of you might be holed up somewhere. Not really. But it was a funny thought.)

Much love always,
Your Julia xxxx

At Mehmet's

Bobbi and I were just eating toast in Mehmet's when the door swung open and Julia came in, trundling her basket in front of her. She parked it up alongside a silent quartet of policemen. They were ploughing efficiently through their full English, no doubt mulling over the latest drama,

251

a shooting up behind Church Street. It was in the paper. A young drug dealer had been shot as he sat in his window.

Julia sat down opposite me. 'I saw you through the window, Sophia, so thought perhaps I'd join you.'

I was suddenly uneasy. I took her some flowers yesterday in an abortive attempt to tell her what I had found out about Chris Muncaster. Of course I ducked it. Maybe in some spooky way she had read my mind.

She ordered coffee from the ever-present Rina. This decisive order was so far from our Julia-and-her-cocktails that I blinked. I blinked too at the sight here in Mehmet's of her changed self. Apart from the chunky basket on wheels she might be just any customer. Her hair swung away from her face in Laura's cut. She had on just a touch of make-up. No lines round her eyes. She was wearing the black pants and shirt from the other day under a short men's mackintosh belted tightly round her small waist. She had a plain silver locket round her slender, lined neck. The only residue from her old self were the sixties boots peeping out from under her trousers.

'You look different, Miss Soper,' said the honest Bobbi. 'More normal. Know what I mean?'

Julia beamed at her. 'I'm like the princess in the forest, dear. Woken from a long sleep.'

'And who was your prince, Miss Soper? The one who kissed you awake?'

'Bobbi!' I warned. Dangerous ground.

Julia stared at her, then nodded. 'No kissing was involved, dear, but I think it just might have

252

been Sophia. She just came into my house one day, looked at my garden, and things started to change.'

Bobbi beamed at her. 'Me too. So I'm the princess in the forest too.'

I had to get off the dangerous ground. A diversion: 'Did I tell you I'm ripping up the carpets tomorrow, Julia? Stephen's going to help me strip the floors. So the dead carpets will have to be in my back yard. At least till we work out a way of getting rid of them.'

'Your poor plants!' she said, holding up her veined hands in horror. 'What about them?'

'That's what I was thinking. I'd hate to hurt them.'

She frowned. 'Should I come and ... well ... guard them for you? While you're working?'

Bobbi grinned. 'A plant-guard instead of a bodyguard! Ace.'

'If you'd do that for me, Julia,' I said. 'Just great.' My glance strayed across the café, past the policemen to the empty shopping basket. 'Still no Pusscat, Julia?'

She sighed and picked up her coffee cup. 'I regret to say he is still avoiding me. He's somewhat disdainful these days. Makes the house very quiet.'

I breathed more softly, with something like relief. This new, modernised Julia was a bit disconcerting. It was nice to see the old eccentric Julia was there underneath.

'I have the women from the Garden Scheme coming this afternoon,' she said, 'to see if my garden really will pass muster for the open day. They say they'll bring posters and leaflets. I'm supposed to distribute them. The woman on the phone said, would I be doing tea and cakes? People do, she said. I hadn't thought of that. I didn't do it last year.'

'Pity Mrs Selkirk isn't here,' said Bobbi. 'She makes lovely ginger nuts. And shortbread.'

'Mmm,' said Julia. 'I had thought cocktails...'

'But there'd be no profit in that,' I put in hurriedly 'Nothing for the charity.'

'Yes,' she said, disappointed. 'You have a point there.'

'I can put leaflets through doors for you,' said Bobbi encouragingly.

My child protection bells rang. 'You can't go round houses yourself, Bobbi. You and I'll do it together.'

'Splendid!' Julia cheered up. 'And Sophia, perhaps you and I and Mrs Selkirk and Stephen can have cocktails after everyone has gone away?' She frowned. 'Perhaps I could ring Gregory. He could bring some of his friends like last year. He has very generous friends. For the charity.'

'Yes,' I said. 'We can count the money and celebrate afterwards with your cocktails.'

'Pity there's to be no cakes,' said Bobbi. Her glance strayed across to the counter where the policemen were queuing to pay. 'Perhaps I'll talk to Rina about it.'

Julia looked at her thoughtfully. 'And is your father still on his travels, dear?'

Bobbi glanced at me. 'He's still away. But he'll be back soon, I'm sure.'

'Good. I'm sure you must miss him. My own dear father died when I was ten... Oh, I'm sorry,

254

dear. How tactless I am.'

Bobbi smiled too brightly. "'S all right, Miss Soper. I'm cool. He's away, is all.' On cue, her telephone rang.

'Sparrow!' She glanced across at us and walked away behind the counter into the narrow vestibule that led to the kitchen. After a few minutes she came back, her face unusually closed off.

'My dad's quite all right: she said. 'Fine.' She looked at me defiantly. 'He wanted a word with you but I said you weren't here.' My bright confident Bobbi had melted away.

'Bobbi!' I scrabbled for my purse.

She stood up, slinging her schoolbag on her shoulder. 'I'm going home,' she said, and charged off.

Julia stood up. 'I'll go too,' she murmured. 'Watchful eye and all that.'

I stood in the queue, waiting to pay and feeling guilty. I thought I knew Bobbi by now. She was a lesson to us all in sturdy self-reliance. But here she was being the ten-year-old she really was, missing her father and feeling isolated in the middle of all of us who were getting on with our own lives. Selfish people like me. What had I been thinking of? I should go to the police and officially get Sparrow listed as missing. I should tell the social services about Bobbi. What planet had I been living on, all these weeks?

I'd just made up my mind to do that when my phone rang. I went into the vestibule to answer. Of course it was Sparrow.

'That you, Sophia?' he drawled.

'You know it is. You rang my number.'

255

'Where are you?'

'At Mehmet's.'

'Bobbi said you weren't there.'

'Well, I was. She said that because she was mad at you or me. Or sad at herself...'

'Are you angry with me, Sophia?' His tone was quiet.

'You bet I am. Your daughter's just rushed off because she can't say how sad and bereft she really feels. You have her thinking she's twenty-five years old, not ten. I'm here between the devil and the deep blue sea thinking the sensible thing is to inform the police you are missing, and that a child has been left alone and perhaps the social services should know.'

There was a prickling silence at the other end of the phone. Then: 'Now listen, Sophia.' His tone was no longer warm and drawling. It was cold and clipped. 'You mustn't do those things. They'll put Bobbi in danger and me in jeopardy. Police, social services – some people there get paid for information. They're not all lily white. And if Olly's bosses have got Bobbi they've got me. Any institution by its very nature is as leaky as a sieve. I need just a few more days, Sophia.'

'How do I know?' I almost wailed the words. 'How do I know you're not a crazy paranoid chancer? Stringing me along. Stringing Bobbi along...'

Another chilly silence. Then a very deep sigh. 'Ask Stevie. Does he say I'm that? And you've met me. Do you really, really think I don't have Bobbi's best interests at heart? She chose you. I trust you. I had to leave her there at the house. They know about Elsie down in Aldeburgh. She's had a visit. A very polite one, but she was visited. That's why I went to see her, to see she was OK. I couldn't leave Bobbi there, could I? She is safest at the flat – which they don't know about – and with you and Stevie. My judgement call.'

I hesitated. 'But she was so unhappy just now, after she talked to you, Sparrow. I think it all came in on her. It's not a game any longer.'

'It was never a game, Sophia. Now, this urge for the police and the social to get involved – are you really gonna heave us all overboard or are you on for the voyage?'

I sighed. 'How can I heave you or Bobbi overboard?'

'So we up-anchor and row onwards?'

'All that.'

'Great.'

'You must keep ringing her, Sparrow. Morning, noon and night. She needs reassurance.'

'She's not the only one.'

When I got to the flat Bobbi was at the big dining table with printed pages and images spread out before her, scissors in hand.

I looked over her shoulder. 'What's this?'

She glanced up at me, her gaze neutral. 'Medieval village. Lords, freemen and peasants. I'm trying to represent it all graphically on one sheet.'

I squeezed her shoulder. 'You're such a clever girl, Bobbi.'

She reached backwards and put her hand on mine. 'You too, Sophia.' She nodded towards the window. 'Now you can signal to Miss Soper that I'm safe and sound. She's been there at her

257

window since I got in.'

I went to the window and looked at the house opposite. Julia was standing there in the gap between the curtains. I waved and she waved back and set about closing her curtains.

'You'll come and stay again at mine tonight, Bobbi?' I said.

She was already shaking her head. 'No, I'm staying here now, till he gets back. If I stay here he'll be safe.'

We all do that, make bargains with the cosmos: irrational, nonsensical bargains calling up some kind of magic to sway the balance of probability in our direction. I did that when I made that last ride to Drina's house: if – *if* she was all right then I'd never feel sorry for myself about my own lost baby or Malcolm's iniquities ever again.

Well, *that* hadn't worked.

'You're probably right,' I said. 'Why not stay here?'

She started to cut around another figure, avoiding my eyes. 'And you can stay here if you want.'

I looked round. 'Are you using your computer?'

She shook her head. 'Enough here to cut and paste all night. A non-technological task.'

'Can I use it?'

She paused. 'Sparrow's laptop is beside his bed. It's a very good one. He'd want you to use that.'

That sounded like another bargain. If someone was using Sparrow's laptop then he will be safe. Cosmically speaking.

'Yeah,' I said casually. 'Good idea. Then I can work here with you? I'll need to go and get my yellow book. Will you be all right?'

She turned and looked at me then, her round eyes very bright, but red-rimmed with recent tears. 'I'm always all right, Sophia. You know it and I know it.'

So Bobbi and I spent the evening in her dining room, she cutting and pasting and creating life in the Middle Ages, me labouring away, transcribing my scribbles into something like decent prose on Sparrow's laptop. In that companionable, clicking silence I became absorbed in my task, transfixed by the energy and life singing towards me from the yellow book, wondering how I'd managed to write all this stuff down: stuff that said something to me, but stuff that other people would relish.

Then finally, at ten thirty, Bobbi made her end of the table neat. 'I'll leave it now. Only a bit more work to do. D'you want tea or milk or anything?' She looked round. 'Where will you sleep? In my dad's bed?'

I was already shaking my head. That would be a bed too far. 'I brought my sleeping bag. I'll bunk down on the long couch.'

'Right.' She came and put her hand on my arm. 'I'm glad you're here, Sophia. Really glad.'

I looked at her steadily. 'It's a pleasure, Bobbi.'

Listening to the whirr of her toothbrush, then the zwing of strange music in her bedroom, I looked at the words on the screen. That was it. I couldn't do any more now. Perhaps tomorrow. No, tomorrow was carpet day, and tomorrow was Stephen Copeland. I followed Bobbi into the

259

bathroom and cleaned my teeth. Then I stripped off, put on my Snoopy T-shirt and crawled into my sleeping bag.

My phone rang. I crawled out of my sleeping bag. 'Yes?'

Stephen: 'Where are you? I called at your house and all was dark. I rang the bell.'

'You're not turning into one of those house stalkers, are you?'

Stephen laughed. 'I just wanted to be sure you were ready for this big carpet peel tomorrow. When do you want to start?'

'Would ten do?'

'Ten would be fine. I'll be there.' I yawned.

'Where are you now?'

'In Bobbi's flat. I'm staying.'

He laughed. 'Then I'm only ten feet above you. D'you fancy a nightcap? Come up.'

I hesitated. 'I don't think so, Stephen. Bobbi's suddenly and uncharacteristically in a bit of a state about Sparrow. I can't leave her.'

'I could come down.'

It was so tempting. I looked down at my Snoopy T-shirt. 'Er, still no. Sorry. I just need to concentrate on Bobbi tonight.'

'Right. See you tomorrow at ten then.' The phone clicked.

I stared at it, disappointed. Snoopy or no Snoopy, it would have been nice had he tried to persuade me to go upstairs for a drink. Or even tried harder to inveigle himself down here for a chat. Even if it had just been about carpets and floors.

Dearest darling Chris,

I was on guard duty today. I told you Sophia was watching the child Bobbi, who seems to be too much on her own, didn't I? Well, the child got herself a bit upset and I felt obliged to track her home and watch her until Sophia was back with her and safe. She's really a very nice child, Chris, and behaving wonderfully, considering.

My mind is in a whirl these days. Getting to know Sophia has been like adding myself to a row of pearls, every one connected. Me then Sophia, then Stephen, then the child and her absent father, then the glittering Laura. Strange really.

Did I tell you I got Mr McAdams to write in my will that, Laura should have my clothes? Clothes are her thing and she seems to put some value on them.

That reminds me. I came across the silver locket you gave me, down behind your cuff-link drawer. I am wearing it now. We look so young in those photos. You're so glamorous in black-and-white. Me, younger even than Sophia is now. I wept for my young self, Chris. I mourned her, that young Julia.

Did I tell you Pusscat is sulking? He is jealous of you, I think. As you are ever more present, my love.

More and more,
Your Julia xxxx

Making Changes

At eight o'clock the next morning I left Bobbi in bed and went along to the Lavender House to clear the floors as far as I could, so the carpets could be ripped up with as much ease as possible.

Julia came at nine thirty and, cigarette in hand, surveyed the yard. 'Not a lot of space here to dump things, dear,' she said. 'Perhaps I should take the plants out altogether for you. They really hate dust, you know, poor things.'

I looked at our careful arrangement: the artfully placed plants and the climbers pegged back to the wall, and shook my head. 'Just too elaborate, Julia. Too much trouble. Let's see what we can do with them where they are. You just keep an eye on them.'

When Stephen came on the dot often o'clock, in neat overalls and complete with canvas tool-bag, I was struck by the uncharitable thought that he might be just too perfect.

Julia eyed him quite severely. 'Sophia and I are worried about the plants in the yard, Stevie. They will not take kindly to being covered by dusty carpets.'

He grinned. 'Won't happen, Miss Soper. We'll put them out the front, then load them into my boot and I'll take them straight to the tip.'

Her face broke into a beam. 'Splendid. They will be pleased.'

He frowned. 'Pleased?'

'The plants. They don't like house dust. They scream at dust.'

He stared at her. 'Well, it's a good job we're taking the carpets straight away, isn't it?' he said.

In the bedrooms Stephen and I worked together quite well, shifting big furniture, hauling dusty carpets and ripping up the old figured linoleum underneath. This had not been lifted in years and there was a lot of compacted dust that started to rise into the air. I had an attack of sneezing and he rooted in his toolbag and brought out two brand-new masks.

'Here, Sophia, wear this. This dust could be toxic. Never know what's been here.'

Julia came up and leaned on the door jamb, watching us. 'You two look like robbers.' Then she gazed at the floor and her face stained with colour. 'That lino was very good, in its day,' she said.

I looked up at her. 'It's coming back in, is lino. You ask Laura, queen of style.'

'Nice girl, Laura,' she said, her face back to normal.

Stephen sat back on his heels. 'These girls from the North,' he said. 'Pure gold.'

She nodded, then drifted away.

So we worked on, me rolling carpets that he had lifted, he using a very dinky claw hammer to lift loose nails. When we finished the back bedroom he stood up by the window, stretching his back. He took off his mask.

'Here,' he said. 'Look at this.'

Down in the yard Julia was sitting on one of the wire chairs illuminated by a ray of sunshine, smoking a cigarette. Pusscat was coiled round her neck like a fox fur.

I took off my mask. 'Oh, good, Pusscat's back. He must have forgiven her.'

'What?'

I explained about Pusscat's desertion. How he stopped speaking to Julia. Or the other way round.

'That is a very unusual woman.'

'Back home we'd call her "a one-off". Unique. Original,' I explained.

'Bit like you?' he said.'

I was saved from answering by the sound of someone – Bobbi, of course – clambering up the stairs over the rolled carpets. When she saw us she burst out laughing. 'You look like you blacked up. Like those stupid show people.'

A glance at the mirror showed this dust-black face with a white mask round the mouth. 'Ugh!' I said, trying to rub the dirt off.

Stephen grinned, his white teeth showing very white. 'You're making it worse.' He looked round. 'Floor should be all right,' he said, stubbing his toe on it. 'Pine. Well dried. Hundred years old, perhaps more.'

Then Bobbi and I were left to sweep out the rooms while he hauled the carpets downstairs and out into the boot of his Volvo.

Bobbi crouched down to hold the dustpan as I – mask back in place – swept up the last of the dust.

She smiled up at me. 'My dad rang. He said it won't be long before he gets back. And he'll ring me morning-noon-and-night and I am to do everything you say.'

'Good. He will be back soon, you know. You

264

mustn't worry.'

'And I telephoned Mrs Selkirk.'

'Did you, now? Why'd you do that?'

'I told her we needed some biscuits for Miss Soper's garden thing. She was very excited. Said she's coming back straight away.'

'And Mr Selkirk?'

'She says he's got a caravan and is looking for sites where they burned witches. "My dear, he's blind to me. The man's unbearable." That's what she said.' The mimicry was eerie. Bobbi got the accent just right. 'So she's coming home today, or tomorrow,' she finished. 'My house is not the same without Mrs Selkirk.'

I took the dustpan from her. 'You're a funny one, Bobbi. You seem to get things just the way you want them.'

She shrugged. 'I thought everybody did that. But then I didn't want my dad to vanish, did I?'

Then there was a clatter at the door and up came Laura, a scarf round her lovely hair, all kitted up to help. She and I, assisted by Bobbi, got the living-room carpet up before Stephen got back at three o'clock, complaining of the queue at the tip.

'So many people with so much stuff. Before long London'll be just one great tip.' He slung a plastic carrier bag on to the table. 'But I brought fish and chips from Islington as a reward for our morning's labour.' He glanced around at Laura and Bobbi, and Julia just coming into the kitchen end from the back yard. 'I only brought three portions. Imagine there'll be enough to share.'

We spread the lot on clean newspaper in the coffee table and all dipped in. I was surprised at my own hunger, then remembered I'd had no breakfast.

Julia, chewing quite loudly, held up a chip. 'This is the first time I've had fish and chips since the day Nixon resigned,' she announced. 'Chris and I ate them on the way home and when we got in Mother had her television on. All that business after Watergate. Remember?'

We nodded vaguely but Bobbi said she knew all about it because they had done it in History at school. It was really History, wasn't it? If I didn't know her better I'd think she was a show-off. But I did know her and she was not. She just said the first thing that came to her head and that thing was usually clever. Or surprising.

After our fish teas we cleared away and Stephen surveyed the floor. 'Should be all right. Bit patchy here and there but no painted border now.' He looked at me. 'We could call it a day, Sophia. I've arranged to pick up the sander at noon tomorrow. We'll get rid of all these nails and things in the morning. So we can start sanding upstairs tomorrow. Then down here on Monday.'

'Sounds OK to me.'

'Right. I'll need at least three showers to get rid of all this dust.'

'I'll come with you,' said Bobbi. 'I need a shower. And I want to finish my project.'

Julia stood up. 'And I need to go home and feed Pusscat. He's coming round but he's still quite snooty. I'm afraid he might be feeling quite neglected again.'

Stephen looked at me. 'I'll pick you and Bobbi up tonight at seven,' he said. 'Did you remember?'

Bobbi looked from him to me. 'Where are we going?'

'A barbecue,' I said. 'To Stephen's friends Emily and Jerry.'

'You didn't ask me about that.' She glared at me.

'I forgot. I thought you wouldn't want to be left alone. Anyway, I'm asking you now. Would you like to go to a barbecue with me and Stephen?'

She grinned. 'Yeah. Cool.'

After those two had gone the house felt empty and hollow. The big room, bereft now of its carpet (tatty though that was), seemed unoccupied.

'Poor house,' I said.

'Darkness before dawn, darling,' said Laura. 'Just think of it with nice shiny stripped floors. It will be so chic.'

'I'm sure you mean shabby-chic.'

'That's it, darling. Your signature style. Now then, can I have a shower, borrow some of your clothes and feel normal? Then we can go out to a clean place with clean floors for a drink and you can tell me why Jack Molloy is so keen to get hold of you.'

'He got hold of me.'

'Tell!'

'I'll do that when we are both clean and sitting in a pub with clean floors.'

Later, in the Fox, it was nice to spend time with Laura, to get a window on the world outside Barrington Street. She talked more than I did but her talk was balm. She was thrilled about Jack's offer to show my work to this agent, and was impressed that I was getting down to it. She was intrigued by

267

the presence of Stephen and wondered whether we were an item.

'He's a bit of all right, that Stephen. And going to a barbecue *en famille*. How cute. How domestic!'

'Aargh. Cute! And we are *not* an item. Absolutely not. He and I are just keeping an eye on Bobbi.'

She glanced at me from under her long black eyelashes, suddenly serious. 'That's a relief. Because I think he's gorgeous. One glance from him and I'm weak at the knees. I fancy making a play there myself.'

I shrugged to cover my surprise. 'Be my guest, love. Go ahead,' I said airily. 'As I say. No item, we.'

But even as I said that I wondered whether I meant it. Whether it was too soon to say this, and whether here I was, cutting my nose off to spite my face.

Then I had a vision of Sparrow Marsh leaning back on his chair in the café, and I was cool about Laura and Stephen. Couldn't happen to two nicer people.

Dear Chris,

I helped with Sophia's house today. We ate fish and chips out of paper! Mother would have been scandalised. They cleared the floor down to that red lino and then ripped even that up. The house is beginning to return to itself. It will be charming when it's done. I have to say at present it is somewhat chaotic. Sophia and Stephen are going out tonight to a barbecue and taking the child. Isn't that nice? Barbecues are where they eat outside. A kind of hot picnic. I don't think we ever went to a barbecue. It always seemed so much colder then.

Oh, I think Puss is coming round a bit. He let me stroke him today and followed me to Sophia's. He is a jealous thing but he is very precious to me. But after all, one has to admit he is a cat, not a person.

See you soon.
Love,
Julia xxxx

The Paragon

Bobbi made three changes of clothes before she felt ready to grace us and Emily's barbecue with her presence. She ended up in jeans, a white cropped top, and shoes with sparkly straps that matched her earrings. She topped this with her school parka and announced she was ready. Stephen curiously echoed her style with jeans and a white T-shirt, which he topped with a battered fawn linen jacket. I wore calf-length green pants and a mint-green blouse with bone buttons. And I put my hair in bunches.

'You look like some kid from school,' commented Bobbi.

'I'm sorry.'

'No,' she said kindly. 'It's all right.'

It didn't take us long to get to the Sillitoes' bulky terraced house in Islington. The house sat straight on to the street but was immaculately painted and pointed, and was obviously a house of some consequence.

Jerry came to the door in chinos and an open-necked shirt. His eyes twinkling welcome, he shook hands gravely with Bobbi and ushered us right through the house, up steps to a long roof terrace facing out over a tree-lined garden. A long table, covered with a cloth in Provencal blue, was laid with cutlery and lit by candles only half-visible because it was still really light. A dozen or so people were standing around talking. Two men were walking arm in arm at the bottom of the garden among the trees.

Emily came to greet us, dressed in a long inky-green dress caught up under her bosom, that neither accentuated nor concealed her considerable bump. I thought of the months following my abortion, when I seemed to see a million plump, flowering women like this. They were on every corner. These women seem to haunt me.

'Sophia!' Emily touched her cheek to mine. 'You look just too, too young. And Stephen!' She kissed him lightly on the lips. 'And you've brought me another guest!' Her eye dropped to Bobbi. She glanced at me. 'What a pretty girl. Is this your daughter, Sophia?'

For a second I was struck dumb.

'I'm Bobbi Marsh. I'm Sophia's ward.' Bobbi shook Emily firmly by the hand. 'I'm her responsibility.'

Emily glanced from me to Stephen to Bobbi, then grinned warmly 'Hello, Bobbi Marsh,' she said. 'Would you like to find something to eat? We have some bits and pieces over here.' She glanced at the hovering Jerry. 'Jerry's dealing with the heavy-duty stuff on the barbecue.' She took Bobbi's hand. 'I hope you are hungry,' she said as she led her off.

A young woman with a ponytail was already at our elbow with a tray of champagne in those round-bowled sixties champagne glasses.

'I'll leave you two to enjoy yourselves.' Jerry gave a military salute to his wife's departing back and made his way across to the barbecue, an elaborate affair built against a wall. A young black man in a chef's hat was already there, expertly turning meat and shuffling around things in silver foil. Jerry was obviously more supervisor than chef.

Stephen sipped his champagne. 'Like a well-oiled machine. Everything around Em works like clockwork. Even a barbecue.'

Despite the fact that I had mentally handed Stephen over to Laura I couldn't stand all this adulation.

'I met Sparrow, you know,' I said. 'I actually met him.'

He choked on his champagne. 'You what?'

'I met Sparrow the other day, in Clissold Park. We had coffee.'

He stood there in silence. Then, 'I don't know if that was wise, Sophia. He didn't want to be around. That was the point.'

'And of course he has to be in charge of everything, hasn't he?'

'I trust him. I always have. He's a fine bloke. And his is a complicated life, but I trust him.'

'I think he likes you too. But do you always do

what he says?'

'Something this elaborate has never been asked of me before. But I do trust him. Something serious is obviously up. So, how did you get to see him?'

'We talked on the phone. I told him I was going to get the social services in. I suppose this got him worrying, so we met.'

'And what happened?'

'He convinced me I shouldn't let the cat out of the bag to the authorities. Or Bobbi.'

'Well, now he's got you doing what he wants. Can't see the difference myself.' He drank off his champagne in one. Then Jerry was bearing down on us again, an open bottle of beer in each hand. 'Here, Steve. Thought you'd like a bit of the real stuff.' He glanced round. 'No need to stand around like lemons.' He led the way to an elegant arbour halfway down the garden, built of some shiny granite, made less chilly with striped cushions.

Jerry settled down opposite me. 'Now then, Miss Sophia. I've been talking to this friend of mine. What he said makes me wonder now just how you have got mixed up with Sparrow Marsh.'

I looked across to where Bobbi was spearing seafood, talking animatedly to Emily 'I thought I said. It was Bobbi. She kind of fell in my lap. She's his daughter and she's kind of adopted me.'

He nodded. 'Ah. Right. Yes. I remember.' He paused. 'Well, my friend gave me the say-so to tell you a few things, in absolute confidence. Only fair, and it might guide your hand. George – a.k.a. Sparrow – Marsh has been working in deep for quite some time...'

'So he *is* a policeman himself?'

Jerry nodded again. 'Poor chap. Almost too useful. Ethnically right. Streetwise. Highly intelligent. But now he's blown and I have to tell you these people can be very nasty So he's been ducking out of sight until they make this string of arrests they've been planning for two years. Two of those people to be arrested are actually in the force.'

'So. It's nearly over?'

'On the cusp, love.' He coughed. 'To be very honest I got to talk to Sparrow on the phone. A fine man. His boss started out with me as a kid, so I had a bit of leeway. But this is completely confidential, love. You've gotta sit tight and stay mum. It's imperative.'

'You were told to stop me blowing it any further?' I said.

'Exactly.'

At that moment Bobbi came running up, a bowl of olives in her hand. 'Emily says would you like an olive and can you come out of this hidey-hole and mingle?' She turned to Jerry. 'And she said would you get off your arse and get back to supervise the barbecue? Nearly ready for serving.'

He glanced at me. 'I apologise for my wife's language. She has this terrible influence on everyone she comes into contact with. Even children. God help our sprog.'

Stephen grinned. 'Hear, hear.'

We followed Bobbi up the steps to the table where the candles were now glittering like fireflies in the early evening dusk. I relaxed and began to enjoy an interesting evening. I found

273

myself beside a young man with a shock of red hair, a plumber who worked on Emily's projects. He told me that Emily was a diamond, that there was never a better time to be a plumber and that his mother was Irish and his father Bangladeshi. 'My mum,' he said, 'makes the best curry in the Northern Hemisphere.'

The woman on the other side of me, grey hair and middle-aged, turned out to have been at school with Emily. She taught art at some North London comprehensive. 'It has its rewards, you may be surprised to hear.' Her partner – she nodded at a small fair woman opposite – was a garden designer. 'She's a good designer, though I say it myself. Bound to be biased, of course. Emily fixes her up with some work from time to time, for which we are both eternally grateful.'

Just when I didn't know how much more of Emily's sainthood I could stand, I was rescued by Bobbi, who came to stand quietly by my chair. I glanced at my watch and then across at Stephen, who was sitting (of course) between Emily and another striking woman who was something to do with their office. I mimed looking at my watch and he stood up. Jerry and Emily stood up with him.

'We have to go, Em,' said Stephen. 'Past Bobbi's bedtime and we have to be up early tomorrow because we're stripping floors.'

Jerry clapped him on the back. 'As long as that's all you're stripping, old lad.'

'Jerry! For God's sake.' Emily rolled her eyes. 'Sorry, Sophia. You can take the man out of the police but you can't take the police canteen out of the man.'

She walked us through the house to the front door, her arm through mine. 'Great to see you, Sophia. And Bobbi. She's a stunner, isn't she?'

At the door she said, 'I'm going into purdah now till after the sprog emerges. But after that we must get together again. All of us.' She kissed my cheek, Stephen's lips, and hugged Bobbi in one swirling movement.

In the car Bobbi announced, 'D'you know what, Sophia? When she hugged me I could feel that baby move. How weird is that!'

Then, there in the dark, travelling through North London, the tears started pouring down my face. I couldn't check them because if I did Bobbi and Stephen would know how much I'd been upset tonight by the paragon Emily, whom even I liked, despite the fact that she lived this dream life and had a living, moving baby inside her and still could pull Stephen Copeland to her side with a mere click of the fingers, the touch of lip on lip.

Later, when Bobbi was in bed, I was on the long sofa when the tears started again. Then, when my mobile rang, I just let it ring and ring. I knew it would be Stephen with an offer of midnight cocoa or even something more exotic. The last thing I wanted to do, tonight, was talk to him clogged up with tears, jealous of Emily and mourning what might have been.

Dear Chris,
It is the middle of the night and I have just had a dream. In my dream I saw Sophia, Stephen and Bobbi going out to their barbecue. But when they had

gone I realised that Sophia had not taken her shoes and I ran, ran through the streets with her shoes in my hand, saying you must wear them, you must wear them. Then there was a bus with bright headlights and I don't know whether it knocked her down or me down. It was a relief to wake up, I can tell you.

And it is a relief now to be sitting here and writing to you.

Good night, my darling.
Julia xxx

The Barter

The next day it rained that steady pole-straight downpour that creeps into every crevice. If the rain had come the day before it would have ruined Emily's barbecue. But of course it didn't. Stephen turned up at ten thirty with a handsome blond man from Crakow, who was clutching a sanding machine draped in a tarpaulin. The two men stood there in the doorway with rain on their eyelashes.

I opened the door wider and they walked in past me and seemed to fill the whole room, the whole house.

'This is Bolek, Sophia. He's our man,' said Stephen. 'He's a wonder with wood. Bolek, this is my friend Sophia.'

I stood helplessly as Bolek put down the machine, clicked his heels and bent over my hand. Then he lifted the heavy machine upstairs as

276

though it weighed an ounce.

'I can't afford this: I said fiercely to Stephen. 'I thought we could do it ourselves, that you–'

'I would have, I promise you. But I had this inspiration. Last year, when he first started out, I drew up some extension plans for Bolek and guided him through the planning system. It was his first job and he's been going on at me ever since to do something in return.'

This touched a chord. 'The Barter!' I said.

'The what?'

I told him about Big Emma and the scheme she set up on the New Dawn. 'They bartered skills. You know, painting for plastering, sewing for gardening, joinering for scribing. There was a board in the community room called the Barter Board. They had the precise currency off to a T. The dole people were not happy, I can tell you.'

He grinned. 'Sounds great.'

'But now I'll have to think of something I can do for Bolek in return. It's a kind of chain, you see. That's the only way it works. You discharge the debt by pushing the favour on.'

Upstairs the machine started and roared through the little house like a fury. Stephen put his hands over his ears. 'You should make yourself scarce,' he shouted. 'About three hours.' He picked up his mask. 'Really, Sophia! Go.'

As he vanished upstairs I stood there on the wet floor feeling redundant. Then I stuffed the yellow book into my bag, picked up my umbrella and went along to Mehmet's. There, over three hours and five caffé lattes, I wrote a story about this social worker who visits this woman in prison, a woman she's been instrumental in putting behind bars.

This is what I really did, of course. I couldn't do it while I was still employed so I waited until after I'd resigned to go and see Mrs Parnaby. Sitting there across the table in the visitors' room, she looked different from the monster I'd built up in my head since she'd been sentenced. And she looked entirely different from the real woman who had stood so defiantly in her elegant black Next suit in court. This woman was pale and shrunken. Her face was smooth and waxen like those of the women on the New Dawn who could only face the days tanked up with tranquillisers.

She frowned at me. 'What are you doing here?'

'I want to ask you why, Mrs Parnaby. Why you were part of the thing that happened to Drina.'

She frowned and looked around the room at the other inmates and visitors. 'They put on their make-up, you know, get dolled up, at visiting time,' she said in a tinny, blank voice. Then slowly, as though she were dragging the words up from a deep well, she said, 'I've told them about it a thousand times but they won't listen. I had this beautiful daughter. She was perfect. Very bright. Such dainty hands.' Her voice became mechanical, singsong. Of course, she had told the tale a thousand times. 'Then when she was four I took her to the nursery school. But at the end of that day the girl they brought to me was not my Drina. She had such dirty hands and the way she looked at you! Wild! Horrible. A changeling. A wild changeling. I tried. I tried to change her, to bring my Andrina back. Darren was very supportive.'

She looked up at me, her eyes gleaming with tears. 'D'you know he sends letters to me every week? He writes me poems. Such lovely poems.' She looked down at her wrist, and started to pull at her sleeve. 'It was no good. The wild thing stayed and my Andrina had gone for ever.'

I had to stand up then, and make for the door. Her plaintive voice followed me. 'You're just like the rest of them. You won't listen. You won't listen.'

The first thing I heard when I got back to my house was the sound of laughter upstairs. Then Bolek came downstairs carrying the machine and behind him, carrying a green plastic sack of sawdust, was Laura. The two of them were covered in a veil of fine dust.

As he lifted the machine into the kitchen Laura, looking peculiarly white, grinned. 'Where were you, Sofe? Skiving?'

'I was sent away to play.'

'I came to give you a hand and...' she nodded towards Bolek, 'came upon this heavenly creature.'

'I bet you did.'

Stephen came downstairs with a dustpan and the long brush over his shoulder like a halberd.

'Anyway, pet,' said Laura, 'we're gonna wash off the dust and go along to the White Hart to have a pint and get it out of our poor parched throats. You coming?'

I looked at Stephen, who was polishing the dust from his glasses with a snow-white handkerchief. 'I don't think so. I ... I've got some stuff to type up.' I was being perverse, of course. I would have loved to go with them for a drink. I was jealous, I suppose. But I was not sure whether I was jealous of Laura for taking over, or jealous that Stephen was having a good time in my house without me.

'And I need to go and see Julia. There was this idea that we might get Mehmet to provide some cakes for her garden day.' I remembered Bobbi's suggestion as I spoke the words. Really it was just a good excuse to sidestep the session in the pub. But now I thought it was not a bad idea.

The three of them washed and hovered, ready to go.

Stephen looked at me. 'I've got you your "handing-on barter".'

'So what might that be?'

'You can teach Bolek's little brother English.'

'English?' I glanced across at Bolek, who was eyeing me sharply.

'He's clever, clever at home.' Bolek's deep voice resonated across the space. 'But English?' He shrugged. 'Only seven weeks now in school. He struggles.'

'How old is he?' I was looking for an excuse.

'Eleven years.' His blue eyes pierced mine. 'But he will learn with you very quick. And when he grows he is to be an architect like Stephen.'

I hesitated.

Bolek looked down at the bare floor. 'I do a very good job for you here. In your house.'

I put my hand on his arm. 'Of course I will. I'll try. But I'm no teacher.'

'Thank you.' He picked up the hand and kissed it. Behind him I could see Laura almost salivating.

As I shut the door behind them I wondered

what was this thing about me and children. All my life they were drawn to me like iron filings to a magnet. When I was quite young I was always recruited to mind children in my grandmother's street. The mothers would come and ask me to take their babies for a walk in their buggies. The children would knock at my door for me to come out to play. That was why, when I started social work, childcare seemed to be the obvious focus. For a time it seemed as though I might be good at it.

And now it was happening again. Now I had Bobbi sticking to me like glue, and here I was making a long-term commitment to a Polish boy I didn't even know.

The mystery, of course, was how could such a woman, a woman who drew children to her like iron filings, allow one child in her care to die a horrible death, and how could this same woman get rid of her own baby like some kind of waste product? How could I have done all that if I was so 'good with children'?

To stop the thoughts crowding in and drowning me I picked up my umbrella. I'd go to see Julia and tell her the Mehmet idea. And if she offered me a cocktail I wouldn't turn her down.

When I got there she was already drinking cocktails. With Doreen Selkirk.

'Gordon Cocktail: gin, dry sherry, lime. I didn't sleep well so I needed a little cheer,' said Julia. 'I persuaded Mrs Selkirk to join me. Will you partake?' She started to pour some into the triangular glass without waiting for an answer. The cat glared down at us from the high Georgian dresser.

Doreen, sitting there like a glorious powder puff in a silver-green gilet of her own making, lifted her glass. 'Hello, Sophia. Are you well?'

The sour amalgam of grudge and guilt seeped away from me and I hugged her, taking in her faint scent of sweat overlaid by some rose perfume.

She disentangled herself. 'Whoa! Whoa! Are you feeling quite well, dear girl?'

'What're you doing here? I thought you were in deepest Suffolk with Roger!'

She groaned. 'Suffolk was fine until a certain person arrived and filled it with witches. I think he draws them to him.'

I thought about me drawing children in my wake.

'So where is he?' I took my drink from Julia.

'Still in the caravan, pretending it's a medieval hut. And he got a job in a bookshop, can you believe it? The bookseller took a fancy to him. I think she likes his accent. It can't be his good looks. Anyway, he handed me the cheque book and said I may as well run things here as he's self-sufficient there.'

'So you're back?'

'Well, I'm on a biscuit mission. Young Bobbi rang and said that Julia here needed biscuits. It was a message from on high. So I'm back.'

'Good thing too.' muttered Julia. She shuddered. 'The country! How could a person like the country?'

Doreen smiled her comfortable smile. 'And what've you been doing to Miss Soper, Sophia? I nearly didn't recognise her. Pure Rumpelstiltskin! I'll have to call Miss Soper Miss Stiltskin

282

from now on?'

'Better call me Julia,' said Julia placidly. 'Much better idea.' She turned to me. 'I see young Stephen was at your house this morning...'

'Doing a job,' I said hurriedly. 'Stripping the floors. He and his friend have gone off to the pub now. Laura's with them. She's been a great help.'

'And...' Doreen looked up at me, 'Bobbi tells me you've had two dates with him. Once at the Savoy–'

'She wore my Jean Muir dress,' interrupted Julia. 'It looked very well on her.'

'They weren't dates,' I said. 'They were, well, sort of comradely ... kind of friendly ... well ... things.'

'Watch it,' said Doreen. 'Don't let him pass you by. He's a nice man. Rather special, I think.'

'Do you love him, dear?' said Julia mildly.

My cheeks burned. Nobody but Julia, who did not live in the real, prevaricating world, could be as direct as that.

I muttered, 'No... I don't know... Not really that. Things are complicated.'

Doreen tried to get me off the hook by hanging me on the other one. 'And how's that fugitive father of young Bobbi?'

My cheeks, I know, went from pink to bright red. 'I ... we've heard from him,' I stuttered. 'I think he'll be back soon.'

She stared at me thoughtfully. 'Good thing too. You're very good with her, dear. But a child needs a parent.' She brightened. 'Did I tell you my Helena is coming to London? Three weeks in the summer. Her father and I talked.'

I began to cool down. 'That's good, Doreen. Very good.'

'Of course, Roger won't like the idea, poor soul, when he actually finds out. But what does he know, stuck down there in Suffolk with his witches and his bookseller?'

Then Julia put an LP of Sarah Vaughan on her record player, filled our glasses again and we listened to that diamond-pure voice in a rare companionable silence.

Doreen seemed more at ease now than any time I'd known her. The more I thought about it the more I realised that everything changes all the time. We are never the same person from one day to the next. Each encounter is a change point, each action a development. You think you remain the same but you do not. Even Julia was changing now, emerging from some weird forty-year chrysalis.

She caught my eye and raised her glass. I did the same. Then in a moment of deep inebriated insight it occurred to me that we are all change-makers for each other and that is a blessing for the human race.

Dear Chris,

That Selkirk woman is quite nice. Not at all like I thought she was in the old days when I saw her going to and from the house opposite. Both less pushy and more caring than I'd have thought She is making what she calls her special biscuits for my garden day and the Turkish café is giving me a tray of cakes they call baklava as well. Young Bobbi and Sophia have fixed that up as Bobbi and her (still missing) father are the friends of the man who has the shop, who's called Mehmet. More pearls on that string. I am suddenly blessed with my friends. And they are your friends too now. All of them.

All my love, darling Chris,

Julia xxxx

PS. Is it too vulgar for me to say how much I long for your body to be here, alongside mine? xxxxx

Viktor

The next day I said to Stephen that perhaps I should seal the bedroom floor while he and Bolek got on and stripped the downstairs. He shook his head. 'The dust rising from down here will ruin it. If you can make yourself scarce for three hours we'll finish down here.' He turned to Laura, who had been there since dawn and was now looking at Bolek from under those wonderful eyelashes. 'You too, Laura. It won't take three of us.'

She put out her bottom lip. 'Men!' she said.

He sighed. 'Don't get sulky on me, Laura. It's not a man thing. It's a skill thing. If it were about writing something you'd be telling me what to do. Give us three hours, then come back and help us prep the floors right through, and seal them.' He glanced at me.

I grabbed Laura's arm and marched her out of the house. 'Come on! Leave them in peace, will you? They're doing me a favour.'

285

Bobbi, when we got to the flat, was still in her pyjamas and deep into a chunky novel about Julius Caesar. She jumped up and asked Laura if she wanted some toast. Laura said no, but could she go on Bobbi's Internet to do a search?

So we spent the morning with Bobbi reading about Ancient Rome and Laura on the Internet looking up Crakow and reading articles about Poles flooding into England and becoming part of the tapestry of contemporary English life. I prowled around the flat and ended up reading one of Sparrow's books about the Maroon Wars against the British in Jamaica.

At eleven thirty Doreen turned up with a tray of biscuits that we had to road-test, in preparation for Julia's garden day. They were delicious and sweet, and somehow compensated for the rain that continued to stream steadily down the windows. At noon it finally stopped and the sun came out to burn the wet patches off the pavements. I got a text from Stephen. *'Done here. Pretty filthy. Yugh.'*

We heard their feet tramping on the stairs and then ten minutes later he and Bolek came back down, showered and changed, hair plastered down, looking like two schoolboys just off the sports field. I had my coat on ready to go home but Stephen said they had already put on the first coat of sealer everywhere except the kitchen and bathroom, where they had stacked the furniture. 'Needs leaving to harden till this time tomorrow,' he said.

'So I'm marooned?' I said. Jamaica, Maroons. Sparrow.

'Just till tomorrow.' He paused. 'Bolek thought we might go and get Viktor. To introduce him to you. Fix up some teaching. You know? The Barter?'

Laura stood up quickly. 'I'll come with you. I'm stir-crazy here.'

When they had gone the sharp-eared Bobbi, not quite immersed in Rome, announced, 'I know a Viktor. He's in the top class at my school. He's very tall.'

'It won't be him,' I said. 'Couldn't be.'

'It's him,' she whispered in my ear when they turned up half an hour later.

Victor was indeed tall for his age, and gangly, with white-blond hair in an old-fashioned crew-cut. He was in that spurt of growth peculiar to boys when his features were temporarily too big for his face. And he wore glasses: exactly the same kind of glasses as Stephen. When you saw Viktor you could see that Bolek hero-worshipped Stephen, right down to the choice of spectacles and career for his little brother.

Viktor bent over my hand in eerie imitation of Bolek, but his face flamed up and when he tried to say something he stuttered and fell silent. At the other side of the room Bobbi closed her book, rummaged in a drawer and produced a set of playing cards. She waved them under Viktor's nose. 'You play?' she said.

He smiled his relief and nodded vigorously. 'I play.' He followed her to the coffee table and watched carefully as she kneeled on the floor and dealt two hands. He kneeled down opposite her and turned his hand over, listening avidly while, with the help of the cards, she explained the English game of gin rummy.

It was both a shock and a relief to see Bobbi with another child. She was so self-sufficient and comfortable with adults that you forgot she was a child. Here she was having such a good time. With all her advantages she was clearly missing out on this.

Bolek was watching me watching them. 'So. Will you teach my little brother, Sophia?'

'Of course. As far as I can. I'll try.'

Laura, perched prettily on the end of the sofa, piped up, 'I've got something I need to leave for Julia but I thought after that we might go to the White Hart. It's nice in there, isn't it? Friendly.'

Stephen was already shaking his head. 'I've phone calls to make, Laura. Things to do.'

Thwarted, Laura frowned.

'That would be nice, Laura.' Bolek smiled at her, then glanced across at Viktor. 'I would like that, but...'

'Leave Viktor here,' I said. 'Me and Bobbi need to get to know Viktor. You go. Get the dust out of your throat.'

Bolek said something to Viktor and the boy nodded, shrugged, and looked back down at the cards in his hand.

Laura and Bolek vanished and Stephen stood in the doorway. 'I'm upstairs if you want me,' he said.

'That's fine,' I said. 'I'll make some kind of start here.'

I heard Stephen's feet stamp on the wooden stairs. He certainly seemed to be giving me space. I didn't know whether to be pleased or piqued about that. Having written him off as a mere friend in my head, I still, perversely, wanted him to feel more than friendly towards me.

I went across to the card-players. 'Can I play?'

Bobbi looked up at me. 'It *is* the Viktor from school, like I said,' she announced. 'He's only been here seven weeks and he's staying with that Bolek and a sister. His mum and dad and his other sister are at home in Crakow.'

I frowned. 'How d'you know that?'

'Viktor just told me,' she said. She dealt three hands and put the pack in the middle. 'Viktor first. He's new to this game.'

I played five hands with them before I cried off and left them to it. Viktor had won three out of the five games. As I went back to my book on the Maroons on Jamaica I thought I might just as well leave Viktor's tuition to Bobbi. After all, she was doing very well so far.

Dearest Chris,

That Laura came across from the Copeland house with a catalogue from a shop called Next. She said I could choose some things and she would get them for me and I could try them on and see if they are OK. I have chosen some pale grey linen trews and a pale grey silk blouse with embroidery. Then there is this white silk shawl. I think you'll like them. I thought they would do for the garden day. I am so looking forward to it.

I am going out dead-heading now, keeping everything up to scratch. So busy.

Love,

Julia and xxx

Shining Floors

On Monday, after seeing Bobbi off to school, Stephen and I walked along to my house to check the floors.

'One more coat should do it,' he said.

We found a paunchy, middle-aged man in a beret knocking on my door. 'They're not in,' he said, as we approached. 'I've been knocking for ages.' He had one of those safe voices: even, low-toned.

I took out my key. 'I'm in now,' I said.

Stephen surveyed the man from head to foot. 'D'you want something?'

The man smiled at me and took out a reporter's notebook, spiral bound. 'Well, I'm writing this book about the Pinder brothers, see? Doomed lives in dark times kind of thing. One chapter is a kind of survey of houses used by them in the 1960s. You know the kind of book – pictures and legends. Thinking of calling it *Parties, Imprisonment and Executions*. Or *The Executioners*. There's a market for these things today.' He pulled a digital camera out of his pocket. 'I already have some pretty decent exterior shots. I was hoping that, very kindly, you'd allow me to take some inside shots.'

Stephen moved so that their faces were inches apart and just touched the man's shoulder with his index finger. 'Not in a thousand years, mate. This is a private house. Leave it alone. Come

290

here again and I'll have some men in hard hats make mincemeat of you.'

The man took a step back and shook his shoulders as though to shake off the imprint of Stephen's finger.

I took a milder tone. 'Can I see your pictures of the outside? I've always thought my house was very photogenic.'

He took his gaze from Stephen and clicked on the viewer on his camera. The Lavender House was captured on his screen, everything condensed to even greater perfection. I took the camera from him to get a closer look. It was a perfect image. Against the clean rain-washed sky the pale lavender, with its white edging, looked cleaner and softer than it really was. The arched windows and neat white door gave it a look of the witch's house in *Hansel and Gretel*. A house of marzipan.

'So, what's the legend about this house then?' I said mildly

The man relaxed, encouraged by my interest. 'I thought you'd know. Word has it that this was one of their safe houses. Word has it that they salted people away here. People they wanted out of their way for a while. They kept them there. They even…' he caught Stephen's gaze. 'They kept them there.'

I clicked a button on the camera.

'Hey!'

Stephen grabbed him as he launched himself at me.

I pressed 'Delete' and one by one watched the images of the Lavender House vanish.

The man shook himself free of Stephen's grasp

and grabbed his camera from me. 'You can't do that!'

'I just did,' I said.

'You can't stop me taking a picture of a house from the street.'

'I have this time,' I said.

'I can take another any time,' he said.

'Not today,' said Stephen. 'Now, get lost, mate. Stop hanging round here.'

The man backed off and started to walk down the street, adopting a comical swagger to show us he didn't care.

As I opened the door I said, 'We'll never stop them taking those outside photos. But I won't let them in.'

'Vermin,' said Stephen briefly. 'Lowest of the low. Forget him.'

I wondered how I'd come to trust Stephen so completely. There had been no brothers in my life. No cousins. My grandfather, when he was alive, was fragile to the point of invisibility. I had no father, of course. There never was a father. My grandmother, till her sudden death, had been the strong one, the reliable one. Malcolm, with his furtive nature, had been the opposite of reliable. What on earth had I seen in him?

We went into the house. Inside, it smelled of toffee and tar. The downstairs room looked bigger, with the furniture piled higgledy-piggledy in the kitchen end. Shorn of its mealy heather-speckled carpet, the floor gleamed rather than glowed.

'I thought you'd like matt rather than gloss,' Stephen murmured. 'If I'd been doing it for Laura I'd have done it with gloss. This is old wood, strips wider than usual. Old as the house, I think. Lots of screws, mends and infills. You'd expect that in a house of this age.'

Here and there the wide boards had been replaced by narrower boards, fixed by countersunk nails now covered with the sealant.

'Bolek did a good job. He said it was a bit of a task here and there to get the level right.'

I realised that Stephen was looking at me anxiously, and started to smile. 'I think it's lovely, Stephen. It has made the whole house right for me. Mine now.'

He relaxed and we got down to work together, lifting the furniture back into its rightful place and rescuing the curtains from their plastic bags and rehanging them. By noon the whole house was transformed: the same as before but somehow very different. Now it really was mine.

Stephen's phone rang. It was Emily.

'Have to go, Sophia,' he said. 'One o'clock video conference with some people in Frankfurt. Said I'd be there.' He glanced around the room. 'All shipshape for you?'

'It's lovely.' At the door I kissed his cheek. 'Thank you. You've made such a difference.'

He looked at me, smiled faintly, even sadly, then left.

The sad look told me that he as well as I knew something had happened to us this morning. He knew and I knew that the unknown had gone out of our relationship. A kiss on the cheek did mean something. It meant we were now just friends. The best of friends. I suppose in every relationship there are points like forks in the road. You can go this way and you can go that way. One fork on the road we were on led to a passionate involvement. The other fork – the one I had stepped on with my kiss on his cheek – was about friendship, less passionate but perhaps more enduring. This morning I had cast him in the role of brother. We were now siblings, good friends, and always would be.

Today he had given me the present of my shining floors. He had made my house my own. I had given him my hand in friendship. Or kissed his cheek in friendship. And that was all. In some ways it was a relief. It was the best road for him and me.

After he had gone I made myself a tall beaker of strong coffee, pulled my yellow book out of my bag, and sat down in front of my computer to transcribe. How wonderful to sit there in my room, now scraped clean of so many layers of its previous existence, to contemplate my stories so far and to mould and develop them into whole entities, separate from their inspiration on the New Dawn.

By three fifteen, when I was due to go to Mehmet's to meet Bobbi from school, I'd managed to transcribe all my new drafts. The book – at least as signified by these first chapters – was shaping up. Soon I'd have something to show. Only God and Jack Molloy knew whether it was any good. Perhaps I was deluded. Perhaps I would have to sign on, or get a job or something. My squirrelled resources would not stretch beyond the end of the year.

I sighed a deep sigh and stood up to stretch myself and look through at the rehung butterfly curtains. The man with the beret was back out there again, taking pictures with his digital camera.

Dear Chris,
    There are still men hanging round that little house of Sophia's. She calls them 'house stalkers'. I have started to worry about her and the little house. They sully it with their presence. They soil the memories I have. I hope Sophia is safe but I would not – could not – intrude by letting her know I worry. I suppose this is how any mother feels, no matter how old their children.
    All love, my darling,
    Julia xxx

Reincarnation

Bobbi isn't in Mehmet's. Rina says she was there earlier, with a boy, very blond with big teeth. 'But they had toast and went,' she says.

'Where? Where did they go?' My panic shows.

'She didn't say.' She flushes. I must be glaring at her. I take some deep breaths and calm down.

'We were busy. I just imagined she went home on her own.' She shrugs. 'She always did that before you came along.'

I touch her arm in apology. 'Sorry, Rina. I'm right off the mark. Keep an eye out for her, will you?'

I run out of the shop towards Barrington

Street, causing a car to shriek to a stop on the High Street. *I will not lose another child. I will not lose another one.* The words drum into the left side of my brain even while my right side is telling me, *Bobbi is not Drina. Bobbi is not Drina.* A split screen in my head.

They are not at the flat. They are not in my house. I run back on to the High Street and in and out of every shop. What before had been charming and colourful now seems threatening. The kind smiles, the genuine puzzlement of the shopkeepers seem false. They are different, after all. Not like me. They could all be in on it, bribed by Oliver Cowell and his mother.

I come to a halt again outside Mehmet's. Rina knocks on the window then comes outside to see me. 'My uncle was just saying he saw something. An old woman walked out with them.'

'What?' My blood freezes at the thought of Oliver's crone of a mother.

'You know that mad old one with the basket and the cat. The one with the kinky boots.'

I hug her, grabbing her hard in my relief. 'Oh. Oh. Thank you, Rina.'

She wriggles free, obviously thinking there is more than one mad woman in Barrington Street.

At Julia's house the cat glares at me from the windowsill. Bobbi answers the door, wreathed in smiles.

'Sophia! We're having punch!'

So they are, she and Viktor sitting side by side on the leggy sofa. 'Thees punch ees verry tasty,' says Viktor, beaming.

Both Bobbi and Julia clap their hands. 'Bravo!'

296

says Julia. 'Good English, Victor.'

I look from the rosy glasses to the rosy faces. 'Julia! You haven't...'

She smiles brightly. 'Just fruit juice, I swear to you.'

I continue to stare at her.

'Well, to be honest, there is a mere liqueur glass of vermouth in there. Just one.' Her smile fades as she examines my angry face. 'Sophia. We were having fun.'

Oh, what the hell. I pick up a glass. 'Can I have one?' Might as well test it.

It turns out to be too sweet and distinctly unalcoholic.

'These two have been wonderful,' says Julia firmly. 'I saw them in the café and recruited them as leafleteers. We have delivered eighty leaflets about my garden open day to selected house-holds.'

'How did you select them?' I am interested.

'Plants in front garden.' Viktor's voice is deep for a young boy

'No rubbish or detritus,' says Bobbi.

'What is detritus?' says Viktor.

'Rubbish. Throwaway stuff,' says Bobbi.

'De-trit-us.' He rolls it round his tongue. 'Is good word.'

'So we came back here for punch and tea-biscuits to recover from our travails,' says Julia proudly 'We were having a conversation.'

I glance at them, one to the other. 'What about?'

'Dying,' says Bobbi. 'I was telling Miss Soper about my mum being a humming bird on Jamaica. And how, if you live an innocent or virtuous life,

297

you become a beautiful thing after you die. If you live a guilty life you come back as something very low, like a worm. And people stand on you.'

'A delightful thought,' murmurs Julia.

'I don't know how accurate—' I begin.

'But Viktor doesn't agree,' says Bobbi. 'He believes in Heaven and angels with wings and all that and the Holy Father. He goes to church.' She makes it sound as though a church is a very weird place.

'Church is good,' puts in Viktor. 'Beautiful.' He sniffed through his large nose. 'Smells very nice.'

'What about you, Miss Soper?' says Bobbi. 'Where do you think we go when we die?'

'Well, we always went to church when I was your age, me and Mother. Hats, gloves, prayer-book in white leather. The whole shebang.'

'Yuargh! Hats,' says Bobbi.

'No need to be rude, Bobbi,' I say, on auto-matic pilot.

'So-ree!' Bobbi winks at Viktor, who screws up his face and tries, but fails, to wink back.

Julia ignores us. 'St Mary's. Morning eucharist or evensong. It was nice. We met people we knew. Chatted. Then Mother stopped going to church about the time the British invaded Suez in 1956. I don't know whether the two events were linked, but I do remember the coincidence.'

'But what about dying, Miss Soper?' says Bobbi, eagerly tracking her first idea.

'Well, like Viktor, I liked church. Beautiful place, nice dusty smells. And in those days I did think that we all went to a Heaven where angels sang in the realms of glory and little children sat by the knee of Jesus. I remember the text "Suffer little children to come unto me".'

'That's nice,' says Bobbi. 'All the children safe.'

I think about Drina and wish I believed all this. Then, ridiculously, I wonder if Drina has been reincarnated as Bobbi but realise my timescale is off. Then my thoughts push back into my own childhood, unfurnished as it was by any church- or chapel-led dreams. For my practical grand-mother 'the dead are dead meat, pet'. For herself she insisted on cremation: 'No hypocritical ser-vices, if you don't mind.'

'But what, Miss Soper,' pursues Bobbi, 'd'you think now?'

'Well, I don't know, dear. I tend to think of the living not the dead. Except for Mother, and she lives on in my mind.' She pursed her lips. 'I hadn't thought about it before, dear, but I'm rather taken by your idea of reincarnation. So nice to think of your mother humming away under blue skies.'

Bobbi looks around us all. 'So what would we like to be if we were reincarnated?' Her glance fixes on Viktor. 'You!'

He shakes his blond head. 'I tell you, Bobbi, I am an angel. I fly in Heaven. Flap! Flap!' He uses his long arms to demonstrate.

'You, Sophia!'

I've had a minute to prepare. 'I think I would like to be a wild horse, somewhere in the world where there are still wild horses.'

'And you, Miss Soper?'

'That's quite a thought, dear. I think I'd like to be a swan. On the river near here. Pusscat and I see them when we walk there. They look so peaceful, so beautiful.' She glances round. 'Where is he? He goes walkabout all the time these days.'

'He's keeping guard on your windowsill,' I say. 'I saw him as I came in.'

'Poor Pusscat. I thought he was feeling better but his nose is still clearly out of joint.'

'And now you, Bobbi,' Viktor's deep voice comes from beside me on the couch. 'What will you be?'

'Isn't it obvious?' says Bobbi. 'I'll be a humming bird with my mum under those blue skies. Then we can have a whole life together, humming birds side by side.'

Julia stares at her, her watery blue eyes very wide. 'D'you know, dear, if you believe it that hard, I believe it will come about.'

It's all getting too heavy for me so I stand up. 'I imagine you two have homework to do. Your brother must be wondering where you are, Viktor.'

He jumps up politely. 'I text him I am at Bobbi's,' he says. Led by her unerring instinct Bobbi does the unthinkable. She stands up and leans down to kiss Julia's cheek. 'You'll be this lovely swan, Miss Soper. I can see it. And Pusscat will be a baby swan, all dark and fluffy, paddling along beside you with his nose out of joint.'

Julia pats her absently on the arm and stands up to see us out. As she ushers us through the door the cat streaks past us into the house and she is already scolding him for his absence when she closes the door behind us.

On the opposite side of the road, Laura and Bolek are sitting shoulder to shoulder on Bobbi's wall, their heads close together. Bolek leaps to his feet and comes to shake my hand.

'Viktor is making great progress. Thank you, Sophia.'

'You can thank Bobbi for that.'

He shakes Bobbi's hand and she says gravely, 'He can say a lot in Polish but I'm afraid he doesn't know enough English yet. Can he stay and do his homework here with me?'

Bolek glances at his watch. 'We have a bus to catch. I'm sorry, Bobbi. It will be after seven when we get back.'

Viktor moves to stand by his brother. 'I come another night, Bobbi. Is late.'

She frowns, then nods and turns away to pull out her door key. 'See you tomorrow, then.'

Bolek shakes my hand again, then takes Laura's and bows over it, nearly kissing it. We watch the brothers saunter away and from the doorway Bobbi says, 'Are you going out with Bolek, then, Laura?'

Colour stains Laura's perfect cheeks. 'Not at all. We just met on the doorstep here. I came here in search of my friend Sophia.'

We go up to the flat and while Bobbi turns on her computer to start her homework, I make coffee and cheese sandwiches to mop up the effect of the punch.

Laura, leaning on the unit beside me, tells me she's the carrier of a message from Jack Molloy asking the whereabouts of his package. 'Something about striking while the iron's hot. And did you really want to get on in the writing trade or not? I said I was coming round here and would pick it up. It was just my good luck to bump into beautiful Bolester. That's his real name. Bolek is

301

his nickname.'

'D'you really fancy him?'

'Who couldn't? Have you got eyes? Let those that have eyes, see.' She picks up a piece of cheese and pops it into her mouth. 'But get involved? I don't know. Very intense, these Slavic types. And anyway...'

'Anyway, what?'

'Oh, nothing. Anyway, d'you have that stuff ready for Molloy? If you have I'll take it. Save you the postage.'

She is very insistent. I leave her and Bobbi eating the cheese sandwiches and go along to the Lavender House for my pages. I shuffle them together into an elastic band and sit down to rattle off some kind of explanation of what the whole book would, or might, end up as. Then I slip them into a Jiffy bag and scrawl Jack Molloy's name on it.

When I get back along to Barrington Street I find the two of them not in Bobbi's flat, but upstairs with Stephen, sprawled on his sofa and floor listening to some bhangra music on his perfect sound system.

He is sitting at the large table, ripping open his post. He beckons me to sit beside him and mouths in my ear, 'Bobbi invited Laura to come up and hear my sound system.'

'So I see,' I mouth back.

'I have some news,' he says.

'What's that?'

'It's Emily,' he grins widely. 'She only had the baby, practically on the boardroom floor.'

I can imagine the scene. All those suits in disarray.

The bhangra fades.

'It's a girl, eight pounds,' he says, his voice bellowing into the now silent room. 'They're calling her Stephanie. How about that?'

Dear Chris,

The days get more and more interesting here. I recruited the assistance of two children to help me with the leaflets for my garden day. One is the daughter of that man opposite, the one who is missing. My friend Sophia has virtually adopted her. She does keep her safe. I have the smallest suspicion that this is very satisfying for her after her dreadful experience with a little girl in Newcastle. The other child who helped today is gangly and very blond. Foreign, somewhere in Eastern Europe, I think. Poland. Wasn't that where your mother came from? There are so many of them around at present now that there is no East or West. Isn't there a line in a hymn? 'There is no East or West. There is no North or South?' Something like that.

Anyway we talked today about death and things, and this has made me think of those big funerals they put on for Roy and Richie. You might have seen them in the papers, wherever you are. All those flowers! Thousands of people. All that sentiment. Church services with tributes. Roy came out of prison for Richie's funeral. Quite a fa-lal about that. Did you see it in the papers? Anyway, Chris, today the child Bobbi, who's very precocious, got us talking about the afterlife. According to her if you have lived an honest and virtuous life you become something beautiful after you died. She thinks her mother is a humming bird in the Caribbean. (Funny, that location, as her mother is the

303

white one.) It seems that if you have been bad you are reincarnated as something really low that people step on. Can you imagine what the Boys would be reincarnated as? One shudders to think. But if one is a vaguely good person, the idea has quite an appeal, don't you think? When the child insisted on my choice, I told her I wanted to be reincarnated as a swan. And the more I think about that, the more it appeals. As well as the beauty and the grace there is one particular thing about the swan that I really like. Can you guess what it is?

Ever your
Julia xxxx
PS. They mate for life.

Prodigal

'At four o'clock this morning twelve houses were raided across London and the South East in the final stage of Operation Tentacle, set up three years ago to flush out a criminal organisation, part of a European-wide network trafficking people, drugs and arms. Fifteen arrests were made and more are pending. Members of the police force are among those who have been arrested. Sources close to the police say they are confident that they have the two men at the top of this operation as well as a significant number of people down the chain. Premises have been closed...' The woman's voice on the radio clipped on.

I rolled over and out of bed in one movement

and raced downstairs to turn on the television to catch a glimpse of the door of Kazoo with some police tape on it. The next scene showed a policeman with his hand on the broad head of a chunky man to stop him hurting it as he entered a police car. The face was pixilated but I'd have recognised Oliver Cowell anywhere.

I went to the stairs. 'Bobbi! Bobbi! Get down here, will you?' I shouted. In two minutes she was there, neater than anyone deserved to be, who was just out of bed. 'What? What is it? Is there a fire?'

'I think it's time we went. We need to get back to the flat. I have this feeling your dad'll be back soon. Come on!'

Her glance dropped to my skimpy T-shirt, Sleeping Beauty pyjama bottoms, then to my bare feet. 'Like that?' she said. 'You look like a scarecrow.'

Five minutes later she let us into number 83. She sniffed and suddenly shouted, 'He's here. My daddy's back!'

'How d'you know?'

'His bike. I can smell his bike. Come and see!' She dragged me to the back hall and there, sitting back in gleaming glory, was a big shiny monster of a motor bike.

Bobbi stroked it tenderly. 'It's a Suzuki RF900. Goes like the wind. Once I went right to Bristol on the pillion. I had to hold on to my daddy very tight.' She looked up at the ceiling. 'He's here!' She pushed past me and raced up the stairs yelling, 'Daddy, my Daddy!'

Following her much more slowly, I came across Doreen leaning against her front door. 'He's back then?' she said.

305

'Seems like it.'

'It'll all change then,' she said. 'Everything changes.'

'I don't see what you mean.'

'You'll see. I'm off this morning up to Big and Bold to give *madame* a choice of the new gilets for the autumn market. I also have this idea about making knitted bags. To be honest I have this secret fear that my gilets are about to go out of fashion. So I need to see if I'm still in business. But I'll be back at two, dear, if you want a shoulder to cry on.'

Cry? Why should I cry because Sparrow Marsh was back?

When I got up to the Marsh flat, Bobbi was suspended from Sparrow's neck, being swung round like the arms of a windmill. Stephen was standing in front of the fireplace watching them, coffee mug in hand, grinning from ear to ear.

Sparrow stopped whirling but Bobbi stayed clutching him. He was wearing a white T-shirt and black jeans. His feet were bare. His skin gleamed. He smiled at me and my heart gave this heavy lurch.

'And here's our guardian angel,' he said. He peeled off Bobbi's fingers and came to shake my hand. 'Sophia.' He paused. 'So nice to meet you at last.'

I took that as my cue and joined him in deceiving Bobbi that this was our first meeting. His hand enveloped mine in a strong handshake. I'm afraid to say I felt faint, like some mincing maiden.

'We've been looking forward to you getting back, haven't we, Bobbi?' I said, waiting a full

306

second before rescuing my hand.

'Yeah. Still, me and Sophia've been all right, waiting for you.' She looked up at her father. 'Sophia and me are best friends.' She dragged him down on to the sofa beside her and linked arms with him.

I glanced across at Stephen. 'It was a team effort,' I said. 'We all helped.'

'Too modest,' said Sparrow, his glance moving between me and Stephen. 'Stevie here says it's all down to you.'

'She played a blinder,' Stephen grinned, and came across to put an arm round me. 'Duck to water, eh, Sophia?'

His arm felt warm, protective, but I still felt uncomfortable. 'It was a privilege.' I struggled to keep my tone light. 'Bobbi and I get on very well.' It sounded too wooden, formal. To my horror I found myself reverting to type. Mild social-work-speak.

'Best friends,' Bobbi said absently, snuggling into Sparrow's arm. 'Me and Sophia are best friends. And I have this new friend, Dad, and his name is Viktor. I'm teaching him English and he's coming on really well. You should hear him. You'll see him later today. We can meet him in Mehmet's. You'll really like Viktor, Dad. He's Catholic and he crosses himself in school, have you ever seen that? He believes in angels, says Mum is an angel in Heaven but I say no, she's a humming bird on Jamaica...'

In all the weeks I had known her I had never seen Bobbi so happy or excited, so vocal in her pleasure. So rosy and childlike. I realised now how she must have contained herself in these weeks while Sparrow was away. I thought I knew Bobbi, but I didn't.

I wriggled away from Stephen and made for the door, babbling, 'I have to go, I have to...' and fled, running down the street, round the corner, not stopping until I was inside my own dear house. I took three deep breaths and went upstairs to strip Bobbi's bed. I tied the sheets in a bundle, then went back to straighten the bed and gather together her things – odds and sods of clothing, pyjamas, brush, toothbrush and soap – into her sports bag. At the bedroom door I looked back. Clean and clear. Bobbi was no longer there. Not a whisper of her. Not a single black curly hair. She was back where she should be.

Now I realised why Doreen thought I might need a shoulder to cry on.

Sitting downstairs at my table, I tried to deal with this canyon of sadness inside. I was happy for Bobbi. She was where she should be. She was happy. But me? I had never felt so alone, so bereft; not as a child abandoned to the care of my ancient grandparents who never discovered where their daughter had fled: not as an abandoned mistress who had sacrificed her child for a lover only out for himself, not even as a failed social worker scrabbling to secure some feeling of worth with Emma and the others on the New Dawn.

The only thing worse than this was finding Drina.

I opened the battered yellow book and tears fell on the open page. I let them fall, as steadily, steadily I transcribed my next story of how

Emma's friend Shirley enlisted her help to deal with the boy who tormented cats.

Later, tears now dry, I looked up through the window to see Stephen's Volvo swing round the corner as he made his delayed start for work. Later I saw Doreen making her way, large checked bag in hand, for the bus into town. By the time I'd finished transcribing, four hours later, my eyes were dry and my hand was steady.

I had managed without Doreen's shoulder.

At lunchtime I avoided Mehmet's and wandered into the bookshop. I picked up the latest Julian Barnes and the latest Pat Barker, thinking that I would now, without Bobbi, have time to read some decent stuff. Just then, on a side shelf laden with dark books on real crime I came across two books about the Pinder brothers. I thought of that house stalker the other day who was about to add yet another to this seamy collection. I picked up the fattest of the books and found a seat so I could take a better look. I turned to the photograph section and flicked through. The people in the black-and-white photographs looked well dressed, chuffed with themselves and enjoying life. The men had the gleam of sweat on their faces. The women looked like passing breezes, mere tarty adornments. They must be grandmothers now. I thought of Oliver Cowell's ghastly mother. What was she feeling now with her darling son in a cell?

I turned a page and came upon a full-page picture of the Pinder brothers, handsome in their own burly way, surrounded by four men. Three of these men had Scots names. The fourth was labelled 'unknown'. I looked closer at it. Then I took it to the window to get a clearer view of a tall man with Brylcreemed hair and longish, fine features. The elegant way the suit hung on his slender figure marked him out as different from the other men standing there. My grandmother had this thing – and a full scrapbook – about an actor called Gregory Peck. This man was his double.

I closed the book and found myself putting it on the desk beside the other books I was buying. I had nothing in my purse, so I had to go out to the hole in the wall to get cash (one of my tight budget rules this year was *no credit*). As I collected my money I glanced up the street to see the backs of Viktor and Bobbi scampering towards Mehmet's.

I wondered where Sparrow was. Back at the flat, sleeping off weeks of tension and flight? Back at the office, discussing with his colleagues the success of Operation Tentacle? I didn't know and I had to remind myself it was none of my business now.

Later, on my way back down Barrington Street, I knocked on Julia's door. She seemed moderately pleased to see me, but I had to wait until she had finished snipping the box hedge round the gravel with kitchen scissors before I could get her full attention. Then we sat at her tiny kitchen table. She poured herself a glass of milk and poured me one without asking.

'Now, Sophia. What are you going to tell me? Something serious by the look on that set face of yours. What's wrong?'

'Nothing's wrong. Everything's right. Bobbi's

father is home at last.'

'I saw. She went to school on the back of that motor bike of his. Her school uniform and a blue helmet. Quite comical. That's very nice for her that she has him again. Parents are too precious to lose, Sophia. Look at my dear mother. She was precious to me even when her marbles were quite gone, poor dear.'

'Yes, I am pleased for Bobbi.' I am sure my voice belied my words.

'But you will miss her,' said Julia. 'Anyone can see that. You'll miss being her one-and-only, I mean.'

'She is just round the corner,' I said. 'I know that.'

She echoed Doreen's words. 'But it will not be the same, dear. You know that too.' She paused. 'I hope Bobbi is not too busy to help me on my garden day. She and that nice little boy promised to help. It's next Sunday, you know.'

'Yes. I remember.' I had forgotten.

'And you'll help? And little Laura?'

'Of course. I'll remind her.'

'Mrs Selkirk called. She has promised me three dozen cakes and four dozen biscuits. She is such a nice woman. I didn't quite realise that at first. And Mr Ahmad in the paper shop has given me a whole pile of paper bags so that we can bag them to sell.'

I peered through the open door of the kitchen to the garden beyond. 'It's really looking exquisite, Julia.'

'Thank you,' she said composedly. 'Now then, did you come to say all this or was there some-

311

thing else on your mind?'

I had forgotten. I scrabbled in my bag and pulled out the Pinder book. I leafed through to find the photo and laid it flat in front of her on the kitchen table.

'I found this. See at the back, right? The man who is called "unknown"? I wondered...'

She was rigid beside me. 'It's Chris. Yes, that's my Chris.'

'I kind of thought ... he's very elegant and handsome. Like one of those 1940s film stars you see in the old movies.'

She put a trembling finger out and ran it down the length of the figure. 'Class among rags,' she said softly. She looked up at me, her large round eyes brimming. 'I never had a photo, you know. It never seemed... I thought he probably had hundreds of photos of himself up there in Yorkshire. But I never had one.'

I pushed the book towards her. 'Here, have this.'

She shook her head. 'I want no book about those Boys. I saw all the stuff in the papers. My mother said it was disgraceful what they said about them. But she didn't know. I don't want that book in my house.'

I was disappointed. 'Then tear out that picture, Julia. Separate Chris from the rest of them. Then you'll have a picture for you to keep.'

'Are you sure?' But she was already reaching behind her into the kitchen cabinet for her scissors. Then she carefully cut Chris out, away from the others, so he was no longer in the picture. Then she closed the book and sat with her hand

312

on his image.

She looked up and smiled faintly. 'Perhaps you would ring Laura when you get home, Sophia? She wants me to order some clothes from that shop catalogue,' she said, gently dismissing me. 'I am so busy here. That honeysuckle needs cutting back just a bit.'

Obediently I stood up. 'Are you sure you're all right, Julia?'

She smiled radiantly. 'I am fine, dear. Never better.' She handed me the book. 'Don't forget this. I don't want any book with those two in it.'

Back home I rang Laura, who – more efficient than I am –had not forgotten the garden day. 'Of course I'll be there. I would do anything for that woman,' she paused. 'And her wardrobe.'

'You are a disgrace to the human race, Laura,' I said calmly, 'although on the way to being a credible good fashionista. And she wants to see you about some catalogue.'

'Mmm. Too late to order stuff. I'll have to take her up to town to buy it.' She paused. 'Oh, I gave your package to Jack Molloy, who seemed un-characteristically pleased that you had come up with the goods.'

I had forgotten about that and suddenly had a deep twinge of panic at the thought of a stranger's eyes reading my pages.

'And...' she said. 'I went on a date with the Beautiful Bolester. Darling Bolek. Polish promise.'

'Was it good?'

'Quite surreal, darling. He took me salsa dancing. Plied me with tequila. Behaved like a perfect gentleman,' she said gloomily. 'Kissed me on the cheek on my landlady's porch.'

'Are you complaining?'

'Yes ... no. I did love it. He's such a dish. The other women were eyeing him up, I can tell you.'

'But...?'

'But I think he may not be for me. That electricity, darling. That sensational spark. Not there. Not within a mile. He felt it, I felt it, this chasm, this lack. Hence the chaste kiss.'

'Ah, well.'

'As you say, pet, *ah, well*. I have been thinking I needed somebody more mature. Someone to take the lead in my life.'

'Like Jack Molloy?'

'Well, he has a certain reptilian charm, I must admit. And the most divine feet. But really, darling, he's been there, seen it, done it, come back and is far too old. There is *older* and there is *old*. He is *old!* And that's without taking the five children and three grandchildren into consideration.'

'Right. We'll cross him off our list. Oh, I nearly forgot. Great happenings here.' I told her of Sparrow's return.

'Jesus! What a tale. What dramas. What's he like, this dad of hers?'

'He's nice ... well, not quite *nice*. More interesting. Kind of dramatic.' I tried to keep my voice neutral.

'I've gotta meet him.' Laura paused. 'What does Stephen think of all these dramas?'

Strange question. 'I think he's cool about it. Pleased. He and Sparrow are good friends, going back.'

'That's nice.' She paused again. 'Well, love,

314

must go. Gotta cook up a piece about banning fox-hunting. Did you know there are actually three people on our course, one of them female, who participate in this ghastly ritual? I got some great interviews, though. Must go. Bye, darling!'

Darling Chris,

Well, here you are. In front of me at last. Large as life and twice as beautiful, as Mother would say. It makes me so happy to see you again, even though your image is always with me, carved right here on my heart. I feel you so close to me now, as though you are there in the next room. How lucky I am in my young friend Sophia. She found you for me and I thank her for that

She and her friends are going to help me with the garden day. Suddenly I have a little family around me. I never thought I would experience that. Life is full of surprises.

Oh, the child's father is back. I don't know why he has been away but I'll ask my Sophia when we have a moment. She'll tell me what the story is.

I know now in my bones that my garden day will be a success. Everything out there is perfect and now I'll have you there. You can go into my mother's silver frame, the one with my father's army picture. Don't worry, he will not be banished. I'll slide you into the frame on top of him. He won't mind. He was always a very reasonable man.

All my love always,
Your Julia xxx

Presents

I saw very little of Bobbi – and therefore Sparrow – in the days leading up to Julia's garden day. One day I saw her on the back of his motor bike on her way to school. Another day I was standing sheltering from the rain at the bus stop when I saw her with Viktor. She ran up and grabbed my arm.

'Where have you been, Sophia?' Droplets of rain stood in her fine halo of hair. 'Where have you been?'

'I've been at home. And now I'm getting on the bus and going to see my teacher from the university.'

'But I thought you'd come round to see me, like you usually do.'

'Can't go on doing that now, Bobbi. Your dad's back. Emergency over.'

'But I've missed you.'

'How is he, your dad?'

She scowled. 'He's great. But he's around too much. I'm always tripping over him. He's on two weeks' leave. He was gunna take me to Aldeburgh to see Great-Nanny but I told him I wanted to stay at home.' She looked me in the eyes. 'Did you know he wasn't really in Security? That he was a policeman? That's the secret.'

'No, not till it was nearly over. I know now.' I felt uncomfortable under her sharp gaze.

She grinned. 'Am I good at secrets or what?'

316

'I'd never have known, Bobbi.'

Viktor was pulling at her rucksack. The two of them had other fish to fry. She looked along the road. 'You waiting for a bus?' Then she squeezed my arm. 'You should still come and see us, Sophia. My dad wouldn't mind, you know. He's cool about me having my friends round.'

I changed tack. 'You're helping Julia on Sunday?'

'Yep. Me and Viktor are either selling tickets or selling cakes. Or both.'

'Good. I'll see you there.' I turned away, looking for the bus.

'Sophia!'

I turned back.

'My dad's been asking me an awful lot of questions about you. I told him what a great time we had in Aldeburgh, and d'you know what? He said he knew about that and he'd asked Great-Nanny all about you and she'd said good things.' She was watching me closely and I was embarrassed at my red cheeks.

'And he did ask me if you and Mr Copeland were an item.' Her gaze was steady. 'And I said I didn't know. I did say I knew Mr Copeland liked you and he should ask him about you. And I thought you two were really just Friends. Like the American programme on television.'

This time Viktor came between us and grabbed her arm. 'Come on, Bobbi! We'll be late.' And the two of them went off, to whatever they were late for.

As I sat on the bus in the usual queue of traffic in Islington I wrestled my mind away from Bobbi

317

and on to Jack Molloy, with whom I was about to have lunch.

As I walked into the restaurant I could see him at a corner table. He stood up and waved me over. He was smarter than usual, wearing a tweed jacket instead of a bomber with his jeans, and even a tie with his checked shirt. He was even wearing shoes and socks instead of the usual bare feet and sandals.

He must know the difference, then.

He shook my hand quite formally and turned to his companion, a smart woman so well presented it was hard to tell whether she was forty or sixty. Her silver-blonde hair was immaculately cut and her jacket draped just so. I didn't need Laura to tell me it was Armani. Even sitting down, she looked very tall. She had a clear, sharp look and a firm handshake.

Jack said, 'Marie Lomax, Sophia Morgan. Sit down, Sophia. We were just looking at the menu.'

I sat down and picked up the menu, which was nearly as big as a tabloid newspaper. The two of them were looking at me as though I were the first course.

Jack pushed up his glasses. 'Marie here has been talking to the course about the arcane mysteries of agenting.'

'Did Tariq ask awkward questions?' I said, knowing my friend of old.

He grinned. 'Doesn't he always?'

Marie nodded. 'The boy was knowing enough. I think his question was something about whether the plethora of cross-cultural novels coming out were a sop to liberal feeling or a genuine literary

318

evolution.' It was hard to tell whether or not she was being ironic.

I couldn't press further because now they both had their heads down over the menu, making a big business over choosing their food. Jack looked up at me. 'Choose! It's on the college, Marie being an honoured guest.'

Later I sat quietly through the main course as they gossiped about mutual friends in newspapers and publishing: arch, salacious village gossip about names I recognised from the papers. I made a good, if silent, audience as I chewed away at a very nice veal dish that I'd chosen at random.

We were on to coffee before my pages were mentioned. At last I was treated to the full beam of Marie Lomax's attention. 'I read your pages, Sophia. I could see they were very much draft...'

I felt so humiliated. I should never have sent them. I didn't know what they were really were myself.

'...But they were original. A fresh voice. Lively. You can write.'

I could have fallen on my knees and worshipped her. 'Thank you,' I said meekly.

She shrugged. 'Don't thank me. Down to you. One can write or one can't.'

She clearly thought my modesty was posturing. I waited. Jack filled his wine glass and took a sip.

'So, when will you have a full draft?' she said.

I plucked a date out of the air. 'September. I'm sure by September.'

'Good.' She bent down and pulled my Jiffy bag from her briefcase, which was tasselled and surprisingly girlie. 'Here you are. I've added a few notes in there as well that might or might not be of use. Get the full manuscript to me by the end of September and we'll see what we can do. I have one or two ideas.'

She stood up. And up. She was very tall. Jack stood up. I stood up. She leaned down and kissed Jack.

'It was fun, darling. Those young minds, Jack! Such a challenge.' She shook my hand again and smiled slightly. 'A big step, Sophia, exiting from the course. Not sure how wise that was. But I'm sure we'll meet again. Write like the wind!' And she was gone in a vapour trail of Guerlain perfume.

Jack grinned. 'Well, she liked you.'

'How could you tell?'

'I can tell. You wait.' He signalled to the waiter for the bill. 'Now then, why don't we have one at the Red Lion? Your mates will be there.'

So they were: Laura and Tariq and the others. They shouted their welcome and Jack bought me a bottle of beer and left. I felt warm, entertained and cared for in the company of my old acquaintances, and began to wonder whether I really had made a mistake, isolating myself in Barrington Street with a mad old woman and a knowing child as my chosen companions.

This feeling lasted only an hour. By then the conversation had veered to some new stand-up comedian, unknown to me, who was apparently a genius. The more they described the brilliant iconoclastic nature of this guy's comedy the more they lost me. I tried to slip away unnoticed, but Laura followed me to the door to give me a hug.

'I'll be there on Sunday!' she said.

'Sunday?'

'Julia's garden day.'

'Oh, yes. Of course. See you there.'

Outside, the crowded pavements were wet from the recent rain but still I decided to walk down to the Holloway Road to get my bus. The walk would clear my head of the fug in the pub. And I could delay the moment when I would open my Jiffy bag on the bus to see just what Marie Lomax had written about my deathless prose.

This buzzing feeling was like Christmas morning in my grandmother's house with the modest pile of presents, neatly wrapped, sitting there on the sideboard. I was not permitted to open them until after dinner and the Queen had had her say at three o'clock. The build-up of excitement was exquisite.

This was just the same.

Dear Chris,

I had not thought I would get so wound up in this garden thing. Last year it was quiet enough, with just Gregory giving me a hand. A few people trickling through the door. No cakes. There are to be cakes on Sunday. And biscuits. I am really looking forward to it. I hope all is well up there in Yorkshire and you are keeping warm as I understand there are winds there today. It said so on the wireless.

All love, dearest swan,

Your own

Julia xxx

Slipstream

Much to Julia's delight there was some rain in the days before her garden day. 'Saves watering,' she told me. 'Pray for it to be dry on Friday afternoon, though, or my grass will be sodden and destroyed by all those feet.'

I'd got into the habit of calling on her every day, though I avoided drinking her cocktails or whisky now, as I was writing every day, encouraged by Marie Lomax's measured, positive comments on my pages. The shrewd tone of her faint praise made me realise that in the yellow book, if anywhere, lay my future.

On Thursday afternoon I was coming out of Julia's house and there by the bus stop was Sparrow Marsh on his motor bike, his helmet in his hand.

He grinned. 'Sophia! I saw you go in there and waited. I never thanked you properly for taking care of my Bobbi.'

I shook my head. 'No need.'

'Have you ever been on a bike?'

I shook my head. 'I did have a pedal bike. Years ago.'

He put on his helmet, reached into the carrier and took out a green helmet and a leather jacket. They were brand-new, too large to be Bobbi's. 'Put these on and we'll take a ride,' he said.

'I don't think...'

'Please put them on.' He tipped his head to one side and smiled. 'Come on,' he said. 'Put them on.' I did as he said, just to stop my knees shaking. He held out a hooked arm. 'Hop on. Hold tight.'

I jumped on and put a tentative hand on his belt. He reached back and pulled my arms so they were right round him. Even through the leather I was conscious of the dense mass of his muscles. The engine roared between my legs, vibrated through my body and we were off. He drove at low speeds through the city streets but still it seemed as if we were flying. There in the tangle of dangerous traffic, I began to relish people's second glances.

At last we left the suburbs behind. He revved the engine and we raced along a three-lane motorway at the speed of light. Then I couldn't think. All I could do was hold him tight. After what could have been anything from ten minutes to an hour he slowed right down and took an exit into a two-lane road where we drove at a more gracious pace through a small town and several villages. Then he turned into a narrower road and suddenly we were in woodland. He eased the bike across greensward and stopped under a tree.

He turned off the engine. Silence. Or the illusion of silence. As my ears adapted to it, the air around me was gradually embroidered with the whirr and trill of birdsong, and the rustle of trees moving and settling in the wind.

'Ouch!' Stiffly, I eased myself off the pillion, feeling as though the engine was still vibrating through me.

He leaped off easily and grinned. 'Well, it was

your first time.'

'First time ever.'

'And d'you like it?'

Really I'd been too busy hanging on and staying alive to think much about that. But I nodded. 'The nearest thing to riding a horse in the open air.'

He took out a great chain and tethered the bike to a small tree. 'You ride horses?' he said.

'No. I used my imagination. But that's what I think it would be like.' I took off the helmet. 'Thank your friend for lending me this.'

He smiled slightly. 'Don't belong to anyone. I just bought it. For you. I thought green would suit you.' He took it from me and watched me shake out my hair. 'You have nice hair,' he said, locking the helmets in the box.

'Bobbi once said it was like barbed wire.'

He laughed. 'That child! What's she like?' he said. He looked upward into the lacey green of the leaves. 'Oak,' he said. He pointed away from the path. 'And over there, hornbeam. Old woodland. The best of England,' he said softly. 'Don't you think so?'

I was so surprised I nearly fell over. 'It's beautiful,' I said weakly. I had a lot to learn about this man.

He nodded towards a break in the trees. 'There's a nice stretch of river down there, through those trees. You'll like it.'

He led the way downwards. The dusty forest floor was still lined with the shrivelled remnants of last year's leaves. I breathed in the damp, loamy air. Then the sound of rushing water penetrated the twittering of the birds and I began to run. The trees opened out to a clearing where a narrow bridge crossed a pulsing stream. Further upstream, where the water was tumbling over rocks, was a heap of stones, a dam made by some child engineer to make the water run higher, faster.

'This place is so ... brilliant,' I said, leaning over the parapet.

'Bobbi loves it,' he said. 'See that dam? She made it last autumn. Still there. She makes things to last. Stevie has his eye on her for an architect.'

'She's a clever thing,' I said, still watching the swirling water.

'Not down to me. She's like her mother.' He paused. 'Kid really likes you, Sophia.'

I knew his eyes were on me. 'That's mutual,' I said, turning to look into those eyes. 'Bobbi gives as much as she gets.'

'She thinks we should be friends, you and me,' he said. 'She told me so. Quite strong about it.'

'I don't see why not,' I said, my mind whirling around, considering what I could or should do when he made his move. Or if he made his move.

'Good.' His eyes moved up the river. 'There! See that fish leaping? See it?'

I turned to look. Upstream, fish were pimpling the surface and now and then one of them flashed, for a second, right up into the air. Glancing sideways at him I knew, despite the drift of the conversation, he would make no move. He was back in neutral, easy in his skin, and I would not be troubled by decisions about how to respond. I relaxed.

Later, we made our way back to the bike and we rode through the woods and out the other side, ending up in a roadside pub, me in front of a glass of beer, he with juice. The only people in there were a few old men at a corner table. They watched us with close interest. Whether it was because of our leathers or our sheer good looks I was not quite sure.

Sparrow and I did talk, though. He told me about his family in Bristol, especially his old grandfather who had come here in 1953. He talked easily about Pamela and her mother, Mary, and Elsie, the nana. He talked of the day Bobbi was born, when he drove Pam to the hospital, with her side-saddle on his bike.

I tried to get him to talk about his job but he shook his head. 'Another time, Sophia. Another time. Plenty of time for those things.'

Over my second beer he got me to talk about my life, to tease out more about the things I blurted out to him on the phone. Everything. He put his big hand over mine when I finally told him about finding Drina. The old man in the corner stirred and coughed.

'Oh, baby,' said Sparrow. 'Now that was hard.' His touch was soft, comradely, and I let my hand lie there, under his.

Then he took his hand away and my hand felt cold. 'And Stevie? He means a lot to you?'

I blushed. 'Yes... I... He's been very...'

He glanced at the big watch on his wrist. 'That the time? Jeez, I gotta go. Promised Bobbi and that buddy boy of hers I'd take them for a pizza after school.'

I was silenced. I could find nothing to say. Then suddenly we were very busy buckling our jackets, fastening our helmets and getting on to the bike. As we roared away I was cursing myself for not handling things the way I wanted. But later, as we moved into the mainstream traffic, I wondered if I knew it myself: what I really wanted.

Even so it was very good to hold on tight to Sparrow Marsh, feel the wind in my face and watch the world stream by like a film on fast forward. This was enough, for the time being.

Dearest Chris,

Well, it's all ready now. The garden is fine. The rain this week had been just right, dense enough to penetrate but light enough not to beat the little faces of my darling flowers.

You know I told you about my young friend Sophia? Well, I thought she and young Stephen might make a go of things. He's such a nice boy. But you know that, don't you? Anyway, I think the father of young Bobbi, who has just turned up again, is making a bit of a play for her. He took her off on his motor bike today. I hope she is careful. I wouldn't like to see her feelings hurt. That happened to her once before, you know. I've become so very fond of her. She makes me think of the daughter I never had. Of course, I know that's quite a mad thought. We live in a world of might-have-beens but there's some comfort in it, isn't there?

Has it been raining where you are? What is that saying, something about the sun shining on the just and the unjust? Does the same go for rain?

All my love always,
Your Julia xxx

All for Julia

On Saturday morning I was just settling down to work when Laura rang to say she was meeting Julia in town to shop for clothes. 'She says she'll come by taxi. She wants something new to wear for her garden day. We did look at the Next catalogue but I thought Peter Jones. D'you fancy coming?'

'No, I won't come, wouldn't intrude on a private party,' I said, more sharply than I'd intended, probably put out by the fact that Julia was arranging something without reference to me. How ridiculous was that?

Laura sighed. 'Oh dear, Sophia! You're mad at me about Stephen. I knew I should have told you.'

Another ridiculous *frisson* of jealousy. 'What about you and Stephen?'

'I confess. We went out together on Thursday. We went to Brixton. He showed me this house he'd designed in this tiny little space. Opens up at the back but at the front it's only eleven feet wide. All glass and concrete with this brilliant central atrium for light. I'm going to pitch it to *World of Interiors* or *Architectural Review*.'

'Well, that is fascinating. But I hadn't heard about you and he ... well ... culture-vulturing. Why should I?'

'Oh. I heard of this house and I asked him.' She paused for a long time, then she said, 'And I'm

328

afraid we had lunch afterwards. We talked for hours. He's so *aware*, Sophia. About design and colour. You name it. I've never talked so much about real things to a grown-up before.'

'Good for you.' I didn't know what to say.

'Anyway, he took me to his office afterwards. Glam place. I met his boss. This super woman. Or should I say Superwoman? Of course you met her, didn't you? She had the sweetest tiniest baby in a basket in the corner. Good as gold. I thought *she'd* make a good piece. "Having It All" and all that.'

'You're such a hack, Laura. Emily is nice.'

'Yeah. Well. I'm pleased you know now. About me and Stephen. I was worried about that.'

'Can't think why. I'm pleased there is a you-and-Stephen. He's nice, you're nice. Shame to spoil two houses, as my grandma would say.'

'Well, I did think you might have had a thing for him.'

'Not really. I like him, like I like Doreen or Bobbi ... or anyone in that house.' I resisted telling her that at the time she was *ooh*-ing and *ah*-ing over the Brixton house I was wandering in a distant forest with the other – more attractive to me – occupant of that same house.

'As well as that, Sophia, he's asked me if I'm going to Julia's garden thing tomorrow.'

'I hope you told him you are. Remember Julia's relying on your help.'

'To be honest, I was flattered at first that he asked me. But then I realised he'd invited Super-woman and spouse, the sprog and half the workforce. All for Julia, and why not?'

'But you really do like him?'

'He makes me weak at the knees. Does that count? Do you mind?'

I thought about the bike helmet and feeling weak at the knees in the middle of a forest. 'No. I don't mind one bit.'

'Phew! Great. That's a relief. Now I can pursue him without a scrap of conscience.'

'Just one thing, Laura.'

'What? You're not going to tell me he's too old for me, are you? I've had enough of that from Tariq.'

'It's not about him, it's about Julia.'

'What about her?'

'The shopping. Don't you go tricking her up all mother-of-the-bride-ish.'

She laughed. 'Would I? I'm a stylist, darling, not an undertaker.'

Five minutes later I was just picking up my pen to start work on a pristine second yellow book open in front of me, when the phone rang. I thought it was Laura again but it was Doreen, asking me if I'd like to go along and help her with the batch of biscuits and cakes for Julia. I took one last look at the empty page and said yes, of course I would. Things were tumbling around me so fast that it was proving impossible to write about Tyneside in 2001.

When I got there Doreen was at it, full steam ahead. The flat, warm with the oven full blast, reminded me of my grandmother's kitchen. The air smelled of vanilla and spice, and the big table was covered with a white sheet. She pointed at six plastic cake boxes on the sideboard. 'Got them at the Pound Shop, a pound apiece,' she said gleefully, handing me a voluminous apron.

On the smaller table at the kitchen end were scales, two large mixing bowls, two boards and a neat row of ingredients in packets. 'Your job's doing chocolate chip cookies and gingerbread men,' she said. 'I've got an almond pound cake in the oven and am making a carrot walnut spice cake. American recipes – so very over the top. We can sell these by the slice.'

I tied on the apron. 'I don't know whether I can do any of this, Doreen.'

She fluttered a floury hand in my direction. 'Don't worry about it, dear. I'll be with you all the way.'

I was just rolling out the ginger mixture when there was a knock on the door and in came Bobbi. 'This smells lovely. Can I help?'

'Certainly, dear. Press out those gingerbread men for me. Sophia'll show you how.'

Bobbi was just pressing the fifteenth gingerbread man when Sparrow put his head round the door. 'Mrs Selkirk? Is Bobbi OK? I have this meeting with my boss this morning. I'm gettin' stir-crazy up there.' He smiled at me. 'You helping, Sophia?'

I felt heat running through my body.

Doreen smiled at him, her round cheeks dimpling. 'Of course she can stay. But I wish you'd call me Doreen. Everyone here does. Otherwise I'll have to call you Mr Marsh and that's plain silly.'

He grinned. 'You're on, Doreen.' He advanced into the room. Towards me. He reached out and touched my cheek. 'Sophia? You're covered in flour.'

And then he was gone.

'Sophia!' said Bobbi accusingly. 'You're very bright red!'

'It's that oven,' I said, rubbing my cheek very hard. 'It's very hot in here.'

Doreen spooned the last of her mixture into the cake tin. 'Oh, by the way, Sophia, Roger's coming back from Aldeburgh specially for Julia's garden day. I thought that was rather nice of him.'

By five o'clock that afternoon I was back at home, scribbling in the yellow book, when a taxi drew up outside and out stepped Julia, laden with glossy carriers and parcels. I went to open the door so she didn't have to put down the parcels to knock. 'Julia! You look like Mother Christmas!'

'Can I show you what I've got? Laura has been such a help. She knows where to find just everything. I even got shoes and new boots. Brassieres! The nice woman in the shop assured me that everything works from the foundations.'

Julia laid her booty along the back of the couch. Laura had done a fairy godmother of a job. The first items revealed were jodhpurs and a matching waistcoat in wheat-coloured fine cord and a butter-coloured silk blouse with big sleeves to go underneath it.

'I thought the blouse was too long,' said Julia. 'But the shop woman said you wear it showing under the waistcoat and out over the trousers. That's how they wear them now. And just look at these boots!' She held up long boots in supple leather. 'They look a bit like my old ones but the cut is entirely different.' Then she pulled out a

332

narrow linen skirt in very pale grey with a matching knit sweater. The shoes to go with them were low-heeled black leather with a cross strap. She held one of them against her narrow foot. 'Aren't these elegant?'

Between them Laura and the shop woman had got Julia just right. I was awed. 'Must have cost a mint, Julia.' Then I felt like a klutz for mentioning money at all. I blame my grandmother. She was always so embarrassingly direct about things financial.

Julia, putting the shoes back in their equally elegant box, looked at me mildly. 'Well, dear, when you have only spent pennies on the pure essentials for forty years, there is quite a bit left in the pot.'

'So, what will you wear tomorrow, for the people coming to see the garden? The grey or the gold?'

She stroked the silk shirt. 'I'm not quite sure, Sophia. What do you think? Shall we wait and see what the weather offers us? My Chris used to say it's always such a leveller, the weather.'

Darling Chris,

I have a confession to make. I did go rather wild today. I went shopping with the young woman Laura, Sophia's friend. You remember? Well, she is a design person and it shows. Going to be a journalist in fashion. She's the one who loved my clothes. The ones you bought me. Remember? She has taken photographs of them for what she calls her fashion archive. It seems that we are all just history to these young people.

So there we were, Laura and I, up West in the old

haunts. Now I have some lovely new things. I chose them with you in mind. I'm sure, when you see them, you'll like them. Do you know I bought jodhpurs? They are really for show but they made me dream of one day going riding with you. Think of it, you and I, side by side!

Terribly busy with this garden thing.
All my love,
Your Julia x

Garden Party

We were treated to a storm late on Saturday night. It started with a firework display of dry lightning. I stood at my bedroom window and watched the sky split three times, creating darkness around it, even in this light-polluted city. Then the dark sky let fall a torrent of rain and I began to worry about Julia. Her plants would be dashed and the work of months would be obliterated.

I opened my window and leaned out. 'Stop! Stop, will you! Think of Julia,' I shouted, before pulling back, my face and hair streaming with rain, feeling very, very stupid. But never underestimate the power of prayer! A minute after my great shout the rain thinned. Two minutes later it stopped.

I towelled my hair and my face and climbed back into bed. It would be all right now. I felt sure of that.

I slept in and didn't get to Julia's until eleven o'clock. The door was wide open and I followed a diminutive grizzle-haired black man into the house. He had heavy baskets on his arms filled with vegetables. I could make out long flat green beans, broccoli, cucumbers and bunches of brassy marigolds. He walked straight through to the kitchen and squeezed by Doreen and Bobbi, who were laying out the cakes and cookies on plates lined with doilies. Julia was out in the garden at a round table, elegant in the jodhpurs and waistcoat, waving her ivory cigarette holder with one hand and arranging plates with the other. Beyond her, the garden looked exquisite, fresh from, rather than crushed by, the night rain. The flowers, plants and shrubs stood to attention, glowing in the brassy noon light.

'Gregory! You precious man. What's this?' said Julia.

The grizzled man laid the baskets at her feet. 'This, Julia, is the best home-grown produce in North London. Should make a few pennies for your cause, whatever that may be.'

She put a hand on the sleeve of his woolly jumper. 'I can see you've been working hard, Gregory.'

He glanced down the garden. 'So have you, girl. Look at that philadelphus – ain't that like some kind of snowstorm?' He stood on his tiptoes to get a better look down the length of garden. 'I see you got rid of the vegetables.'

'Gregory.' She nudged the nearest basket with her new boot. 'How could I compete with you?' She took his arm. 'Come and see what I've done.'

The two of them made their way down her garden. Now and then they stopped, so Julia could bend down and cup a flower in her hand, as you would the face of a small child. Gregory brought his head close to hers and the soft rumble of their voices joined the twitter of birds, the roar of distant traffic, and the rumble of the nearby train, in what counted as Sunday silence in this city.

'Aren't they sweet, those two? Isn't he the good old boy who helped her do the garden in the first place?' Doreen was standing beside me, a plate of cookies in each hand.

Bobbi was beside her, balancing the huge carrot cake, now divided into plump slices. 'You look nice, Sophia,' she said.

'Thanks, Bobbi.' Probably inspired by Julia, I had made a special effort, trying on three different outfits before settling on jeans and a low-cut pale green top under a fitted plum-coloured velvet jacket I'd bought when I first came to London.

Bobbi examined me closely. 'My dad's coming this afternoon, you know. Said he had to support the cause.' She looked me in the eye. 'He's seen his boss and he's going back to work on Monday. Says he's stir-crazy, stuck at home with me.'

'Bobbi! I'm sure he's not...'

She placed the carrot cake at the dead centre of the table and arranged the biscuits on plates around it. 'Don't you worry, Sophia. He's not gunna be lurking around criminals any more. So he says. He's at some desk solving crimes with a computer and a telephone. It's just for the time being, he says. Myself, I think it won't be for long. He likes a bit of action, does my dad.' She looked me in the eye again. 'He asked me if you'd be here this afternoon and I said you'd be bound to be, as you were Miss Soper's best friend.' She took off her apron and handed it to Doreen. 'Gotta go. He's making spice dumplings for dinner. Haven't had those for ages.'

Doreen removed her own apron and folded it with Bobbi's. 'Me too. Roger's waiting for me.'

'He's there? Home to stay?'

She smiled grimly. 'Quite the reverse, my dear. He came specially to tell me he's fallen in love with the bookseller, that *we* were all a mistake, et cetera, et cetera. And I'd recognised it before he did, aren't I clever? And he quite understood now about me missing my Helena. And so on. He does go on.'

'So how do you feel?'

'Me? Numb, I suppose. Changed.'

'So what will you do?'

'I'll wait till Helena comes in the summer. Show her London. Then I think I might just go back with her. Be near her. Be a counterbalance to the geography teacher.'

I couldn't think of a thing to say.

'Don't worry about me, my dear. I'm sure that in the end I'll see Roger as a bit of an episode. A mid-life adventure. I'll go back, get a job and an apartment, take Helena back and...' her voice faded.

'Start on the next adventure?' I said.

Her brow cleared. 'Yes. That's good. Start on the next adventure. You should try an adventure of your own, Sophia. Isn't it time?'

I laughed. 'That's not impossible.'

Then Julia and Gregory stood before us. Julia

337

beamed. 'Thank you, Mrs Selkirk ... Doreen. It all looks very beautiful. So kind of you. Now, Gregory and I are going to have a cocktail. Will you join us?'

We turned down her offer and made our way out. 'One of her cocktails and I'd be begging Roger to stay,' said Doreen grimly.

One of Julia's cocktails, I thought, and I'd be rushing across the road and asking Sparrow Marsh if he would take me on his bike for a spin to the forest.

Instead I hopped on to a bus to Islington and made my way down to the canal, where people were enjoying the best of the fine day, taking their dogs and their children for walks. There were children on their own down there, hanging around, playing desultory games, waiting for something more exciting to happen, walking the line between charm and threat that children seem to occupy nowadays. On the canal one or two of the boats were occupied. You could peer down at people playing house on a Sunday afternoon. One boat was kitted out as a studio and a man was painting down there.

I was just relishing being on my own among strangers with no responsibility for anyone when a little girl jumped out in front of me, urged on by her mates who were leaning against the bank. She stood there staring me down until I was inches from her, then leaped out of my way, her laughter chiming with that of her friends.

Then, as I walked on, my mind was filled again with Drina. In my time in the Lavender House that image of her coiled in her stinking cage had begun to fade. Now it was back again, nailed there behind my eyes. I felt sick. I also felt guilty at letting her slip away. I started to worry that if I didn't keep Drina properly in my mind, she would not exist anywhere any more, except as a news cutting or Internet file, to be dragged out by someone like Tariq every time child abuse became a hot issue.

How wonderful, I thought now, if Drina had grown up to be a naughty girl, lively enough to torment adults on a canal path.

Then as I made my way back up to Upper Street I conjured up the image of Bobbi in her overlong apron, holding up the carrot cake like a crown. I stood very still on the narrow pavement and, by conscious effort, laid that image of Bobbi over the wretched one of Drina and stayed there, eyes closed, until Drina faded and there was only Bobbi there.

'Excuse *me!*'

I opened my eyes to a woman in an Afghan jacket trying to get by with a double push chair. I leaped on to the road into the path of a car that had just turned the corner. It screeched to a stop ten inches from me and the driver opened his window and shouted at me to get out of the fucking way. The woman in the Afghan told me to watch myself, lady, and went on her way.

Back on the pavement I looked at my watch. Two fifteen. I was late for Julia's two o'clock opening. My grandmother always said disaster came in threes. Today there was the naughty girl bringing back the nightmare of Drina. Then there was me nearly getting killed on the road.

Now here I was, late for Julia's big day.

When I finally got back to Barrington Street the house and garden were full of people. Viktor was serving tea out of the kitchen, Bobbi was selling lists of Julia's plants that she'd printed on her computer, Doreen was selling cakes and cookies, and Gregory was just packing the last of the beans into a cornet made of newspaper to sell to Mr Ahmad from the newsagent's.

Julia came towards me out of the crowd. 'Sophia! I thought you'd forgotten us.' She kissed me warmly on the cheek – a new thing. Her lipstick was sticky. She smelled faintly of rum and was all benevolence so I knew she would be holding no grudges at me being late.

Past the borders, through the archway (presided from on high by a glaring Pusscat), down on the gravel circle at the bottom of the garden, I could see Emily Sillitoe sitting on one of Julia's blue wire chairs with her baby on her lap, Jerry hovering at one shoulder. Beside her on the other wire chair sat Laura with her finger in the baby's miniature clutch. Just behind them were Stephen and Viktor's brother, Bolek. In the splash of deceptive light at that end of the garden these men might have been father and son.

My glance focused in on Laura, bent over the baby, the sheet of black silken hair shading her eyes from view. I could see now she was flirting with them all – the Sillitoes as well as Stephen and Bolek. A smile forced itself to my lips. My grandmother would have called her a little minx.

'D'you want a cup of Viktor's tea?' Suddenly

340

Sparrow was at my elbow, graceful in the blue cashmere sweater I'd spotted in his wardrobe. His bare feet were in deck shoes.

I lifted my eyes to his. 'Tea?' I said weakly.

He had a china cup in each hand. 'Young Viktor is a very good salesman. Said if I bought a coffee I could have a tea at fifty per cent of the going market price. He's gonna make some business-man one day.'

I ordered my knees to stop shaking and took the coffee.

Sparrow nodded towards the group on the gravel circle at the bottom of the garden. 'Smart group, ain't they? Like they were posing for a Marks & Spencer ad.'

I laughed. 'That would appeal to my friend Laura. The one with the hair. Magazines are her thing. I was just having a smile at her flirting with all of them at once. Stephen, Bolek, Emily, Jerry. Even the baby.'

'So who are the couple with the baby?'

'Emily and Jerry Sillitoe. She's Stephen's boss and Jerry is one of your lot. Retired.'

'Sillitoe? So that's the legendary Jerry Sillitoe. A great cop, legend has it. He's the one who checked me out.'

'I asked him to do that. Sorry.'

'Right.' He took a sip of his tea. 'D'you mind?'

'What? About the baby? I–'

'No. About your friend flirtin' away there with Stevie?'

I tried innocence. 'What do you mean? Do I mind that my dear friend is just being her charming self?'

'Don't you mind that she's down there charming old Stevie?' he said bluntly.

I decided to play it straight. 'Stephen's my good friend. He's been kind to me and I feel protective towards him. I'd hate it if Laura were messing him about. But I think she really likes him. And one way to get his approval is probably to make a fuss of Emily's baby, who's named after Stephen. She's not daft, our Laura.'

He laughed out loud.

I frowned. 'Is that funny?'

'I'd forgotten you were from the North. Call a spade a shovel, do you?'

'Don't be so bloody patronising.'

He held a hand before his face. 'Sorry! Sorry, pax.' But he was still smiling. 'Why don't we go and break up that pretty picture?' He put his arm through mine. 'Or create a new one?'

Laura stood up as we approached. Her cheeks were rosy. 'Sophia!' she said, giving me a hug. 'Look at this precious little thing.'

I touched the back of the baby's hand. She was like nothing so much as a kitten: contained, perfect, innocent. My gut ached.

Emily said my name, smiled regally, and put up a cheek so I was obliged to kiss her. 'Well done!' I said to Jerry. He grinned. 'It was tough!' he said. 'Couldn't have got through it without Emily here.'

She smiled up at her legendary policeman. 'You are a darling old softie,' she said.

I introduced Sparrow. He and Jerry exchanged brief comments on some mutual acquaintances and left it at that. I relaxed. They were obviously very comfortable with each other: members of an invisible club, like golfers or football fans.

Laura moved across to stand beside Stephen to be introduced, putting a proprietary arm through his. He smiled at Sparrow and winked. 'Rather a change from life "in deep", Sparrow! A garden party!'

Sparrow already knew Bolek through Viktor but still he shook hands with him in that vigorous way men have.

Bolek looked across at me. 'The floor is satisfactory, Sophia? You like it?'

'It's wonderful. So clean. Makes all the difference.'

He glowed with quiet pride. 'And the trapdoor, it is no problem?'

It seemed to me then that the whole world went quiet. The bustle of people in Julia's garden faded. The birds stopped singing. 'The trapdoor?' I said.

'The trapdoor. Down the left near the wall. I levelled it and screwed it down. That floor was a beast to level. So many different sections. It is so in many old houses.'

'I didn't see any trapdoor.'

He smiled, his white teeth gleaming. 'So! I am the good workman from far away.' He turned to Stephen. 'Is that not so?'

Stephen nodded. 'Bloody good.'

'And I say there is a trapdoor.'

'But ... but...' I spluttered.

Bolek frowned. 'I am sorry, Sophia. Did I do a wrong thing?'

Laura's eyes were gleaming. 'Tell them, Sophia. Tell them about the house stalkers.'

Uncomfortable with all their eyes on me, I

343

managed to get the story out, about the creepy Pinder-obsessives and the tale of a trapdoor.

'You asked me about them, the Pinders,' said Jerry thoughtfully. 'I remember that. This was the reason why?'

I shook my head. 'I asked you about the Pinders because of Julia.' We all looked towards the border near the house where Julia was pointing out her fabulous climbing abutilon to a pair of ladies in straw hats who were hanging on to her every word. 'I think I told you. Julia knew the Pinders quite well. Her boyfriend was one of what they politely call now "their associates".'

'Yes. There was this Chris Muncaster,' he said. 'Now gone the way of the just and the unjust, I fear.'

I looked around for somewhere to put my cup and saucer. Laura took it from me. 'I need to see it now,' I said firmly. 'That trapdoor.'

Bolek nodded. 'I'll come with you and show you.'

'You'll need gear,' said Stephen. He threw Bolek a bunch of keys. 'Lockbox in the back yard,' he said. He was definitely staying here with Laura on his arm. How things can change in a few days.

So it was Sparrow, Bolek and I who went along to the Lavender House to check on the trapdoor. Sparrow looked around the downstairs room. 'This is nice,' he said. 'This is where you work? It's very smart.'

I shoved the papers on the table to a neater pile by the computer. 'It's all just improvised,' I protested. 'No funds. I had to make something of what was already here.'

He helped me to move the sofa and the chair and then the rug out into the kitchen end of the room. I looked down at the gleaming floor. It was a mish-mash of boards, broad and narrow, patched here and there with brand-new boards, stained down to match. Bolek knew his stuff.

I looked closer at one of the older sections near the wall. I kneeled down and looked even closer. 'Here, here it is.' I looked up at Sparrow. 'D'you see this? How the hell did I miss it?'

He looked down at me, the glimmer of a smile in his eyes. 'Sophia...'

At that point the door crashed open and in came Bolek with a chunky electric screwdriver in one hand, a toolbox in the other. 'Now,' he said. 'Shall we do it?'

Sparrow put his hand on my shoulder, a searing touch that I did my best to ignore. 'Are you sure you want to do this, girl? It's screwed down and secure there. Do you really want to do this? Open the box of tricks?'

'I do,' I said grimly. 'At least I'll have something to say when those men in anoraks come round. That'll be very satisfying.' I nodded across at Bolek. 'Do it!'

He set about unscrewing the countersunk screws and then finally, with a grunt, began to lift a section out of the floor. 'I took off the old hinges,' he said. 'Had to do that to make the floor lie flat.' He grunted again and the whole thing came up, leaving a gaping hole.

I leaned over and stared into a dark space below. Then my gaze pulled back upwards again to the edge of the hole, lined with old wood, perhaps as old as the house: the reason why the trapdoor had fit so snugly. 'What's this?' I said, running my fingers over strange ridges worn into the old wood.

Sparrow kneeled beside me and his hands followed mine. 'Well, baby,' he sighed, 'I wouldn't swear it but...'

Suddenly I knew what the ridges were and a wave of revulsion tore through me. I gagged and had to press my fingers to my lips to stop myself from being sick. 'They are scratches.' I finally got the words out. 'Someone was scratching, scratching to get out of this hole. Someone was left there.' I hauled myself to my feet. 'There must be a...'

He stood up, grabbed me and held me close. His voice was in my ear. 'Listen to me, Sophia. There's no body down there. The smell's wrong. It's dry down there. It smells of dust. That's all. No *body*. Believe me I would know. I've been where there were bodies.'

My eye suddenly rested on what was clearly the top of a ladder. I wrestled myself free and grabbed a torch from Bolek's toolbox. 'I'm going to look down there.'

'No, Sophia,' Sparrow protested.

But I had my feet on the top rung and step by step I let myself down into what was a box of a room, ten foot high, ten foot square. There was a mere glimmer of light from a narrow grille that must, I reckoned, be on my front path, somewhere near Julia's pots of geraniums.

I flashed the torch around the walls, throwing light on peeling remnants of old distemper.

346

Hooks hung from walls and the ceiling, I suppose the kind used for hanging meat, in the old days. An old card table, the dust on it pie-crust hard, scattered with scraps of paper. At its centre a jug lay on its side, in a position of surrender.

I rubbed the dust from one piece of paper and in the torchlight made out a name. And another. And another. Just her name. *Julia. Julia. Julia.* My breath caught in my throat.

Sparrow scuffled his foot on the floor, disturbing the film of solidified dust. He forced my torch hand downwards. 'Uh huh! We need to get out of here, Sophia. Something happened here. See that? Looks like gravy browning? I'll put money on it being blood. Old blood.' He gripped my shoulder, hard. 'Out!'

I lifted the torch and flashed it round again. In the far corner was a lumpy shape. It could have been a dusty old dog. It wasn't that. It was a dusty old coat, rolled into itself and neatly folded over. I picked it up and the air thickened even further with dust. I coughed.

'I tell you, leave it,' said Sparrow urgently. 'You have to leave it. You need the police here.'

I spluttered, trying to get my breath. 'I've got the police here, haven't I? Anyway, it's my house; the things in here are my things. You can't tell me what to do with my things.'

When I got upstairs, watched by a tight-jawed Sparrow and an intrigued Bolek, I lay the coat across the chair. It was a big heavy thing. Opening it up I could make out the silk Crombie label. It was that old-fashioned style that some of the boys were wearing again. Tariq has one. Far too

347

big for him but he says that's the style.

This one was different, though. I fingered the buttons. They were not like those on Tariq's coat, which were brown as conkers, in polished leather. These buttons were some kind of metal. They had a military crest on them and were all neatly sewn on, the insignia on each one set upright on the dusty coat.

Sparrow groaned. 'You shouldn't mess with it, Sophia. You're contaminating it.'

Ignoring him, I reached into the deep inside pocket and pulled out what I thought at first was a birthday card. But it was an invitation from Lord and Lady Menderes, Sloane Square, to a cocktail party, six till eight, 5 July 1969. I turned it over and the back was scrawled with writing that meandered drunkenly across the card. This time he had managed more than the name. I peered closer and read out loud.

'My darling, darling Julia, I am here in this place we know so well. But the dilemma I am in could be something and could be nothing. The boys think I have transgressed and it's hard to convince them they are wrong. This could be the last letter I'll ever write, or a mid-term note that you will never see and you and I will go on our merry, merry way. But, darling girl, here in the dark (hence bad writing) I tell you that I love you and always will for ever, my darling girl. Chris xx PS. I'll see if I can get one of these goons to deliver this. A snowball in hell comes to mind. I love you, I lov

'It finishes there,' I said.

Bolek whistled.

'Poor pilgrim,' said Sparrow softly. 'I wonder who he was.'

'I know just who he was.' I was on the edge of tears. 'I know very well who he was.'

Then I started to shake. Sparrow pressed me down on to the couch and sat beside me, his hand over mine. He glanced at Bolek, who replaced the trapdoor without screwing it down.

'What do we do now?' he said.

'We wait until Sophia is OK, then we decide, the three of us,' said Sparrow 'We just wait. I could be wrong but I think what we have here is a crime scene.'

One Life

In the end we didn't say anything to anyone about the cellar. I worked hard at persuading Sparrow and Bolek to keep quiet just for now, until I managed to say something to Julia. And today, I pleaded, just wasn't the day to say something to Julia.

I looked Sparrow in the eye. 'Let Julia have her garden day.'

'That's OK, Sophia. Don't worry.' He touched my arm and for a second there was only me and him in the world.

He looked across at Bolek, who shrugged. 'No hurry,' he said. 'No hurry.'

Then we went back to help clear up after the big garden day. The only visitors still in the garden were the two ladies in straw hats, who were at the bottom of the garden sunning themselves on the blue chairs on the pebble circle. The Sillitoes and their baby, and Doreen were nowhere to be seen. Stephen and Laura were retrieving doilies and cake-papers that had drifted into the borders. Bobbi and Viktor were in the kitchen counting the money and placing it in a biscuit tin printed with roses.

Bobbi looked up, winked at me and kept counting the notes and coins.

Laura came across, clutching a carrier bag of crumpled doilies. 'Well? What about this trapdoor? Did you find one?'

The scratches on the trapdoor sat there like lead in my mind. 'Nothing much. Just an old trapdoor and a dusty cellar. You could hardly tell it was there.'

She grinned. 'Was it all dank and spooky?'

'I wouldn't say that. There's a kind of air vent to the path. It was quite dry, really.'

Stephen took the carrier bag from Laura. It was somehow an intimate gesture. 'Laura and I are going up to the Heath for a walk. How about you two?'

That 'you two' was interesting. I didn't even glance at Sparrow but he saved me from answering. 'Thanks but no thanks, Stevie,' he said. 'We've got plans of our own.'

Laura raised her eyebrows at me but I kept my face blank.

'Where's Julia?' I said.

'Inside somewhere, with her buddy Gregory and his friend, I think.'

We finished clearing up and stood by the glass kitchen door. The heat of the day was thinning fast. The clematis on the back wall rippled in a fresh breeze.

We watched Viktor, and Bobbi, who was chanting, 'Eighty people through the door at two pounds, making one hundred and sixty pounds. And seventy-three pounds for plant lists, tea and cakes. That's two hundred and thirty-three pounds in total. How good is that?'

'That's great, honey,' said Sparrow. 'Just great. Now, Sophia...' He took my arm.

I glared at him. 'We can't spoil Julia's day,' I muttered. 'We just can't!'

Then Bobbi picked up the rose-painted tin and we all crowded into the sitting room where Julia, cigarette in one hand and glass in the other, was holding court for Gregory and two of his allotmenteers. Bobbi held up the tin and announced the profit.

Julia put down her glass so she could clap her hands. 'Bravo, dear! Aren't we clever? Last year I took one hundred and twenty pounds. You have all made such a difference. And Mrs Selkirk ... Doreen ... with her biscuits.' She looked across at Gregory. 'She's from deepest Berkshire, you know. She knits and makes biscuits.'

He let out a wheezy laugh. 'You gotta tell her they were dee-licious,' he said.

'So everything's sorted, Miss Soper,' said Stephen. He was holding Laura's hand.

Julia picked up her glass. 'Stay!' she said. 'Have

a drink with us to celebrate a wonderful day.' She looked rosy and content, and much younger than her years.

'No,' I said, desperate at the thought of deceiving her while drinking her cocktails. 'We've got to go our various ways. Plans. You know.'

She nodded and Gregory nodded with her. 'These young things, Julia,' he wheezed. 'They have lives of their own. Same with my grandkids, you know? Lives of their own.'

'I'll come to see you tomorrow,' I said. 'If that's all right?'

She was still smiling. 'Yes, dear,' she said. 'But could you make that very late? I'll probably have a little lie-in. Mother wouldn't approve, but it's been a very busy day.'

She turned back to Gregory and we trooped out of the house. Bolek, after conferring with Viktor, went off for the bus, Bobbi and Viktor let themselves into number 83, and the rest of us stood on the pavement.

'I'll go and get the car,' said Stephen. 'I had to park it way down Brooke Road.' He looked at me. 'Sure you won't come, Sophia? And you, Sparrow?'

Sparrow shook his head. 'Me and Sophia's fine,' he said. 'We got plans.' He looked at me. 'I'll just go check on Bobbi,' he said, and bounded into the house.

Stephen strode away and I looked at Laura. 'Well, well, you and Stephen.'

She shrugged. 'He's cute.'

'I thought you'd fallen for Bolek,' I said.

'Stephen's more interesting. The better bet.

More...' she paused, 'long term.'

I suddenly started to worry about her. 'Are you sure? There's Emily, you know. Even if they are just friends.'

She laughed. 'If I didn't know you better, pet, I'd think you were warning me off. But then...' she nodded towards the house, 'I see you have other fish to fry.'

'Stop changing the subject.'

'I can see why you're putting a warning sign around that Emily. She's stunning, grown up, successful, fertile, and what's more she's a nice woman. Makes you sick.'

'Aren't you worried about that?'

She shook her head. 'That thing with her and Stephen is already withering on the vine, you'll see. Trust me. So anyway, what about you and...?' Again she nodded towards the house.

'We barely know each other.'

'Are you kidding? I could feel the chemistry the length of Julia's garden.'

'I...'

Our conversation ground to a halt as the subject of our conversation came out of the house and strode down the path.

'Bobbi's set up a game of chess with Viktor,' he said. 'I told her we'd only be an hour or so, Sophia. If you wait, I'll bring the bike round.'

I glanced at Laura. 'Where are we going? You didn't ask.'

'OK. Will you come for a ride on my bike?'

'Go!' said Laura.

'Yes. I'll come for a ride.'

'Right,' I said as he vanished back into the

353

house. I wanted to object to his cavalier management of me and my time, but I couldn't do that with Laura standing there.

At that point Stephen drew up in his dusty Volvo and Laura climbed in. He wound down the window. 'Sure you won't come with us, Sophia?' The late sun clipped his rimless glasses, making his face look naked and innocent.

I shook my head. 'I don't think so, Stephen.'

As I watched his car make its way into the streaming traffic and down Barrington Street, I knew that was one life that I was waving away. I think I could have had a life with Stephen, even with the shadow of Emily around us. But not after I'd met Sparrow Marsh. Even if nothing happened between me and Sparrow, just by existing he'd managed to rule out Stephen altogether.

Darling, darling Chris, too tired and to be honest a little too far gone to write, but I've had this wonderful, wonderful day with my friends. My only wish is that you were here to take off my boots like you used to. I will love you for ever and ever and ever, J xxxx zzzzzz

Jaunting

I make Sparrow wait while I go along to the Lavender House to change my velvet jacket for a thick sweater, change my shoes for boots, sling a scarf round my neck and pick up the grey gloves

354

with pink bobbles on.

While I do this I wonder how I have managed to fall in love with a man I have only seen three times. Not oh-yes-good-for-a-date-man. Not oh-yes-good-for-five-dates-man. This is really, really oh-dear-I've-fallen-for-this-person-for-life. Man!

This is just what happened to Julia all those years ago and look where that got her. Talking to her cat.

Back downstairs I feel compelled to kick over the rug and take another look at the trapdoor. My hand hesitates over the drill, still lying there. I could always screw the whole thing down again and pretend all this has never happened. But I couldn't do that. Julia has a right to know. To know about the coat and where we found it.

From outside comes the squeak of the motor bike's horn. I cover the trapdoor again with the rug.

Sparrow is sitting there with the green helmet over his arm like a basket and the leather jacket draped over the pillion. Pleased that he cannot read my recent thoughts about him being my I've-fallen-for-this-person-for-life-man, I put the gear on, clamber behind him and grab him round the waist.

'Nice gloves,' he says. 'My favourite colour, pink.'

'Doreen Selkirk gave me them,' I say in his ear. 'The first time I met her. She made them. I followed her off the bus on that first day. She's the reason I ended up here in Barrington Street. For a story.'

'God bless Doreen Selkirk,' he murmurs, then

the engine drowns out his voice altogether.

We drive through the narrow back streets and head north on the High Street and on, on, out of town. I lay my head on his back and let the streets, the shop-fronts with their tumble of goods, the churches, the mosques, glide by in a blur. Then we even leave suburban streets behind and I close my eyes, give myself up to the speed and the sweet vibration of the bike through my body.

When I open my eyes we are on a road by a stretch of river, some tributary of the Thames, I suppose. The road begins to meander and Sparrow slows down. We put-put our way through two villages and eventually stop in the third beside a pub with seats and tables outside. Next to the pub, in a mown field, half a dozen boys are playing a scratch game of cricket in tracksuits. A cluster of girls watch them.

Sparrow parks the bike and we jump off. 'Now then, Sophia? Something to eat? To drink?'

I twist and straighten my body to get the feeling back into my muscles. 'Nothing to eat. A beer will do.' I am suddenly shy. I can't look at him.

'Inside or out?'

The sun is still out but the wind is up and I'm cold from the ride. 'Inside.'

He goes for the drinks and I find a seat by the window where I can see the river and the children playing. He brings beer for me and orange soda for himself. 'Seen too much blood on the road to take a risk,' he says, catching my glance.

'Very grown up,' I say, finally pleased to be meeting those bright, questioning eyes.

'If that's a compliment, thank you.' He toasts

me with his glass. 'Now, the business of the trap-door,' he says. 'Just what's this about Miss Soper? You know her more in a month than I do, or even Stevie, who's been here on or off for all his life. Me, I thought she was just another old crazy. London's full of 'm.'

'Julia's not crazy. Not in the least.' Then, sitting there, relishing the very sight of him, I tell him everything about Julia, from the first cocktail to the last beautiful plant in her garden. I tell him all the stuff that Julia has let slip about Chris Muncaster and the blanks that Jerry Sillitoe has filled in for me. I tell him about Laura taking Julia in hand and coveting her vintage wardrobe. I mention how lonely Julia has been. How enclosed, frozen in mourning. How now there is a thaw.

'And it's you who broke that ice?'

'She and I took to each other from the first.'

'Like you and my Bobbi took to each other?'

'Well, that was more like Bobbi took me over from the start. But yes, that day – Doreen, Julia and Bobbi, and the Lavender House – I knew my life was changed.'

'What is it about the house?'

'Well, I'd been made homeless that day, and there was this house inviting me in. It seemed meant. All mixed up with Bobbi and Julia, of course. But it seemed inevitable that I should have the Lavender House.'

'And now it seems that the Lavender House means more to Julia than just planting up your yard?'

'It's a roundabout thing. The house has something to do with the Pinders, those crazy house

357

stalkers showed me that. And the Pinders defin-itely had something to do with Julia's Chris. I found a book with a photo of them all together. And now there is the cellar and Chris's note and his coat.'

'And the old coat really belonged to this Chris guy?'

'I'm sure. It's there in the note. The one he left in the pocket. His letter to her. I know it's his, so, sadly...'

'Yeah. Now we know what happened in the cellar.'

'His blood,' I say, miserable now. 'Like rust on the floor.'

'And Jerry Sillitoe's certain, says there's been no trace of the bloke? Not then, not since, home or abroad?'

'No trace.' Tears are standing in my eyes.

He puts his hand over mine, just there on the table. 'He's a sound man, honey. He'll know.'

'Jerry said he'll be in concrete now, way below ground.' So, Chris is not up in Yorkshire some-where, preferring a county life to life here on Bar-rington Street with Julia. He is dead. Probably dead within hours of Julia last seeing him, forty years ago. He didn't leave her. He was dragged away. I need to tell her that. Tell her all of it.

'I'll have to tell her, Sparrow. Tell Julia.'

'You're right. And there should be an investi-gation.'

I pull my hand away from his. 'Even after all these years?'

'Especially after all these years. Procedure...'

'Procedure?' I look out of the window where

now two girls are playing catch with a spare cricket ball. They're the same age as Bobbi. And Drina. And Drina – she'll always be ten years old, just as Chris Muncaster will always be thirty-six, no matter how old Julia gets. Procedure did not help Drina. And procedure will not bring Chris back to life. He'll stay vanished, no matter how many policemen go through their procedural motions. I look back at Sparrow. 'What good would procedure do for Julia?'

'The word nowadays is "closure". Julia gets closure after all these years of not knowing whether to mourn or not. She'll know that he's not absent but dead. *Closure.*'

'Yaargh! What an ugly word.'

'But people need to move on.'

'Julia is moving on. She's stopped wearing hot-pants. She no longer walks her cat in the basket or talks to it. You saw her today. She has friends who live in the here and now. She lives in the present day. When I first met her she was living in 1969.'

He runs a finger over the back of my hand. My skin itches. 'Seems you're quite a catalyst, Miss Sophia,' he says.

I drop my hand into my lap. 'It's Julia we're talking about. I know you're one of them but why do we need to get the police in on this? I'll show her the coat and the note, so we're not keeping the facts from her.'

Now it's my turn to grab his hand. 'Please, Sparrow. Let's just leave this where it is. I'll talk to Julia. She'll get her closure, I promise you. She's just escaped from the past where she's lived too long. Now – now you want to shoot her back into it. It'll be in the papers. Those house stalkers'll have a field day. Everyone will know her story. They'll make her a guy. She'll be laughed at. Oh, she'll be pitied, but it'll be that gloating, pious pity that makes you want to vomit. It'll be resurrected Pinder fever. The place will be crawling with stalkers, official and unofficial.' I shudder. 'My Lavender House will never be the same. They will destroy it.'

He is squeezing my hand, holding it almost too tight. 'Listen. The sad thing is that that house will never be the same for you anyway, now, will it?' He pulls my hand till it touches his chest. 'You really care, don't you, Sophia?'

I wrestle in vain to retrieve my hand but he holds on tight and says, 'OK. You say no police. Then I say no police. D'you know you could make a man admit to murder with those eyes? And that voice. The same as I first heard on the phone, that soft voice from the North. Bobbi couldn't resist you. She's already given me a lecture about not scaring you away. Even old Elsie told me to treasure you. How can I say no to you now?'

'You won't get into trouble?'

'Only with my own cop's conscience. Who else knows? Just you. Me and Bolek. And he didn't quite catch on what was really happening.'

I finally rescue my hand. 'Good. Now I can relax,' I say, more calmly than I feel.

He grins. 'Well, then. Another drink?'

When he comes back with the drinks I have calmed down enough to ask him again about Pamela and how they met. I've heard it all from Bobbi and Elsie, but it's nice to see his eyes light up when he talks about her, to hear the pride in his voice at her cleverness: how the memory of her makes it easier, not harder to bring up Bobbi on his own.

Then I find myself talking about Drina and my life in Newcastle, about my grandmother and my friends up there on the New Dawn Estate, about my little flat and its garden.

We sit there as the light fades, absorbing facts about each other's lives like sponges, storing them away, creating a living context for the thunderbolt of recognition I think we both felt when we met.

Finally we are standing outside the pub, getting kitted up for the journey home. He says, 'Why not stay with us tonight, Sophia? The Lavender House is not the right place for you tonight. Just till this thing's sorted.'

I think of the trapdoor, still unscrewed. 'Well...'

He shakes his head. 'No strings, honey. I'm not laying some kind of lure. Just offering sanctuary, that's all. We have all of our lives for the rest to happen.'

My heart sings.

When we got back Viktor had gone and Bobbi was waiting for us, snakes and ladders set up on the low table. She grinned up at us. 'Thought a nice game might be restful before bed. I made cheese sandwiches in the kitchen, Dad. Can you get them?'

When he'd gone she pulled me down beside her. 'So, are you and my dad an item, Sophia?'

I flushed. Charming as she was, she thought too much, knew too much. 'Bobbi, I...'

'I just wanted to say it was cool with me. It was in my plan as soon as I saw you. I saw this kind of fit. Like in a jigsaw. You know?' Then I saw the anxiety in her gaze and realised at last that so much of this confidence, this precociousness, was about survival.

I was saved from answering by Sparrow shouldering his way through the door, carrying a tray of hefty sandwiches and three cans of Coke.

I won the Snakes and Ladders twice and Bobbi threw her hand in, yawning dramatically, saying all this garden stuff had just done her in and she was just desperate for her bed.

The melodrama of her exit left us both embarrassed. Sparrow got up, put on some cool jazz, and poured us both some wine. I drank half a glass, then suddenly we were dancing together in the small space between the couch and the deep window At first we moved in that awkward-casual way that strangers have when they first dance together. Then within minutes our bodies became more familiar with each other. Our movement became easier, more intimate, as though we had danced together all of our lives.

My own, my darling, darling Chris,
I watched Sophia and the man called Sparrow. I could see them dancing in the window of the middle flat. You can tell in a second that they're made for each other, those two. They are so different but they are a match. Just as you and I were a match.
I sat there in my window, clutching my strong coffee, watching it like it was a scene from a film. Roman

Holiday. *We saw that film together. Do you remember?*

Sorry for the wobbly writing. I have to confess I'm a little bit tipsy after that session with Gregory & co. And my mind is now too full of those times you and I had in the little house round the corner. The one Sophia calls the Lavender House. My body aches with it, for it. For you. Our own private place. Eating, dancing, making love. No Mother, no Richie or Roy Pinder to queer our pitch, even if it was their place and all you had was the key. I remember some nights you were a bit jumpy in case they turned up. But perversely, even that added to the fun.

And do you remember, after all that loving we came along here and had cocoa with Mum? Our secret. Our secret place. Do you remember?

I do.

Your loving

Julia

PS. I made the back yard beautiful with plants and flowers, for Sophia and for you.

Howling

The morning after the garden day I woke up in Sparrow's bed at eight to find a six a.m. note from him saying he had gone to work.

Once I'd shaken the fuzzy joy of the night before out of my head, I remembered my eleven o'clock appointment with Julia. I couldn't dodge that any more. At the gate I met Stephen and we shared a few thoughts about the garden day and how good it was.

'You OK, Sophia?' He eyed me carefully.

'Fine.'

'Good. Well. I'm off to Zurich tonight, but I'll be back at the weekend. See you then.'

I turned to go.

'Sophia?'

I turned back.

'I'm really pleased you turned up in Barrington Street. Seems you've shaken us all up.'

I thought of Julia. 'And is that a good thing?'

'It can only be a good thing.' Then he smiled his small wry smile and turned to walk to his car.

Watching him I thought that falling for someone is such an eccentric thing. I could so easily have fallen for Stephen but I didn't. I fell for someone who wasn't there but cast a long shadow forward in my life. And I was happy.

Then I ran along to my house to shower and change into mundane day clothes, before returning to a demure Bobbi, who said yes she had slept very well. Her dad had gone to work and she was just ready for school. I saw her out to school, went back home and chilled out with some cornflakes and coffee, and considered just what I was to say to Julia about all this mess.

I was on my fourth cup of coffee when I came up with the only, the most banal, answer. Be direct.

I was at Julia's door at eleven o'clock on the dot. She answered the first ring. Despite the lack of make-up and the scraped-back hair she was smiling gleefully.

'Did you have a nice evening, dear?' she said.

Of course I coloured. 'Yes. Yes. Very nice.'

She led the way through, Pusscat weaving through her legs. 'I saw you dancing in the window with Mr Marsh. You moved really well together, I thought.'

I continued on quickly, 'And you, Julia. How are you after your great day yesterday?'

'I think it was wonderful, dear, but I only remember a few things, to be honest. Too many cocktails with that incorrigible Gregory, I'm afraid.' She sounded very composed. 'I had to drink coffee to come to before I could go to bed, if you see what I mean.'

She led me into the kitchen. 'I'm in here making myself more strong coffee. Do have some.'

I hitched myself on one of her tall stools but refused the coffee. I sat quietly watching her drink hers. When she had drained the last drop I said, 'I want you to come with me, Julia.'

'Where?'

'To my house.'

'Your house? Is there something wrong, Sophia? Are you ill?'

'I'm good, very well. But I want to show you something. Something very difficult.'

'Is there a problem?' She frowned.

'Just come!'

She stood up. 'Don't be silly. How can I go anywhere looking like this? I never go anywhere barefaced.'

So I had to wait while she put on her make-up and teased her hair out of its unbecoming ponytail.

'Now!' she beamed, putting her arm through

mine. My heart ached for her. 'Are you sure you're all right, dear?' she said.

'I'm fine.'

When we let ourselves into the Lavender House I asked her about Chris. She frowned. 'Chris? I told you about Chris. All about him.'

'Tell me again.'

She sat down and went through it all again. And again, her love for him radiated from her. She glanced round the room, seemed about to say something, then stopped.

'And he just vanished?' I said.

'Into thin air,' she said. 'I was always so very sure he went back to Yorkshire. You know. Away from the Boys and their troublesome demands. All that London trouble. Away from me...' Her voice tailed off. 'Perhaps he thought I was part of all that London trouble. Perhaps he'd just had enough. He was always, well, just that bit un-predictable. Still, he was wonderful to me. Truly wonderful.' Her voice had dropped to a murmur, almost a whisper.

I walked across and moved the black plastic from the big coat that lay on the chair. I held it up and sneezed as the dust came away from it. She stood up and touched it, running her painted fingernails over the buttons. After a very long time she said, 'Do you know, I sewed these on for him, myself. His regimental buttons. His own regiment. A kind of joke, I think, on Richie, who bought the same coat but had no right to buttons like these. Not that that would have worried *him*. He had his own dark regiments around him...' She was talking very fast, almost spitting in her haste to push the words out.

I held on to the arm of the coat. 'So this was Chris's? His coat?'

'It certainly is. As I said, I sewed on those buttons.' She looked round. 'Is he here?'

'No, no, love.' I forced myself to keep my voice steady. 'It's just that I found this coat. Here in this house.'

She looked to the left, to the right. She peered behind me, bewildered. 'Where?' she said. 'I helped you clean this house, Sophia. There was no coat.'

'You know I had the floors sanded? Well, Bolek, Viktor's brother, found a trapdoor. There's a cellar underneath here, Julia.'

She looked at the floor, clutching the coat to her. 'This was in there?'

There was a long, long silence.

'Can I see?'

I pulled up the rug. 'There, see?'

'I want to see this cellar.' She let the coat fall to the floor. 'Let me see.'

'Bolek took the hinges off,' I said. 'You'll have to help me.' Using a claw hammer from the toolbox I managed to lever the trapdoor from its housing and between us we lifted it and leaned it against the wall.

She peered inside. 'I can't see anything.'

I handed her the torch. She flashed it right past the scratch marks into the void below. Before I could stop her she was on the ladder and making her way down.

I stood with my hands balled into fists, listening to her stumbling around, muttering words I could not hear. Then she emerged, covered in dust, clutching the scraps of paper with her name on. She sat down heavily on the arm of the chair. 'The Boys used to have people here, you know. People on the run. Giving them breathing space, Chris said.'

She looked around. 'Chris and I sometimes came here, you know. Just the two of us. He had the key. And he was here before he left. You know that, don't you, Sophia?' She held out her hand, palm up. 'He was here. These notes are from him. Just my name. He was calling for me but I could not hear. I did not answer,' she said dully.

'He wrote something else,' I said. I took the invitation card from the pile of paper on the desk and turned it over. 'Here's a letter of sorts. It was in the pocket of the coat.'

She took it from me, held it close to her eyes and read it. Once. Twice. Three times. 'Well, that's it then,' she said. 'Those mad men killed him. Or one of their lieutenants. One of the dark regiment. Same thing. I wonder what they thought he'd done to them? Wouldn't have to be much for that Richie. You could be his best friend, then he would do terrible things on a whim. My own mother liked him but he was mad as a barrel of monkeys.'

'I'm sorry, Julia,' I said miserably. I couldn't tell her the thing about Chris and the police. Too much information.

'What have you to be sorry for?' she said sharply. Then she shook her head. 'I was so sure Chris had gone North, you know, and I made myself accept that. That he'd gone back to the bosom of

368

his family and I must not pursue him. I could not.'

'But now at least you know he didn't leave you. He would never have left you.' A straw grasped.

'No. They grabbed him away for their own mad reasons.' She leaned down and touched the coat where it lay on the floor. 'I am thinking now that I realise exactly when it happened. There was this night when those boys called at my house. Well, Richie did. He was out of his head on something. Perhaps even some perverted notion of guilt. Chris loved him, in his way. So there was Richie, banging at the door, yelling through the letterbox. Screaming. Swearing. Then poor Roy came along and scooped him away. He was always cleaning up after his brother. Then they drove away in that American car of theirs, past the house on the corner, this house of yours. The place where Chris and I had such sweet times. They slowed down just by here. Then they went. Right out of my sight. Out of my life.' Gently she lifted the coat from the floor and pressed it to her. 'You know, those two were done for, even then. The net was closing in. It was in the papers. Not long after that they were arrested for murder. Not for murdering Chris. No, not Chris. Some other villain that they knew about. They got long stretches. Both dead now, of course.' She raised her eyes to mine. Her mascara had run, pooling her eyes in dark shadow. 'But they weren't the only ones who had to endure a life sentence, were they, dear?' she said finally with the barest glimmer of a smile.

I tried to take the coat from her but she clutched it to her chest. That was when a sound

369

came from the cellar below that made my blood freeze: a strange inhuman howling. Julia's face crumpled and she started to sob.

'Christ!' I said.

Then Julia's brow cleared. 'Of course!' she sniffed. 'Pusscat. He just can't climb up ladders. You can get him, dear, can't you?'

Her courage made me brave and I took the torch and scrambled down the ladder. And there he was, hissing and spitting in the darkest corner. After three failed attempts I scooped him off the floor and literally flung him up through the hole.

I could hear Julia say, 'Oh, Pusscat, how could you? Scaring poor little Sophia like that!'

I climbed up again and heaved the trapdoor across the space, and flung the rug over it. 'That's it!' I said. 'Never again.' I was filthy and my hands were stinging where the cat had scratched me. What a monster he was.

When I looked at her, Julia had the coat over one arm and Pusscat over her shoulders. He was purring. 'Now, Sophia,' she said softly, 'I think I should go home, don't you? It's been such a very long morning.'

Oh Dearest Chris,
This has all been such a waste. Such a waste.

A Smudge of Lipstick

When Sparrow got back from work I worked on him about not telling his bosses about the cellar with its famous criminal associations. I went on and on about saving Julia from weeks of torture by the press, about her part in Chris's story. I knew Tariq would have given his eyeteeth for such a story. It might even have shaken the languorous Jack Molloy out of his barefoot sandals.

Still, my powers of persuasion did not put a stop to Sparrow's enquiring mind. The next day he came back from work with an interesting tale.

'No use being stuck behind a desk unless you can have a play with the files and get on the phone, is there?' he said, eyes sparkling.

'Go on!' I said. 'What is it?'

'Julia's Chris Muncaster was a piece of Jigsaw.'

'Jigsaw? What's that?'

'Name of an operation they had in the end for nailing the Pinders. They formed a special squad for the task. Jigsaw Squad. Very original.'

'You boys do like your games,' I said.

'D'you want to know or not?'

'Tell me!'

'Those brothers had wriggled out of dozens of serious charges. Witnesses terrorised. Policemen pacified with bungs.'

'So what was this Jigsaw?'

'Jigsaw was about putting together specific

371

crimes with places and people. All pieces of the jigsaw. See? In the end Muncaster supplied some of the pieces for us, for the police at the time. Seems he wanted out, to get out of their world. The boys wouldn't let him, so he turned to us.'

'He wanted to get out to be with Julia. He was a spy. Like you were when you were undercover.'

This offended him. 'No, not like me, Sophia. I'm a pro, doing my job, not informing. Big difference.'

'So, he was a turncoat?'

'Seems like.'

'And the boys found out and they ... got rid of him?'

'Seems like.'

'D'you think I should tell Julia that?' I said. 'Would it make it better or worse?'

He lifted his shoulders in an elegant shrug. 'Ball's in your court now. You're the one insisting on not blowing it. You would know better than me whether she should be told or not. Isn't she your friend?'

'I'm sorry but I think Miss Soper has to know everything.' Bobbi's voice came from the corner where she was sitting with a laptop on her knee. She'd turned down an offer of the cinema from Bolek and Viktor, opting rather to keep her eye on us. Sparrow and I had told her now that we liked each other and wanted to spend more time together. And at least until the matter of the trapdoor was sorted I'd be staying with them. Bobbi said she was cool about that but said I must promise her one thing.

'Anything, Bobbi,' I said.

'Just don't act like you're my mother or some

stupid stepmother thing. I came before Dad. I found you first, not him.'

'Friends first, then, Bobbi.'

'Friends first.'

'That's all right then.'

'Like I say, you've gotta tell Miss Soper. Like Martin Luther King said, The Truth Will Set You Free. Miss Soper needs to be free.'

Sparrow and I exchanged glances. He ruffled her hair. 'Honey, if you weren't lovely you'd be terrible.'

I could have kissed him there and then. When he was around Bobbi lost her tough precocious edge and she became a child again.

On my second day at number 83 I had a phone call from Laura saying she was in Zurich with Stephen as he had asked her and it would be a mistake to turn down such a good opportunity for copy. Jack Molloy thought so too and had given her leave.

'So is it the opportunity you're after, pet, or Stephen?'

'Sarky cow! How can you ask that? He's sweet, gorgeous, grown-up and I'm madly in love.'

'Nice,' I said.

'Nice for you too, I hear. Stevie tells me you've moved in.'

'Not quite, but ... well...'

'I rest my case. We'll be back on Saturday. Dying to see you. Both of you. Lots to talk about.'

'Yes, lots. See you.'

So it was nice staying there with the Sparrow and Bobbi, savouring the taken-for-granted notion that our lives would be together. It was really hard for Sparrow and me to keep our hands off each other although Bobbi's presence kept things reasonably cool. But then, of course, when we managed to be on our own, the glorious fireworks started. Again and again.

On my second day there I came upon Doreen in the hallway and she invited me in for coffee. Her flat, shorn of Roger's mess, was neat and sterile, as though she herself were planning to move out. She shook her head when I asked if she planned to go rather than have Helena to stay, saying things were OK, despite her work not selling.

'I've hooked up with this woman who is opening a wool shop in Islington. She says knitting is now becoming a pastime of choice and that's where the future lies. Not knitting for the *hoi polloi* but kitting them out so they can knit for themselves. So I'm to work for her two days a week. It will be so interesting. I've never worked in a shop before.'

'Great. You can settle down again.'

She shook her head. 'Not really. My Helena is still coming in July so things are on hold till then.'

'You could meet someone new.'

She was already shaking her head. 'Men! To be honest, dear, I've had enough of them. One husband who forgot how to love me, and then Roger who only really ever loved himself. I'll stick with my daughter. Such love never dies.' She leaned forward and smiled her sweet smile. 'And I'll stick to my friends.'

I found myself blushing. 'That's nice, Doreen. Just think, if I'd never followed you off the bus I'd never have found the Lavender House, or Barrington Street.'

'Or Mr Sparrow Marsh, of course. I see you two are certainly close now.'

'Seems like,' I said, echoing Sparrow's own phrase.

'And what does Miss Bobbi think about that?'

'She's cool about it.'

'She would be. After all, she fell for you first.'

I laughed. 'That's just what she says.'

Doreen replenished my coffee. 'And what about Miss Soper? Is she cock-a-hoop after her garden day?'

My heart lurched. 'Oh, there is something.' Even as I wondered whether I should tell Doreen, I began to relate the story of the cellar, and the link it had in Julia's life.

'So it was my job to tell her. It's obviously hit her for six. And now I've more to tell her. I've knocked on her door three times but she doesn't answer.'

'Keep trying, dear. She must know about all of this,' said Doreen soberly. 'Otherwise you're treating her like a child. And there's no respect in that, is there?' She paused. 'How dreadful for you. Will you ever be able to live in that house, with that story attached to it?'

That thought had been haunting me for days. Twice in the last two days I had taken an alternative route to avoid passing the Lavender House. That was a thing to be faced, but not yet.

I was just coming out of number 83 when I saw Julia clipping up her front path and going into her house. I ran across and knocked on the door. I hammered on it in frustration. I shouted. But still she didn't come.

I spent that evening sitting on Sparrow's sofa, his hand in mine. Becoming this close to someone, without hurry or subterfuge, was quite a new thing for me. It was dawning on me now that being together was not just about the physical closeness of making love, of going to sleep and waking up next to someone. It was about what might look like superficial things: discovering how neat he was getting in and out of his clothes, how he whistled and talked to himself in the shower. How he liked only very pale toast and only played lip-service to football. And although I knew of it from her own mouth, his closeness to Bobbi was a revelation. They worked together like two well-oiled parts of a machine. They spoke in an encoded, affectionate shorthand of words, looks and gesture that was almost impenetrable at first.

It would have been easy to feel shut out of such intimacy but in their own way each of them was generous in making me feel included. Bobbi was not even much fazed by the thought that Sparrow and I were sleeping together. I think it was good that she and I met first. She'd be quite capable of getting rid of any girlfriend she didn't approve of.

I mentioned this thought to Sparrow. He grinned his broad grin. 'That theory ain't never been put to the test, honey,' he said. 'And never will be now.'

It was on the Thursday after the garden day that I finally caught up with Julia in the queue in the Pound Shop. She was wearing her hotpants and had Pusscat in the basket. She had a chemist's bag under her arms and was buying a feather duster with a long handle. She smiled brightly when she saw me.

'Sophia! How are you, dear? Such ages since we talked.'

'So it is. I've missed you, Julia.'

'Have you, dear?' She handed over a fiver and got her change.

I paid for my washing powder and ran after her, managing to keep pace with her right back to Barrington Street. I had to be persistent, refusing to let her outmanoeuvre me by walking more and more slowly.

'How have you been, Julia?' I said finally.

'Me, dear? Oh, the usual. Lots to do. I'm cleaning the house now from top to bottom. Oh, I must tell you the garden ladies were thrilled by the contribution. I told them it was all down to good friends and neighbours.'

We were at her gate. 'I really need to talk to you, Julia. I want to talk to you about Chris.'

'Chris?'

'Your friend Chris Muncaster.'

'Well, then, dear. Go on. Tell me.'

We watched as the cat leaped out of the basket and stood guard at the door.

'I can't tell you here, Julia. I need to come into the house. To tell you there.'

'I don't know about that, dear. Pusscat's getting very cross with himself these days. Doesn't care to have me out of his sight. Very chary of anyone coming in.'

I took her arm. 'I'm coming in with you, Julia. And if I have to fight off Pusscat to do it, I will. I've survived his scratches once and I can do it again.'

She shook off my arm and pulled out the key from the string round her neck. 'All right, dear. All right! On your own head be it.'

The house smelled of bleach and Fairy Liquid. The hall was sparkling. Through the glass door I could see the kitchen was spotless. There was no offer of tea, milk or cocktails. She led the way into the sitting room and sat down with her knees together on the chair. I sat on the spindly-legged sofa.

'Well, dear?' she said.

I told her about the Jigsaw Squad. 'So you see, Chris was trying to rid himself of the brothers, for things to be all right for you and him. Don't you see, Julia? To be with you in the ordinary way.'

She looked at me quietly for a while. 'Well, dear, I always knew Chris was a good man, in his own way. Weak in his own way too. Under their spell. But don't you think I'd rather have him alive doing a bit of crooked driving, or carrying this or that to Amsterdam, than under concrete on some motorway? Don't you think I'd rather have him in prison than that? Don't you think I'd rather have had him grow old, whether it was alongside me, or in some distant place?' She paused. 'Even in Yorkshire, riding to hounds.'

I felt reprimanded. Julia had never seemed more sane. 'I'm sorry, Julia.' I was near to tears.

She smiled her sweet smile. 'Don't be sorry, my dear. Never be sorry. You've brought such colour into my life in these few months. You know what I mean. My life before was in black-and-white, like those old films. But with you it was full

Technicolor. I'll be forever grateful for that.' She stood up. 'Now,' she said briskly. 'I have to get on. So much to do.'

I stood up miserably. Then to my astonishment she reached up and kissed me on the cheek. 'Don't brood!' she said briskly. 'Get on with your life. Take a lesson from me. That way lies madness.'

At the door she said, 'One thing, dear. Please don't bang on the door like that and shout through the letterbox. It brings back such bad memories.'

I stood on the pavement and rubbed my cheek and looked at the red smudge of lipstick on my fingertips. Julia's Red. No mistaking it. Then I looked across the road and there in the first-floor window was Sparrow, his arm round Bobbi's shoulder. They were both grinning and waving at me to come in, come in!

I waited for a space in the traffic and dodged across, racing into the house and up the stairs two at a time to join my own, my very precious ones.

Dear Sophia,

It was lovely to see you today. I'm sorry I forgot my manners and offered you nothing to eat or drink. My mother would have been ashamed of me. I'm sorry I had to hustle you away but there is so much to do to be ready for my journey to see Chris at long last. It's been such a wait but now that is all at an end. Don't worry about your lovely Lavender House. The Boys will have won if you let all that long-gone business spoil it for you. You won't have to live there too long, believe me. I have made an arrangement. One thing that gives me

379

great pleasure is how at last you have put behind you the bad things that happened to you in the North and are so settled here among people who care.

Love always,
your friend Julia xxx

PS. I hope little Laura enjoys the clothes I've left her and that you enjoy this house, which I have made nice and clean for you. I know you will take care of it and of my dear plants, especially philadelphus. Oh, and please be tolerant of Pusscat. Just give him time. He will come round.

PPS. Tell young Bobbi that I loved her story of the humming bird on Jamaica and that this really is my swansong.

Acknowledgements

Writing a novel based outside my home turf of the North of England has been one of the great pleasures of this book. The extended hospitality of Debora Robertson and Sean Donnellan during my research period, and their inside-track knowledge of London life in general and North London life in particular, were crucial to me in getting the context right. Thank you especially to Debora for sparking the whole thing off by finding the Lavender House in the first place and to Sean for helping me with his brilliant location photographs that crowded my pin-board right through the writing of the book. They are inspirational.

Thank you to Harriet Evans at Headline for her brilliant support and for taking care of my precious novel with such insight and rigour; to Yvonne Holland for her meticulous line editing and her understanding of my intentions in the book; to Gillian Wales for continuing to support my endeavours in this work, even though this time it is not set in the North, and to Juliet Burton for, as always, keeping me steady.

Finally – though he won't want a mention – an

especial thank you to Bryan, whose genial, unselfish support continues to smooth my path in this sometimes impossibly driven life of writing, travelling and teaching.

Wendy Robertson
Bishop Auckland 2007